I Stopped Time

JANE DAVIS

1 - SIR JAMES'S STORY

BEGINNINGS

I grew up motherless. That isn't to say my mother was dead. 'Conspicuous by her absence' was the phrase I heard my father use as I listened at keyholes in hope of answers. Theirs was a lengthy marriage. The fact that she chose to take no part in it didn't detract from his sense that she was his wife. Yes, he had frequent lady friends, perfumed, interchangeable. None replaced her. My mother remained the love of his life - except, that is, for racing cars, an open stretch of road and, of course, the lure of speed.

I couldn't help but feel I must have done something terrible to cause her to go, but my father frequently assured, "You were hardly capable of anything more ghastly than crying too loudly. Or too often. No, it was me your mother left." But he failed to provide an adequate explanation of his crime, claiming to have bought her the best money could buy, even allowing her to pursue her career - against his better judgement. What *was* I to think?

"Think of the boy!" I shrank into my seat at the sound of my grandfather's bullish proclamation over the cut-glass and cruets. "I can't understand why you don't divorce her."

My father slowly applied a napkin to one corner of his

mouth. His response was measured, dry: "I wouldn't expect you to."

"Frankly, I never understood why you had to marry her in the first place!" Never one to waste time listening to the other side of an argument, the older man forked food into his mouth as if his was the last word.

"I know you'd have preferred me to throw in the towel with some obedient little debutante, but," and here my father turned his focus to me, exaggerating the width of his cow-brown eyes, "your mother *was* exciting. And very beautiful."

My grandfather inhaled his Claret, spluttering, "*Excitement!* That's not what one looks for in a wife!"

"'*Til death us do part* was the promise I made. And I haven't managed to kill myself yet."

"Despite your confounded tomfoolery! Look here, in my day a man would have taken a woman like her -"

My father coughed a loud protest.

"Do you dare censor me? One can only hope," my grandfather's eyes singled me out, flashing terror into my soul, "young James here will learn from your mistakes!"

"Son." I found my hair being ruffled, my father's voice assuring, "Don't listen to anyone who tells you it's a mistake to marry for love."

"Oh, come *on!* What utter rot!" The table shook as my grandfather's glass crash-landed, the stem snapping under the weight of his forearm, adamant that it was my father, and not he, who was responsible for the wreckage Mrs Strachan fussed over.

Is it possible to miss someone of whom one has no memory? No, I missed the *idea* of her. Like the Rome I learned of in Ancient History lessons, a mother was an idea in the minds of men. Sometimes differing substantially from the reality.

From the age of eight, I boarded. Once I overcame the

anxiety of separation, this masked the situation. Increasingly, as I grew older, it was an annoyance that school was interrupted by holidays rather than the other way round. It was then that a mother's absence became most apparent. My father - who, in many ways, remained a boy himself - cut a dashing figure as he picked me up at the end of term in whatever incarnation of a prototype he'd been working on, all leather-coated, moustache and goggles, revved up for the next event on the calendar. Never a moment to lose, we rushed from the *London to Gloucester Trial* to Brooklands for the *Round the Mountain Race Meeting*. While he denied himself pause for thought, I pondered that perhaps a woman as exciting as my mother might have enjoyed our escapades.

I met her once when I was about ten. Only the once.

My father and I were visiting Brighton for the annual speed trials that took place along a mile of arrow-straight road when he caught sight of an advertisement for a photography exhibition.

"Well now!" The name on the awnings wasn't one I recognised. Grabbing hold of my upper arm, he raised his free hand to halt the traffic. "This looks like fun, James. What do you say?"

"But you said we were going to have -" I was not expected to say anything, that much was apparent. The harshness of his glare retracted the promise of ice cream.

We shuffled as part of a compacted crowd from one black and white memory to another. And there she was: another exhibit to be admired from a carefully roped-off distance. Weightless coral chiffon, skin like cream, bobbed hair the colour of autumn.

"Why, Kingdom!" She appeared animated, but I was bored by the affectations women made for my father's benefit. They talked their various ways into his drawing room to see for themselves the lie of the land - the habitat of this almost-available and most amusing of men - only to find the errant son lingering in the doorway, seen but not heard; forever eavesdropping. "You should have warned me..."

"*Why, Kingdom!*" I was exaggerating her voice inside my head. "*You should have -*"

Pushed in front, my father's hands clamped tightly on my shoulders, I shrank as every vertebra in my back was compressed. "Son." He cleared his throat: three noisy syllables. "This is your mother."

There had been no warning. I had prayed for this moment, but now it had arrived my jaw dropped, my throat constricted.

She exhaled my name - "James?" - as though it were part of her she couldn't bear to be parted with.

I swallowed hard, looking from this woman, a tableau not unlike one of her own photographs, to my father's face, uncertain how he expected me to react. "I - I don't recognise her."

"No." His grip relaxed, knuckles cracking in my ears. "Not your fault. No reason you should."

The shudder of the woman's breath was audible. Her pale blue eyes pooled. I watched her lips tremble, before she covered them with a slender-fingered hand. Everything else was utterly still, the moment suspended.

"Move along!" As an attendant's shout broke the spell the shuffling recommenced, carrying us in its wake. I wasn't ready, still trying to absorb that *this woman was my mother.*

Desperate for another glimpse, I rotated my neck like an owl. She was on tiptoes, straining to make herself seen above heads and hats, between shoulders.

"James!" I heard her call above the steady murmur, slightly louder now. "James!" Not the voice of someone who would abandon me, but increasingly desperate.

Holding on to a brass post for support, I leant out across the thick twist of rope. "Mother? *Mother!*"

Seeing me, her expression of panic softened. She smiled, pressed two fingers to her lips and then turned the fingers towards me, rippling. I blinked hard, capturing the gesture: her fingers, lips, the wave.

Two shrill blasts of a whistle cut through the echoing space. "Back, please! Stand well back!" But it was my father's hand that grabbed my collar. Reluctantly releasing my grip on the brass post, I was air-lifted back among the crush, watching my damp fingerprints evaporate.

"I'm sorry, Sir." Shame-faced, I bowed my head, anticipating punishment. "I only wanted -"

"Son! I thought I'd lost you."

My head swivelled back in the direction we had come from. "Can we - ?"

"Perhaps next time." His hands were already steering me into the flow. So there was to be a *next time*. "She hasn't been taking proper care of herself. Very drawn, don't you think?"

The room was overbearing; the high ceilings gave the sensation that the walls were closing in; the general murmur became an elevated din.

"I don't know."

Shuffling people, jostling for position, crushed in from all angles.

"What's that you say? Speak up!"

My toes treading on the heels of the shoes in front, my nose pressed flat against the coarse tweed of a jacket, the terrible weight of my father's hands, and to see what? Pictures of boring old things. There is no place for nostalgia in a boy's vocabulary.

"Can we go now, Sir?"

"Yes, let's. It's stifling in here. Coming through!" My father began to hack his way through the jungle of legs, setting free a blizzard of excuses, issuing me with instructions that were impossible to follow. Pushed, stretched and stumbling, I was manhandled into a marble clearing. We navigated the echoing corridors, guided to the exit by a misshapen rectangle of daylight, cut with a bold-shaped shadow.

Framed in the doorway stood a grey-haired soldier with loose red skin around one eye that looked like a turkey's wattle, and whose left trouser-leg was tucked under at the point where his knee should have been. An image far more striking than any I had seen that day, both repulsive and fascinating. I was unable to tear my eyes away. My father executed a neat little jig, but the man stepped forwards. "Kingdom." He planted his crudely-fashioned crutch firmly. "I'm glad you felt you could come."

"Well, look who it isn't!" Puppy-like in his enthusiasm, whatever followed would be a lie. The tone was one my father reserved for people he'd been trying to ignore. "Didn't see you there. We're just popping out for some air. The boy's feeling faint."

"I'm doing the same myself. Not my thing, crowds. We only expected half this number. Still," the man inhaled on a cigarette, "shouldn't grumble. We stand a fair chance of turning a profit."

"Well -" My father nodded, taking a sideways step.

The soldier seemed unprepared to let him escape so lightly. "Down for the speed trials?"

"That's right. Fine venue, Brighton."

"And don't tell me. You must be young James!" The soldier smiled down at my drop-jawed recoil, but I was surprised to find a hint of nervousness reflected in his rheumy eyes.

"Yes, this is my son." My father held me back protectively.

"You must be very proud of him." Whatever the man had seen to make my father proud wasn't clear to me: I was distinctly average in everything from hair colour to ability on the cricket pitch. "Did Lottie…?" He nodded rapidly, looking away and scratching one side of his face.

"Briefly." Whatever this single word conveyed, it drew the man's gaze. My father and the crippled man locked eyes, what passed between them remaining concealed. Shielding my own, I looked out of the arched porch: the onion-topped domes of the Royal Pavilion glowed brilliant white against the violent blue of the sky; gulls' silhouettes circled and looped.

"Like to swim, young man?"

I twisted back, surprised that the soldier was addressing me directly. He stood erect, a hint of the military man he had once been.

"Yes, Sir."

"You should ask your father to take you to Saltdean. The new lido's jolly good. Of course, I can only go round in circles." He noticed me staring at his limp trouser-leg, and saluted: not the response I expected. "Don't look so worried. I didn't let them get my favourite one."

He appeared to be keen for me to laugh, but it seemed impolite somehow, and so I stood stupidly, my mouth twitching.

"Anyway, we really must be getting along." Stepping into the soldier's shadow, Father squeezed his arm. "Glad to see you looking so well. Come along, James."

"Who was that?" I ran to catch up with my father who was striding off down the sun-bleached pavement. Our shadows stretched long and thin, all the way to the street corner.

"Just an old Tommy your mother's taken under her wing." He looked left and right distractedly at the junction, seeming to have forgotten what was next on the agenda. "Good sort, your mother."

I remembered her eyes, her hair, her gasp, and wondered what it would take before she decided to take me under her delicate chiffon wing. Not the loss of half a leg, I hoped.

2 - LOTTIE'S STORY

BRIGHTON, 2001

"And what words have you chosen to have engraved?" Wishing to put my worldly effects in order from the comfort of my bed, I had opted for Mr Marsh of Marsh Littlejohn Solicitors on account of his mobility rather than his reputation. My initial reaction was that Mr Marsh must have sent one of his clerks. We eyed each other with suspicion from our respective vantage points: mine, propped up on a mountain of lace-sheathed pillows, the variety the young assume old ladies crave; his, loitering beyond the foot of the bed. Inching forwards, he introduced himself, touching my rice-paper hand, instantly withdrawing his own.

"*The* Mr Marsh?" I rasped.

"The same." His smile was a blend of pride and embarrassment, as though accepting a prize on the sports field.

I checked myself: there was someone - once - who hadn't dismissed me because I was too young. "You've done well for yourself."

"If it's not rude to ask, how old are you, Miss Pye?" He adopted a voice designed for conversing with deaf foreigners. "It... says... here..."

I interrupted. "Old enough to make a will. And there's no

need to shout for my sake. I have a fully-functioning hearing aid." Credentials established, I nodded to the chair by the side of my bed. "Make yourself at home."

His silk-lined jacket unbuttoned, its tails flicked upwards, a truce of sorts was drawn. He took a slim notebook from his briefcase and, consulting his watch, jotted down the time. "So, what's your secret?"

I hesitated. "My secret?"

"You must have good genes, obviously, but is there anything else?"

"I suppose you'd like me to tell you the path to longevity is lined with whiskey bottles!"

"Preferably."

"Then let's leave it at that. I imagine you're charging by the hour."

My choice of stone, the place of burial: these things were easily settled.

"Your headstone, Miss Pye?" Mr Marsh prompted.

The question wasn't unreasonable. Given the purpose of our meeting, I should have been prepared. Now, I hesitated.

"You must have thought about it." He conveyed a growing impression of anxiety as our interview proceeded, his eyes straying frequently from my face to his wrist. I know how I appeared to him. I experience that self-same shock every time I'm forced to acknowledge myself in a mirror. The face that stares back belongs to what used to be described as an 'old crone'. The witch from Hansel and Gretel. Hollow eyes peering blankly out of the workhouse window. Skin dissected by etchings, stretched so thin it clings to the contours of my skull and gathers in folds around my neck, like a sock that has lost its elastic. Hair so fine it is beyond grooming. But it wasn't always like that. *I* wasn't always like that.

"How would you like to be remembered?" Mr Marsh prompted. Inserting itself into my filing cabinet of thoughts, his question seemed to relate to appearance. I was surprised he was unable to detect the red-headed girl inside my much reduced frame when I felt her presence so vividly. "Beloved wife and mother?" he suggested.

"No!" I averted my gaze while I recovered myself. "Hardly for me to say."

"Hmm." He repeatedly clicked his ballpoint pen - his thumb accustomed to constant texting, no doubt - narrowing his eyes in careful thought. "I take your point." The pen scratched the surface of his notepad.

"What's that you're writing?"

"A fail-safe."

"Saying what, exactly?"

"In loving memory."

My skin went cold. "Cross it out."

"If you're undecided…"

"Please." I felt my nails digging into my palms. "Just do as I ask!"

His expression suggested he thought my protest disproportionate. "Then, can I suggest we keep it simple? Your name and the dates, perhaps…"

An involuntary noise escaped me, interpreted as dismissive. Silently, hands unmoving, Mr Marsh waited for me to expand.

"I had hoped it would be someone else's job to do this, but they've all gone. No one to remember me now."

"All of them?" With the lick of a finger, he scooped back layers of notes in search of a fact to refute what I had said. He didn't have to look far before his finger tapped on an earlier entry.

Though I doubted he'd ever lay eyes on my gravestone, it was because of James - the only blood relative I have ever known - that it was vital to get it right. "To be honest, Mr Marsh, I've never had much faith in words. Words are what lies are made of. I trust only what I see with my own eyes - which is considerably less than it used to be."

After I dismissed his brief lecture on the history of the law with the announcement that that my son, too, was a solicitor, he remained determined to coax something out of me.

"What about poetry? Literature?" And then, unknowingly, he struck gold. "You're not telling me you've lived as long as you have and you don't have a good story or two."

There was a time I liked to quote that the past always falls victim to the present but, in my case, the reverse is now true. The room seemed to darken, the urge to close my eyes and retreat into memory almost overwhelming. Before television, before the wireless, before even cinema, stories were our main form of entertainment. My favourite stories were true, those that had Daddy shaking his jowls and declaring, "You couldn't make that up if you tried!"

"Three," I gasped, fighting to earmark my place in the moment, not to slip backwards until I had the luxury of being alone.

Mr Marsh's startled expression suggested he hadn't expected anything so specific. "I beg your pardon?"

I felt light-headed in my breathlessness. "I have three stories."

"Well, then." A quick recovery, pen poised, he thought he had arrived at a neat solution.

"I'll need time."

"Time?" It was as if I were Oliver, asking for more.

"Yes. To think. Orson Welles hit the nail on the head when he said that a story is almost certainly a lie."

"I understand." Leaning back and folding his arms, Mr Marsh showed no signs of departure. "Whatever you decide will be there for all eternity."

I had to spell it out for him. "Give me a week."

He raised his eyebrows dubiously.

"Don't fret. I'm not going anywhere until we've settled this."

Looking doubtful, Mr Marsh collected his belongings, pointing questioningly to the door as if an alternative exit might have opened up. "Perhaps you'll give me a call when you're ready."

Closing my eyes, the reel began to run; flickering images coming into focus, the slightly speeded-up world of silent movies with its exaggerated expressions. A red-headed girl in a seaside resort at the birth of a new century. The sounds, the sights, the smells, the vastness of the sky and, below, the writhing sea, stretching to infinity - or France, whichever came first. Brighton! Mine for the taking.

"Tell me the one about Phoebe Hessel!" I would demand of Ma, whose stories took on the rhythm of dough being kneaded, accompanied by the clatter of kitchen pans.

I had discovered Phoebe during an elicit game of hide-and-seek in the oldest churchyard in Brighton. Tracing the lichened dates beneath the tangle of ivy, the calculations I made, counting on fingers and then out loud seemed, to me, incredible. "One hundred and eight?"

A hand was clapped on my shoulder. "Got you!"

Declaring loudly, "You can't have, because I'm not playing," I ran all the way home, clattering up the stairs to the kitchen.

"Ma! Ma!"

"What's that terrible to-do about? Is that you, Lottie?"

I recovered my balance with one hand on the doorframe, and panted, "I've just discovered the oldest woman that ever lived! Only she's dead now."

Bent over the table with a rolling pin, Ma merely turned her head, apparently unimpressed. "That must be Phoebe Hessel you're talking about."

"You've heard of her?"

"Ask around town and you'll still find people who remember Phoebe selling gingerbread at the foot of Old Steine. That's where Prince George first came across her."

"A prince?" Gawping, I slipped into my seat at the table.

"*The* prince. But it was her early life that was a mystery. Some say, after her mother died, her father dressed her as a boy soldier so she could follow him into the army. But she would tell anyone who cared to listen how, at the age of fifteen, after she fell madly in love with a private from the King's Lambs, she disguised herself as a man. And together they fought, side by side."

Like a child with a picture book, I learned Phoebe's story by heart, but it had the ring of a fairy tale when Ma told it: "When asked how she kept her secret for so long, she said it wasn't safe to tell it to drunken men or children because they always tell the truth. Instead, she dug a hole big enough to hold a gallon and whispered it to the earth."

"Tell me the part about the highwayman," I begged, aware of every revision to the original: each stretching or concealment of facts.

"What highwayman?" Distributing flour liberally with flicks of a wrist, Ma pretended not to remember it was Phoebe's evidence that brought the notorious James Rooke to justice.

"Josie tells me."

Gripped tighter, the rolling pin hesitated mid-air. "Does she now? Then Josie and I will be having words."

What Tennyson saw fit to immortalise in poetry, Ma thought too gory for children's ears. If I couldn't have the highwayman, a hero among villains, I was going to have the next best thing: "Tell me the one about how you found me!"

I was never under any illusion that I was Ma's real daughter: I was so much more important than that. This was understood by the name I called her. I couldn't say 'Mother' as other children did because it was never in doubt that I'd had a mother of my own. So in one of England's southern-most towns, I used the northern version.

"If you're not careful, child, I'll put you back where you came from."

"Just one more story."

She raised her eyes in despair. "Lord, give me peace in my old age, if it's not too much to ask! Sit yourself down again, child. You're making me dizzy."

I sat, my elbows on the table making circles in the flour, chin resting in my hands, halo neatly in place. "Please, Ma. I am sitting nicely, like you said."

She closed her eyes and, while she drew breath, I held mine in readiness for a hasty retreat in case my nagging produced what I no doubt deserved. Ma pursed her lips, giving no clues as to her decision. "I had always longed for a little girl - don't ask me why - but it wasn't to be. My lot was to have boys but, one by one, I lost them to consumption." A bowl landed heavily on the bleached white surface in front of me; translucent cubes of lard nesting on a bed of soft white flour. "Hands?"

Keenly, I held them out for inspection: fronts, backs and nails. "Make yourself useful, then. Breadcrumbs, fine as you can get them! And try not to get it in your hair like last time. Now, where were we?" Ma returned to her aggressive style of rolling. "You arrived in a late summer storm when all the fine folk had taken to the seafront for their afternoon strolls. The storm came on so sudden that everyone was caught out. Slanted rain made light work of cotton dresses, feathered hats wilted, and silks clung like second skins. I hurried along the promenade, clutching my shawl, while people darted here and there in search of shelter. Holiday-makers huddled in shop doorways, abandoning broken parasols as they raised their hands to hail hansom cabs. Even the fishermen took to the arches, which just goes to show.

"I counted the seconds after I heard the rumble of thunder to see how far behind the lightning was. If someone had told me lightning can strike miles from the centre of a storm, I would have told them not to be so daft. I wasn't afraid for myself; it's not as if I had any good clothes to ruin. As the pavement cleared of running feet, I faced the elements, blinking back raindrops. Thinking I was alone, I watched lightning fork into the swollen sea, still some distance off. The rain seemed to be easing when I became aware of a woman pushing a perambulator up ahead."

I fidgeted: the first appearance of my mother.

"Don't wriggle if you want to hear the end of the story, Lottie." Ma slapped the wrist nearest to her, a warning glance. I angled the bowl so that she could inspect its contents. "Still too lumpy. You're not done, not by a long way, Missy. Now, where were we?" Wiping her brow with the back of her hand, Ma left a telltale trail of powdery white. "The woman, she looked like a holiday-maker from behind, all fashionable-like, holding onto her fancy hat, dress nipping her in at the waist while its skirts dragged along the pavement, heavy with water. Both ruined! While everyone else had taken cover, with waves crashing about her feet, she continued her walk to the end of the promenade. As you know, I've got no time for tourists whose idea of disaster is a heel gone down a pothole, but this woman seemed equally foolish when there was a child's safety at stake. 'Madam!' I called through the rumble of thunder." She shaped her hands into a megaphone to demonstrate. "'Let me help you find shelter for the little one.' Just as the woman turned, open-mouthed with surprise, lightning pierced the sky and struck the wet pavement." My breath was suspended in an inflated moment. "I watched helpless as she was lifted into the air like a rag-doll and thrown into the street right in front of my eyes. Freed from her hands, your carriage continued its journey towards the sea. There was no time to think.

I ran after it and grabbed the metal handle, just as the front wheels reached the place where the pavement drops away. There you were, wrapped in white and screaming at the top of your lungs."

"Show me, Ma." Grabbing her hands, webbed together with the makings of pastry dough, I peeled away her fingers to reveal scarred palms. "Are you sure it didn't hurt?"

"Ruined the nerve endings, the doctor told me. Never felt a thing in them since. Now, look at the mess you've made! What did I tell you, Lottie?" She attempted to shake me off. "Do you want to go to bed without hearing the ending?"

Conceding that I didn't, I meekly returned my hands to the bowl.

"By this time, an audience of black umbrellas had gathered. They were none too keen to get too close to the poor lady where she'd come to rest in the sludge left behind by the horses and the rain. It was a white-haired gentleman who stepped forwards to do the decent thing, covering her with his cape, God bless her soul.

"No one knew who your mother was. When she wasn't claimed or reported missing, they assumed she was a fine lady on a day-trip from London. 'Would you mind taking the baby home while we track down the father?' a policeman asked me. 'I wouldn't want to be blamed for sending her to the workhouse if she doesn't belong there.'"

Satisfied with the explanation that my mother was a fashionable lady from London, I was taken aback when a semicircle of sly-faced tormentors disguised as seven-year-olds trapped me in a secluded alley.

"Oi, Red-head! Think your mother was a lady?"

I looked up to an open window two storeys above, but saw only a small rug that had been hung out to air.

"You know what sort of woman God strikes down with lightning?"

My hands sought refuge behind my back, finding the roughness of brickwork.

"Prozzies."

I swallowed.

"Who else wouldn't be missed?"

"Lottie's mother was a prozzie."

This crude refrain was taken up, filling the narrow space.

"So what if she was?"

Heads swivelled. Alfie West, mop-haired wearer of hand-me-downs, had dared breach the line of attack. He thrust out a hand, a life-saver. Hauling me behind him, he hissed, "Get yourself off home," and then provided a verbal shield. "What's it to you? Oldest profession in the world. More than you can say for dustmen, Charlie Brazier. And remind me what your mother does, Ethel? That's right: milk lady."

"But it was your mother told mine!"

"My mother repeats a lot of stupid things she hears. It doesn't make them true."

Charlie Brazier squared up, feet a shoulder-width apart, and squashed his nose sideways against the back of his hand. "Let's get this right. Are you calling your own mother a liar?"

"Kiss my arse!" Alfie simultaneously threw the first punch and turned to me. "You still here?"

Seeing my escape route, I scampered home, blubbering incomprehensibly. Ma was in the yard, clothes pegs in her mouth, but she soon had me up in the kitchen, legs dangling from the tabletop. Pacified by a jam-coated spoon, I was implored to talk sense.

"Stuff and nonsense! Children say all sorts of cruel things without thinking." Ma's verdicts, always final, came with backing from on high. "I doubt God still deals in lightning bolts but, if he does, he'd have a better bowling-arm than they credit him with. Why, he'd have had the lot of them by now! Listen to me, Lottie. Your mother was in the wrong place at the wrong time, that's all. Could have happened to any one of us." (I suspect that she was thinking of herself, so close to the centre of the storm and yet spared.)

"It wasn't just children," I persisted, licking the spoon. "Alfie West says he heard it from his mother."

"Oh, that Mrs West!" She hugged me close, strawberry-daubed cheeks and all. "She's always picking up scraps of gossip. Just say for argument's sake that God chose to punish your mother - and I'm not saying he did, mind. He chose to save you for greater things."

Her message was clear: God had a purpose for me. It was my job to work out what it was.

3 - LOTTIE'S STORY

BRIGHTON, 1910

Daddy stood back, surveying his handiwork with a critical frown. *Kate and Sidney Pye's World Famous Steak and Kidney Pies* curved in gold-edged lettering on the plate-glass shopfront, and underneath, in the shape of a smile, *Accept no imitations*. Whether lit or not, his pipe, rarely extracted from his mouth, now rose and fell. "What do you think, Nipper?"

"It's beautiful!" I cried in admiration, clasping my hands.

"But will Ma like it?"

You might not think a fishing port would be the place for a pie shop, but even if you loved the smell of the sea and all of the aromas carried inland on the wind, folk can't live, breathe and eat fish seven days a week. Even the fishwives who sold the catch straight from cradles on their heads queued to spend their hard-earned coins at our shop. Wiping his paintbrush with turps, Daddy winked at me. "Everybody loves a pie."

I never really understood why. Most folks survived on stew. On Sundays it might be rich with a sheep's head or bullocks' livers but all that was left by Fridays was gravy. In my mind, pie was only stew wearing a hat. And although Ma's piecrust was crisp and golden and melted in your mouth, there was no mistaking stew for anything else. Still, the filling that went into her pies was special. Slow-fried onions the colour of toffee-apples mingled with chunks of topside steeped in best Sussex ale. ("Wasted," lamented Daddy, looking on longingly in hope of the dregs.) Mushrooms and kidneys were thrown into the pot, but all sorts might find their way into the mixture. And, the thing was, you couldn't inspect the filling until you'd parted with your money.

On cue, Ma appeared behind me. "Well, let's have a look at your masterpiece." Her smile performed a trick of acrobatic proportions, promptly standing on its head. "I thought we'd agreed to put something about 'health-giving properties' underneath!"

"Now, we *didn't* agree, Kitty. If you remember rightly, what I actually said was there's no proof -"

"Who needs proof? Everybody knows it's just puff. Anyway, you didn't mind 'world famous.'"

"We have our share of foreign visitors, but the line has to be drawn somewhere."

"No one's died after eating one of my pies," Ma protested, as if this were something to trumpet about. She operated a strict three-stage warning system but, bypassing step one, Ma moved straight to her steeliest glare, leaving Daddy to reflect.

Consulting a cloud, he exhaled. "Not as far as we know."

Knowing we would both pay the price of Ma's displeasure, my mind raced to chores left undone. *"That bucket's no use to anyone empty."*

Although bird-like in stature, Ma was equipped with a great booming voice designed for keeping order, and she wasn't one to hold back, not with opinions or admonishments. Daddy, who knew he could be absent-minded, was patient when her moods descended.

"What have I done wrong now, my dear?" he would enquire smilingly.

"It's not what you've done, it's what you *haven't* done!" she exploded.

But, on the whole, the household ran like clockwork. "What we'd do without that woman I'll never know," Daddy remarked, but once she was out of earshot he was inclined to add, "I've a few ideas of my own."

"What's that, Daddy?"

He crouched down to my height, his bones groaning with resistance. "Ma's trouble is that she thinks work's a cure for everything, even a broken heart. But I wake with the sound of gulls in my ears and long for the sight of the ocean. I see old pals I've known since I ran barefoot, and I ask myself, would the occasional pint of ale really do any harm?"

"Whose heart's broken, Daddy?"

He sighed and pulled me to him. "Both of ours, Nipper: your Ma's and mine. But we've got rather too good at hiding it from each other."

Although his sons were never far from Daddy's mind, I thought of myself as more than adequate compensation. I set about the task of convincing Daddy by throwing my arms around him whenever the occasion called for it - and sometimes when it didn't, to keep him on his toes.

Muffled by his striped apron, I sulked, "But why does Ma always have to be the one who says what goes?"

"If I had my way, I'd be up on the Downs every afternoon and nothing would ever get done. We all have to do things we don't like, Nipper. I'd be lying if I told you otherwise. Doing right is what's important."

"But how do you know what's right?"

"Your Ma puts me straight, that's how." He kissed my frown away. "I'm joking with you! The right thing is the one that nags away at you and won't let go until you give in."

It sounded very much like Temptation. "How do you know it isn't telling you to do bad things?"

He chuckled. "Chances are, the bad things are those you want to do but shouldn't and the good things are what you don't want to do but should."

"Are adults' answers always so confusing?"

Daddy thought for a moment. "I'm afraid so. Not everything in life is clear-cut. It would be nice if it was. Sometimes, all you can do is make a decision and hope it's the right one."

I hoped for facts when I asked questions, and I asked an awful lot of questions. There were facts that I understood at the time. Already, I was arguing with the one that said I had a life of domestic service to look forward to until I married and had a home of my own to clean.

Ma had attempted to tame me by making sure I knew how to sweep the hearth, light the fire and to make use of the cinders to polish cutlery: "There's nothing worse than being unprepared, my girl. And if you have a head start, all well and good."

The responsibility of making sure the coal bucket was full was usually a job for a son but, in the absence of her darling boys, Ma declared dubiously, "You'll have to do." So instead of curling into a tight ball at first light and waiting for the frozen condensation on the inside of the windowpane to thaw, I was the only girl who trailed behind the tip carts with a dozen boys, hair still a-quiff from their pillows.

"Go home, Red-head!" They broke away from scavenging for stray lumps in the gutters to lift the layers of my hems with their sticks - sticks that also encouraged lumps of coke to fall off the cart. "Get back to scrubbing floors."

Prepared to turn an occasional blind eye, the coalman's patience was tried until he would snatch a stick out of the hand of a boy and turn on us. "I should inform on the whole bleeding lot of you!" There were no complaints. Most parents considered their sons' temperaments would be improved by a good beating. Even if Alfie West was under orders not to go home empty-handed, his mother had no sympathy: "I didn't tell you to get caught, now, did I?" she'd say, dragging him indoors by the ear.

"They're right, Lottie," Alfie said. "I don't like to think of the end of that stick going anywhere near you. There's more than enough driftwood on the beach to keep your Ma happy."

Swapping cobbles for shingle, I picked my way between upturned boats draped with nets and the brightly-coloured bathing machines owned by the fishermen as a sideline. Lamenting the days when there were hundreds of fishing boats, they complained to the tourists they rowed around the harbour that their industry was in its death throes.

"Yours are the only death throes I can see," I apologised to the bulging-eyed fish whose silver tails thrashed in nets.

You can try to forget the sea if you live in Brighton, but it never forgets you. There's a reason you feel most at home on the beach. You become a reflection of the wildness. The fishermen understood how I felt.

"I survived a storm," I boasted, convinced of my invincibility, as the wind lashed at my hair and salt coated my skin.

Their pipes nodded at the corners of their mouths as they concurred: "Oh, you're a fisherman's daughter. No doubt."

Home was all I knew. Children put up with disapproval, because we were always warned worse was hiding round the corner.

"If you can't find something useful to do, get out from under my feet!" Ma would yell. "And I don't want to see you until teatime!"

I didn't wait to be told twice. As far as the arches of the viaduct, the streets were mine; from the stench of the slums, through the narrow back-alleys to the grand Regency avenues lined with exotic palms. In a town designed for pleasure there was always plenty to do. An Italian organ-grinder pushed a tottering monkey dressed in a red waistcoat into the crowds with a collecting cap. Punch and Judy shows drew gasps on the promenade. There were cockles, whelks and jellied eels to gorge on. We had strong men, escape artists, bearded ladies and dwarfs. But, for me, the greatest spectacle was the fashionable folk who strutted the length of Madeira Terrace like peacocks. Our visitors rode the electric railway from the Palace Pier, or took one of Campbell's paddle steamers, not realising *they* were *our* entertainment. I lapped up every exquisite detail: the pearl buttons, the puffed sleeves, the feathers and bows, the delicate lace trim, the whitest gloves. These women had chambermaids to dress them. Road sweepers rushed to their assistance so they didn't ruin their good shoes. They glanced out from beneath wide-brimmed hats to make sure they were being watched by the right sort of people, and, if you weren't the right sort, they thought nothing of saying, "I'll thank you not to stare."

You could mix with royalty, film-makers, actors and music hall stars in Brighton. I had no shortage of choices when searching for my Great Purpose, and, slowly, I began my process of elimination.

4 - SIR JAMES'S STORY

SHERE, 2009

I didn't react when my mother's solicitor wrote to inform me of her death - hadn't known how to react, if I'm honest. I'd presumed she had died many years ago. I lost my father when he was sixty-seven, back in 1959. Not racing, as I'd always feared, but as a spectator. It was the excitement that killed him. My mother was his junior by eight years. Who would have expected her to live another half century? She must have been, what...? 108 years old to my eighty-seven. It hardly seems possible.

I had no idea she'd known where I live. Even old friends had failed to track me down to Shere, a small Surrey village hemmed between the A25 and the North Downs. A ramshackle scattering of overhanging gables, timber beams and crooked elevations, dotted around the ancient churchyard of St James's. Clear waters from the Tillingbourne trickle idly through, dissecting Middle Street in front of the award-winning public conveniences complete with their ivy-trailing hanging baskets. Here, a short walk with the dog in tow, pausing on the bench to feed the white-tufted ducks, followed by a paper and a pint qualifies as a good day out. At weekends our tranquility is shattered by the rumble and roar of Harleys and

Morgans. Noisy Americans in search of the quintessential English experience get as far as the stocks outside the Black Swan Pub before being lured inside by chalked promises and rumours of smugglers. Do I share the right of the locals to be disgruntled when I too sought a timeless retreat? I like to think I do my bit by lending my name to the petition to make Church Square traffic-free. (I can so rarely park outside my own house - a double-fronted affair with a dubious history as the local vicarage and one-time brothel.) But as a resident of only twenty-two years, I am still eyed with suspicion, as if it were my ill-gotten money that funded Pathfields housing estate that continues to defy the architect's optimistic prediction that it would 'soon weather in'.

It was through this insubstantial network of roads designed for nothing wider than a horse and cart that the man from *Parcelforce* was obliged to wend his way. I imagine he looked over his shoulder through a wound-down window to ensure he wasn't leaving evidence of his passage on the fleet of shiny 4 x 4s.

A silvery vibration from my glass cabinet preceded his knock. Restraining Isambard by the collar, his paws determined to claw a path to freedom on the tiled floor, I answered the door.

"Sir James 'astings?" The man asked, all tattoos and open-collared uniform shirt, shifting his weight from one trainer-clad foot to the other.

"Yes?" I looked disapprovingly at his van, its engine idling.

"Sign here, please." Without eye contact, he thrust a miniature etch-a-sketch and a finely chiselled plastic implement in my direction.

"What am I signing for?" I noticed he had a perfectly good HB pencil behind his ear.

"You don't think they tell me, do you?" He hoisted up his trousers by the waistband, sniffing. "I'm just the delivery man."

The resulting signature bore no resemblance to the letters I thought I had traced.

"Excuse me." Mrs Smythe-Jenkins approached with a slight bend in her legs, nervous as only a woman in designer heels on cobbles can be. "Do you know how long you're going to be? I can't quite squeeze past."

"As long as it takes, love." Turning back to me, the delivery man raised his eyebrows, lowering his tone. "Plenty of room - if she knew the width of her vehicle."

I stood by, growing increasingly dumbfounded as, sideways shuffling and with beads of sweat standing prominently on his forehead, he deposited box after box in my narrow hallway. "There must be a mistake."

"You said you're Sir James Hastings, didn't you?"

"What on earth are they?"

"Bleeding heavy, that's what!"

He loitered optimistically, but I recoiled from the idea of tipping him for something I hadn't ordered. "You've been paid, I take it?" I asked.

"Yes, Gov -"

"Then I think we're done." I watched his face fall, then, raising one hand, nodded an apology to Mrs Smythe-Jenkins. Sitting in her open-topped BMW she anxiously checked her Rolex. Always picking up here and dropping off there, experiencing life vicariously through her daughters. Probably the closest she ever came to sitting still, her distress was only too apparent. I heard Isambard retreat, nails clipping down the hallway, commencing his oval circuits of the dining room table. "Basket!" I hollered after him, feeling the need to holler at someone.

The boxes were sealed with blue plastic bindings that would have challenged Houdini. I hadn't had the scissors out since last Christmas's wrapping frenzy - couldn't imagine where they might have got to - so I retrieved a nail clipper from the bathroom cabinet and launched an attack on the first accessible box.

Lifting the cardboard flaps, I frowned: "What the devil?"

Tightly packed with s-shaped polystyrene chips, it housed a number of hinged wooden boxes containing green glass plates, the precursors to photographic negatives. In the second were folders of photographic prints - hundreds of the things - carefully catalogued decade by decade. I found notebooks filled with diagrams and words. Scrapbooks containing newspaper clippings. A lifetime's memorabilia. And here, a letter written ten years ago on tissue-thin paper in spidery scrawl, its envelope taped to the side of box one.

'To my own sweet James,'

The greeting made me bristle. As a young boy, I had dreamed of being addressed in that manner.

'It is my greatest regret that we spent so little time together, but there never was a right time to invite myself back into your life and explain why I left. Anything I might have said began to sound unacceptable, even to me. I don't expect it will be any comfort for you to hear that there hasn't been a day when I haven't thought of you.

I was deeply saddened to hear of your father's passing. He was a good man - and I was a foolish young girl who could never have given you everything you deserved. I hope that you have known happiness, but if not happiness, a sense of usefulness that gives life purpose. There is much to be said for keeping busy.

I used to think that I took photographs to record people and things that might otherwise have been lost. Now I tend to think that I was simply justifying my own existence. Perhaps, if you look hard enough, you will find my reflection in them.'

There was more if I had cared to read on, but I felt the walls closing in, the space-shifting sensation reminiscent of that claustrophobic art gallery where, for the briefest of moments, I had been pushed in front of a beautiful lady and told she was my mother. Hands shaking, I struggled to put the letter back in its envelope, to tuck the flap back inside.

"Pub!" I shouted at Isambard, who, familiar with the command, appeared leather lead in mouth, metal chain trailing. At the same time, I grabbed my stick.

We walked the few yards across Church Square, past the war memorial where the wreath that I'd laid for Harry Patch, one of the last veterans of the Great War, had seen too much autumn. I had been deeply moved as I watched him break the silence of eighty years, his memories still so raw as to summon tears. It has since struck me that he would have been only slightly older than my mother. Why was it I felt no similar sense of kinship with my own flesh and blood? Distracted by brewing anger I told myself that I had not been forgotten. Worse than that - my mother had been thinking about me but *still* there was no invitation. And now - now! - that she felt the need to *apologise,* her main concern was that I had been making myself *useful.*

Stepping inside the comforting dimness of the pub, I ducked under one of its worm-infested beams that supported the weight of history. The threadbare carpet, rustic tables and wax-encrusted candlesticks suggested an authentic experience; the á la carte menu otherwise. I was relieved to find our favourite table, by the crackle of the open fire, vacant.

"Lie down!" I pointed as I stood at the low bar. Isambard sunk meekly to the floor, the black tip of his nose resting on his front paws, sombre eyes trailing me.

A beach-blonde newcomer enquired, mid-spin, "What'll it be, mate?" in such a way that I wasn't sure he was addressing me. He turned, puffing out his cheeks as he made what passed for eye contact.

"Pint of *TEA* please. And a bowl of water for the dog, if it's not too much trouble."

Hearing of his demotion, Isambard lifted one disapproving ear.

"Coming right up." The barman punched the touch-screen of the till, picked up a pint glass and threw it, catching it in the other hand. "That'll be £3.45."

I examined the glass of amber liquid that he deposited on the bar towel in front of me. "I'm afraid it seems to be cloudy."

"Give it a minute to settle, mate. Yes?" He began to serve a neat woman dressed in tight jodhpurs and gleaming riding boots who already had her red leather purse open, and whose smile had an apologetic quality, as if she was sorry for disturbing him. "Two lattes for table three, please."

My patience in short supply, I held the glass up to the artificial light filtered through the classic malts. "I'm telling you, it's off."

Frowning, the barman consulted a passing colleague whose v-necked t-shirt exposed crevice-like cleavage. "Mate." Standing in front of the spitting espresso machine, his back to me, he briefly inclined his head towards the glass. "Does that look cloudy to you?"

She barely gave it a glance. "Give it time." Polish, from the sound of her.

Aware that I was overreacting but unable to stop myself, I raised my voice: "Is there *anyone* here who knows a thing or two about beer? I don't suppose, by any remote possibility, that there are any *English* staff left in this establishment?"

Table conversation temporarily suspended, heads strained in my direction displaying appalled expressions.

The barman leaned on the bar, his elbow aggressively close to my hand, and lowered his voice. "Listen, mate, if you've got a problem…"

"You're damned right, *mate*. If you'll give me my money

back, I'll take my business elsewhere."

"Gladly." His palm hit the bar in front of me, depositing three pound coins and a handful of coppers underneath. I pocketed the money, slapping my leg and grabbed my stick. "Isambard. Come, boy!"

"And by the way: you're barred!"

As eyes were hastily averted, there was much shaking of heads and tutting as I stumbled on the doormat. "You know, the young come in for all the flack, but I find it's the older generation who have no manners these days," I heard one voice exclaim to an eager hum of agreement.

Not a regular among them: no hint of sympathy. Doing what I had sworn never to do, I walked uphill to the William Bray, newly renovated, which I always associate with being stripped of character. Greeted by a sign that announced, 'Only guide dogs allowed', I was about to turn away in silent protest when a barmaid dressed plainly in black sailed through the door. As she arrived on the patio area at the bottom of a small flight of steps, Isambard took a healthy interest, sniffing her where no dog should sniff a young lady in polite company.

"Isambard, no!" I tugged at his lead and turned to her. "I must apologise -"

Laughing, she deposited her tower of plastic ashtrays on a round umbrellaed table and stooped down to fuss over him. "He's just being friendly, aren't you, boy? He *is* a boy, isn't he?"

"He most certainly is."

"We used to have a German Shepherd just like him, down to the black snout." Having located the drool-inducing spot behind his rust-coloured ears she had him under her spell.

"Don't tell him that! He thinks he's unique."

As her close-fitting t-shirt rode up to reveal the base of her spine, I liked her all the more for the absence of a Celtic tattoo.

She glanced over her shoulder at me and grimaced. "He

may be right. We had to have ours put down six months ago."

I was torn between awkwardness and sympathy. "Ghastly business."

"How old is he?"

"We're not entirely sure. The animal sanctuary bullied me into taking him. Must be ten years we've been together now, a couple of old strays."

She smiled apologetically. "Did you see the sign?"

"I have to say, I'm not keen on leaving him outside."

"Tell you what, seeing as its quiet and the boss is out, you can bring him in just this once." Making quick work of the steps, she held the door open and stood aside.

Stealing past, Isambard clipped across the green-grey slate tile. The bar was airy and empty; not a juke box or slot machine in sight. As I perched on a leather barstool, a clatter of pans and shouts of laughter filtered through from the kitchen.

"You're Sir James, aren't you? I heard you were a Black Swan man."

"Truth told, I've had a falling out with the barman. I shall have to apologise if I want to show my face in there again."

"You never know." She took her place behind the bar against a backdrop of bottles that avoided the impression of clutter. "You might prefer it here."

I thought I wouldn't appreciate the minimalism, but I found myself running my hands over the smooth surface of the bar, a single piece of oak that had been allowed to retain its natural curve.

"Bitter?"

"Please. If you don't mind."

My eyes were drawn to framed black and white photographs showcasing architectural details from the village: close by, a fragment of lettering from a gravestone; on the opposite wall, a precariously tilting chimney. My mind drifted to the contents of those boxes.

Angling the glass and pouring with an easy confidence, the barmaid followed my lingering gaze. "If you like them, there's more next door in the restaurant. Mainly of motor racing. The guy who owns this place? He's into all that."

Given that we were the only two people present, it would have been awkward not to chat, but the search for common ground - beyond a love of dogs - seemed futile. "They say he's the *Stig*, don't they?"

"Don't tell anyone but *Top Gear*'s not really my thing. I'm more a *Stig of the Dump* kind of girl."

"I suppose you'll tell me I should have heard of him."

Her expression one of incomprehension, she placed the pint on the bar in front of me. "That was *only* my favourite book when I was growing up."

"I thought you were going to tell me he's a rap artist! You see, that's the problem with not having children."

"No nieces or nephews?" she asked.

"Only child," I explained.

"Me too."

"Ah!" I reached for the glass appreciatively. "Now, *that's* what I call a pint." I took a sip. Having investigated - and rejected - the possibility of sitting in front of the log burner, Isambard settled by my feet. "I feel at home already." I tapped my chest with a little in the way of pride. "My father was involved in motor racing, you know."

Wincing slightly, the barmaid rested her elbows on the bar. "I'm more into the photography side of things. The older the better."

I was intrigued to see her eyes take on an eager glow. "Is that so?"

"We're doing the Twenties at college. There's this stuff by Cecil Beaton you wouldn't believe. If I hadn't seen the proof, I would never have believed people back then looked so modern. That's why photographs are important. 'The camera never lies.'"

"Load of tosh. What about all of that paint-brushing the magazines do?" As she looked momentarily confused, I back-tracked. "What did I say?" It was such a long time since I had conversed with anyone under the age of twenty that, in my panic, I had chosen the wrong word. But I also found that I was smiling.

"You mean air-brushing! But they didn't have that back then, did they?"

"Beaton did his share of doctoring, I can tell you. This generation of women aren't the first to want to look taller and thinner."

"*Really?*" Elbows slid across oak towards me conspiratorially.

"I wonder," I said, looking at her anew. "You say you like old photographs?"

"Love them," she replied luxuriously.

"Then I've just taken delivery of something that might interest you." I shook my head, dislodging a memory of the delivery man. "Forty-two boxes of the stuff, would you believe?"

5 - LOTTIE'S STORY

BRIGHTON, 1910

Long before doubt was cast on Ma's story of my beginnings, I woke on Sundays with the feeling that something terrible must have happened. With no toys, laughter or work to distract us, there was nothing to look forward to. Gone the comfortable weekday layers, dressing was a penance. I laid out my best frock and petticoat, starched and steamed to cardboard perfection.

"Lottie, don't make me late for church!" Ma knocked on the bedroom door, her gloved hands impatient for something to be getting on with.

"Know thine enemy," I quoted, resigning myself to the inevitable; counting the hours until bedtime when I could wriggle free.

"Now, don't you look pretty?" She slapped my fingers away from my collar as I emerged.

"But it's cutting into my neck!" I flounced downstairs, the effect Ma desired ruined by an unsaintly scowl.

Daddy silently sympathised, standing at the kitchen doorway, pulling down his own stiffly-starched collar to display raw skin.

Church was followed by Sunday School. While I read Bible

stories, Ma enjoyed her only weekly outing, visiting an old friend in a sanatorium. She never seemed to get any better, this anonymous friend. Asked, "How was she?" Ma sighed her standard-issue response: "Much the same."

Daddy wasn't the church type. "Don't you believe in God?" I had asked, horrified to have learned the severe punishment for non-attendance.

"Well, now." Daddy packed his pipe tightly. "My god is nature, and nature is at its most powerful when it's shaped like a wave, buffeting the jagged rocks." It was understood between us that his Sunday ritual involved donning his best collar and tie, paying his respects to the fishermen and looking out to sea. Being a man, he understood politics and science. He'd done his best to explain Darwin's theories to me but, after I endured repeated nightmares populated by rats the size of hippopotamuses, Ma politely requested he stick to politics.

After he turned his attention to educating me about 'Votes for Women', she was equally nonplussed. "Give over, Sidney. When would I find time to chain myself to railings?"

It was only after Ma explained about my Great Purpose that I started paying attention in church. She hoped it wasn't too late to replace all the modern ideas Daddy had been pumping into my head with the Ten Commandments. The reason for her anxiety only became clear over time. I had thought I was a permanent fixture in the Pye household, but one Sunday, after throwing my arms around Daddy's neck as he bent over *The Gazette*, I asked, "What are you looking for?"

He rubbed his eyes and sighed loudly. "You're old enough for an honest answer."

It had been a throwaway question, brought on by boredom. Now he had my undivided attention.

"I've been placing advertisements in the paper in the hope that we might trace your real daddy. Every week, I search the columns to see if anyone has replied."

Arms dropped to my sides, leaden. "But - but you told me I was your little girl! I thought you wanted me. "

"And you are, Nipper, you are, but…"

In my experience, explanations beginning with buts were lies, and I haven't heard much in my long life to change my mind. I flew to my room, where my head remained buried face-down under a pillow throughout Daddy's attempts to console me, until my tear ducts ran dry. I drifted in and out of sleep to the sounds of the business, serenaded by customers stopping on their way home from the music hall.

"Oh, I do like to be beside the seaside,
Oh, I do like to be beside the sea…"

"Is that one of your own, Eddie?"

"It's the new one by Mark Sheridan. Haven't you heard it?"

"Now, when would I get the chance to hear new music?"

The crackle of greaseproof paper, snatches of high-pitched laughter, the chink of coins being slipped into the till: these were my lullabies.

"You awake, Sid?" Ma's hissing voice on the other side of the paper-thin wall woke me.

"I wasn't." The springs of the big bed creaked.

"I'm worried about that girl," Ma whispered.

Daddy's voice was exhausted. "I thought she was old enough to understand."

"Oh, she'll have forgotten all about it by morning, you'll see. That's not what's on my mind. What I was wondering was… could she take after her mother?"

"She's a good girl. You've seen to that. Now, can we get some sleep?"

The bed creaked again. "Sidney?"

"What now, Woman?"

"That *Natural Selection*. Is it in the blood?"

More squeaking of springs. "Good*night*, Kitty!"

It might have been Ma's generous administrations of cod liver oil, but I could barely recall a day's illness. Still, something was wrong with me, serious enough to be reserved for whispers. All the more reason to pray, I scrunched my eyes shut and pressed my palms together with renewed levels of concentration. And then I took to wondering if church on Sundays was enough to keep me out of the fires of hell or - worse still - the workhouse.

My Saturday afternoon wanderings resulted in newfound fascination with the nuns of the Community of the Virgin Mary; strange, romantic figures who glided through the streets in crocodile formation, blinkered like the rag and bone man's horse. When I tried to engage one in conversation, a woman pulled me aside, keeping a firm grip of my elbow while she berated me: "You oughtn't to do that. They won't answer you, you know! They've taken vows of silence."

Released, I cradled my wretched arm in the other, nursing my biceps in an exaggerated manner. "What's a Vow of Silence?"

"They're not allowed to speak except to pray."

"Why's that?"

The woman's nostrils flared. "It's unnatural for a little girl to ask so many questions." But, unwilling to let the opportunity to display her superior knowledge pass, she was quick to relent. "It's so they can hear God when He speaks to them."

My own Vow of Silence got me into trouble.

"I'm talking to you, young lady!" Ma's fist hit the table, making the mixing bowl jump. "And I'll thank you for doing me the courtesy of replying."

I got on no better at school where everything was learned parrot fashion. Sent home with a rap across the knuckles and an instruction to "Pray for some intelligence," Ma assumed the worst and added a clip round the ear to the equation. Two undeserved punishments were too much to bear and, clutching the side of my head, it was with howls that I broke my vow.

"Now then, Nipper!" Drawn towards the commotion, Daddy appeared in the doorway.

"Oh, Daddy!" I flung myself into his apron, sobbing. "I tried really hard."

"I think it's time we had a little chat." He herded me towards my bedroom and ensured I was deposited onto one of the twin beds, a sobbing, shoulder-shuddering wreck. He sat on the opposite mattress, arms folded across his knees. "Why don't you explain what went wrong."

"I - I - I -"

Daddy applied one hand to each of my shoulders. "Deep breaths." He demonstrated the process.

"I took a V-vow of Silence," my voice quavered. "But no one would let me keep it."

"What did you want to do *that* for?" He held me at arm's length, wearing a half-amused expression.

"It was so I could hear God telling me about my Great Purpose."

"What *are* you talking about, you daft child?"

I tried to keep my explanation simple. "Ma says God saved me for a reason."

Daddy's face turned a violent shade of puce. An angry serpent-shaped vein throbbed on the side of his forehead. Holding my breath, I anticipated the worst.

"Lottie, Lottie!" He sighed, drawing me to his chest and wrapping me up in his arms. "Isn't it enough that you make me happy in my old age?"

"You mean I'm to stay?"

He rocked me. "Of course you are! What would I do without you?"

But that wasn't all he had to say about it. I listened through the wall. Daddy rarely raised his voice, so it was quite a speech for him.

"It's got to stop, Kitty! You've filled the child's brain with candy floss and she's taken it to heart."

"What do you expect me to say when she comes home with ugly gossip?" Ma began protesting in her wronged tone of voice.

"No more, not another word! She's already got her head in the clouds, and when she comes crashing down to earth it will be your fault, do you hear me?"

From then on, I kept my search a secret. Joining the end of their crocodile, the nuns led me to the front of an imposing fortress in Queens Square. It was entered through a gothic gateway, with a hexagonal turret and crenulated pointings. I carefully mouthed what had been stencilled on the wall: 'St Ma-ry's Home for Fe-male Pen-i-tents'.

I could hardly ask Daddy what it meant so I saved the question for Sunday School, where Mr Lesley, a serious man of retreating hairline and overcrowded mouth, allowed sensible questions asked in earnest. Loitering patiently in the shadow of the organ-loft until the others had left, I asked, "Excuse me, Sir, but can you tell me what a Pen-i-tent is?"

"Well, Lottie, it's another word for a sinner who's seen the error of his ways."

I was confused. "Are the nuns from St Mary's sinners?"

I was alarmed to find I was the cause of Mr Lesley's dramatic change in colour. "Why do you ask, child?"

"The sign says it's for Female Pen-i-tents."

His relief was immediate. "I see why you're mistaken. They run a home for fallen women who would otherwise be destined for the workhouse." He hurried to cross himself. "There but for the grace of God…"

"Amen," I concluded, this gesture of dismissal making me reticent to ask Mr Lesley what a fallen woman was. Next week, perhaps.

It wasn't long before I found myself outside St Mary's

Home again. I was waiting for a nun to emerge, when a couple of young ladies stepped out of the front door.

"Shall we make a run for it?" Walking under the arch, one laughed - apparently intoxicated by the blast of sea air which swept her blonde hair across her cheek. Closing her eyes in pleasure, she inhaled deeply and expelled a satisfied *Ah!*

"Here!" The second noticed me, narrowing her eyes and pointing. "What are you looking at?"

"You're not nuns," I said cautiously from the cover of a tree lopped so brutally it was hard to tell if it had started life as an acorn or a conker.

The first put her hands over the round hard bulge of her stomach, throwing back her head. "They wouldn't have us."

"Are you fallen women?"

The pointing young lady approached. "Think you're better than us, do you? What are you? Nine?"

"I'm ten," I swallowed, backing into the tree trunk. Close behind me, a horse clipped past.

"I give you a year in service, then you can come back and call me names." With this haughty retort, she disappeared inside the front door.

"Don't mind her." The other leant back against the wall. Her smile was sad around the edges, like a delicate scrap of frayed material. "I don't expect you know what you're saying."

"I don't," I agreed enthusiastically. "I was told nuns and fallen women live here, and you're too pretty to be nuns."

"You're sweet." She traced a slow semicircle in the dust with the toe of her boot and reversed the action. "There's some like Connie who were daft enough to believe the promises men made them. And there's others like me... you could say I'm a volunteer, I suppose." Air caught in her throat in the form of an *hmf*. "Not that it feels like it now."

I must have looked confused, because she smiled that sad smile again. "This place is for unmarried mothers and prostitutes. Dear now, I really shouldn't use that word with you."

Prostitutes were a fact we lived with, each neighbourhood boasting its own brothel, butchers and bakery. Despite this - my parents being older, having no brothers or sisters to enlighten me, and being too embarrassed to show my ignorance - I only had the vaguest idea of what was involved. "Some people say my mother was one of them. I was saved from the workhouse."

She looked genuinely pleased. "And what's your name?"

"Lottie Pye. As in *Kate and Sidney Pye's World Famous Pies*. Only they're not my real parents."

"Well, Lottie Pye." She reached out and shook my hand, quite seriously. "I'm Felicity."

"Felicity who?" I asked, just as the door opened inwards and, behind her, through the gateway, I saw a fierce square frown framed by a wimple.

Felicity put one hand under the swell of her stomach while she righted herself. "Just Felicity."

The frown spoke, its voice flat. "It's time."

"One moment please, Sister." She turned to me.

"Perhaps you'd prefer to find alternative accommodation where the rules suit you better than ours."

Knowing she couldn't be seen, the young lady pulled a face and stuck out her tongue, then whispered, "What do you say if one day I come by and try one of those pies of yours?"

The choice between the fierce frown and the sad smile was one of the easiest I ever had to make. "Oh, yes!" I said.

screen, skirts trailing seconds behind. "Oh, I'm terribly sorry! I didn't see you have company."

"Lottie," Mr Parker introduced me. "This is my model -"

But before he could go any further, the young woman cried, "Lottie, what are you doing here?"

"I had no idea the two of you were acquainted. This young lady has been promoting our establishment, Felicity. We were settling our accounts when I decided to try her in front of the camera. She's the most interesting child I've seen in a long time."

Without her finery, Felicity had been an exceptionally attractive young woman. Lipstick and rouge only emphasised the paleness of her skin.

"We're old friends." She walked towards me with a smile and playfully whisked away the fan. "It's time you were off home, Lottie." She deliberately brushed the feathers against my nose. "You know how your mother worries." Fussed and patted, I was herded through the curtain before she cut the air with a sharp whisper. "Does your mother know you're on your own with a gentleman?"

I must have hung my head to hide a tear, because she cupped my face. "You've done nothing wrong, Lottie. But remember, *this* side of the curtain in future."

I was confused. Felicity had no qualms about being alone with Mr Parker. It seemed unfair that, having been allowed a glimpse of what lay beyond the office, it was to be snatched away from me - by someone I thought was on my side.

Idling home, I detoured via the arches where the fisher-men smoked pipes and mended nets. Even in silence, I sensed their camaraderie. Life for them was shaped by nature and necessity. Their grandfathers and great-grandfathers had followed the same routines, and they expected their sons to do the same. They would pass on their skills and traditions and, at the very last, their boats. Being part of a great cycle was worth the hardships of a life spent at the mercy of the sea. If they had avoided danger, the fishermen all knew someone less fortunate. I had heard told many times about a storm in Folkestone that claimed three lives, despite the efforts of those who braved the squall trying to rescue them. Their women-folk stood staring blindly into the blackness. Nothing to do but wait and pray, tortured by thoughts inside their heads.

At home we had routines, but they had no design beyond the business of living. With Daddy and Ma working so hard, it didn't seem reasonable to ask, 'What's to become of me?' Because, always older than the parents of children I knew, Ma's back never straightened as it once had, and Daddy now perched on a stool behind the counter.

An idle half hour's thinking-time unravelled. Arriving home, I found Ma's folded arms and furious expression bar-ring my way. "And where've you been?"

"The front," I ventured, pulling up just beyond the reach of her arms.

"And before that?"

Cringing, I hung my head. It was best to endure her wrath, waiting to learn what she knew.

"We've had a visit from that fine friend of yours." Ma formed the word 'friend' as if she had a bad taste in her mouth. Without knowing Felicity, the fact that she wore make-up would have identified her as one of three things: an actress, a prostitute or a woman so modern she'd taken leave of her senses. "I don't care to hear how you met her, but she clearly knows you well enough to be concerned for your welfare. She tells us you were having your photograph taken." And as if this wasn't enough. "By a Mr *Parker!*"

There was little point in denial: I imagined proof might exist. "Yes, Ma."

"She said you were alone in this man's studio. Did I under-stand correctly, Lottie?"

Avoiding the glare of her bulging eyes, I strained my head further downwards, prepared to flinch at the swipe of a hand. "Yes, Ma."

"Do you really think that's the place for a respectable young girl?" She didn't wait for an answer before turning her head to Daddy, who was pretending to be busy rearranging bags of flour. "Help me out, Sidney!"

"Oh, you're doing very nicely, my dear."

Ma closed her eyes and sighed. "You mustn't go placing yourself in a position where you could be taken advantage of." There it was: the suggestion of sinister goings-on that no one saw fit to expand on. "Do you understand?"

"Yes, Ma," I repeated, for fear of sounding ignorant, and hoping to shorten the length of the toasting.

"At least that's a blessing! I don't want you to have anything more to do with this Mr Parker, do you understand? If you must recommend a photographer, Mr Fry is far more appropriate. If he's good enough for the King, he's good enough for tourists."

I was only too happy to escape to my room, where, by standing on my bed, I could access a view of rooftops and sky from its one small window. But while Ma was trudging up the stairs I heard her muttering to herself, "That girl's attracted to every undesirable in town! If we're not careful, she'll come to no good - just like her poor mother."

8 - SIR JAMES'S STORY

SHERE, 2009

Isambard's sharp bark alerted me to our visitor's arrival. A little out of practice at receiving guests, I stole a moment to check the contents of the tea tray. Cups and saucers from a china set that saw infrequent use, the silver apostles' teaspoons, sugar cubes (white and brown), a small jug of milk, plates: all present and correct. I had also unpacked one of my mother's boxes that contained photographs from the Twenties, selecting a number I thought might appeal, given the barmaid's interest in Beaton.

"Not too late, am I?" she asked brightly, lowering a set of earphones and leaving them hanging. The muted sound of a drum still beat while she fumbled inside her jacket pocket to silence it.

"No, no. Bang on time."

As Isambard administered his own enthusiastic form of welcome I realised, foolishly, that I had forgotten to ask her name. "Sit!" I reverted to my icebreaker, and Isambard's haunches dropped, his tail sweeping the floor. "Shake hands." And he padded both front legs for balance in preparation for this small trick.

Delighted, the girl bent down and shook his paw with

mock-seriousness. "How do you do? What's his name?"

"Isambard. After Brunel."

"That's quite a mouthful." She observed him shrewdly. "Mind if I call you Izzy? You look like an Izzy."

"You have me at a disadvantage," I apologised, trying to avoid frowning at her familiarity. No doubt she would soon be addressing me as 'Jimbo'.

"Don't worry if you're busy packing." She nodded at the unavoidable mountain of cardboard boxes that were insulating the hallway. "You didn't say you were moving."

"No, they'll have to carry me out of here. It's simply that I forgot to ask your name."

"It's Jenny." She laughed, tucking a stray strand of hair behind one ear. "Jenny Jones."

"Well, come in Jenny Jones." I stood aside to make way. "Make yourself at home. First door on the left."

I had chosen the dining room, having the advantage of a large table and lacking the clutter of my sitting room. Its putty-coloured walls were the backdrop for my father's various trophies and his treasured grandfather clock with its walnut casing, which had belonged to his father before him and his father too, but would end its descent through the Hastings clan with me.

Pausing in the doorway, I followed Jenny's line of vision to a glass case on the sideboard. It contained a bedraggled yellow-eyed bird with a blue-black head, rust-coloured back and gold speckled wings. Stuffed. "What's that?"

"Barnabus? He's a pheasant. A relic from my childhood." I didn't like to mention that it was my father who had shot him.

She crept forwards. "Doesn't he give you the creeps?"

"Not in the least. I suppose you could say we're old friends." I moved alongside her and leant against the edge of the table for support. She seemed reluctant to take her eyes off the bird, as if he might move as soon as she wasn't on her guard.

Resisting the temptation to laugh, a smile stole across my lips. I laid two plates on the table and offered her a slice of date and walnut loaf. "Help me out here. It's organic."

It struck me that it would be as well if Jenny didn't look any closer at Barnabus. A friend of my father had arranged to have him stuffed and, as a joke, had had a brass plate engraved with the inscription, *A bird too stupid to live*. These were men who understood camouflage, a flock of birds rising noisily from a perfectly good hiding place at the snap of a twig a sure sign that the species was overdue for extinction. Pulling a linen tablecloth from a drawer in the sideboard, I said, "Tell you what. I'll cover him up. Take a look at the photographs. They're what I asked you here to see." I flapped the cloth into position, pulling on the corners to ensure the plaque was safely concealed. Nodding in response to Jenny's enquiring face, I encouraged, "Go ahead. Pick them up."

Her hand poised mid-air, Jenny was distracted by a tinny arpeggio and, pulling a slim mobile phone from her pocket, slid back the black cover. "Hello." I felt my brows pull together, irritated that she'd chosen to answer. "Course it's me. No, I'm busy. Call me later. I don't know what time. When I'm finished here, I suppose."

I looked at her with raised eyebrows, thinking she might take the hint and turn the device off.

"I told them to call me back." She shrugged, as if I had been unable to hear every word. Determined to say something, I had manoeuvred my mouth into position when the phone in the hallway started ringing.

"Nightmare!" She smiled sympathetically. "It's like they can see you, isn't it?"

I exhaled, exasperated. "Do excuse me one moment."

As I listened to the deacon repeat the arrangements for the Harvest Supper, covered in unnecessary detail at the previous Thursday's committee meeting, I heard Jenny enthuse,

"No way!" and, checking my smile, I remembered why I had invited her.

Hearing my return, she twisted her head towards me. "They're *awesome*."

She had confirmed my instincts. "Do you think so?"

"Ye-ah!" Wide-eyed, she nodded. "Where did you get them from?" Jenny held the photographs as you would an old gramophone record, and placed them on an orderly pile of her own construction.

"They were my mother's. She was the photographer."

"She was a *photographer!* Do you know who any of these people are?"

I shrugged. "No idea, I'm afraid."

I had deliberately placed portraits and fashion shots on top and Jenny smiled as she said, "I love Vintage. Don't you wish you were born in another age?"

"You're forgetting: I was." I levered myself slowly into a chair with a slight groan, dropping the final inch or so. The grandfather clock clicked loudly, then rang out the quarter hour. "Shere is the only place I've found where you can actually step back in time. Have you lived here long?"

"I was born here." The weight of Jenny's sigh implied this was longer ago than her appearance suggested.

Intending to lighten the mood, I added, "There's life out there beyond gymkhana-land."

"Real stuff happens here too." Such a sad little comment that it humbled me. "Anyway," she continued with a defiant flick of her hair. "You *chose* to live here."

"Ah! Guilty as charged. I tried the real world and it wasn't what I thought it would be."

A truce negotiated, Jenny returned to the slow rotation of the photographs. Standing to pour the tea - milk for her, lemon for me - I pondered that keeping myself to myself had made me forget how deeply the young feel everything, so outwardly sure of themselves and yet so fragile.

When I heard her intake of breath, loud above the ticking of the clock, I knew that Jenny had reached what I had dubbed 'The Nudes'. I have always found Kenneth Clark's distinction between being naked and nude useful: to be naked is to be deprived of clothing, implying the embarrassment we feel in that condition, whereas to be nude has no uncomfortable overtone. In reality, the women in the photographs weren't nude. Like *Rokeby Venus*, they were positioned, draped and lit, so that only so much was revealed - not at all daring by today's standards. But, in the context of the other folders' contents, unexpected to say the least.

"I hope you're not trying to shock me, Sir James," Jenny quipped, the urge to say something outweighing the wonder of what she held in her hands. Her failure to put the prints down on the table betrayed a refusal to be parted from them.

"I don't find them shocking." I wasn't worried that she would question my motives. Anyone who listened to local gossip - and, in a village the size of Shere, that meant everyone - would know I've never been interested in young girls.

She laid a couple of the photographs side by side on the table. "Have you noticed? There's no underwear in sight. Not a single suspender. No stilettos." Jenny had detected what I hadn't been able to pinpoint. In classical art, the nude is intended to show the perfection of the human form. With photography, results are instant, rarely considered to be that finer thing we call 'art'. "There's something" - she shook her head - "innocent about them."

"Precisely!" I was delighted she had grasped it immediately. "Like Eve before her encounter with the serpent."

Jenny narrowed her eyes and her face became a thoughtful frown. "These photographs weren't taken for men."

"Not for a mass audience, certainly. I imagine they were private commissions."

"Was there a *mass audience* back then?"

"I take it you're asking about pornography?"

"I suppose I am," she ventured, not remotely nervous.

"Then, yes - almost as soon as photography was invented. With no controls, it was openly displayed in shop windows in certain quarters of London. That was the driving force behind the Obscene Publications Act of 1857: the need to protect the young and the weak."

She glanced upwards for as long as it took to laugh. "People like me, you mean?"

"Women, yes - and impressionable young working-class men. Porn was only acceptable in the hands of educated men."

"Who were beyond corruption, I'm guessing."

I raised an index finger as a conductor would a baton. "And then Queen Victoria - whose name has been hi-jacked to refer to prudish values when she was anything but - blew the whole thing out of the water by buying a work featuring some rather attractive nudes called *The Two Ways of Life*. It was by a Dutch chap…" The act of clicking my fingers did nothing to jog my memory. "Never mind. It was Prince Albert who took a shine to it. Royal approval wasn't enough for some. When a copy went on display in Edinburgh the half containing the nudes was curtained off."

Her head tilted to one side, Jenny exclaimed, "You didn't tell me you were an expert!"

"Oh, I'm nothing of the sort." I dismissed the notion. "Censorship is what interests me."

Jenny's focus remained firm. "Do you see what I mean about how modern the people looked, compared with photos of people taken in the Seventies with their collars and flares?"

"I think it's the quality of the photographs that makes the difference. The first automatic cameras produced some terribly grainy results. But yes. Yes, I do."

"They're very… emotional. Is that the right word for it?"

I nodded. "Emotive, I'd say."

"You get the impression your mother was in on a secret. But she can't have *known* all these people, can she?"

"I imagine they were clients. Or models."

The blue stamps on the backs of the photographs, each signed and dated, appeared to capture Jenny's imagination. "1923! You must have been very young then."

"Very." I almost choked on the word.

She had arrived at the bottom of the pile. "Are there any more?"

"Remember the boxes in the hall?" I asked.

"Never!" she exclaimed.

"See for yourself."

I remained seated while she disappeared. Cup and saucer in hand, I listening to the repeated sound of cardboard scraping against cardboard, the light rainfall of polystyrene chips on the tiled floor. When Jenny reappeared she had placed one hand over her mouth as if in disbelief. Above, her eyes were gleaming.

"I didn't quite believe it either," I said, laughing dryly. "I've only just scratched the surface."

"What are you going to do with them all?"

I shook my head, "To be honest, the thought overwhelms me. When you mentioned your interest in photography I thought you might have some ideas."

"They belong in a museum," she mused. "Only they're almost too personal. I saw an exhibition of this guy, Lartique, once. That was kind of similar. You might have heard of him."

"No. You'll find me hugely ignorant of all photographers with the exception of your friend Beaton and a young chap - actually, he's probably not so young now - called Bailey." Noticing Jenny's impatience to continue, I waved a hand in her direction. "Don't let me sidetrack you. Lartique, you say? That sounds like a French name."

"He came from this eccentric family of inventors. Because he wasn't well as a child, he was given a camera to keep him quiet. His early shots are full of uncles paddling about in wine barrels in a lake, all dressed up in shirts and ties and braces, with these handlebar moustaches." Jenny had become animated, her hands manipulating imaginary facial hair. "There's one of his brother up to his waist in water in this big black tyre. He has flippers on underneath, but on top he's wearing a tweed suit with a handkerchief in the outside pocket, an explorer's hat and these little dark goggles, like the glasses Lennon wore." She frowned. "You're asking yourself, who *are* these people? But the answer's in front of you. You're looking at a family album." Her eyes narrowed and she leaned forwards, supporting her weight on her hands, a shoulder-width apart. "I don't suppose…"

I raised my eyebrows. "Try me."

"No. It's way too cheeky."

"I can only say no."

"I have to find a project for my college course. I don't suppose you'd let me put on an exhibition of your mother's work? I - I'd help you catalogue it first, of course."

Caught off guard, I hid my reservations behind a question: "Do you really think people would be interested?"

"They love stuff like this." She changed tack suddenly. "Hey! I bet you're in here somewhere."

"Only as a very young boy." I had been surprised by the number of photographs of me that I wasn't aware existed. My father had displayed a few on top of the baby grand in the drawing room, enough for me to recognise myself as an infant.

"There must be more…"

Jenny was so enthusiastic, I felt I had to tell her. I tried to keep it simple in the hope she would understand that an old chap like me finds this sort of thing difficult. "I'm afraid

I didn't know my mother awfully well. In fact, these are all I have of her."

"I'm sorry," she said, her head on one side.

Thinking I was closing the subject, I added curtly, "Yes, well. That's just the way it was. You don't miss what you never had."

The clock ticked loudly, punching holes in the silence.

"Did she die when you were young?"

I pursed my lips, rubbed my mouth, feeling the beginnings of stubble. "Just over a month ago, actually."

Jenny's eyes wandered in a slow arc of mental arithmetic. "But she must have been…"

"One hundred and eight." I finished her sentence. "The collection spans eighty years."

"You didn't know her?"

"Only what my father told me, which was sparse to say the least." I had tried not to ask too many questions to spare him the pain. I suspect his motive for volunteering little was similar.

Jenny's eyes turned in the direction of the hallway. "Your mother's story is out there in those boxes." She looked at me, hesitantly. "If you want to find it, that is."

I surprised myself. "I suppose that might not be such a bad idea. I only know half the story of where I come from."

"And the exhibition?"

"You've caught me at a moment's weakness. But why not?" As I shrugged, she offered a raised teacup so that I could clink its edge with mine. We both drank. "Yes, why not?"

9 - LOTTIE'S STORY

BRIGHTON, 1910

"What have you done to get yourself into trouble?" Alfie West sidled up to me one afternoon, elbowing me sharply in the ribs.

"Oh, Alfie!" I stamped one foot in frustration. "I'd just got that nice couple to notice me and now you've gone and frightened them off. 'Sides, I haven't got the slightest idea what you're talking about!"

Alfie was unrepentant. "It won't take you long to find another tip. This is urgent. There's a smart fellow in a black suit going round and showing folks a photograph of you."

The thrill of the forbidden made my stomach cartwheel. "Where?" Climbing onto the bottom railing, I peered down onto the Lower Esplanade, following the line of Alfie's outstretched arm. There, Mr Parker was weaving between the stall holders, hovering in front of the rifle range and the men supping their pints outside *Welcome Brothers*, tipping his hat before interrupting couples linked together by their arms. I had thought I wouldn't hear any more about Mr Parker's glamorous world once I had returned to the bustle of the promenade, hailing cabs or directing folks to the Post Office. It seemed I was about to be proven wrong.

"He's asking if anyone's seen you. I told him I never clapped eyes on you."

I stepped down from the railings as a gull alighted on a post close by, taking up position as sentry. "That's Mr Parker. I'm not supposed to have anything to do with him."

"Shame," Alfie shrugged. "I don't 'spect you've ever seen a photograph of yourself."

I shook my head, thinking of Ma's regular lectures about the repercussions of causing offence to God and bringing disgrace on the family, the order of priorities never entirely clear. "Can't."

"You looked really pretty."

"I doubt it!"

"Don't take my word for it. Go on! What harm can looking do?"

My resolve wavered. But we didn't need to approach Mr Parker. He was striding up the stairs in our direction with one hand raised, as if hailing a Hansom cab. A little out of breath, he smiled at Alfie. "You've found her! I'm indebted to you, young man. Well deserved."

Alfie's eyes flashed as Mr Parker reached into his pocket for a coin. "You're welcome, Sir. Any time."

"Lottie, I thought you'd be curious to see how your photograph turned out." He held it up for me, his expression expectant. I felt a turning over in my stomach. Tinted to highlight the colour of my hair, the pale blue of my eyes and the turquoise of the peacock feathers, Mr Parker had not only stopped time. With my weekday clothes disguised I might have been the daughter of a lady.

"I've taken the liberty of displaying it in my studio. People want to know if it's for sale. Some would like their portrait taken with you, and I've even had a tentative enquiry to see if you're available for advertising. So you see, there's a serious discussion to be had."

The impossibility of the situation dawning, hope escaped like sand in an egg-timer.

"Well, Lottie?" Mr Parker was asking, knees bent and hands on thighs. "What do you say? Shall we go and talk to your parents?"

Alfie adopted the role of spokesperson. "She's an orphan."

"Your guardians, then…"

I was grateful to Alfie - a boy with a sixth sense for opportunity - but, unable to see any way round it, I blurted out, "My guardians say I shouldn't have anything to do with you."

Sighing with disbelief, Alfie clapped one hand over his eyes.

"What?" Mr Parker laughed, taken aback. "Am I such an ogre?"

I shook my head. From its post, the yellow-eyed gull stared at me with disdain.

"Then it must be possible to make them see sense."

Alfie winced. "With respect, Sir, you haven't met Mrs Pye."

"This is your future we're talking about, Lottie! What do you intend to do when you leave school?"

I had thought about it, arriving at the conclusion that there was nothing to be gained by growing up. I would rather run away to sea than contemplate a future in domestic service, where I could expect to work a sixteen-hour day and (here I use the term that remained a mystery) face the prospect of being taken advantage of.

Mr Parker was flapping his arms enthusiastically. "This is a wonderful age to be involved in an industry involving scientific research and entertainment. Right now, inventions are being patented that will change the way we live. Cameras! Cinema! Motor cars! Flying machines! Don't you want to be part of it?"

"Yes!" said Alfie, jumping up and down in his bare feet.

Crouching down to my level, Mr Parker enquired. "And

you, Lottie? What will your answer be?"

It sounded so much more inviting than domestic service. "Yes," I whispered, surprising myself.

"Then, we must summon a little courage. Show me where you live!"

As we arrived at the end of my road and I pointed to the painted signage of our shopfront, Mr Parker laughed heartily. "*Kate and Sidney Pye's World Famous Steak and Kidney Pies!* I've been here before. This is a good omen."

Daddy was standing outside in his green-striped apron, polishing the window aggressively with vinegar and newspaper.

"There you are, Nipper." He smiled, tired-eyed. "Ma would tell me off for calling you that when you're almost a young lady. So, how was the sea today?"

"Nice and calm with little white horses." I reached into the pocket of my pinafore and pulled out a perfect pink shell. "This is for you."

"Well, now." He turned it over in his hand, examining it closely. "It's amazing that something so small can be so perfectly formed. Ma would call this proof of God's existence."

"And what about you, Mr Pye?" Mr Parker asked, lifting his hat.

Daddy did a swift double-take. "My apologies, Sir. I didn't see you there. What can I do you for?"

"I've come to talk about Lottie."

"Lottie?" His expression was one of bafflement. "I hope she's been behaving herself."

"Absolutely. She does you credit."

"Glad to hear it." Daddy shook the hand that was offered. "I didn't catch your -"

"Nathaniel Parker: photographer." Out of politeness, Daddy could hardly snatch his hand away when he heard who was standing in front of him. Mr Parker produced a business card. "Your daughter was kind enough to recommend my studio to tourists, but I haven't had the pleasure of seeing her recently. Until today, that is."

"I'd better find my wife." Slipping the card into the pocket of his apron, Daddy hastily brushed his mouth with the back of one hand. "Lottie's her department. I just do as I'm told."

He shouted for Ma, who plodded heavily down the stairs, beetroot faced, greying hair escaping from its pins. "What can be so important that you've called me away from the kitchen?"

"My dear, this is Mr Parker." Daddy executed an embarrassed introduction, his eyes unable to settle. "He's here to talk about Lottie."

Ma's nostrils flared. "There's nothing he can possibly say that I want to hear." Arms folded across her chest, her eyes were at their steeliest, her lips tight.

"That's a great shame -"

On seeing the photograph that Mr Parker held up, Daddy's face softened.

"Because you're denying your daughter a marvellous opportunity. With a face like hers, she could be a model. Or an actress."

Having always been teased about my appearance, I looked at the portrait a second time, but Ma barely gave it a glance: she knew exactly what she would see. "Her face is going to get her into trouble one of these days."

Until then, she had never suggested there was anything wrong with my face. Certainly nothing that deserved the glare she normally reserved for insect-life.

"Who's to say that won't happen when she's serving behind the counter of your shop at night? Or in service - where she'd be beyond the scope of your influence. It could happen when she talks to strangers in the hope of earning a few pennies. Think about it," he appealed. "Would it be so very terrible if Lottie's face appeared in an advertisement for Pear's soap?"

My eyes brimming with hope, I saw only Ma's age and prejudices reflected back at me. Mr Parker's well-meant reference would have brought Lily Langtry to the front of her mind: an actress who became mistress to the Prince of Wales. If Ma told the story, she would have made it sound as if the cause of Lily's undoing was advertising soap. "Run upstairs, Lottie," Daddy said. "This discussion doesn't concern you."

Shoulders tight and head low, I brushed between Ma and Daddy but, with my face and future being debated, I crouched behind the counter, straining to listen.

"Mr Parker," Daddy began. "Lottie's been prepared for a life in service. I'll thank you not to go confusing her with horror stories. And, while we're at it, what were you thinking of, inviting a child into your studio? I mean to say!"

"Mr Pye," Mr Parker replied evenly. "Lottie and I had a business arrangement. Naturally, she was curious to learn about the equipment. From what I've gleaned so far, I think your daughter has enormous potential. I don't say that out of charity. Although I prefer to think of myself as an artist, I'm a businessman first and foremost."

"It's not respectable." Ma shuddered, thinking her proclamation self-explanatory.

"Forgive me, but I don't understand your reservations. It's a hard life you have in mind for her. I appreciate the fact that you've made plans, but plans can be altered. I know what I'd prefer for a daughter of mine."

Ma, who was not accustomed to being challenged on matters of morals, raised her voice. "Then I can tell you don't have any daughters, Mr Parker!"

There was a pause before Mr Parker spoke in a strangled voice. "I *had* a daughter, Mrs Pye. A wife and a daughter."

It seemed that I wasn't the only one who didn't dare breathe in the expansive silence that followed. On all fours, I peered out from my hiding-place to see Ma's chastened head bowed in a stance that felt all too familiar.

It was Daddy who finally felt obliged to speak. "I - I see. I'm terribly sorry, I'm sure."

"Yes, well." Raising a fist to his mouth, Mr Parker cleared his throat, but his voice was altered. He spoke hastily, as if he couldn't wait to leave. "I'm offering to take Lottie under my wing. Come and see for yourselves what I have in mind for her. If, then, you don't feel it's right, I'll bow to your judgement. But, please - I beg you - don't dismiss it out of hand. Now -" He replaced his hat. "I've taken up enough of your valuable time. You know where to find me."

Had he rehearsed it a hundred times, Mr Parker couldn't have made a more convincing speech.

10 - LOTTIE'S STORY

BRIGHTON, 1910 - 1911

"So?" Alfie landed heavily beside me on the sea wall then jumped down onto the beach below.

"I blame the King." I sulked.

"The new one?"

I snorted air through my nose. "I was talking about King Edward!"

"But he's dead."

"Exactly!" I had always liked Edward VII for all his beautiful lady friends and his portly stomach. Shortly after Mr Parker's visit, he succumbed to bronchitis and something called Smokers' Throat on account of the thirteen fat cigars and twenty cigarettes he enjoyed daily. Then, hearing his horse had won the 4.15pm at Kempton Park, he collapsed. "Decisions about daughters' futures can't be made while the country's in mourning. Apparently."

"I didn't think your Ma had any time for Edward."

Relenting, I giggled. God was often asked to save the King in church. While everyone else was busy murmuring their *amens*, Ma had been heard to mutter, "Save him from himself, dear Lord."

"Appearances." I tapped the side of my nose. "I *did* think

"We have each other, and that's more than enough. Remember when we first met, Lottie? You told me people thought your mother was a prostitute. What made you say that?"

"They said that being struck by lightning was God's punishment."

She laughed. "If that were true, he'd have got me first!"

"Who else wouldn't have family to come looking for them?"

"I have family. They come calling every time they're short of money! Maybe your mother was just all alone in the world. It happens."

"I want to do the right thing," I said. "I don't want to let Ma down."

"You're a good girl, Lottie, but in this world you've got to take care of yourself. Your folks aren't as young as they were. They won't be around forever. Think about it."

13 - LOTTIE'S STORY

BRIGHTON, 1911

Mr Parker did his homework. Whilst developing my portraits, he came across a series of photographs of a little-known actress who had been reported missing in early 1901. Born in Bermondsey, she was christened plain Agnes Coin, but she had adopted the stage name of Rebecca Lavashay. At the time of her disappearance, she was on tour with the musical comedy *Florodora*, which had triumphed in London.

Hailed the most beautiful women on stage, the original *Florodora* girls had married millionaires. This increased the attraction of the parts on offer; young actresses queued day and night to audition. Agnes was the least experienced among them and her voice wasn't the strongest heard, but the priority was to cast six girls who were five foot four and weighed 130 pounds. As well as matching these requirements, something about Agnes's eyes earned her a part. She didn't disappoint. Given an audience, this shy novice was transformed.

The Brighton shows sold out within hours. In return for the promise of glamour and romance, audiences were prepared to indulge an unlikely plot, which globe-trotted from the Philippines to a Welsh castle.

The Brighton chorus girls were wined and dined until they were almost too exhausted to rehearse but, as far as we know, none of them married millionaires. Much to the annoyance of the tour manager, his leading lady was forced to 'retire' from the show.

Scandal only heightened the tour's success. Fortunately, every girl in the show knew the lead's lines. Each was given the opportunity to audition in front of a paying audience. When the chorus line was reduced from six to five, spectators barely noticed the difference. If anything, the men's lyrics asking the ladies if there were any others like them at home made more sense. As part of a group, Agnes had disguised her auburn hair. It was important that none of the girls outshone the others (or, rather, that they all shone equally). When her turn came to take the lead, her true colours revealed, the audience was charmed. A glowing review in *The Gazette* proclaimed her a bright young star. If the manager harboured any lingering doubts about who to cast as his leading lady, it was the queues of rose-laden men outside her dressing room that tipped the scales in Agnes's favour. He knew what he had within his grasp - if only he could limit her expectations.

This didn't make her popular among the cast. No one likes an overnight success. But Agnes had that rare thing you can't teach: star quality. Her off-stage shyness translated into a dignity that failed to respond to criticism and, in time, might have earned their respect. It wasn't to be. When Agnes failed to turn up for rehearsal in Bournemouth, the manager chided the company that she had been unable to cope with their bickering. Privately, he blamed the lure of London's bright lights.

"But what if the real cause of her disappearance was the curse of the leading lady?" Mr Parker asked.

Felicity smiled gently at my blank expression. "I think what he means is that Agnes fell pregnant."

Certainly, there had been no shortage of suitors. Rejected by the remainder of the cast, if anyone needed companionship after curtain call, it was Agnes.

"Ma won't like it." I struggled to explain her opinion about the low moral character of actresses.

Pacing energetically, Mr Parker tugged at his beard: "What we need is a good tragedy!"

Tracking Agnes's trail to London, Mr Parker discovered that her parents had died in the workhouse. Previously they had run a pub called *The Lamb*, but trade suffered after a violent brawl, followed weeks later by flooding from the Thames. Sued by the freeholder for outstanding rent, they moved into a simple room near the docks. Mr Coin arrived home most days empty-handed. Accustomed to the life, he drank what little he earned. When her parents could no longer afford to keep her, Agnes was taken in by a distant uncle who had lost his wife and was looking for a housekeeper. She ran away, preferring to take her future into her own hands.

"I suspect the man was a brute." Mr Parker reported causing Felicity to bite her lip. "With only her face to recommend her, and options limited, Agnes chose the lesser of two evils."

"It's too convenient." Felicity was sceptical. "An actress who can be placed in Brighton seven months before her death, but wasn't recognised? What about those queues of men?"

"People have surprisingly short memories," Mr Parker answered. "In some cases, opportunely short. But given that we're a holiday resort, our man may well have already left."

Or - as I often thought but kept to myself - perhaps my mother wasn't recognisable after her accident.

"So!" Mr Parker clapped his hands, a welcome distraction. "Are you ready to meet your new mother?"

My mouth feeling uncommonly dry, I swallowed, unable to speak.

"Put her out of her misery!" Felicity said.

"These are your photographs." He began by laying them out on his desk, side by side. "And, these I acquired from a contact at *The Gazette*." I shivered as, underneath, he laid out a series of portraits of the most beautiful lady I had seen in my short life: fragile, delicate, kind-eyed. My mind was cartwheeling: this was the face I had been searching for my entire life!

"Ignoring the difference in your ages," Mr Parker encouraged, "see if you think there's a likeness."

A clear resemblance seemed to leap out at me from the page. Largely, I admit, it was a case of hair length and colour, both of which might have been altered.

"Eureka!" he cried.

"Lottie." Felicity placed one hand softly on my forearm. "This is a publicity story, that's all. I wasn't a trapeze artist. In fact, I've never even been to the circus."

But, at that moment, I would have believed anything Mr Parker told me.

Two weeks later, an article appeared in *The Sunday Gazette* about the uncelebrated actress Agnes Coin, her disappearance, and surprising new evidence that had recently been unearthed.

Returning from church at midday, we found Daddy at the kitchen table, the newspaper spread out in front of him. Tobacco flavoured the air, and I couldn't smell the sea in his hair when I threw my arms around his neck.

"You're too old for that, young lady!" Ma scolded.

"Leave her be," Daddy replied. "She's my little girl."

Tight-lipped, Ma paused in front of the age-dappled mirror to smooth her post-hat hair. "You shouldn't indulge her," she said, determined to have the last word.

Daddy released the stem of his pipe from the grip of his

teeth and tapped the seat next to him. "Sit down, Kitty. I have something here to show you."

"I've no time for newspapers." She knotted her apron tightly around her broadening waistline. "Dinner won't cook itself."

Daddy had learned how to attract Ma's attention, and it wasn't by jumping up and down or raising his voice. "You'll make time for this," he said softly. Their eyes collided in understanding.

"Lottie, find something to do for half an hour. And for goodness' sake, try not to ruin your dress," she said. "I'll just pay a visit, then I'll be with you, Sidney."

"Make that an hour, Lottie." Daddy smiled as Ma's footsteps retreated downstairs to the backyard. "Pay my regards to the sea for me. I didn't get the chance this morning."

"You're not ill, are you?"

"I'm quite well, child. I just needed thinking time."

Too old for kisses, too young for adult conversation, it was obvious I was becoming an inconvenience; one who ate too much, harboured too many opinions. Bypassing a young mother who was wearing out a square foot of paving-stone, patting the back of a wailing infant, I wandered downhill. Wind-chased clouds allowed intermittent appearances of strong sunlight, dappling the cobbles in fast-shifting shadow. En route to the arches, I filled my lungs with salty air as gulls looped and dived overhead.

My ears burned as I saw Alfie West hanging around near the railings in a tight gathering of slouching, elbow-leaning boys. He straightened up, touching the peak of his cap. "Oi, oi, Lads! Here comes Lottie Pye in her Sunday best."

Propelled by an unidentified hand, he staggered forwards into my path.

"Hello Alfie."

"Where are you off to at this at time of day?"

"The usual." Barely-disguised sniggering escaped from behind cupped hands. Feet apart, I flicked back my hair defiantly. "Making myself scarce."

"Want to do something?" he asked.

I shrugged, biting my lip. "Don't mind."

"There's gratitude for you!"

Alfie saw the unwanted tear that had welled up, even though I turned away. He lowered his voice so that our bawdy spectators couldn't hear. "I won't ask no more if you don't want me to. Just do me a favour and walk with me as far as the steps."

I swiped at my eyes. It was too much to be expected to explain the feeling of constantly battling change when nothing could be done to defeat it. Life seemed to be shaped like a curve, the future elusive. "It's not that. I like you asking."

"Then let's skim some stones."

Whistles squeezed out from between fingers followed us. Alfie shot a triumphant grin over one shoulder. As we launched pebble after pebble into a sea that was as grey as my thoughts (Daddy called it 'rearranging the beach') I asked, "What will you do when you leave school?"

"They say there's a war coming."

"Who says?" I laughed, it sounded so unlikely; barely pausing from the business of releasing another missile which sank with a hollow sound.

"It's been all over." He shrugged as if the idea didn't bother him. With the grace of a ballerina, he extended an arm and placed one foot carefully behind the other. We watched the stone skim the surface in a series of light bounces before it disappeared in a ripple that barely left a blemish.

"Would you fight?"

"If I had to. I wouldn't want to be the only one left behind."

I shivered. "I'm glad Daddy's too old," I said at last.

"You'll be fine, Lottie." I wasn't sure if Alfie was referring to war or the future in general. "One of these days I'm going to look up and see your name in big letters on a poster. And I'll say, 'Oh yes, I know Lottie Pye. In fact, I was there when she came to school with her petticoat tucked into her draws.' That was quite a sight."

"You liar! You never did!" I knocked him sideways with a firm shoulder shove.

"Didn't I now?" He rocked back against me, grinning.

"Coming?" I asked, my feet scrambling against stones.

"I'm not done yet."

"Suit yourself. I'm going home for my dinner."

I scampered up the stairs near the Free Shelter Hall, passing through the centre of a loud bachelor party dressed in boaters, dickie bows and buttonholes, and holding cones of whelks and mussels. Looking back from a vantage point at the top of the railings, I saw Alfie propped up on his elbows, scanning the horizon. If I worried about the future, it was even harder being a boy. So much was expected of you.

I arrived home, not to the normal smells of the kitchen at Sunday dinnertime, but to the embers of a fire, two empty teacups and anxious faces.

"Sit down, child," said Daddy, removing his pipe from his mouth. The bite marks around the stem were multiplying daily. "We've something here to show you."

"Is it about the war?" I asked, looking at the newspaper on the table.

Ma's cheeks reddened. "Who's been filling your head with nonsense?"

"Alfie West -"

"Alfie West, expert of everything! That'll be his father talking. It's men who dream up reasons for wars and women who are left to pick up the pieces."

Daddy appeared amused by Ma's passion. "Spoken like a true feminist, my dear."

For a working woman who held the purse strings, he couldn't have chosen a greater insult. "Feminist? Not me! Giving us all a bad name."

"Let's not get sidetracked." Daddy's nervousness was apparent. There were damp circles of perspiration under the arms of his good shirt. His hand felt clammy as he took one of mine. "Lottie, you know how we've been trying to trace your real family. Well, I think you need to look at this. It's an article about a young actress who was reported missing early in 1901. They assumed she'd taken herself off to London, so nobody looked too hard for her. But given her appearance and that she was beginning to make a name for herself... why don't you just read it?" He turned the newspaper 360 degrees and I came face to face with the photograph of Agnes I had studied only weeks earlier. I was aware of two sets of eyes concentrating on me, looking for signs of recognition.

Pretending to misunderstand, with deliberate vagueness, I said, "She's very beautiful."

Daddy pointed to the words underneath and swallowed. "Yes, but does she remind you of anyone? Look at the description: 'As part of the chorus, Agnes was forced to disguise her copper-coloured hair...'"

Ma reached out a hand to touch a lock of mine and drew her bottom lip in. She was strangely silent, as if she was none too keen for me to learn about my real mother.

"It's the dates, Lottie," Daddy persisted. "Do you see? She was here nine months before you were born. It would make sense for an unmarried mother to return after the birth. To search for your father."

Ma looked as uncomfortable as I had ever seen her at the reminder that my mother was unmarried.

I employed all of my acting skills. "You think this is my mother?"

"We'll probably never know for certain." Daddy shook his head. "But we think it's worth contacting the newspaper to see if they have any more information."

I nodded my consent.

"We wondered if Mr Parker might be able to help."

This was unexpected. My eyes flicked up in time to observe Ma loosening the collar of her blouse as if she was overheating.

Daddy continued. "It would be best to go to the newspaper with a photograph of you taken from the same angle so they can see what we can see."

The bell rattled and a familiar voice reached us from the shop. "Anyone home?"

"We're closed!" Ma shouted down, her voice gruff, then, to us, she tutted, "What can Josie want?"

"What your friend always wants," Daddy muttered, weary rather than annoyed. "Tea. Several cups of it."

The approach of laboured footsteps suggested that she would not be put off her mission. "Have you seen *The Gazette*?"

Ma sighed in exasperation. "We're looking at it now!"

Accompanied by huffing, a breathless Josie appeared at the door, one hand in the small of her back, the other brandishing a rolled copy of the paper. She barely gave my parents a glance: it was my face that interested her as she waddled over to the table. "I've known you all your life and there's no doubt in my mind," she said, jabbing the photograph with a finger, as if she were responsible for the discovery. Glancing at Ma, she said as an aside, "Tell me if I'm interrupting."

It was only then that I realised how upset Ma was. "Lottie, I remember the day I found you, thinking you were the answer to my prayers. Whatever happens, we'll always be your family."

"You don't know how lucky you are, my girl," Josie clucked, taking a seat in front of the dying fire. "I don't suppose there's a brew on the go?"

14 - LOTTIE'S STORY

BRIGHTON, 1911

"I'm delighted you've decided to take me up on my offer." Mr Parker greeted Ma and me in the office of his studio, both dressed in our stiff Sunday best on a Thursday. "Let me give you the grand tour." He whisked the velvet curtain aside.

Ma, seemingly unimpressed by the treasure trove, looked at him with embarrassment. "I'm here as a customer."

"I'm terribly sorry, I must have misunderstood. Do take a seat." He drew back the comfortable chair at the small side table.

Complying, she handed him the article, pointing to the photograph of Agnes. "Perhaps you can tell me how much it would cost to have a portrait of Lottie taken from the same angle as this one."

"No, I insist." Mr Parker waved her away when she reached for her purse, looking from me to the newspaper article and back again. "This is remarkable! They're too alike for it to be a coincidence."

"That remains to be seen." But if Ma was wary to commit herself, she seemed charmed by Mr Parker. Holding the teacup that was offered at chest level, little finger airborne, she sat as if riding side-saddle.

"Faces are my business, Mrs Pye. At Art College, we used to draw a grid on the blank canvas to help us focus on each feature. I still see a grid in my mind's eye whenever I look at a face, and I can tell you that the spacing of Lottie's features is virtually identical to this other young lady's. I have to say, she was a great beauty. Do you have any idea what became of her?"

"We believe she was killed - here in Brighton."

"No!" Mr Parker stopped what he was doing, his face a perfect match for his funereal attire. "Do you know how it happened?"

"We can't be sure." Here, Ma appeared to blush. "But if Lottie *is* her daughter - and I'm not saying she is -"

"No," he intervened.

"- I was actually there at the time."

Mr Parker lowered himself into a chair next to Ma, appealing earnestly. "You can't leave me in suspense."

Lubricated by tea, she continued. "It was the lightning that got her. She was walking on the promenade with her baby in a perambulator."

"But I remember reading about that! You were quite the heroine."

Ignored, I toyed with garments on the clothes rail, gravitating towards a silk dress.

"Sadly, it was all I could do to rescue Lottie in time." Ma put her teacup in its saucer and placed it on the table.

Mr Parker followed her gaze to her lap. "Your poor hands!" he exclaimed.

She drew them into her sleeves, her tone now subdued: "My reminder that it never does to be vain. There's not one of us who can't say, *there but for the grace of God.*"

"Quite so. It seems doubtful that..." Lowering his voice, Mr Parker leaned towards Ma conspiratorially. "Lottie's father will come forward. If he was a..." Pausing to frown and glance up at me, he reduced his volume even further. "...young man, it's more than likely he would have a family of his own by now."

Ma matched his whisper. "That's not what this is about. It can be difficult for a child not to know where she's come from." She covered her mouth with a hand briefly to compose herself. "We've been the subject of the most distasteful gossip - by people who should know better."

"I'd like to help, Mrs Pye," Mr Parker said as he ushered us out. "I have contacts at the newspaper. No doubt they'll want to publish Lottie's story. It's important it's presented in a tasteful way. Why don't you and I discuss this further when the photographs are ready?"

When I looked back through the door, I thought I saw Mr Parker wink at me before he pulled the blind down. The fish had taken the bait.

If Ma had thought that setting the record straight would end the gossip, she was mistaken. My classmates' reaction was similar to that of the cast of *Florodora*.

"You always thought you were better than us."

Too proud to cry, I bit down on my bottom lip and held my head up, giving a good impression of just that. Only Alfie saw through my act.

"Ignore them," he advised. "There isn't a girl here who doesn't want to be you and a boy who wouldn't kiss you given half a chance."

I laughed, letting down my guard, my head dropping.

"So can I?"

"Don't be daft!"

"Doesn't matter." He shrugged. "I've told them all you're my girl anyway."

"You've got a big mouth, Alfie West!"

"How else could I make sure the others would leave you

alone? Plus, they all like me, so they'll have to talk to you eventually. Want to skim some stones?"

"Can't," I sulked. "I've got chores."

As I dragged my feet along the seafront, I could feel people's eyes following me, their whispers barely concealed behind parasols. I felt like thanking every single one of them not to stare. Alfie walked upright, meeting each enquiring look with an obliging grin. "See that?" he said. "You're already half famous."

"Don't stare back!" I scolded.

Ignoring my concerns, he raised one hand in a wave. "I'm enjoying myself. Tomorrow, I'll be no one again, but today I'm the boy who's walking down the road with the girl from the front of *The Gazette*."

I tried not to lift my eyes from the pavement. "I hate this," I said.

"Better get used to it." Alfie used the same arm to bring the traffic to a halt and then pretended to sweep the road in front of me, the ripe smell of horse manure blending with marine odours. "Now, promise me you'll smile."

I exaggerated the tilt of my chin and grimaced for Alfie's approval but, after he had tipped an imaginary hat, I ran home.

"Here she is!" Daddy announced my breathless arrival at the shop door to the small gathering who were examining my photograph while waiting in line. Some, it seemed, had just come to hear Daddy's side of the story. I didn't wait to hear the end of the question, "How does it feel to be…?" before I clattered upstairs and threw myself face-down on my bed.

Daddy knocked on the door a while later. "Well, then," he said, perching on the other single bed under the eaves. The angle of his back would have been forced to mirror the slope of the ceiling as he addressed the pillow that covered my streaked face. "I've been proud of you today, Lottie. Business has never been better, that's for sure. So what's eating away at you?"

"No one would talk to me at school, apart from Alfie. Then everybody stared at me on the way home."

"Is that so? I can understand why people might be looking, but why wouldn't your friends talk to you?"

I came out of hiding. Light penetrating the curtain cast the evening shadows I privately thought of as being 'the boys'. His focus on me, Daddy seemed oblivious to their presence. "Alfie says it's because they're jealous."

"I see." He scratched his head. "You do know that, if you have your photograph taken for the magazines, it might be like this all the time?"

Throwing my legs over the side of the bed, I adopted the best position for sulking: elbows on knees and chin in hands. "If I was a lady, I could wear a hat and no one would recognise me."

"Then a hat it is!" His pipe rode up and down. "For now, you'd better go and help Ma before she explodes. She's taken it on herself to make double quantities - that's an awful lot of pastry. I'd ask you to stay home from school and help tomorrow, but there'd be no shortage of attention here."

"Do you think I could get used to it, Daddy?"

The pipe was set aside for thought. "A soul can get used to anything if they put their mind to it. It's whether you want to, that's the question. Now, run along, scallywag, or neither of us will have a future worth worrying about!"

15 - SIR JAMES'S STORY

SHERE, 2009

Jenny put the scrapbook containing the newspaper article down on the dining room table, her eyes low.

"I'm sorry." She turned away from me, blinking back tears, those that escaped taking on the colour of her eye make-up.

"I didn't realise you'd find it upsetting. Here." I held out the cotton handkerchief that had been tucked into the breast pocket of my jacket, and she took it reluctantly. "Go on. I always have one at the ready."

She was far happier when Isambard, sensing a change in the atmosphere, sacrificed his dense coat so that she could bury herself in it.

I chose to extract myself. "This calls for a pot of tea."

While I was still busy in the kitchen, wondering if I was cold to have remained detached from my mother's story, Jenny joined me. "Thank you." She deposited the creased handkerchief on one side. "I should explain -"

The narrow space felt claustrophobic: a reminder of disappearing fingerprints, the smell of heavy tweed. "No need." I felt the need to fight my way back to a space where oxygen was in greater supply, looking uselessly about for a rectangle of light to guide the way. "All over now."

"No, I'd like to." As Jenny struggled to begin, I loosened my tie and unbuttoned my collar. "You see, my mother died of cancer when I was eight. It's not the same, I know. But I couldn't help thinking what it must have been like for this little girl - probably the same age as I was when I lost my mother - to find her story after looking everywhere."

I searched for the words of sympathy expected from one who has lived longer and to whom loss is an acquaintance of old. Instead a wave of irritation flooded over me: if my mother had really understood loss in the way Jenny suggested, why had she allowed history to repeat itself by leaving? But it wasn't the time to talk about myself. I fixed my face into a serious expression. When I faced Jenny she was smiling - sadly, but smiling nonetheless: "We've got more in common than you thought. We both grew up without mothers. You didn't know that, did you?"

The words escaped before I could think about them. "You're terribly brave."

"No." She shook her head. "I'm not. They had to make me talk about it, and even now…"

I broke the silence. "Do you think it helps? All that talking?"

She faced me across the narrow room, no wider than a passageway, leaning back on the work surface. "It's got to, hasn't it?"

"I don't know. When I was a lad you were expected to keep your feelings to yourself. Saved you from getting worked up."

"The whole point is to work through them," she said, reaching past me for the tea tray. "Let me take that." Before I could protest, she was walking back to the dining room, making light work of what would have proved a struggle for me.

I followed, bypassing a stack of cardboard boxes. "No

point upsetting yourself if you don't have to." Intending to open the window, I found that an estate car parked on the kerb was obscuring my view of the square.

"Oh, so you'd prefer to bottle it up?" She challenged, glancing up from the tea that she was pouring.

Flustered, I deliberately changed the subject as I took a seat at the table. "Is it just you and your father at home?"

She nodded. "We get on alright, you know?"

I wasn't sure that I did: my own father was hardly a typical example. Jenny interpreted my silence as the sign of a good listener. She handed me a cup and saucer. There was a slice of lemon on the side, just as I liked it.

"Mum was only thirty-seven. They tried to prepare me. My dad said I should be proud of her. She sat up in bed reading magazines and wearing a turban. Even her eyelashes had gone by then. It must have been awful for her, but I just got used to it. All the time that she was trying to say goodbye, I was furious with her for not trying harder to get better. I thought she should do it for me. I didn't want to have to be proud of her. I just wanted her there when I got home from school."

Unprompted, a vivid image of my father appeared in my mind. I had been called to the headmaster's office with no explanation, and suspected I had been reported by a prefect for a breach of rules sufficiently serious to warrant his personal attention. When I saw my father standing there, hands clasped behind his back, I thought, *This must be worse than I imagined.* Racking my brains, I conjured up a suitably remorseful expression. My father's advice on how to survive school had been, "Remember the golden rule: never get caught. If you are, I shall disown you."

This was a transitional year during which I went from being in awe of my father to being slightly embarrassed of him. He didn't resemble other fathers, wearing neither suit nor tie for the occasion. His hat was a leather skull cap, goggles raised to the level of his forehead; his main item of clothing a long tan leather coat, battered and weathered and oil-stained. ("Worn in," he called it. He was furious when Mrs Strachan threw it out. "It was just getting how I like them!" he'd bellowed.) There were muddied knee-length boots on his feet rather than polished brogues. He dangled a fat cigar. Never giving the impression that he understood how out of place he looked, he leant back against the oak panelling drumming his fingers, impervious to the headmaster's practiced glare.

"Ah, Hastings," Old Granger began. He was balding in the least attractive way, and his right hand frequently fingered the thinning hair that was combed ineffectively across his pate. "Your father's here to collect you."

My heart threatened to break free from my ribcage. Expulsion, then. I hung my head waiting to learn what I'd done to earn this fate. Technically, I had little doubt I deserved it, as did a high proportion of boys. I just wasn't aware I had broken the golden rule.

"I'm afraid your mother's unwell. Your father will fill you in on the way, no doubt." Granger's raised hand twitched twice in the direction of the door before finding its way back to the strands of hair.

Surely only something life-threatening would require my presence? I felt a wave of panic in the pit of my stomach for this woman I had only met the once. It appeared my father's summation that she hadn't been taking care of herself was correct. I had been promised a 'next time' - prayed for it - but I wouldn't have prayed at all had I known my mother would have to be ill before she asked for me.

My father coughed loudly. "You'll need your warm coat, son. I've brought the bike."

My hesitation while waiting to be dismissed earned me an exasperated, "Well, Hastings, don't stand there gawping. Do as your father says!"

Encroaching on Mr Granger's side of the desk, my father gravely offered his hand. "I'll write if there's no improvement by next week."

The response was blunt: "The less disruption to the boy's routine, the better. The best place for him is in school."

My father's days of being told how to behave by headmasters were long gone. He attempted to lower his voice, but it remained audible to anyone within a ten-foot radius. "I'll be the judge of that." I felt the weight of his hand on my shoulder. "Come along, son."

As our feet crunched on the gravel drive, he clicked his tongue as if approaching a horse. "Like her?" he nudged me. Parked diagonally in front of the main entrance and attracting looks of longing from a small gathering of Seniors was his latest acquisition: a Brough Superior, sleek in black and chrome with a sidecar shaped and suspended like a boat, coated with a healthy splattering of narrow country lanes.

"Out the way, chaps!" My father aimed his arms at the stragglers as though parting the Red Sea. He threw the skirt of his coat aside and straddled the bike. "In you hop. Gloves and goggles on the seat. No time to lose. *British Empire Trophy* at Brooklands, one o'clock. The clever money's on Eyston."

"So there's nothing wrong with M-mother?" I stammered, aghast.

"Wouldn't have thought so. Except that she never ate properly." He adjusted his goggles. "Didn't believe in lunch, would you believe?"

I shrank into the sidecar, pulling the collar of my coat up.

On seeing my relief Father turned on the engine, laughing above its purr. "Come on, James! Keep up." In recognition of my continued discomfort he conceded, "Difficult chappie, your Head, isn't he?" It was almost as if I had made a poor choice of school for myself. "*Why?* he asks. None of his blasted business! I shall spend time with my son whenever I damn well please. Understand this: people generally deserve the lies they're told."

It wasn't an age when you took the feelings of a young boy into account. If your son was considered sensitive, you teased it out of him.

"You got on with your dad didn't you?" Jenny was saying. "It sounds as if he was fun to be around."

Just then I was remembering the relief, the humiliation of the day's lesson; the hatred I allowed to fester the length of the journey, before, acknowledging where my loyalty lay, I transferred it to the store of grievances against my mother: this, too, was her doing.

"One didn't *get on* with one's father!" When I saw how Jenny shrank into herself, mirroring the stance of my younger self hunkered down in the sidecar, I instantly regretted my outburst. She had just shared something personal with me. I would have to give a little to win her back. "He wasn't an easy man, you see. But he *was* terribly exciting. It was there, just beneath the surface: that intention to win at all costs."

Despite my years, it would have felt like a betrayal to say that, exciting though he was, I found my father's recklessness frightening. I loved and feared him in equal measures, but more than that: I feared *for* him. It could only be a matter of time before he fell foul of his own golden rule and was caught out. I imagined it happening as he steered a prototype into the steep-sided bend of the banking, or as he plummeted from the seat of a plane while looping the loop, or as he accepted another drunken bet that he couldn't do the impossible. How best to explain that the sensation I most associated with my father was a dredging of my guts? I shouldn't have had to feel responsible for both of us: that was his job. Something else I couldn't help but feel *she* was responsible for. Other men had a wife's calming influence to prevent them from doing these things.

16 - LOTTIE'S STORY

BRIGHTON, 1912

Mr Parker threw the magazine down on his desk when he saw the advertisement in print. The soap manufacturer had only used my photograph as the basis of an illustration. I was unrecognisable. "If I'd known that was all they had in mind, I would have refused. Do you know what this is, Lottie?" He stabbed the page with an index finger, as if it were contaminated.

"An advertisement for Wool Soap?" I ventured timidly.

"No!" I took a step backwards as he brought both fists down on the desk. "It's an advertisement for Lottie Pye who happens to use Wool Soap! Except we can't tell whether it's Lottie Pye or..." He waved his arms about, plucking a name from the air. "...Isabella Hardy-Ramsbottom." He shook his head at the sight of me sniggering behind the palm of one hand. "You must take this seriously! We have to think beyond the next job if we're to make the leap from *The Gazette* to *The Lady*."

"But Lily Langtry appeared in advertisements long after she was famous."

"That was different! She was paid to endorse products - all because there are women foolish enough to believe that, if they use the same soap as Lily Langtry, they'll start to look like her."

An appearance at a local parade as Queen of the May ending with the opening of a branch of *Liptons* was greeted by mixed reception. There were those who thought the arrival of a convenience store was the answer to all life's problems and those - Daddy included - who feared local shops would suffer.

"The family should have stood together on this. I look a bit daft if I protest at the planning meeting - only to find my own daughter cutting the blooming ribbon!"

All in all, my contribution to the household income was rather less than if I had spent my Saturdays taking tips from wealthy tourists. It was no longer considered appropriate for me to loiter on corners like a 'street urchin' (to quote Mr Parker). Instead, I wore my Sunday best on a Saturday and stood outside the studio come rain or shine, trying to convince tourists to have their picture taken with the 'soap girl'. Apparently, it was good practice for me to sit in front of a camera. I wasn't sure what I should have been practising, other than trying my best not to blink. The sole consolation was that my Sunday best was grander than it used to be, thanks to Mr Parker's generous clothing allowance. Dispensing with layers of petticoats, I wasn't permitted to do anything to get my dress dirty. The irony was, now that I had freedom of movement, I was no longer allowed to move. Rather than envy me, girls from school whose normal habit was to ignore me came by to mock, malice barely disguised by sympathy.

"Aw, shame you're not allowed down the seafront no more," I was repeatedly reminded. "Just as it's getting *interest*-ing." The word ripe with meaning, they broke away giggling. There were rumours of kisses being sold underneath the pier - by the same girls who had accused my mother of being a prostitute.

Days passed when I didn't miss the adventure and

irresponsibility of it. Days of distractions when Felicity and I flicked through fashion magazines together and she experimented on me with make-up and beauty spots. Days when she showed me how to dress my hair, how to stand with my shoulders back. Days when she demonstrated how to find my most flattering angle in front of the camera.

"This is a photographic studio, not a beauty parlour!" Mr Parker would protest.

"Do you want your models to look their best or don't you?" Felicity asked, unrepentant.

"Oh!" He threw up his hands. "Sometimes I despair!"

The first photograph I ever took was of Felicity with Harry standing on her lap, their heads angled and touching. This was not Felicity flirting with the camera, showing her best side or dressed in Paris fashions. It was a mother and son, pure and simple. Mr Parker called it *Madonna and Child.*

"You've captured something there," he admitted as he scrutinised her expression. "You have an eye for this." But I was even more pleased when I saw him open the door for Felicity and bid her good evening as if she was a proper lady. That was the real magic of photography.

It was a year of change, when the impossible became reality. In 1912 I saw my first biplane, a contraption that looked too spindly to take to the skies, composed more of air than machine.

"It's unnatural, that's what it is!" Ma proclaimed her verdict at supper. "There's never a thought for the grief these daredevils cause when they do themselves an injury."

To David Lloyd George's declaration that, "Flying machines are no longer toys and dreams," Ma's reaction was, "If the Good Lord had meant us to fly, he would have given us wings."

"He *is* giving us wings!" Daddy was barely able to contain his excitement. "They've just arrived a little later than the rest of the equipment." But as he read the account of how Bleriot had flown the Channel while still using crutches after an earlier crash, and got lost in the Kent fog without a compass to guide him, Ma's arched eyebrows spoke for her: he was a fool - and nothing would convince her otherwise.

It was Claude Graham White who was at the controls of the bright blue biplane, chased over the Downs by grown men and boys waving cloth caps. I caught my breath at the sight of it, light-headed. The lettering on the wings spelled out *Wake up England*.

"What's it mean?" I panted, struggling to keep pace with Alfie while avoiding rabbit holes. In turn, he wanted to keep up with his brothers.

"He's showing how easy an attack from the air would be. Even the navy can't keep us safe."

Another impossible thought: the might of the British navy was a fact, like God and Empire.

In the middle of it all, there came that dreadful day in April when I heard rumours of the sinking of the Titanic and was drawn to the seafront as if by some magnetic force. Finding Alfie, I stood staring out to sea like a tortured fisherwoman waiting for news of her missing husband. Under a moonless sky, countless souls had slipped beneath the icy depths, while the lucky ones, shivering in eveningwear and nightclothes, listened to the screams and then - worse still - to the terrible unbroken silence that followed.

We stood silently among the fishermen who knew first-hand about the fury of the sea; the treasures it surrendered and the sacrifices it demanded in return. We stood even as the rain fell and foam crept around our feet, pebbles grinding and shifting under them.

We stood again to acknowledge a smaller tragedy. In August, a young Scoutmaster was accompanying a party of Sea Scouts on a camping expedition to Leydown. All were experienced boatmen. Hit by a sudden squall, the entire crew was thrown overboard. Among the first to be hauled into a lifeboat, the Scoutmaster made it his business to dive back into the waters. A father of two saw him holding one of his sons' heads above water, whilst the other clung onto a dingy. Saved - or so he thought. All younger than Alfie and me, the nine dead were no different from us: none of them saints. Over one million attended the funeral, but we stood to honour Percy Baden Powell Huxford - named after the Chief Scout. Swept out to sea, he couldn't be buried alongside his friends.

As I shivered, I felt Alfie's cold hand clasp mine. Unable to decide if it would rescue me or drag me under, I held tight. Children of Brighton, we were also children of the sea. What would happen to us over the next few years no longer seemed to be within our control.

17 - LOTTIE'S STORY

BRIGHTON, 1914

August 3rd 1914 began as a hazy summer's day, the air shimmering protectively over calm waters. I was sitting alongside Felicity and Harry, our backs pressed against a wind-break. The most remarkable thing had happened in recent weeks. After a year's determined practice with a camera, Mr Parker had lent me a portable model he didn't require for studio work.

"I know you'll look after it," he said. "Just make sure you pack it away safely every evening."

The seafront was the perfect location for new subjects. Rows of striped tents and bunting provided perspective. Abandoned straw hats became donkey-fodder. Young women dressed in puffed-sleeved blouses reclined on the shingle as casually as their discomfort permitted. The Beach Orator, dressed in black cassocks and bearing a striking resemblance to Oscar Wilde, lifted one arm dramatically, his enthusiastic sermon drowned out by the jagged strains of Blind Henry's accordion. Cloth-capped, Harry was absorbed in his selection of the choicest pebbles, discarding those that weren't shiny enough for his liking. Spider-like, I bided my time, adjusting the camera's controls for distance, speed and aperture. I practised with moving targets, taking the photograph when my subject reached a carefully-chosen background. The pier too obvious, a particular cloud formation and a wooden post dressed in seaweed was to form the centre of mine. I tracked the approach of a fine-silhouetted bearded gentleman from twenty yards away, feeling my neck redden as I realised my victim was considerably more attractive than I had envisaged. Ten yards… eight… six… and wait... a step further … Click! Distracted by the noise, he frowned, his head darting about looking for its source. Felicity shaded the camera from view with her hat, her economy of movement failing to draw attention to me. Instead Harry, happy with his growing collection of pebbles, was oblivious to the man's glare.

"Carefully!" Felicity grabbed one of Harry's hands and removed its content when his throwing became too enthusiastic. "You'll do someone an injury."

Looking at her with horror at the injustice, his face contorted as his wails increased in volume.

"You great big baby! Come here." She held her arms open and he scrambled into them, whooping as she spun him around. "Oh, good Lord!" she exclaimed, her voice tempered with chill, one hand cupping the back of Harry's head. "We'd best head home, Lottie."

I turned to see what had caused this sudden change: a paperboy wearing a placard announcing, *Britain is at War*. I glanced around at the beach; deckchairs were still straining under the weight of men in suits, trousers rolled up to their knees, and women whose faces were shaded by large hats and parasols. There was no sense of panic; nothing to suggest that anything had happened to spoil a perfectly good day out. It would have taken the appearance of a warship on the horizon to send the day-trippers, who had spent good money on train fares and chair hire, scurrying back to London a moment earlier than scheduled.

I knew this was an important moment to capture, the moment of change Mr Parker had spoken of: the normality of the undisturbed holiday-scene with the horror of the historic message. "Five minutes," I said, scrunching an urgent retreat.

"Lottie! Oh!" Felicity threw up her hands, frustrated, but I was already setting up the shot. My lens fell on a couple who would form my foreground, framing the paperboy. I measured the distance in my head, checked the light, set shutter speed and aperture, knowing how the slightest error could ruin the shot. Then I waited for the moment when the paperboy shouted the day's headline and the couple looked completely absorbed in each other, without a care in the world. I breathed, just as I had been taught. At the last moment, a black dog entered the viewfinder and startled the young lady. Too late: my finger was already pressed down on the shutter.

"It's ruined!" I lamented as I trudged dispiritedly back towards Felicity, redistributing pebbles with each sinking step.

"Too bad. That's your lot." She looked at the horizon and sniffed, kissing Harry's blonde head. "How can all these people just sit here as if nothing is happening?"

But not everyone was complacent. A group of Royal Navy Volunteer Reserves ran whooping into the shallows, the waves breaking against their thighs, launching their hats skywards as if celebration was in order.

"Lads!" shouted one. "How about getting our fortunes told?"

Passing close by, his trousers plastered blue-black to his legs, one pursed his lips. "Got a kiss for us before we go, ladies?"

Stepping out of his way, I clung to Felicity's arm. "Why don't you come home with me? Daddy will know if there's anything to be done."

A tight gathering swarmed around the counter, little business being transacted. "There you are!" Daddy interrupted the senate. "Afternoon, Felicity. How's young Harry?"

"Growing up too fast, that's how he is, Mr Pye!" Discreetly, she extracted an errant finger from his nostril.

Daddy had grown fond of Felicity in recent months, although Ma remained wary of a woman who was so kind and yet did such a dreadful thing for a living. She liked her criminals to have evil glints in their eyes and her saints to wear polished halos so there could be no confusing them.

"Any more for any more, folks? No?" Daddy emerged from behind his counter to hold the door open. "Then I've got family to see to and you should be off to see to yours."

"What do you make of the news?" Felicity lowered her voice as he turned the sign from *Open* to *Closed* and followed behind her on the staircase.

"It's been such a long time coming, I'd half convinced myself it would never happen."

"Is that you, Lottie?" Ma called from the kitchen. "Get yourself in here and let me take a look at you."

"Hello, Mrs Pye. I hope you don't mind me -" Placing one hand over her mouth, Felicity averted her eyes.

Ma wasn't one to ignore a distressed soul, no matter how low her opinion of her was. She stood, patting Felicity on the shoulder, offering her own seat and eying Harry, whose hands gripped the tabletop in close proximity to her labours, with suspicion. "Well, now. You're more than welcome. Lottie, make yourself useful and pour more boiling water in the pot. Have you been into town, Felicity?"

"The seafront. We came straight here the moment we heard. Honestly, you wouldn't know anything had happened!"

Her verdict confirmed, Josie's tone was smug. "Exactly what I said! Barely a ripple."

Daddy intervened. "There's a meeting at the Town Hall

tonight. There's no point any of us getting worked up until we hear what the mayor has to say."

The tea poured, Ma asked, "Haven't you got something to be getting on with, young lady?" a sure sign there was adult discussion underway that didn't concern me, while a small boy who had crawled under the table could safely be ignored.

I found Mr Parker in his office, fountain pen poised above inkwell. He lifted his head to see who had rattled the bell. "Ah, it's you, Lottie! I suppose you've heard the news? I've shut up shop, business was so slow."

"Does that mean you have time to develop my photograph?" I asked optimistically.

Mr Parker expelled his intended objection with a sigh. Removing his glasses to rub his eyes, he said, "Why not? I'll go mad if I spend another minute staring at this ledger. I've done the same set of calculations three times and come up with three different answers. None good, I might add."

There was nothing I liked more than standing in the semi-darkness, watching images come to life in the chemical tank. I flinched as I saw the smudge of black dog appear, his nose buried in the young lady's dress like a pig rooting for truffles, her hands thrown up in horror.

"Well, now!" Mr Parker held the dripping print, praise indeed. "I like what you've done there. You've captured an historic moment, but there's humour too."

I could hardly admit that the dog was an accident.

"I wonder if *The Gazette* would be interested in this for tomorrow's edition. What do you say?"

The first indication that my work might be saleable, I brimmed with pride.

Mr Parker hesitated, rubbing his beard. "Of course, it would have to appear under the name of the studio. I'd have trouble convincing them this is the work of a thirteen-year-old girl."

The photograph appeared on the front page the following day under a quotation from the mayor: 'Brighton Will Not Panic'. In typeface so small I thought only Daddy, Ma and Felicity would notice it, they printed, *Photograph by Lottie Pye of Parker's Photographic Studio*. But Alfie had been on the lookout too and brought a copy into school, grinning. "I see your name's in the paper again, Lottie."

Confiscated by the teacher, she was rather less impressed. "Is there nothing Lottie Pye can't do?" She held it by the corner between two fingers and dropped it into the waste-paper bin, while the rest of the class rocked back in their chairs with unnecessarily animated laughter. She narrowed her eyes at me, demanding: "Twelve times' table. Let's see how you get on with *that!*"

But it was the end of school for Alfie and me. We had reached the age of thirteen and there was nothing more they could do with us. We had made the mistake of teaching ourselves to think when all that was required was to recite parrot fashion.

"No more excuses that the rain has washed away your homework," I said to Alfie as we took our slates home for the last time. "What will you do now?"

"What I always do," he winked. "Keep out of Mother's way and get by."

Nobody was better at talking themselves into anything than Alfie West. It was no surprise to find him standing outside the studio door, face scrubbed to a pink sheen, hair oiled and combed flat, dressed in the black uniform edged with red piping that had been worn by hundreds of boys who had come to have their portraits taken. I had come to enquire about my own future since no one seemed prepared to discuss it with me.

"Miss Pye." He tipped his hat, opening the door.

"Mr West," I replied haughtily, but when he caught me

peering at him through the plate glass he cast me a self-satisfied grin.

"There you are, Lottie!" Mr Parker snapped back the velvet curtain on its brass hooks. "Plenty to do today. You've seen young Alfie, I take it? He thought a respectable establishment shouldn't be without its bellboy. Now he'll have to prove he can pay for himself. Of course, with another member of staff to support, we shall all have to work harder. Now where did I put that do-dad? *You* know, the thingamajig?" He began lifting paperwork randomly, depositing it on different piles. Seeing my desolate expression Mr Parker said, "Come along, Lottie, I can't have my best model with a face like a month of Sundays. If you could just help me find my..." He snapped his fingers and sighed noisily. "Where is the darned thing? Someone must have moved it! When there was only me, I knew exactly where everything was."

Turning to leave, I trod on something wedged in the narrow gap between two floorboards. I crouched down to retrieve a small screwdriver, used for making minuscule adjustments. "Is this what you're looking for?"

"Ah!" He took it without comment.

Feeling it wasn't the time to broach the subject of my future, I reached for the door handle, only to find the door opened outwards by Alfie, letting in the startled cry of gulls.

"And where are you off to?" Mr Parker demanded, hands on hips and of stern expression. "On the first day of your apprenticeship!"

"My apprenticeship?" I gasped, astonished.

"I assumed your mother would have told you."

With huge effort, I managed not to launch myself at him.

"She said that if I didn't have anything definite to offer, you would be taking up a position elsewhere. So in the space of a day, I've gone from no staff to two. More fool me!"

Felicity chose that moment to appear. Harry was dangling

from her arm, one finger exploring the cavity of his ear. "Do you mind if I have a quick word with Lottie? I need someone to watch Harry for a couple of hours."

"Well, she can't!" Mr Parker barked, then, on seeing Felicity's astonished expression, relented. "Oh, bring him in. He can make himself useful. I'll try him out in front of the camera."

"Oh?" Setting Harry down, she pressed both of his arms to his sides.

"I've been asked to produce a set of postcards for young women to send to their sweethearts on the front line. Horrible sentimental things. We can throw in a few of him pining for his daddy."

Looking flushed, Felicity lowered her eyes.

"Oh, look now..." Mr Parker began.

Felicity raised her face, a fixed smile in place. "Harry, you do whatever Mr Parker tells you." She ruffled his blonde hair, one hand trailing along the wall as she left.

"Blast!" said Mr Parker. "That was tactless of me. I shall have to make amends."

18 - SIR JAMES'S STORY

SHERE, 2009

Jenny handed me a photograph of a proud young man in an RAF uniform standing in front of a Lancaster III. "This isn't your father, is it?" she said, implying that she thought it was.

I looked at him; he stared back, confidently grinning, unblinking. Almost a stranger, a fresh-faced young man with his whole life ahead of him. "Well, I'll be!" I exclaimed. "Wherever did you find this?"

"In the box I've just opened."

"Let me take a look." Pulling back the cardboard flaps, I saw that its contents were different from the others. Inside were bundles of letters, some of them in my father's hand, others in my own.

But Jenny was clasping the photograph, her eyes widening with recognition. "This is you!"

"Good looking young chap, wasn't I?" I tried to make light of it as my trembling hands touched rediscovered things I had never thought I would see again.

"You were a pilot?"

"Royal Air Force. My father told me you got a clean fight from the air, not like the poor buggers on the ground. He'd seen action in the Great War, so he knew what he was talking about. Turned out, it was some of the better advice he gave me." My mind was elsewhere as I shuffled bundles of envelopes. "What the devil?"

"Is something wrong?" Jenny hovered at my shoulder like a wasp at a picnic.

"I never once wrote to my mother. How on earth did she get hold of my letters?"

"Another mystery. My mother wrote a letter for me to open on my eighteenth birthday. Full of everything she thought I'd need to know."

I acknowledged her distractedly. "Obviously didn't trust your father to come up with anything sensible."

"Maybe not. Could have done with most of it five years earlier. I had to grow up a lot quicker than she thought."

"Never once had a letter from mine. Not while she was alive anyway." I selected an envelope at random in my father's handwriting, noting the Brighton address. After unfolding the sheet contained within, I read silently, aware of the rhythmic movement of my lips.

"My dear Charlotte,

More news from the boy enclosed. I must say he seems to be bearing up remarkably well, which is more than I can say for myself. I'm a bag of nerves waiting for the postman! It makes me wonder if Father was the same, but his letters were always full of what ho, up and at 'em. I'm not sure the old goat suffered a moment's doubt in his life.

Excellent meeting at the House about the rights of handicapped servicemen. The testimony from your good man proved most useful. Do send my regards.

Your loving husband."

"Well!" I sat back in my chair and, setting the letter down on the table, covered it with one hand.

"Anything?" Jenny asked from the far side of the room, where she had made a tactful retreat with the excuse of filing photographs in new wooden-fronted cabinets, using a combination of my mother's sub-sections and her own mysterious system of cataloguing.

"Well I never," I repeated, a little shell-shocked. "My parents were in contact. All those years and I didn't know it. Not once did she ask for me. All it would have taken was an invitation."

"Why did you wait?" Jenny demanded. "It works both ways."

I shook my head wearily. "My father was always willing. She only had to ask."

Jenny carefully withdrew something from the drawer in a sly hiss, then forcibly slammed it shut. After the involuntary shudder of my shoulders had settled, I was surprised by the marked alteration in her appearance. "Then he was just as stubborn as you are!"

Having made a concerted effort to control my own outbursts, I was taken aback at her display. "I - I beg your pardon?"

"What I'm trying to say is, perhaps she thought she didn't have the right to ask. She was the one who left. Maybe your father had to offer."

"My father did everything for me!" I began to protest, unprepared for this ambush that seemed to have been pre-prepared, waiting only for the command to attack.

"Oh yes, everything!" Her eyes rolled. "Except allow you to see your mother, that is!"

"Your trouble is you're judging him by today's standards. It was extremely unusual for a man to raise a child by himself in those days. I was lucky not to have been farmed out to spinster aunts."

"And *your* trouble is that you've never given a moment's thought to your mother's point of view!"

"I beg your -"

"You worshipped your father, while she was always the villain!"

"What do *you* know about it?" I exploded, red-faced, but Jenny was undeterred.

"Quite a lot, actually. All of this!" Placing a small pile of photographs on the table, she deliberately sent them spinning in all directions. Her hands at shoulder level, she cast her eyes about the room at the growing piles of debris we had created, while the boxes in the hallway appeared as mountainous as ever. "I don't know what *you* see in your mother's work, but *I've* been looking at the world through her eyes! Have you even noticed what she chose to photograph when she wasn't working in her studio?"

"I, er -"

Jenny shook her head at me while I stammered, unable to lift my eyes from the table. "Middle-aged women and young boys! Mothers and sons: everything she didn't have."

"Perhaps they made interesting subjects -"

"I've tracked the dates on the backs. First we have the women - or perhaps I should say 'the mothers.'" She snapped a number of photographs face down on the table in front of me, the dates clearly written, not within the official stamp of Parker's studio, but in plain blue ink. "Then we have a gap of several years. But when we come back, the subjects change: boys this time. 1927. 1928. 1929. And here. 1930. Look at them! See how they're getting older?" Impossible to argue, I nodded feebly. "I'm willing to bet they're almost the same ages you would have been. Your mother spent the first part of her life looking for the mother she never knew. Then she spent the second part of her life looking for the son she never knew. I wouldn't call that the actions of someone who didn't give a shit. Would you?"

She had my attention. I could hear Jenny's laboured breathing as she stood over me while I turned the photographs over one by one, greeted by marble-playing, donkey-riding boys; taken from the position of the puppeteer, laughing faces raised to watch a Punch and Judy show; a boy with his arm forever poised to skim a stone; a delivery boy astride a bicycle, one foot on the raised pedal, ready to push away from a standing start; a Boy Scout with the tips of two fingers in his mouth, about to whistle. Time frozen. For me, every face the ghost of a childhood friend who didn't see the war out. But that wasn't what my mother had been looking at, I could see that.

Jenny took a seat, arms folded, her eyes ranging the far corners of the room. Flushed, she wore the look of someone whose outburst had taken her by surprise, but who harboured no regret. She pressed her point, insisting I react. "Do you see now?"

"I - I don't know what to say," I said at last, leaning back in my chair and rubbing my eyes before returning both hands to the table: humbled. "Once again, you've shown me something I didn't realise."

Pacified, Jenny reached towards the hand closest to her, but stopped just short, letting hers settle on the table, fingers splayed. "Perhaps just these few pictures - out of everything we've found - is why your mother left you her collection." She repositioned her face so that it was impossible for me to avoid her gaze. "You must be able to see how much she missed you."

19 - LOTTIE'S STORY

BRIGHTON, 1914

We were under strict instruction to stay smiling in Brighton but, as months passed without victory, concern and fear crept behind the cheery facade. "Won't be long now," turned into, "What can we do to help?"

"It says here that the Allied forces have retreated to Paris." Daddy now used a national newspaper as a placemat while he paused to eat his evening meal.

Ma barely looked up from her kneading. "Is that good news?"

Daddy batted pie-crust crumbs from his moustache: "I don't know any more. It's just words."

To be honest, cartoons of the elderly Tommy called 'Ole Bill' made more sense to me. I memorised them from Mr Parker's copies of *The Bystander* so that I could describe them to Daddy. "Ole Bill's sitting next to a hole in a wall, while his officer asks who made it. 'Rabbits?' Bill says."

"Rabbits!" Daddy roared, throwing back his head. There was nothing like laughter to take the edge off. Sometimes you forgot there was anything to be afraid of.

"That's enough words for one evening. Life goes on," sighed Ma, but she didn't have to watch her husband or sons pack their bags and leave like Mrs West did.

"Will you fight?" I asked Mr Parker.

"It won't come to that," he replied cheerfully. "People with their own businesses will be the last to be called up."

Like a fool, I believed him.

There were hardships for those left behind with nothing to offer the London incomers who reported that trenches were being dug to counter imminent invasion. Resourceful women took in washing from the local barracks, instructing children to rummage through uniform pockets for cigarettes and sweets. When food was in short supply, they sent their youngest to the army camp at Shoreham with patched and fraying pillowcases, instructing them to "Stand there and look hungry." Many didn't have to act. Wives resorted to the pawnbrokers. Nothing was safe: neither their absent husbands' Sunday best, nor the bedsheets.

I did my bit by knitting khaki socks for the troops. By Christmas I had two misshapen tubes that Ma took one appalled look at and despaired, "Who do you know with feet shaped like that? Unpick them and start again!"

Never before had living on the coast made us feel vulnerable. Every morning as I collected driftwood, I expected black warships to darken the horizon, angry flying machines to fill the sky like bats. No longer lingering, I feared the moment when the air-raid warning would send us scurrying. But you can't live in constant fear. There were still moments when staggering customers sang us half-remembered segments from the music hall, still raucous laughter between Ma and Josie over a pot of tea, and still small discoveries as I learned how to perform feats of magic with light and chemicals. Breathtaking moments as ghost-like images appeared in the developing solution before taking on solid form, and Mr Parker exclaimed, "You've captured something there, Lottie!" Moments of optimism when he said, "There are two parts to photography: the emotional and the technical. You have the emotional. My task is to teach you the technical." Sometimes, whole days passed when we needed newspapers to remind us we were at war. And then, our false sense of security was shattered by news of the bombardment of Scarborough - a seaside town, not unlike ours.

"Holes were blown in the ten-foot castle walls, which collapsed as if they were made of timber." Daddy scanned, eyes zigzagging. "The old beacon on Castle Hill, used for centuries as a look out… The lighthouse had to be demolished…"

"How many are dead?" Josie demanded, unimpressed with talk of history and buildings.

Daddy traced a finger down the page. "Seventeen. Many more wounded. They've called it a murderous attack on an unfortified town. *All the world should know.*"

Suddenly it was our war. I knitted harder than ever, while Alfie's sixteen-year-old brother Eddy signed up to join his older brothers in the fight.

"It's a disgrace," fumed Mr Parker when Alfie delivered the news unemotionally the next day. "Boys fighting men's wars!"

"If you're prepared to say you're eighteen, they'll take your word for it," he shrugged. "The recruitment officer gets his shilling whether it's true or not."

"What did your mother have to say?" I asked.

"Same as she said to the others: 'Come home safe.'"

I watched the war edge closer as Brighton's most famous buildings were transformed into military hospitals. The Royal Pavilion, used on special request from the King; the Dome, its rows of metal hospital beds placed underneath chandeliers and gold leaf so that, when patients woke, they thought they were in paradise; a new sign was erected outside the Workhouse at Elm Grove - Kitchener General Indian Hospital. But the wounded soldiers who began to arrive just before Christmas would be the most unexpected sight of all.

"I have an assignment for you," Mr Parker announced. "Alfie, you can carry the equipment. I want Lottie to photograph the parade."

"Aren't you coming with us?" I asked.

He turned away from me, unconcerned. "Call it an experiment."

"But... don't you want to see the Indians arriving?"

"I don't need to. I'll have your photographs to look at."

I stood open-mouthed.

"Do I take it you don't think you're up to the task?" Mr Parker asked.

"No, Sir!" I replied.

"Well, then. Get organised and make sure you're there in good time."

When I was ready to leave, he said, "Remember, Lottie. Preparation: backdrop, light, shutter speed, aperture, subject matter and..."

I scrunched my face up to think. "Feel the picture," I said trying to bury the nerves that threatened. Good nerves, I told myself.

"Don't let me down," he said, an unnecessary reminder of the faith he was putting in me.

The route was tightly packed all the way from the railway station to the Royal Pavilion. As the crowd jostled and surged, Alfie instructed them to "Stand well back," as if he were accustomed to giving orders just as well as the policemen dotted along the route. Through the viewfinder, I witnessed the sedate approach of the military ambulances keeping pace with the walking wounded. White-turbaned heads were held high, dignified men in thin khaki uniforms unfit for an English winter. Some walked with sticks, hunched lopsided over crutches; others were dressed with white triangular slings, small sails in a sea of men. Facial hair varied from dark beards far longer than the fashion to clean-shaven chins with wide moustaches; skin tone from Welsh coalminers' to West Country farmers'. A tense hush descended over the crowd until one bright spark piped up, "They're a long way from home, aren't they?" It was the first time the Indian army had fought outside its own country. Although we were accustomed to foreigners, few of us had come face to face with an Indian.

"They've had to provide separate water taps and lavvies for the Hindus and Muslims."

"You don't say! I only hope our lads are being treated as well abroad."

Occasionally a face stood out from the others, crying out to be at the centre of a picture: a turn of the head; a pair of intelligent eyes; barely concealed pain. These were my first impressions of the effects of war: an empty sleeve hanging limply; a man wearing a head bandage that covered both eyes being helped along by a fellow soldier. We had been taught we were superior to these men, that they needed the British to run their country for them. Was that why Mr Parker had wanted me to look at the scene with my camera's eye? Without understanding, I could only take the shots. But, in the end, it was my photographs that asked the questions.

"Well, now," Mr Parker said. "Put a camera in the hands of a child and you see the world with their wonder."

What was considered exotic soon became commonplace. The sight of hundreds of men prostrate in prayer on the lawn in front of the Dome was something we learned to tell the time by. Because a child wasn't taken seriously, I moved unhindered and took the photographs I wanted, realising that a pale-skinned, red-headed girl was as much a novelty to the Indians as they were to me.

"Red-head," I said helpfully, pointing to my hair and smiling when they repeated it with varying degrees of accuracy.

And when my photographs appeared in *The Gazette* under

Mr Parker's name, I knew it was a sign I was improving. It was only when some of the convalescing Indian soldiers visited the studio to have portraits taken to send home that there was ever any friction between us.

"Red-Head," they insisted.

"No, no," Mr Parker explained slowly, pointing to his own chest. "*I* take the portraits. *My* studio. *Me*. Mis-ter Par-ker. You understand?"

Scowling, they conferred in their own tongue with much shaking of heads, and turned towards the door as if to leave.

"Fine!" Mr Parker said, frustrated in defeat. "I will find Red-Head."

20 - LOTTIE'S STORY

BRIGHTON, 1915

"The Lord giveth and the Lord taketh away. Blessed is the Lord."

A solitary wail emanated from the front of St Nick's. In my naivety I was embarrassed for Mrs West at having let herself down in front of the congregation. As the organist allowed a chord to swell, a tapping sound at the end of my pew distracted me. I turned towards the stained glass windows, where Alfie was silhouetted, a halo surrounding him.

"Coming?" he hissed.

Ma's eyes were tightly closed in prayer. Undecided, I glanced in her direction before shuffling sideways along the bench.

"What about your mother?" I whispered, already rising to my feet.

He shrugged. "Can't stand the sight of me. Says I remind her of him. You with me or not?"

"Alright," I said, deciding I would have to accept whatever punishment Ma devised for this previously unheard-of offence. As we were still tiptoeing down the side aisle in an effort to hush our echoing footsteps, the vicar commanded,

"All stand for the final hymn!" Amidst low murmurs and general shuffling we burst into bright sunlight. The oak door closed behind us with a resounding boom, stifling the opening line of *Guide Me O Thou Great Redeemer*.

Outside among the long seeded grass that grew between the gravestones, Alfie addressed the mound of loose earth that surrounded a freshly dug grave. "She says Lloyd George is a murderer."

We trudged downhill in silence, both knowing where we were heading. Alfie's gaze was fixed firmly on the cobbles. Five weeks of sleeping in the trenches had been too much for poor Eddy. He had caught typhoid fever and was dead within two days. Heart failure at the age of sixteen: an old man's disease.

On the beach, we located a lonely spot where we would be ignored and, straight-backed, faced France. I slowed my breathing to the rhythm of the waves. They retreated, pulling small clutches of pebbles in their wake. Reaching for Alfie's hand, I heard him sigh: nothing more. Part of him was absent. Long after the point when I felt like fidgeting, I stood tall: when the wind whipped hair across my face I didn't tuck it behind my ears; when my lips dried to the point of splitting I didn't wet them.

Eventually, a shivering Alfie dropped, picked up a pebble and tossed it aside. "Said he was off to see the world. All the idiot saw was a ditch!"

Only when his practiced hand was happy with its choice of stone did he sit with his legs splayed in front of him, taking aim: a bouncing bomb fired at Le Havre. This was no game. I crouched down on my haunches, hugging my knees, watching in silence.

"What's it all for, anyway?" Alfie asked, not expecting a reply.

I could have quoted any number of authorities. Helping our friends in Belgium, the politicians said. 'We can't just allow the Germans to seize a free country.' But wasn't that what we'd been doing for hundreds of years? Except that we'd called it 'conquering' and used words such as 'glorious' to describe the expansion of our Empire? I had listened to the vicar's words about the righteousness of war, but what about 'Thou shalt not kill'? And if there really was a God, whose side was he on? The only thing you could rely on was what you saw with your own eyes. Alfie's final missile skittered across the surface and sank like a dead weight, then he trudged up the beach, hands in pockets.

I stood, my feet sinking as I turned to ask, "Where are you going?"

"To see if Mother's ready to look at me."

Similar scenes were re-enacted all the way from Land's End to John o' Groats. Away from Ma's hearing, Daddy looked up from the newspaper wearily, rubbed his eyes and acknowledged, "I'm glad my boys didn't live to see this." Away from Daddy's hearing, Ma crossed herself: "Thank God my boys died at home where they belonged. At least we had bodies to bury."

I made my way to Mr Parker's studio, alone.

Mr Parker pulled the curtain aside. "Ah, there you are, Lottie. Was it a good memorial service?"

I sat down in the leather chair, my shoulders leaden. "Awful."

Perching on the corner of the desk, Mr Parker's trouser-legs rode up and displayed an inch of sock above his polished boots. His voice was saturated with knowing. "That's how it should be if the vicar does his job properly."

In spite of myself, I found that I was crying.

"Come now." Mr Parker pulled a handkerchief from his breast pocket, using it himself. "Believe it or not, at times like this, work is the best place to be. Let's not waste those tears. Sit for me."

But dangers lurked in dark corners for those who didn't fall victim to Kitchener's pointing finger. For perhaps longer than I realised, food had been harder to come by. What was available was costly. Ma was defiant: she refused to increase the price of her pies. "Folks would prefer less steak than to fork out more of their wages," she insisted, tight-lipped.

"Steak?" Daddy threw his hat down on the kitchen table on returning from the butchers. "There *is* no steak! And without steak, there'll be no steak and kidney pies."

"We'll get by." Ma carried on as if there was no cause for concern. "What about Mr Lee?"

Mr Lee was the local poacher, known by everybody, rarely identified by name.

"He says he's never seen the like before. People are sending their lads onto the Downs to catch rabbits."

"Well, then," Ma said, as if Daddy had stumbled on the solution.

"When would *I* have time to...?"

"I'm just saying: there's still a choice."

Daddy's rising colour betrayed the effort involved in holding his tongue until Ma retreated to the back yard. Then, trembling in frustration, he said, "I'm too old to be running around looking for supplies, let alone chasing rabbits! See what I mean about having to do things you don't want to, Lottie!"

I knew that things were tight. I saw even less of my earnings than usual, until one day, when I handed my envelope to Ma, she slipped it straight into her apron pocket. "We've all got to make sacrifices," she said. "I'll need you to serve in the shop in the evenings as well."

"I don't mind helping Daddy."

She couldn't look me in the eye. "Daddy won't be there."

"But what will I tell people? They expect to see him." Daddy held court, entertaining them with stories and offering comfort when good news was in short supply.

"That he's doing his bit for the war effort, same as everyone else." Ma stopped what she was doing to quip. "Unless *you* fancy catching a few rabbits, of course."

I didn't.

I witnessed first-hand how slow business was. People didn't arrive in the numbers they used to. They were busy queuing at the National Canteen where food was cheap and hot.

"How's it going?" Ma called downstairs from the kitchen.

"No one's been in for the last couple of hours. Shall I lock up?"

"What? Have you got something better to do?"

Longing for the warm glow of the embers I heard Josie laughing, as if it was a great joke.

"Come closing time, there'll be a rush. You'll see."

When the bell over the door rattled, I stopped blowing on my hands and hopped off the stool behind the counter. "Can I help you?" I asked the two ruddy-faced police officers who emerged hunch-shouldered from the darkness, bringing a blast of Arctic air with them.

"Hello, Lottie." One removed his helmet, and cradled it against his chest. Since my photograph had taken pride of place in the shop, everyone seemed to know me. The other leaned on the counter: embarrassed - or so I thought. "It's Kitty we're after."

"I'm serving this evening." I smiled as instructed: enough to be polite, no more. "What can I get you?"

"I'm afraid we're not here for our suppers. We need to talk to your mother."

Slow footsteps plodded down the worn wooden tread, and Ma appeared in the doorway. "Evening, George. I thought I heard a familiar voice." She nudged me. "Didn't I say business would pick up? Now, what will you have? It's on the house."

"Hello, Kitty." The officer without the helmet winced. "Sit yourself down a minute. We've come about Sidney."

Ma's face fell and she lowered her voice. "It's just a few rabbits, George. Surely you can turn a blind eye..."

George walked around to the service side of the counter, his voice gentle. "We're not here about rabbits, Kitty."

"Oh?" She sank onto Daddy's stool.

"There's no good way of telling you this, so I'm just going to say it: there's been an accident."

She pushed herself back to her feet, understanding his meaning before I did. "Is he at the hospital?"

The officer called George took both of her hands in his and made a careful study of them. One of his thumbs traced the outlines of her scars. "Not the hospital, no. That's the dreadful thing with these blackouts. A car coming along the Ditchling road missed the bend..."

The other officer took up where he had tailed off. The one who had faced the door. "Ended up in the ditch where your husband was hiding."

Ma snatched her hands away and they shot up to her face.

"Both killed outright."

As she fell, George caught Ma in his arms and gently lowered her to the floor, asking urgently, "Got any smelling salts?"

"No." I tried to swallow but my throat was knotted, every cell of my being fighting what I had heard.

"Then we'll need sweet tea." George scooped Ma up from the floor - like a child in his arms, she was no weight at all - and carried her upstairs. Josie cried out as they entered the kitchen. I was ignored, unimportant. He was not my real father.

Perched on the end of my bed in the boys' room - despite the fact that I had slept there for over fourteen years, it remained their room - I addressed the ghosts that hung from the eaves. "Daddy's on his way to join you. Look after him, you hear me!" Their presence that had once, as a newcomer to the household, gripped me with fear, and was still sometimes oppressive, offered the only available comfort.

With the sound of weeping, I knew that Ma had recovered from her faint. It was Josie whose tears fell like an ocean. Ma, abandoning her tea, gathered a shawl around her shoulders and, securing her Sunday hat with a pin, said, "I'm ready to go and see him now, George."

"Are you sure, Kitty?" George asked, his eyebrows knitting together.

"We've been together these past fifty-five years," she said, dignified. "I'll not desert him now."

But there was an unstoppable voice inside my head that said, *this is your doing. Yours!* Even as I reached up and opened the casing of the clock on the mantelpiece to still its arms and covered it with a white cloth, it insisted, *He was only there because* you *made him go.*

21 - LOTTIE'S STORY

BRIGHTON, 1915

Ma, having always been the strong one, shrank daily until she was incapable of making the slightest decision. In stark contrast, Josie - who Daddy had always considered a confounded nuisance - arrived each day at sunrise and stayed until the last swaying customer had been served. Finally, deciding it was hardly worth going home, she gave notice on her rented room. After years of appearing not to take very much in - other than tea by the gallon - Josie made up for Ma's newly acquired forgetfulness by nagging her to add salt, prompting her to stir. I was glad of her presence. Part of me, however small, still wanted to blame Ma for Daddy's death.

It was Josie who waved me off in the mornings: "We'll be fine. The last thing we need is you getting yourself fired for being late."

But I was no fool. Bravado couldn't disguise the fact that my wages weren't enough to keep a faltering business afloat. I volunteered before I was asked. "What about renting out the boys' room? There's no shortage of people looking."

Wincing, Ma looked to Josie who weighed the pros and cons with the angling of her head and a tightening of her mouth.

"It doesn't matter where I sleep. I'll curtain off a corner of the kitchen," I suggested.

"Oh, I don't know," said Ma, but it took her less than a day to decide.

"Tell me, how's your mother coping?" Mr Parker asked. I was getting used to conversations when the participants didn't look each other in the eye.

"Fine," I replied, knowing full well Ma would be mortified at the thought of anyone discussing family business.

"I was half expecting you to tell me you were needed at home and couldn't work here anymore."

I attempted to joke. "How would you manage without me?"

"That's what I've been asking myself! I don't mind admitting, you and Alfie have been a godsend. Having the two of you to teach… it's reminded me what it is I'm doing and why."

"And why's that, Sir?" I hesitated in my sweeping of the studio floor.

"Because I love it, of course!" He slapped his thighs. "It's the books and the cleaning and getting customers through the door that I used to detest. Now those things take care of themselves, I have time for the things I enjoy. I've even started painting again. So, I'd be very sorry if you had to leave me, Lottie." He looked at me sincerely. "But I would understand."

I cornered a small pile of dust. "Things will be better once we find a lodger."

I heard Mr Parker's sigh. "I see. Leave it with me."

For Felicity, moving to a room above a shop was another step towards respectability. She and Harry needed very little, she said. To be honest, Felicity was the one person I didn't object to giving up my room for. If Ma had been a bit sniffy at Mr Parker's suggestion, her resistance levels were unusually low.

"Better the devil you know," Josie advised.

"In all honesty, the devil is the last person I'd imagined having to stay."

"I think you're going to find it useful having Felicity here." Mr Parker accepted the cup of tea that was offered with a gracious smile, having helped Felicity transport her possessions. "You'd be surprised at the people she knows."

Furtive glances exchanged, Ma was almost speechless. In the background, we could hear the sound of Felicity singing to Harry.

"I do hope…"

Mr Parker brushed her reservations away with a swipe of his hand. "All in the past."

It was the next day when Ma was approached by a local farmer called Lockley who was prepared to sell his produce directly for a discount.

"Profits being what they are, it makes sense to cut out the middle man," he explained unconvincingly. From the size of his stomach, I observed that he hadn't felt the pinch of rationing. When Ma told him she'd want it delivered - seeing as she no longer had a husband who could collect - the poor man almost choked on his tealeaves.

Felicity chose that moment to position herself in the doorway. "What a lovely surprise, Mr Lockley!" she exclaimed. Her hip resting on one side of the frame, her hand on the other at shoulder level, Mr Parker couldn't have staged her more prettily.

"Felicity, what are you doing here?" Mr Lockley's voice was unnatural and he fingered his collar.

"This is home. Harry and I live here now."

Mr Lockley turned to face Ma, resigned. "Evenings do you? I'm often down the road for my pint anyhow."

"You have a deal." Ma brushed her hands free of flour before extending one to Mr Lockley. "Could you show Mr Lockley out, Felicity?"

"My pleasure." She stood sideways, smiling.

"I'm more than capable of finding the door." Mr Lockley hesitated, compared the size of the gap in the doorway with his girth and barged past, almost carrying Felicity with him.

Groceries came to us in much the same way. Ma said Daddy was looking out for us, but I knew better.

As part of the bargain, Harry gained two grandmothers who were more than happy to watch him when Felicity quietly kept her appointments. Felicity didn't volunteer information about where she was going and Ma didn't ask, worried what the answer might be. We became a household of women, somewhere other women sought hot tea and refuge. To my surprise, I even found Mrs West sitting in Daddy's chair on the eve of his funeral.

"Come to pay her respects. We seem to have more in common these days," Ma explained, blowing out the candles that she had lit for the sake of appearances, fearful of waste.

Gradually, I had allowed myself to feel Daddy's absence. I tried my best to hold my tongue when Josie sat in his chair or used his chipped cup, telling myself these were just things. I had retrieved his pipe from the mantelpiece and, fitting my teeth into the indentations his had left, sucked any last traces of his breath. I had carried it to the beach and sat among the fishermen on an upturned barrel, mirroring their positions, one foot resting on the other knee; politely ignored now that I was no longer a little girl to be toyed with and teased.

"Of course, it wasn't as if he was your real father," Someone wearing brown lace-ups with a slight heel spoke to me as I emerged blinking from the funeral service. Ma hadn't encountered any difficulties in persuading the vicar that Daddy deserved a Christian burial after she explained that his religious instincts had been gradually eroded by the loss of his sons.

Alfie, who had kept a respectful distance, was by my side at once. "It's not like Joseph was Jesus's real father either."

The air froze with a sudden hush. I raised my puffed eyes to see whose face matched the shoes. It was the mayor's wife. I had always found her irritatingly dimpled and smug.

"Well!" she exclaimed, appealing to our betters in anticipation of support. "I was trying to say something kind to the poor girl!"

In the shade of an ancient yew, dozens of hands poised to throw the first stone but Alfie could have chased tigers that day. "Lottie doesn't need your sort of kindness."

"What business is it of yours, young man?"

"Well, let me see." He held his chin, deep in thought. "So far I've lost a father and three brothers in this war. I'm learning fast what the right thing to say at a funeral is. And that wasn't it - not by a mile." Alfie turned to me. "Coming, Lottie?"

I glanced back towards the church door where Ma was solemnly thanking people for coming, her face veiled by borrowed black lace. "Later. She might need me."

"Take your time," he said, replacing his cap. "You know where to find me."

"At least I've still got you." Alfie and I were sitting with our backs against a breakwater, elbows touching. The dusky sky was violet. He had sat there for hours in waiting, huddled inside his inadequate jacket, ruddy cheeked. Silent and subdued moods had taken him more often since the telegrams started to arrive. Alfie's old joking self made fewer appearances. Although he had little to say for himself, I didn't think anything of it. This was a solemn vigil, not a holiday outing.

"I'm going away, Lottie," he announced at last.

His meaning unmistakable, my eyes followed the trail of his words until the wind carried the last lingering letter out to sea.

"Say something." He turned to me miserably. "Anything."

"Today, you tell me! Why?" I demanded. A simple enough question: impossible to answer. When Alfie didn't respond, I continued, "It isn't as if you believe in the war. You hate everything about it!"

Hanging his head, he said. "Remember those Leydown boys? It's like we said back then: I just don't see how I'm any different from the rest of them."

"Have you told your mother yet?"

"No. And I'm not going to until after it's done."

"She won't let you go." I was confident I could rely on Mrs West to put her foot down.

"Yes she will," he said, his voice heavy. "She can't stand being around me."

"And me? Did you even think about me?"

"Of course -"

I clasped his face in both hands and pulled it towards me, kissing him, stubborn and closed-lipped; the only way I knew how. My beach-damp hair lashed at his cheek. I inhaled him, his salted skin, the goodness of him, then I pushed him away. "There! Now you've got what you've always wanted."

With a pained expression, he put the back of one hand over his mouth as if I had slapped him: "Write to me?"

Stunned that the kiss had made no difference, I shook my head violently. "I won't write letters." There were lies in words. I never wanted to write what I thought someone else wanted to hear, or read a letter wondering what was missing.

He looked up, his eyes questioning. "My mother can't write, *you* know that. If you don't write to me, no one will."

And I couldn't stand it. The sight of the sky reflected in those honest eyes. Not if this was to be the last time I would see them. "I'll come here every day and I'll look over to France, and I'll collect a pebble to remind me. And when you come back… well, you'll have to help me put them back, because I won't be able to carry them all, that's for certain."

Already, I was spouting words I had little faith in. My eyes were growing blind, nothing that blinking could remedy. I felt one of my fists being prised open as Alfie peeled back stubborn fingers one by one, and the shape of something cold and curved filled my palm before he folded them back. "Here's the first one."

Listening to his stony retreat, my eyes closed, I imagined his back becoming smaller and smaller, and, with my head bent over my knees, I gave in to great sobs that shook my coiled frame. By the time I was ready to open my eyes and see the picture in my mind, Alfie was gone.

"Come home safe," I whispered to the darkness.

The next morning, when he wasn't keeping guard on the flagstones outside the shiny black door, I knew: he really was gone.

"Do you think it's too large for young Harry?" Mr Parker said, watching me square the shoulders of his empty uniform carefully on the wooden hanger. "I shall miss Alfie, for all his cheek. He said I wouldn't regret taking him on, and he was right."

"Yes, Sir," I mouthed, unsure if I spoke the words out loud.

"I gave him a copy of your photograph. I hope it was the right thing to do."

I swiped at the corners of my eyes. "Shall I bring your tea now?"

Mr Parker sighed. "It's all right to talk if you'd like to."

"No, Sir. Thank you all the same."

"I know how worried you must be -"

"Then answer me this," I demanded, fuelled by anger. "Don't you feel bad that another boy has gone to do what should be your job?" Shocked by my outburst, my hand flew to my mouth. "I -"

Instead of erupting, Mr Parker was hesitant, bringing a curved index finger to rest in the incline between his lips. When he withdrew his hand, he bit on his upper lip and slowly reshaped his mouth. "Lottie, it's time I was honest with you. I feel terrible that *anyone* has been asked to fight. Terrible. And never more so than now. But I have a fight of my own, and my fight is against war itself. I'm a conscientious objector. You know what that means, don't you?"

I nodded, not trusting myself to speak. I had heard much talk of cowards, but I had also seen what war did to men through the lens of my camera.

"I've had my call-up papers and I've done what I can to resist. Now it goes before the Board."

The waiting - the seeming inevitability of it all - became unbearable. It wasn't only Daddy my thoughts turned to when I saw an empty chair. Each day I collected a pebble for Alfie. My collection grew until I had to move it from a bucket by the fireplace to the back yard. Until I realised that, deep down, I believed Alfie was as dead as Daddy. All that was missing was the telegram. The sight of my lopsided pyramid was a calendar measuring the days. How long do you go on collecting pebbles in memory of a loved one? Is six months enough? A year? I could no longer answer Ma's question, "What are you going to do with those things?" or laugh at Josie's suggestion that I was collecting missiles so we wouldn't be found wanting when the invasion came. It was pointless, the war. Pointless! So when the pebbles became playthings for Harry, who used them to construct roads for his toy cart, I didn't scold him as if they were precious things. It was the time they represented that was precious. By then I understood why Alfie had gone: it is easier to leave than be left behind.

And then came the morning when Felicity burst from the studio in tears.

"Felicity!" I called after her, as the door shut out the mournful screech of gulls.

I edged back the velvet curtain to see Mr Parker sitting at the side table, his forehead resting on one hand, a crumpled letter suspended from the other. When he looked up I closed the gap, holding my breath.

"Lottie!" he called out, having seen me. "I'll have to tell you sooner or later."

I approached him cautiously, hands behind my back.

"Sit, sit!" He was impatient with emotion. I perched on a plump chair, uncomfortable with so much in the way of comfort.

"My dear girl, the Board have given me a choice: join the medical corps or face a court martial. They've left me no option. The studio will close at the end of this week."

"But what about our work?"

"We knew this day would come. I'm afraid it will have to wait until this wretched war is over."

"I could keep things going..."

Mr Parker stopped me with a sigh. "Lottie, truth told, you're a far better photographer than I'll ever be. I'm simply an opportunist while you - I have my suspicions that you could be a great artist. But there's the paperwork, the licence, the rent. It's too much to ask of a sixteen-year-old girl."

I smiled through my tears. "What about Lottie Pye Limited?"

"Lottie Pye Limited will have its day, I have no doubt, and I hope to be part of it. But in case you feel you have to go your own way, I have some things I'd like you to have. Firstly these." Flat-palmed, he slid a leather folder across the table towards me. "Your portfolio. Photographs of you. But more importantly, your own photographs and newspaper cuttings."

As I turned them over one by one, he said, "You've come

a long way from that little girl who walked through the door with dirt smudged all over her face." I was about to protest, but Mr Parker continued. "And there's something else." He stood and walked to the darkroom, returning with the hand-held camera and sincerity in his eyes. "Will you do me the honour? I won't need this where I'm going." I looked at him, open-mouthed. "You're to have the keys so you can use the darkroom. And in return, I expect you to tidy up once a week. My solicitor will contact you should anything change." I must have lowered my guard because he added, "Believe me, this is not my choice."

I let my head drop to my chest.

He sighed deeply. "You and Alfie and Felicity, we've made a good team and I shall miss it. I shall miss you. You'll write to me, I hope? I expect to hear great things of you."

"I'm sorry, Sir. I won't write letters."

"Of course, I forgot. You and your collections. What will you collect to remind you of me, I wonder?"

"Images, Sir. I'll collect images."

"Well then, I shall look forward to seeing them." Mr Parker stood and trudged towards the darkroom. When he spoke again he didn't turn to face me, but his voice was so old it wouldn't have surprised me to discover that his hair had turned grey in that instant. "Perhaps you'd send Felicity back to see me when she's feeling better. There's something I'd like her to have. Your Madonna and Child - I hope you don't object?"

"No, Sir."

"Why is it," he barked, one hand resting on the doorframe of the developing room, "that you *insist* on calling me Sir?"

"Because it's what I've always called my teachers. And you've been the best one by far."

"Then I must try not to be so irritated by the sound of it."

Mr Parker turned then and, if his face was not quite smiling, it was a plausible imitation. "I envy you, Lottie. A person who doesn't exist on paper could disappear. Start again somewhere else."

I knew it was the last time I would see him for a long while. If Alfie West could lie about his age, so could I.

22 - SIR JAMES'S STORY

SHERE, 2009

"What was your war like?" Jenny asked.

We had been sorting through a box of faded and yellowing picture-postcards designed to be sent to the front. They featured my teenage mother together with an older version of the blonde-haired boy we had seen elsewhere and another older model - quite lovely - who posed as his mother.

"I signed up as a pilot. It would have been, oh, 1941."

Jenny's eyes widened. "Talk about having to grow up fast! You would have been younger than I am now."

"I was called up at eighteen - although I wasn't allowed to take part in ops for a year. The Germans had control of the skies, so there was a huge pressure to get us airborne. Not many pilots had teaching experience and, more often than not, the weather was blooming awful. I lost almost as many pals in training as I did fighting."

"Did you fly in the Battle of Britain?"

My smile was a wince. Blame Churchill: it was what everybody wanted to know. "No. Mainly raids over the other side of the water: Kiel, Bremen, Le Havre. I took part in the Market Garden campaign. Bombing roads and bridges. Dropping dummy parachutists to throw the enemy off the scent."

I gasped at a sudden flashback: a shell bursting in front of the cockpit. There was just enough time to shout, "This is it, lads!" and grab hold of the safety harness before the burst, suspended over the nose of my Wellington, grew from the size of an orange into a great, dark, flame-spewing mass. As it exploded, the aircraft lurched and shuddered. We entered splinter clouds that hung like black puffs. Debris hit the armour-plated shield behind my head as the windscreen shattered. I absorbed the damage to the aircraft through my hands on the control column, each jolt and vibration, while the splinters ripped through metal. Flying glass grazed the side of my face. I felt no pain but my vision was obscured by blood, Williams swabbing at its source before I even needed to ask.

"Nothing to worry about," he said, using familiar words of comfort. I was lucky. The splinter had narrowly missed my left eye.

I had never known anything like the bond between men who faced the possibility of death together on a daily basis. And yet, at the end of the war, after shaking hands by the side of a narrow Surrey lane, we went our separate ways.

"See you around, I expect," was the last thing Williams said to me, with a brief shoulder slap. I never saw him again.

Like so many memories, this one had taken on the mantle of a dream. It belonged to another lifetime, together with the image of my mother's face, her hand over her mouth; the old man silhouetted by the gallery doorway; a man on a bridge walking away.

I glanced up to find Jenny frowning at me, concerned. "Headache?"

My hand had moved involuntarily to the slight depression of my scar, proof that the memory was real. "Shall we get on?" I asked.

Jenny shook her head. "You never give much away, do you?"

"No heroics for me. You had to treat it like any other job. I did what I had to do and got out of there."

As we continued sorting through our individual boxes I felt silence grow between us, suffocating, like ivy. Occasionally, I glanced up to find Jenny looking away, sometimes feeling her eyes dart towards me. Laughing, as though I had suddenly thought of something amusing, I felt compelled to take the shears to it. "I'll tell you something, though. I met Clark Gable once."

"The one from *Gone With The Wind?*"

"I only know of the one. He was serving with the US Air Force, based in England."

Jenny leaned forwards, resting on her elbows. "What was he like?"

I stopped and thought. "Actually, he was the most charming man. It wasn't every day you walked into the mess and found a famous star. He and his crew were making recruitment films to send back home. 'Carry on as normal, boys. Drinks are on the bar. And *try* to look as if you're having a good time.' A minute later, he was swamped. Everybody wanted him to say the famous line they'd pushed past the censors. It sounds mild today, but to hear 'damn' said on film back then was shocking. 'Emphasis on the *give*, that's the trick.' It kept us busy for a good half hour, trying to get it right, until he stopped us, 'Boys, boys, you'll do me out of a job!'"

"Did you speak to him?"

I shook my head. "I don't know if you've ever met someone you really admire, but if I was to say anything, I didn't want it to be trivial. You see, Gable had joined up after his wife was killed in a plane crash. Lovely woman. You don't get over something like that." I paused, blinking away images of planes spiralling downwards, smoking tails, men reduced to names on war memorials. "I wanted to tell him I was so very sorry, but the atmosphere was one of free whiskey and cigars. Then, there was a moment when I realised he was acting. His laughter was too hearty to be genuine. For no more than a second, our eyes met over the heads of the men and he let his guard slip. I nodded to him, raising my glass slightly: the smallest gesture. Then I turned away and let the poor man be. Later, when he was leaving, he slapped me on the back. 'Gotta go,' he said." I heard myself sigh. "We make war so that we may live in peace. So said Aristotle."

"Do you think that's true?"

I sighed. "Honestly? I don't know any more. Mind you, it was easier for us to live with ourselves than those who fought in the First World War. Poor blighters didn't know what on earth they were fighting for."

"Are you talking about your father?"

"Not him! My father thought the war had been arranged for his benefit, so that he could learn to fly! My grandfather didn't approve, you see. There was a Navy tradition on his side of the family going back generations. He would never have paid for my father's licence."

"It doesn't sound as if your father was afraid of anything much."

I laughed. "He was a hard act to follow, I'll grant you."

"You were a politician, weren't you?" The inflection was missing: it was a statement of fact. Jenny reddened and turned her attention to the contents of the box in front of her.

Watching her bite her bottom lip, I felt myself frowning. The clock ticked. "For my sins. Thought I'd try and carry on what my father began. He had a whole raft of lost causes."

"I Googled you." Jenny tucked her hair behind one ear, a nervous gesture. "Did you know you have your own Wikipedia page?" To my raised eyebrows, she explained, "It's a kind of on-line encyclopedia."

"I had no idea I'd made such an impression. Another good reason not to buy a computer, if you ask me."

Mrs Smythe-Jenkins had been very vocal on the subject the last time we met in the Post Office queue: "You must sign up for broadband. I don't know how I ever managed without my weekly shop on-line."

"Like the rest of us poor sods, I'd imagine," I said for the benefit of the poor woman behind the counter, relying on people needing a pint of milk and a packet of Hobnobs for unexpected visitors to keep her business afloat.

"It sounds as if you were hounded out of your seat," Jenny persisted.

Anyone who had read the newspaper coverage would have had a fairly comprehensive account of the events leading up to my 'retirement' from parliament. I wasn't looking for sympathy. "Don't you believe it! I resigned."

"It wouldn't happen like that today."

"Perhaps it should! Where's the dignity in waiting to be asked?"

"But Lord Longford supported you -"

"*What!*" I almost choked. "He approved of my resignation, no more! Did this Wikipedia of yours tell you that Longford called people like me *handicapped?*"

"I don't see what was so -"

"I resigned to escape this line of inquisition. You can't possibly understand what it was like back then."

Arms folded, Jenny was adamant. "Not unless you tell me, no I can't."

I sighed loudly, airing the frustrations of an old man who'd missed an opportunity to do something worthwhile - something he believed in - because of a moment's carelessness.

Jenny shrugged. "Doesn't matter. I thought you *wanted* to talk about it."

"Why would I want to *talk* about it?" I barked.

Her raised eyebrows were a reminder of my nanny. *'Temper, temper.'*

"It was a long time ago," I said, a feeble substitute for an apology. "Attitudes were very different." As always, it was easier to draw on someone else's experience. "Do you know, in 1959, a gay musician called Liberace was awarded £8,000 in the High Court after the *Daily Mirror* implied that he was a homosexual? The words they used were outrageous, of course. 'Fruit-flavoured, mincing, ice-covered heap of mother love', was my favourite extract, if memory serves. But they were only saying what was obvious to everyone."

"You mean he denied it?"

"He'd taken them to court to force a retraction. He would have been ruined otherwise. People had stopped going to his shows. He went from the top of his game to the bottom almost overnight. But the words Liberace used were equally offensive in their own way. He said that he was against the practice because it offends convention and it offends society. Mind you, saying that, I don't know that *I* was any better. I was there at the trial and kept quiet. Perhaps, if people like me had stood up to be counted, attitudes might have changed quicker."

"And you?" She enquired gently, eyes like searchlights.

"You don't give up," I sighed, relenting. "It was 1968, if you must know. A year earlier, I would have faced criminal charges. And yet, in its own way, the timing was awful. My draft bill on the rights of the disabled was nearing completion. My father had worked to get ex-servicemen back into employment. The forgotten twenty-one million who returned from the Great War alive but maimed, expected to be grateful. I met hundreds who lived behind closed doors for fear of being shunned; who couldn't even access the services designed for them. Something of an outcast myself, I thought I understood how they felt. My father's work was interrupted by an untimely death.

Mine? By a man with a zoom lens, professing to serve the taxpaying public. It was his duty, he claimed! Once upon a time, 'duty' involved wearing a uniform." I shook my head. "This was a private matter. Thankfully, by then, I had no one to worry about disgracing but myself. I thought that by resigning when I did, the bill might be pushed through."

"What happened?"

"It was shelved. The issue didn't come to the fore again until the Nineties, and by then it was blighted by this blasted obsession with political correctness. Do you know, last week I read a questionnaire at the doctor's surgery that asked people if they *feel* that they have a disability, can you believe?"

"Thank you." Jenny was smiling at me. Then, having made me delve into old memories, at the precise moment my mind chose to linger, she was ready to move on. Placing a photograph in front of me, she said, "Here's a good view of Westminster from the bridge. 1917, it says on the back. Look at all that barbed wire."

I scrutinised the familiar image of politics and tourism transformed by the trappings of war. "Right in the middle of the fighting."

She placed a second photograph on top of the first: a man on the bridge, the camera facing Big Ben. "Any idea who this is?"

I pretended to study the uniform of the Volunteer Fire Service. But it was another face I saw. Another man on a bridge. My eyes clouded over and I swallowed.

"N-never seen him before."

23 - LOTTIE'S STORY

BRIGHTON TO LONDON, 1916

'Dear Ma,
    I am going to London to look for work. I will
    write when I am settled to let you know my address.
I would not even dream of leaving if you did not have Josie
and Felicity to help. I have left the key to Mr Parker's studio.
Hopefully Felicity will not mind sweeping up once in a while,
knowing how much Harry enjoys playing with the props. Please
do not think me ungrateful. I mean to make you proud.
    Yours, Lottie'

Stealing into Mr Parker's studio, I selected a few items to supplement my Sunday best: a parasol, white gloves and enough
make-up to enable me to present myself as Charlotte Lavashay, a young lady of eighteen. I spent the night in a chair,
unable to find a comfortable position. Overcoming my dread
of letter-writing, I rejected numerous drafts, before settling
on those few simple lines. I locked the door behind me in
the hush of first light, with head bent low and occasional
sidelong glances, bidding farewell to the familiar geography
of my childhood. Early enough to see the Indians prostrate in
prayer in front of the Dome. Early enough to see the sparks of

the fishermen's first pipes. The gulls were still a distant echo. The only people I encountered were night owls, betrayed by their pale skin.

I approached our shop where, inside, the household would still be slumbering: Ma, her face a frown, arms pinning the blankets neatly around her; Josie next to Ma, open-mouthed, snoring; Felicity, her face whitened with cold cream, her tresses wrapped in rags; Harry, bedclothes flung off, horizontal, fearless. I sealed the key in the envelope and posted my coward's goodbye.

Aboard the train, clutching my belongings, my stomach was a tight knot. Blurred backdrops of grass-covered fields and ripe crops sped past dotted with cows and farm buildings. Lulled by the rocking of the carriage, I took more of an interest in the stations we passed through and the face of my suited companion when his newspaper sank below the level of his bowler. Removing his pipe, he cleared his throat at every thunderous turn of a page, as if expecting to be asked to read out loud at any moment. The rhythm of the train, the regular turning of the page and his throaty cough became my musical accompaniments.

I showed my ticket to the conductor in what I imagined was the manner of a seasoned traveller, smoothing the raised edges of the punched hole with a thumbnail, and then my eyes must have glazed over. When I woke to my travelling companion's noisy folding of his newspaper, we were passing gardens behind neat terraces of houses, blackened warehouses, tall-chimneyed factories: a subdued sepia palette. His pin-striped legs brushed against my knees. I watched how he wrestled with the carriage door, adopting a two-handed approach.

Finally, after traversing a great brown river, I felt the force of the train braking, slowing down, arriving! My own two-handed attempt to tackle the latch yielded no result.

Recommending common sense to myself, I opened the window and pushed the handle downwards from the outside, finding that it gave - far too easily. The door flew open with me still attached, leaning through the open window. My bicycling feet failed to find solid purchase. Refusing to let go of my precious cargo, I swung outwards. My arm was wrenched, my head collided keenly with glass, then I was propelled backwards - but not far enough! Slipping between platform and train, my thoughts turning to Daddy and Alfie, hands gripped me underneath my arms.

"I've got you!" a voice announced close to my right ear.

With new kinds of pain to distract me, I heard myself cry out. Knees were bruised and skin tore until, freed, I shot out like a cork. My landing cushioned, I found myself lying on top of a grown man. Still clutching the handle of my bag, I rolled to one side, too shocked for embarrassment. There was movement as my saviour sat up laughing, brushed himself down and stood, surveying the damage to the elbows of his uniform. "That was a close shave, I must say! You've knocked the stuffing right out of me."

I raised my head to look at him. For a moment it seemed that he stopped breathing altogether. "I'm most dreadfully sorry -"

"Just as well I still had my lid on." He rapped on his tin helmet. "Voluntary Fire Service at your disposal. Are you injured?"

"I - I don't know." I bit my lip, shocked and tearful, wondering why I had embarked on this foolish journey when I could have been at home enjoying a cup of tea.

"Let me give you the once over." He smiled. His uniform gave me confidence, his ordinariness comforting. "Where does it hurt?" he asked.

Everywhere, I wanted to say.

"You appear to be in one piece but that's going to be quite some bump, I'm afraid."

We were jostled from every angle by day-trippers and troops, intent on wrestling their way along the platform to join the train for its return journey to Brighton. I swiftly withdrew one hand as the brass wheels of a heavily-laden porter's trolley trundled close by. "You're going to be trampled to death if we leave you where you are. Put your arm around my shoulder," he commanded. I felt his arm circle my waist, the warmth of his breath when he asked, grinning, "Shall we dance?"

With some nervousness, I straightened my legs, wincing and limping as we began to weave through the crowds.

"We should get you checked over by a medic. Where do you live?" he asked, hesitating by the barrier to take stock.

"I've only just arrived," I said, fearful of spending what little money I had on doctors' fees. "I'm here to find work."

"Admirable. We need all the help we can get. Your rooms, then?"

"I'm fine," I stammered. "You've been too kind already."

"All the same. At least let me offer you a cup of tea. There's a café in the forecourt. I don't know about you, but I'm absolutely famished. I came here straight from the night shift to meet my cousin, but the blighter hasn't shown. Just as well I hung around, by all accounts." He offered me his hand and I took it briefly. "The name's John Miller."

"Charlotte Lavashay." Said out loud, it sounded too big to fit a battered and bruised girl from Brighton.

"Well, now, that *is* a coincidence! My mother's name is Charlotte."

"People call me Lottie," I admitted. "I don't mind either way."

"And Lavashay? Where does that come from?"

"My mother, of course."

Frowning, he laughed. "Surely you mean your father?"

I blushed, making my excuses. "That bump on the head must have been worse than I thought."

"Then you must do as you're told."

Arriving at the café, I sat at a table obediently, my bag tucked underneath my seat. John removed his helmet, laying it upside down on the checked tablecloth and using it as a receptacle for his gloves. Underneath, once his unruly hair was smoothed back in place, I saw a good forehead above dark eyes, a clean-shaven face, humour despite the tiredness.

He beckoned to a passing waitress. "A large pot of tea, when you have a moment and…" He turned to me. "Let's treat ourselves. I fancy some eggs. Poached do you? Poached eggs and toast for two. And ice with something to wrap it in, please. We have a bit of an emergency on our hands, you see."

Bending to inspect my forehead, the waitress winced. "Ouch, that looks nasty. Be with you in a jiffy."

As we waited, I watched a steady flow of men in khaki and listened to the blur of passing voices, both English and foreign.

"So," John leaned towards me. "How's Brighton faring?"

"Most of the time you'd hardly know there's a war on. Except for the blackouts." Aware of my own intake of breath, I continued. "And the fact that half our men are missing. Mind you, we've had it easier than some."

"And who is 'we'?"

"My mother and I. My father passed away last year."

"Army or navy?"

"Neither," I said with a subdued smile. "He was in the wrong place at the wrong time." When John raised his eyebrows, I faltered, "It was a motor car…"

"Gosh, I am sorry." He placed one hand on the table.

Embarrassed by its closeness, I inched mine away, changing the subject. "Have you been called up?"

"They wouldn't have me!" He laughed. "All this time I had a weak heart, would you believe? It never held me back on the cricket field, but apparently I'd be a liability. I do voluntary fire duty a couple of nights a week, standing on top of the Houses of Parliament armed with my trusty bucket of sand. Shame it's pitch black because the view would be marvellous." He looked down, expression pained. "But in all seriousness, I get fed up of explaining. If you're out and about dressed in civvies and you've forgotten to wear an armband, people think nothing of being rude to your face."

In the station forecourt, within view, there were several recruitment posters on display: 'Every fit Briton should join our brave men at the front'. 'Come into the ranks and fight for your King and Country - don't stay in the crowd and stare'. 'You are wanted at the front. ENLIST NOW'. Women volunteers thrust leaflets into empty hands, asking, 'How do you feel when you see another man wearing the King's uniform?' I felt my mouth twitch as my thoughts wandered to Mr Parker.

"I was out with a pal who was home on leave when he was handed a white feather. You should have heard him! He didn't half give her what for - asked her if she wanted to hear what it was really like at the front. I don't mind telling you, I could have cheered." John pulled a silver case from his uniform pocket and angled it towards me. "Smoke?"

"No, thank you."

He tapped the end of the cigarette on the table before lifting it to his lips, waved a match and, narrowing his eyes, inhaled deeply.

I leaned forwards, embarrassed that I might have caused offence. "You must accept my apologies. I have a habit of asking too many questions."

"Oh, I hope you didn't think I was talking about you!" He sat forwards, flustered.

I watched a woman volunteer gaining on a man who had side-stepped her. "Perhaps when they've been to as many funerals as I have, or seen the state of some of the men arriving home, they wouldn't be so pushy."

"Frankly, I doubt it," he said sadly. "Ah, here's our waitress with the ice. That's terribly kind, thank you."

John laid the checked tea towel on the table, making a neat parcel of ice cubes. "Nifty little trick I learnt from our housekeeper." He looked up, grinning.

As he applied the cold compress to my forehead, I gasped.

"It's probably easier if you grab hold of it." He took my hand and put it in place. "Here. Like this. If you won't see a doctor, you should at least get some dressings on your grazes." He held up his hands. "I *know!* I'm making an awful fuss, but if this is to be my good deed for the day I'd like to make a half decent job of it. Dib-Dib and all that. Tell you what! Why don't you come back to my house and I'll see if we can't sort you out?"

Every moment that I delayed, I risked losing my nerve. Already, the return train to Brighton was very appealing. "Oh, I don't know… I should really…"

"All aboard!"

"I'll have to deliver you into Mother's capable hands because, as soon as I've had my eggs, I'll be ready for my bed." On cue he stifled a yawn, and I was reminded how exhausted I felt. "Excuse me! She's expecting me to bring her some company. Seeing as how my cousin hasn't shown, you'd be doing me the most enormous favour."

"Here we go, Miss." The waitress bent her knees and slid the tray onto the table. "Tea and eggs for two. Shall I pour, Sir?"

"No, I'll be Mother." John smiled, the handle of the pot already in hand.

After we had eaten in amiable silence, he sat back smoking, observing me through narrowed eyes. "Forgive me for staring. You have the most extraordinary face."

Instinctively, my hand located the contours of the bump on my forehead.

"Oh, dear me, I'm not doing very well today. That was jolly clumsily put." John laughed. "I meant that, even with a few bruises, you're quite beautiful."

"I don't know about that. I'm told I'm *interesting.*" Seeing it wasn't an attempt to flatter, I brushed my embarrassment aside. "You see, I work as a photographer's model."

"Is that so?" He drew on his cigarette looking bemused, and I wondered if Ma was right that it wasn't a respectable occupation.

"That was only part of it. I was apprenticed to a photographer. But after Mr Parker - my tutor - was called up, the studio had to close."

"So that's how you came to be here?"

"Is there much call for photographers in London?" I asked, my mission suddenly seeming futile and vain.

"I'm afraid I have no idea. But you could ask Mother. In fact, if you've finished..." After putting some coins in his saucer, John replaced his gloves and helmet.

I placed my cutlery neatly in the middle of my plate, mirroring his, and gingerly pushed myself to standing.

"Here! Let me carry your bag," he offered, stooping to retrieve it before I could object. "My motor is just around the corner."

My second ride in a motor car. In my part of the world that would have made me a seasoned traveller. In London, where engines outnumbered our four-legged friends, I was a novice. I tried to remember the advice about sitting upright, but John's erratic style of driving required more in the way of hanging on to the dashboard.

Immediately, removed from the false station environment, I tasted soot. I smelt dust in the place of salt; heard the coo of pigeons instead of the cry of gulls. Bicycles, motor cars and electric trams competed with horses and carts for road space. Newspaper boys with placard shields cried out: "Get your

Daily Express. Four German Zeppelins downed by British storm."

"That's the spirit!" John declared. "If we can't zap 'em, our weather will."

As we merged with the melée of traffic, I counted buildings six storeys high, saw archways, spires. Gaps and brick dust where houses had stood. A property opened up like a doll's house, furniture still intact on sloping floors. People loading possessions onto hand-held carts. Buildings without glass, not yet boarded up. My photographer's head turned this way and that, framing each wasted image I would have liked to capture.

"Ghastly muddle, isn't it? Most of this damage was done on the nineteenth of October. So far, we've been lucky. Nothing within half a mile of us." I didn't know it then, but I had missed the final Zeppelin raid on London by only a week. "Of course, the worst damage, we managed to do ourselves when the munitions factory at Silvertown went up. You should have heard it! Boom! All of Greenwich lost their windows."

"We've had nothing like this in Brighton." Although open-mouthed, I wasn't concerned for my safety: a girl who has escaped a lightning strike has little to fear from bombs.

Despite the chaos and cacophony, people were going about their various businesses, navigating debris as if it was no greater an inconvenience than waiting to cross the road. Frowning men with bowler hats swung black umbrellas in opposition to stiff legs; a woman in a bus conductor's uniform threw her head back, laughing at a joke; bow-legged boys kicked a tin can between them as they queued for bread when they looked as if they should have been in school; a nanny pushing a baby in a pram paused to allow an elderly lady to coo.

"Not far now," John said. "You really mustn't be nervous of Mother. She can come across as quite fierce. Used to be a suffragette, you know, but she gave it up overnight. I asked her if it was the violence that upset her. 'Good Lord, no!' she said. 'I couldn't bear to be associated with those dreadful vandals who set fire to the tea pavilion at Kew.'"

His chatter was a background to the strangeness. The claustrophobia that gripped me wasn't fear, but the sudden knowledge that the sea wasn't at the end of this street, or the next. There was no shore I could keep vigil on, just brick wall after brick wall, towering umpteen storeys high. And yet, as thoroughfares surrendered to quiet squares with wrought-iron gates offering views of lawns and benches, some with old men and young women digging temporary allotments, I let my mask slip. And when we drew up outside an elegant stone terrace with a balcony at first floor level and steps leading up to a shiny front door, I looked at John's dusty uniform and his motor car afresh, and understood. He wasn't an ordinary Londoner at all.

24 - LOTTIE'S STORY

LONDON, 1916

"Mother!" John called out from the cathedral-like hall, abandoning his helmet on a highly-polished side table, where, rocking, it took on the appearance of a tortoise shell. "I'm home!"

"In the drawing room!" a voice replied, clipped and lively. "Is Edward with you?"

"He wasn't on the train."

"Oh, I do hope nothing has happened to him!"

"Ah, Martha." John addressed a uniformed girl who had appeared silently from a narrow staircase to the left. I blinked with recognition: I could have been her, a girl in a plain black dress and pinafore, hair pulled back severely from her face, dark shadows under her eyes. Younger than me. Certainly younger than the age I had intended to lay claim to.

"Good morning, Sir." Her trained eyes fell on the offending tortoise, chapped hands clasped in restraint.

John handed her his overcoat. "This is Miss Lavashay, our guest. She's had a little accident. I wonder if you wouldn't mind asking Mrs Bellamy to take care of her cuts and bruises. Charlotte, Martha will show you where to have a bit of a wash and brush up. The blue room, perhaps?"

"Yes, Sir," Martha said, her eyes lowered.

He turned to me. "Come and find us when you've made yourself comfortable."

I was shown to an upstairs bedroom with papered walls and rugs on the floor and a delightful blue and white china washstand. When I asked where I could find some water for it, Martha said, "Oh no, Miss, that's not for use. It's an antique."

I looked around me, confused. "But, where shall I wash?"

She smiled. I noticed she had no trouble meeting my gaze and looking me up and down, hesitating at the sight of the toes of my scuffed boots. "You're not from around here."

"I've just arrived from Brighton."

"Very good, Miss." Martha opened a door which I had taken to be a cupboard. "Your private bathroom. There's a clean flannel and fresh towels on the side."

"Thank you," I said, looking in wonder at this room with its china basin and bath with their own hot and cold taps. Water shot out in a torrent and I stepped aside, turning off the tap. "Martha?" I called after her.

"Miss?" She reappeared.

I struggled to arrange the concerns in my head. "Do they treat you well here?"

She frowned, bemused. "Why yes, Miss. We're in demand now there's a war on. Truth is, I'm half afraid that if I leave to join the war effort, my position won't be here for me when this dreadful thing's over."

I saw that she was living the life she had been brought up to expect; took pride in it; valued it in her own way. And there was I: a fraud.

No sooner than I had pressed a wet flannel to my grazes, breath held and eyes watering, there was a knock at the door. An older lady swept in, bringing a breeze of efficiency that I recognised from Ma's manner.

"You must be Miss Charlotte," she said as I hurried to

cover my legs. "I understand you've had a little accident this morning. Sit yourself down and let me take a look at you."

Although I was in safe hands, Mrs Bellamy didn't concern herself if she was a little rough in the process, or if the iodine stung like billy-ho. I closed my eyes and let her go about her business with as little complaint as possible.

"Mind you keep those bandages nice and clean and I'll change them tomorrow." She stood up. "Will I have Martha unpack your things?"

"Oh, I shan't be staying…" I protested while examining her tidy handiwork.

"I'm sorry, Miss, I must have misunderstood. I brought your bag upstairs. You'll find it on the stand."

"Thank you. John said I was to join him when I was finished."

"I'll show you the way, if you're ready." Her curtness suggested disapproval. Immediately, I felt foolish for having sounded so familiar.

She led me down the curved sweep of the staircase to a double doorway off the entrance hall, my boots struggling to find purchase on polished marble.

Mrs Bellamy knocked twice, leaving her hand hovering in anticipation of a response. After a brief pause, she pulled the door outwards and stood aside. Before I could absorb the dimensions of the room, the chandelier, the plush soft furnishings, I heard John's laughing voice: "Out she shot, and the look of horror when she found herself lying on top of me… it was a picture." His back towards me, the point of his elbow was resting on the arm of a chair and, in his hand a cigarette, blue smoke curling. His mother - handsomely dressed in what I presumed was widow's garb - brought one hand halfway to her mouth, coughing discreetly. She was every bit as formidable as John's description: unnaturally straight-backed; unhurried and economical in her movements. By contrast,

John swung his whole torso around, leaning over the arm of his chair, his face animated for a man who had declared himself in need of sleep. Stubbing his cigarette out in a china ashtray (I checked underneath later: it was Wedgewood), and releasing a final stream of smoke, he sprang to his feet. "Charlotte, do come and meet my mother. I've just been telling her about my heroics."

"Mrs Miller." Unsure where to place myself among all this grandeur, I opted to nod and smile rather than risk offering the wrong hand. "I'm embarrassed to have made such a nuisance of myself."

"Delighted, my dear," she said, her voice more restrained than the one she reserved for her son in private. "I hope that Mrs Bellamy has been able to dress your war wounds. She's usually very capable."

"Very," I echoed.

John smiled. "I've fallen victim to Mrs B many a time. I expect you can barely move for bandages."

"Do sit next to me, my dear." Mrs Miller patted a cushion on the settee.

My eyes fell on the khaki wool resting in her lap, and I saw common ground. "I see you're knitting for the war effort." I made a nervous start, hands neatly stacked. "Are they socks?"

"Lord, no! I couldn't bear to look at another sock! These are mittens for the milkladies."

"You must be most awfully good at it. I haven't mastered heels yet, let alone thumbs." I said what I had to say and then waited, determined not to let myself down by asking too many questions.

John was leaning back in his armchair at an angle, his legs crossed. "You must let her teach you. Mother, Charlotte is from Brighton."

She smiled at last. "I was trying to place your accent! It's been years since I was last there. We used to visit when I was a girl. I always enjoyed walking in the park around the Royal Pavilion."

"It's been turned into a hospital for the Indian soldiers now."

"So they tell me. I hear the whole town is overrun."

I hesitated at her meaning. "Not overrun, no. I could show you if you like."

She looked as close as I imagined she ever came to being amused. "However do you mean?"

"I have some of my photographs with me. A few of them have been published."

"Ye-es." She nodded as if giving her decision serious consideration. "I would like that very much." As I stood to retrieve my portfolio, she addressed her son: "You can leave us now, John. We'll be able to make do without you for a couple of hours. I'll ensure Charlotte doesn't go running off without saying goodbye."

"I'll hold you to that," he said, cupping a yawn with one hand. "You must excuse me: I'm absolutely dead on my feet. But I should like to see those myself later."

When I returned with my leather portfolio, Mrs Miller was seated at a table in an alcove under the window, a pair of half-moon reading glasses perched on her nose.

"The light is so much better over here," she explained. "Of course, you have such wonderful light on the coast."

Thinking of the dimness of the kitchen, I said, "We're very fortunate," as I placed the folder in front of her, next to a copy of *The Lady*, and moved the photographs of me aside.

"Not so fast, if you don't mind!"

"I don't think you'll find them very interesting."

"Let me be the judge."

"I hope to be a photographer."

"All the same, I should like to see them." From the manner in which she held out her hand, I surmised that Mrs Miller was a woman who wasn't used to being refused. "My son tells me you're a model."

I handed the pile to her and watched as she took the corners of each print between forefinger and thumb, and I grew steadily from a girl with wistful eyes to a young woman who appeared on picture-postcards destined for the front line.

"This isn't of you." Mrs Miller hesitated at one of the photographs of Rebecca Lavashay in her stage costume. She leant backwards slightly, putting a certain distance between herself and the photograph, and then repositioned the reading glasses on the end of her nose. "She looks familiar somehow."

"That's my mother," I explained. "She was an actress."

"An actress, you say! I adore the theatre. Quite beautiful, isn't she? Do you have a portrait of the two of you together?"

I placed a photograph of my face taken from the same angle next to the one of my mother. "That's as close as I ever got, I'm afraid. She died when I was very young."

"Oh, my dear, I'm so sorry to hear that." Mrs Miller appeared distracted. "Lavashay, Lavashay." She clicked her fingers. "Do you know anything she might have been in?"

"She played the lead in *Florodora*. Her Christian name was Rebecca."

"Of course! Ridiculous story, but wonderful music. I saw it once here in London, and again in Brighton. I dare say it's possible I saw your mother on the stage."

"Do you remember anything about it?"

"Oh, my dear, it's far too long ago and my memory isn't what it was. Tell me, was Lavashay her real name? It sounds French."

It suddenly struck me that I should have been using the name Coin. "No, that was her stage name. I don't know why she chose it. She was christened Agnes Coin."

"Oh." She dismissed my offering like a sour taste. "Now, here we are. I recognise this."

Mrs Miller had moved on to the photographs I had taken during my apprenticeship, holding them up to the light to examine them. Those of Ma and Daddy outside the shop and Felicity with Harry were cast aside, so insignificant that they were unworthy of comment. Those of the wounded Indians seated outside the entrance to the Dome were subjected to particular scrutiny. "They're not like us, are they?" She hesitated at a picture of Mr Parker. "Your father?"

"My tutor." I corrected her. "He's in the medical corps."

"Handsome man," she said matter-of-factly.

When she had finished, she folded the arms of her glasses back and set them on the table in front of her, and I sat with my hands on my lap waiting for her to pronounce her verdict.

"Tell me, what is your plan?" she asked plainly.

I thought she deserved an honest reply. "I intend to visit every photographic studio I can find and ask if they are looking for an apprentice so that I can continue my studies. I'll offer myself as a model to pay my way."

Mrs Miller seemed hesitant, a pained expression creasing her brow. "Let me be frank, my dear. You'll find it hard living alone in London. My son has taken a shine to you, I can see that and, like most mothers, I will do almost anything for my offspring. Within reason, of course. From what you've shown me, it appears that you have promise. What I propose is this." She slowly exhaled while I held my breath. I had expected nothing. "I will show your portfolio to some of my circle. I know a young gentleman who has photographed Lady Diana Manners and Gladys Cooper - to say nothing of Mata Hari, although that's hardly something to shout about at the moment. The point is, he'll be in a better position to judge if you have what it takes - either as a model or as a photographer. You'll like him. Peculiar little man, but terribly amusing. Who knows? He may have something to offer you himself. In the meanwhile - forgive me for asking - but how do you intend to support yourself, my dear?"

I let my head drop.

Mrs Miller sighed. "I thought as much. It so happens that we have an embarrassment of spare rooms and those with spare rooms are expected to do their bit for those made homeless by the war. Something I haven't quite got round to."

My mouth had fallen open during this speech. "That's far too generous," I protested. "I can't take you up on your offer -"

"But you must. I insist." She drummed out a solution on the table with her fingers. "We will say that you've been bombed out. But I do need to clear one thing up. Who is this Lottie Pye whose name appears in the newspapers?"

I saw her expression take on a new significance. "Pye was the name of my guardians. It's how I was known in Brighton."

"Well, my dear, I think this is the last time we need to refer to her. Brighton is in your past now."

25 - SIR JAMES'S STORY

SHERE, 2009

It was the first Saturday morning in a month when Jenny hadn't knocked on my front door. The clattering of the letter box a false alert: another pizza delivery leaflet advertising two super-dupers for the price of one. Although there was no formal arrangement, Jenny's visits had become routine. I had altered my schedule to accommodate them. Sharing my impatience, Isambard kept vigil by the front door, occasionally padding back to the dining room to deliver a progress report.

"It doesn't look as if she's coming today, old chap," I said. "Must be working."

For the first time, there was something I particularly wanted to share with her.

Waiting always makes me nervous. By the age of thirteen I had witnessed enough accidents to understand that racing drivers weren't invincible. I loved the masculine world of the workshops at Brooklands: men who spent days scratching their chins over blueprints; those with visions of shape and form, who hammered and welded; the mechanics with their heads under car bonnets, up to their elbows in grease; those who breathed life into metal. I was less than happy at the side of the racetrack, although I would never dared to have let it show. Nerves bred nerves. I persuaded myself that it was my concentration alone that kept my father's car on the track. If I turned my head away or let my thoughts drift, the consequences would be terrible. Sometimes it was enough to make me forget my fear for a fraction of a moment.

When my father didn't arrive to collect me from school at the end of term, I was not annoyed as a boy with a bank manager for a father might have been: instead I was anxious. With no word by mid-afternoon and unable to reach him at home, I approached the bursar to borrow the train fare. My luggage stowed at the station, I walked the last mile of the journey through rain that hammered the pavements from a diagonal slant.

"I expected you hours ago!" Mrs Strachan spilled a misshapen rectangle of electric light into the porch, continuing to hold the door open after I had wiped my feet and hung my overcoat to dry. She clucked at the sight of the dripping vegetation and overflowing gutters and looked both ways expectantly. "Isn't your father with you?"

"He didn't show. I came by train."

"And you've no luggage?"

"I couldn't carry it. It's at the station."

Our eyes met in understanding but, faced with questions or practicalities, Mrs Strachan was a woman who chose practicalities. "You must be starving. Get yourself out of those wet things and I'll find you something to eat."

Standing in stockinged feet five minutes later, my hair roughly towel dried and combed into shape, I dismissed the dining room table with its two places set for dinner. "Would you mind if I joined you in the kitchen, Mrs Strachan?" I handed over my sopping trousers, noticing that she had already stuffed my wet shoes with scrunched newspaper and paired them together, close - but not too close - to the fire.

"Let's get those on the clothes horse. I've put the kettle on to boil," she said brightly. "Nothing brings a man home faster."

But it didn't.

She deposited buttered bread and a thick slab of fruitcake in front of me "Something to keep you ticking over. You'll have a proper meal with your father."

The grandfather clock in the hall chimed eight o'clock, nine. Mrs Strachan allowed her anxiety to show only in terms of the spoiled beef and potatoes that she scraped into the bin, shaking her head. Before she untied her apron for the night, she assembled a supper of cold meat and pickles. Loyal to our family at the expense of her own, she was insistent that she could stay.

"I'll be fine," I assured her. "There's enough here to feed an army."

"Well," she said reluctantly. "If you're sure."

Alone, I sat in a high-backed chair in the hall watching the minute-hand lap the ivory clock-face in slow motion.

When my father's key eventually turned in the lock and his face appeared, its expression was grave. His eyes couldn't meet mine. Controlling myself, I stood to greet him as expected. "Good evening, Father."

He dragged his feet, sloth-like, before depositing the bag he was carrying in the hall. "Ah. Son. You made it home. I knew you'd be fine."

Ignoring his saturated leathers, he sat heavily on the matching chair to the other side of the grandfather clock, put his hands on his knees and let his head droop. Water dripped from the ends of his hair onto the tiled floor.

"Dreadful day. I couldn't get away. Wouldn't have been right."

My father had taken his new car, known as Gertie, out for its first run. The results had been so promising that he'd taken her up to 129 miles per hour. When his chief mechanic, Jock, had asked to take her for a spin, he could hardly refuse. This had been a joint labour of love, of late nights in shiveringly cold workshops, of sweat, blood and much cursing. Gertie was almost as much Jock's creation as my father's. Mechanically, the vehicle was sound. It was the left rear tyre that disintegrated. Of course, the weather hadn't helped.

"Poor bugger didn't stand a chance. Pour me a whiskey, would you?"

I could already smell alcohol on his breath. "There's supper..."

"Just the whiskey, there's a good chap."

I refrained from saying, "It could have been you." There was no need.

Another half hour passed, *The Times'* crossword finished but for thirteen down, I was loitering in front of the dining room window again, coming face-to-face with a walker who peered through the glass as if I were a museum exhibit. I snarled deliberately, quietly satisfied when he stumbled backwards on the uneven pavement. Dressed in a tou-tou and wellingtons, midway between ballet and riding lessons, Mrs Smythe-Jenkins's eldest was crossing the square. She bared her teeth in retaliation with the addition of stiff-elbowed Tyrannosaurus Rex arms. Waving, I wished I'd thought of that.

Still no sign of Jenny. Well, I wouldn't stay in all day listening to the grandfather clock dispense minutes tick by tick.

"Get your lead, boy." I patted Isambard's flank, grabbing my walking stick. "We're going out."

We ambled alongside the gentle clear waters of the Tillingbourne, past the allotments where scarecrows with terracotta pots for heads and CDs strung on lengths of washing line did little to deter ravenous crows. Through the gate, I released Isambard from his lead so that he wasn't restricted by my pace. Each paw placed carefully, he scouted ahead and then dutifully doubled back to make sure I was still following. The path gave way to flattened grass and we turned left to walk slightly uphill.

Autumn was slow in arriving, but the avenue of sweet chestnuts was rusting to a glorious hue. Isambard wasn't so daft as to bother the horses. Sad-eyed and elegant, they were grouped around a fallen trunk, every muscular inch like a Stubbs tableau but for the occasional spasm of flank and flick of tail. I nodded to a fellow dog-walker: a mirror image dressed in wellingtons, tweed cap and Barbour, hands clasped behind his back.

"Beautiful day," he said, and I supposed it was.

His black Labrador sniffed Isambard's hind quarters enthusiastically, who circled to avoid the unwarranted attention, barking sharply before breaking into a stately trot.

There was a solitary bench under a tree, a simple affair made from a single plank resting on two stumps. On that plank sat a girl, her hands tucked inwards under her thighs, head leaning forwards, face hidden behind a curtain of hair. Isambard stopped at a respectful distance and dropped his flank, waiting to be summoned. Jenny looked up, dazzled by the low sun, a little bewildered. She lowered her earphones, and he edged forwards, a paw-width at a time.

"Mind if we join you?" I enquired, coming to a halt behind Isambard. "The old legs aren't what they were."

We sat in silence, Jenny offering no explanation for her absence. Eventually I levered myself to standing and announced, "There's a pint waiting for me at the *George IV*." It hadn't been my intention, the bench being far enough for my ancient bones, but I needed an excuse.

"It's my mother's anniversary." Jenny looked up, squinting through the sun's rays that had filtered through the leaves. "She liked coming here."

Now she decides she wants to talk! I thought. Hands on thighs, I sat back down: "I must say, it's a fine view."

The steeple of St James's rose from the treetops and, as we sat, there was a ripple of church bells; a false start, like the rewinding of a tape, before the full sequence played out.

"There's a wedding," Jenny ventured.

"Then we're well out of it. The square will be heaving."

She turned her head in my direction and scooped the hair that had fallen forwards back behind her shoulders. "Ask me, I dare you."

"Ask you what?"

"How I'm feeling." Disappointment contorted her features and she turned away. "You can't do it, can you?"

"It's not that I can't," I insisted. "It's just that it's… unnecessary."

"Unnecessary?" Her voice was dull-edged.

"You've come here to remember your mother on her anniversary, ergo -"

"*Ergo?*" The word was said with disdain.

"You think I have no empathy because I don't ask how you're feeling?" I heard myself snap. "Just because I don't talk about emotions doesn't mean I'm completely devoid of them."

"How come this is about you all of a sudden?" she retaliated. "I *needed* you to ask. Did you think about that?"

I hesitated before replying. "You're clearly upset. You came here to be alone and we've interrupted you." I stood, but Isambard, sensing that our exchange was unfinished, repositioned himself, lifting his muzzle onto Jenny's knee. She threw her arms around him, burying her fingers in his mane and resting her chin on the top of his head. They looked up at me saucer-eyed, accusing.

"Actually, I came here because my Dad had his girlfriend to stay last night and didn't want to be reminded what today was. It's the first year we haven't done something together. Just the two of us."

I sat down again, feeling more and more like a reluctant yo-yo. "What would you normally do?"

"Oh, you know. Go to the cemetery. Take some flowers." She cringed. "I've never been on my own before."

I had yet to visit the cemetery where my mother had been laid to rest, flowers or no. It seemed inappropriate somehow to visit another person's grave, but I knew I had to ask the question. "Where's your mother buried?"

"Over at Dorking."

It was a good drive and Jenny had no transport. "How would you get there?"

She shrugged nonchalantly. "There's a bus."

"If you don't mind which day you arrive!" I slapped my thighs. "Come along. I'll drive you."

"But you were on your way out..."

"It wasn't important. This is."

We turned back in the direction of the village, Isambard, Jenny and I, walking in respectful silence. Occasionally a question took shape in my mind then dispersed. Too personal. Too hard to answer. Despite Jenny's insistence that talking is good - talking 'helps' - I maintain that words are not the best tools.

As we neared the florist's, a cramped affair overflowing in metal buckets onto the pavement, I asked, "What were your mother's favourites?"

"I don't know." Coming to a halt in the doorway, Jenny stooped to examine the contents of one of the buckets. "I always gave her daffs for Mother's Day. My Dad takes roses. I thought he'd bought some for her yesterday. Looks like they were for his girlfriend."

A betrayal involving flowers met with strong disapproval from the woman behind the counter, which manifested in a heavy sigh. Arranging stems in a plastic bucket, the florist twisted their heads sharply as though they were chickens' necks.

"What would you like to take her?"

"Something yellow. That was her favourite colour. I like these." Jenny bent over a bucket of large daisies with chocolate-coloured centres, and made her selection one by one, dripping water as she formed a bouquet. She held it up for my approval. "What do you think?" As I reached inside my pocket, she stopped me. "They're supposed to be from me."

The cemetery slumbered in the shadow of Box Hill, chalk and flint, a few degrees cooler than the ambient temperature. A short distance from the row we had been walking towards, Jenny gripped my arm. Someone was there before us. Two people to be precise: a man emerged from the place where he had been laying a bunch of yellow roses on the gravestone. Unable to see either of their faces, I looked at Jenny's. Eyes brimming, she bit her bottom lip, shaking her head. I wheeled her around and we returned to the car. Isambard paced the boot, fretting at Jenny's distress.

"Your father's girlfriend?" I asked, lending her another initialled cotton handkerchief.

She blew her nose loudly. "Look at the state of me! I don't know if I'm upset because I thought he'd forgotten, or because he brought her instead of me."

"I take it he hasn't brought previous lady friends here before?"

"There haven't been any. Not that I know of."

I raised my eyebrows. "And you're what? Nineteen?"

"Almost twenty."

"Well! The man's practically a saint!"

"Your father liked his girlfriends, didn't he?"

"Oh, yes," I agreed. "Of course, I made it my job to hate every single one of them. I rather think I frightened them off."

She laughed. "You think I'm being selfish."

I shook my head. "No, your reaction is perfectly natural. But she must be special, whoever she is."

"Why d'you say that?

"Put it this way: it wouldn't be my idea of a hot date."

Suddenly determined, Jenny reached for the door handle. "Coming?"

We approached the graveside more confidently this time. I held back, occupying a slatted bench under the twisted trunk of an oak, while Jenny stooped to position her daisies next to the roses. Then she stood to the right of her father, who placed an arm around her shoulder, hugging her to him, as if it was the most natural thing in the world to be standing at his wife's grave with the two most important people in his life. I was surplus to requirements.

Contemplating a crow atop a lichened stone angel, my thoughts wandered to my father's funeral, that unseasonably cold day in July 1957, the wreaths not unlike those of racing champions in laurel and carnations, the crowd of colleagues, the cards from well-wishers, all welcome distractions from the fact that I was conscious I should have been feeling more than I actually did. There was no welling of grief. I wasn't overcome by a sense of loss. The stomach-churning anticipation - the dread of waiting - was finally at an end. I was ready to accept the fact that my father was gone, having spent my entire life preparing for the moment with every glance at a speed dial, every lap of a track, the launch of each shiny new prototype. And if I had been unable to mourn for my father in the way expected of an only son, wasn't it only right that I should feel less for the mother who had abandoned me when I was a baby? Who saved every letter and photograph, but never once asked to see me? Jenny's golden head was resting on her father's shoulder. I thought of how she had tried to teach me to look at my mother's photographs as if I was looking through her eyes. I had the will. I just didn't know how to. Perhaps if people hadn't always left, I would have had more practice in the art of forgiveness.

Feeling increasingly like an intruder, I returned to the car where I must have fallen into a doze.

Driving close to the kerb in the Kings Road area, I saw the shine of PVC, fishnet stockings. The engine idling, she leant into the driver's window and blew smoke in my face. "Want some company?"

"No, thank you."

"Don't tell me you want to know the time. Not one of them, are you? I see. Left after the traffic lights. Say Bridget sent you. 'Ere, don't I know you?"

I avoided her gaze. "I wouldn't have thought so."

"I seen you somewhere. 'Aven't you been on the telly?"

"You must be mistaken."

It was always the creeping around and the lies. These were things I had shut out for years. Ever since he had walked away from me on Westminster Bridge saying it was over, and I waited. Waited for him to turn back and tell me he had made a mistake. I had been ready with words of forgiveness, but he didn't give me the chance. That was my final view of him: a man on a bridge, walking away. I was too young to have a memory of my mother leaving. That later image has somehow become linked with her departure, as strange as it may seem. The newer memory superimposed on the place where the old should exist. Layers, one on top of another. Since then, I haven't given anyone else the opportunity to leave: save for a sedate German Shepherd, who I was assured was on his last legs, I haven't invited anyone to stay.

Isambard sharply barking a welcome, there was a tapping at the passenger window. I righted my head and stretched across to unlock the door. "All done?"

Jenny slid into the seat beside me, her hands in her lap, and then twisted quite deliberately to face me. "I want to thank you," she said.

"Don't mention it."

"No, I have to. If you hadn't offered to bring me, I wouldn't have known that Dad's met someone special. Special enough to want to bring her here."

"Do you think you could grow to like her?" I asked, thinking of those powdered faces and the greasy smudges of lipstick left on my cheeks.

She shrugged. "I could get used to her."

"Good enough. Don't you want to go with them?"

"They invited me to lunch but I thought I'd leave them to it."

"Quite right. Don't want to overdo it. Clunk, click," I said and she buckled up. We pulled away, under the arch of the flint-stoned gatehouse and back in the direction of the town centre. *Costas* and *Cafés Rouge* blurred as one, much the same as any other town centre but for the distinctive raised pavements and railings. As we turned onto the old London ring road, I upped a gear and the car purred along happily, winding past cricket greens and thatched bus shelters, crumbling brick walls and topiary hedges, through the villages of Abinger Hammer and Gomshall with their welcoming pubs and roadside cottages.

"If you have time," I ventured, hesitant to break the thoughtful silence. "I'd like your opinion on something."

"Oh?"

"Something in my mother's boxes." I winced. "It can wait if there's something you'd rather do."

"What is it?"

"I'd prefer to show you. If you don't mind, that is."

I left Jenny sitting at the dining room table with the half dozen sepia photographs while I distanced myself with the excuse of brewing a pot of tea. I was uncomfortable at the thought of looking at naked photographs of my own mother with her.

When I returned, she had arranged them next to a selection of my mother's Aphrodites, Graces and Venuses; those beauties who were considered to have a civilising influence. I hadn't imagined that Jenny would have been excited by my latest finds, but she was bright eyed.

"Well?" I asked. "Perfectly dreadful, aren't they?"

"Don't you get it?" She was almost beside herself as I stood peering down over her shoulder. "Just look at the differences. The photographs that your mother took of other women are full of life and joy and... they're not exactly sexy, that's not the word I'm after." She clicked her fingers. "Help me out. You're the one with a dictionary for a brain."

"Sensual."

"Right: sensual. It's not as if the ones of her are obscene or anything. I mean, she's still beautiful. They're just..." She twisted round to face me, turning up her nose. "Well, they're just not very *good*, are they?" I saw nothing to celebrate, much the reverse, but Jenny tapped the table triumphantly. "*These* are what really turned your mother into a photographer."

"I'm sorry." One hand on my forehead, I closed my eyes. "You're going to have to spell it out for me."

"It was knowing what it was like to feel cheap that made her want to make her clients feel... I don't know... powerful, beautiful. Everything that comes across when we look at her photographs of other women."

Subtle changes seemed to occur in the images in front of

me, as if they were developing in a tank, taking on new form and shape. I knew that Jenny's instinct was right. I picked up one of my mother's photographs of another woman. "You're saying *this* is how she would like to have been photographed?"

"Exactly!"

"Thank you," I said, removing my glasses. "You know, I think it's time I paid a visit to my mother's grave."

26 - LOTTIE'S STORY

LONDON, 1918

Some would say I fell on my feet in London, but I enjoyed far less freedom than I'd been accustomed to. Having presented myself as a young lady, I was expected to act like one. The girl who tramped wild and windswept listening to fishermen's stories was silenced. Even her name was unmentionable. Everything that didn't belong in London was consigned to a box. I surprised myself at how easily my life was compartmentalised.

In turn, Mrs Miller was as good as her word. Introduced to her circle, I supped morning teas in drawing rooms, rattled a collection box for Princess Alexandra's Rose Day, helped run Crutch Days for wounded soldiers and enjoyed dinners that would have been lavish by peacetime standards. Mrs Miller sat on the edge of fashionable Society. She placed the blame entirely with her husband; he did nothing to ingratiate himself to the better class of people his business brought him into contact with. The family was 'new money', earned through enterprise and sheer hard toil, and now slipping through the hands of the third generation.

It was Martha who had explained to me about the Millers' marriage. I admitted I had assumed that Mr Miller, referred to in almost reverential tones, was the late Mr Miller. "Dead? Why on earth would you think that?" She laughed away my misunderstanding as she pinned up the hem of a second-hand skirt for me.

"But Mrs Miller dresses like a widow."

"That? She's sworn to wear black for the duration," Martha said with a certain pride in her voice. "She's not touched a drop of alcohol neither."

"When do you expect to see Mr Miller?"

"Christmas, I 'spect."

"Not before then?"

"He's a busy man. There!" She stood up. "You're all done."

"I see," I said, inspecting the results of her efforts in the mirror, and not understanding this peculiar idea of marriage at all.

"It's like Mrs Bellamy says." Martha lowered her voice to a discreet whisper, even though there was no one to overhear. "They get on fine provided they don't see one another. It's been like this for the past twenty years, apparently."

It had never crossed my mind to question whether Daddy and Ma *got on*. They had built a business, argued with each other, comforted each other, laughed together, stuck together. After fifty-five years without spending a single night apart, Ma was lost without Daddy. He had been her strength. Clearly, the rules here were very different.

Martha leaned closer, her reflection joining mine in the mirror. "They say Mrs Miller never got over the shock of childbirth. She was none too keen to repeat the experience."

Her husband distracted by business, Mrs Miller threw her efforts into entertaining ("Nothing compared with the Americans. My dear, they make us look like amateurs!") and considered it a mark of recognition of her own hostessing skills when a gilt-edged invitation landed on her doormat. Of course, the war meant that certain economies had to be tolerated, but this, too, had its advantages. To anyone who would listen, she said, "If you can't afford a portrait by Augustus John - and, my dear, who can? - a Charlotte Lavashay might be the next best thing. Have I introduced you to my houseguest?" And lowering her voice discreetly, she exaggerated the movement of her mouth. "Ve-ry talented."

If her friends and neighbours couldn't assist, some of them knew friends of friends: artists, photographers, magazine editors. I was subjected to the same scrutiny as my photographs; eyes cast over teeth, flank and rump. When my first wage packet was forthcoming, I did what I had always done and offered it to the woman in charge of the household.

"Don't insult me, child." Mrs Miller brushed me aside. "You're my guest."

"But I must contribute…"

"Nonsense! Besides." She looked straight at my footwear, previously unmentioned but now, apparently, a source of offence. "You need new shoes."

It might have been gloves or underwear or a new hat. I did as directed, following Mrs Miller's advice that Peter Jones had a terribly good assistant in the ladies department. Whatever was surplus, I sent home to Brighton. Felicity wrote that Ma understood why I had come to London: the wages were higher.

All this in return for the simple understanding: I was not good enough for her son. Mrs Miller knew of no better way to ensure I ended up in John's arms than suggesting this to his face. She had me where she could keep an eye on me. There, she extended every kindness in the expectation that, when the need arose, I was to reject him. She harboured no qualms about offering his services as chauffeur and guide. When I told Mrs Miller how much I missed the sea, she insisted that John drove me to the beach near Tower Bridge where children shrieked on a few square feet of imported sand, dipping their toes in the brown water. Too tired to go and see a theatre production of *A Little Bit of Fluff*, she urged John to take me in her place. Lottie Pye, still in mourning for Alfie, wept silent tears, but Charlotte Lavashay was seen on the arm of John Miller.

He was like no other man I had had close contact with. Ten years my senior, when not in uniform his style was elegantly understated, not as showy as those who tried to create an impression on the promenade. Good-natured and charming as only a man who hasn't known hardship can be, he pandered to his mother's every need, and she could do little wrong in his eyes.

"I told you Mother would like you," he had said on the day of my arrival, before kissing her on the cheek. "I just knew you'd love Charlotte."

Neither of us uttered a word of denial. Besides, for my part at least, that would have been a lie. Mrs Miller was as amusing as she was wise and, if blunt, what she said was usually true.

John confided in her in ways I had never dreamed a son would confide in a mother, entertaining her with the goings on among his circle. Subjects that would have been unbroachable around our kitchen table in Brighton were very much on the London menu.

"I can't see what he sees in her - and poor Emma is completely in the dark."

"I find it far better when your father keeps me in the dark. Anything else is simply bad manners."

He brought friends and their wives or lovers home for her inspection, fuelling the next day's commentary on clothes and breeding. Models invariably met with Mrs Miller's approval when chosen by other men.

"Quite charming. And did you hear what she had to say about Mr Asquith at Epsom? Apparently he's the most dreadful tease, the naughty man."

Those with potential were always wrong for their current partners. "Eleanor's so refined. And Marcus is such a bore. Johnny, she's exactly the sort of girl I can imagine you with. Wouldn't you say so, Charlotte?"

"Oh, Mother..." John intervened.

"Shush, John!" Mrs Miller turned to me in encouragement. "I'm interested in Charlotte's opinion."

"I liked her," I ventured, non-committal.

"But you don't agree?"

Enjoying a good argument, Mrs Miller expected to be stood up to, and then to crush her opponent. I had no hesitation in saying, "She was beautiful, but she's too reserved. John needs someone far more lively."

"She'd come out of her shell. Marcus doesn't encourage her as he would."

"Listen to the two of you pairing me off!" John threw down his newspaper, with a pretence of annoyance. "I'm still in the room! Besides, it's completely academic: I'm not the least bit interested."

"That's just the problem! When was the last time you brought a girl home to meet me? At this rate, I may not live to see my own grandchildren."

"You're insufferable, Mother! I shouldn't have to point out that I brought Charlotte home not so very long ago. She's sitting right under your nose!"

"Oh!" Mrs Miller raised her hand to her face in amusement. "You don't mean to say?" She hooted disbelievingly, making a pantomime of looking from her son to me. Unable to prevent it, I felt my colour rise. "I didn't think - my dear, I mean no offence - but really!"

"Now, hang on!"

"Really, John, it's fine." Smiling, I braced myself to hear my list of faults. "None taken."

"Charming though she is, I thought Charlotte was one

of your waifs and strays. This is most terribly awkward. It's entirely inappropriate that you allowed me to invite her to stay - and to encourage you to go out, unchaperoned! If I had thought for *one* minute…"

Having heard more than enough, I pushed myself to standing and prepared my excuses. "Perhaps I should…"

"That won't be necessary." John strode across the expanse of floor that separated him from the door and, with a glance at his mother that might have withered a lesser mortal, slammed it behind him. As the crystal on the sideboard vibrated with a silvery tone, a self-satisfied smile forming on her lips, Mrs Miller resumed knitting mittens.

There were many things I would like to have said - that it was unfair of her, cruel - but I was a guest in her house.

She met my gaze. "Do you think it *wrong* that I take an interest in my son's welfare?"

I was reluctant to reply. "Perhaps I should see if -"

"Oh, sit down, Charlotte! We both know where that would lead. No, I suggest we say nothing more about this. It will pass."

I had a simple choice: accept the situation or leave.

For the first time, women were being paid the same as men. Although working for the war effort was difficult and often dangerous, they had more spending money than ever before. I was growing in demand as one of the new faces that sold women powder and rouge - no longer seen as an indicator of lax morals. My body showed them how to wear the new brassieres, how to make utility-clothing feminine. The sight of my ankles exposed beneath the new calf-sweeping skirts was intended to make them rush out and purchase stockings. Just as I was becoming recognisable as a model was not the time to think about leaving. I bit my tongue and pleasantries were resumed, just as Mrs Miller had predicted.

As advised by Felicity, I always asked to keep the clothes from my assignments.

"But why?" Mrs Miller had asked. "It seems terribly vulgar, even in these days of rationing."

Feeling worldly, I replied, "Aside from being useful currency, a friend of mine told me it's the quickest way of finding out what kind of modelling job you're applying for. If the mention of clothing is an issue, it might not be the kind of work I'm interested in."

"Well, I'm sure you have far more experience of this sort of thing than I do." Arching her eyebrows, Mrs Miller posed the question: "But is it not *inevitable* that a certain amount of nudity is required?"

I felt my neck flush, remembering my promise to make Ma proud. "I've managed to avoid it so far."

"You're trying to break into *artistic* circles now. You only have to look at the history. If you remember what we read the other day, the nude *is* a form of art. Of course, it's a matter of personal judgement -"

John, increasingly perturbed by the direction of the conversation, exploded. "Mother!"

Mrs Miller didn't drop a stitch. "Honestly, John, I hadn't taken you for such a prude. Do you imagine Botticelli and Raphael drew from memory?"

"Freddie is *hardly* Botticelli! Don't listen to her, Charlotte. You shouldn't feel pressured to do anything you don't want to."

But listen I did, because art appreciation had formed the greater part of Mrs Miller's attempts to educate me, and the nagging voice inside my head told me she was right.

"Don't be such a bore, John! She'd be perfectly safe with Freddie. I understand he's one of those homosexuals I've read about. I dare say it goes hand in hand with an artistic temperament."

A homosexual might have been a member of religious sect as far as I was concerned. Still, it dawned on me that there was nothing to be gained by limiting myself to the 'safe' jobs. Controversy was what made the art world thrive. Plus, there was a more pressing issue. Having failed to secure an apprenticeship, I had nowhere to develop my photographs, and I possessed little else to bargain with. Freddie had been derisory at any mention of my own work, his mocking tone suggestive of imagined amateurish efforts.

"I was published in the newspaper!"

"And what newspaper was that, pray tell?" he sneered.

"*The Brighton and Hove Gazette*," I responded with a certain pride.

"Oh, the *provincials?*" Clasping his hands at chest level, Freddie laughed as though he had thought I was making a joke at my own expense, then seeing I was hurt, said, "That's something I'd keep to myself if I were you."

And so when Freddie next raised the question of "that little subject you are so tactfully trying to avoid," I asked, "You say it's for a private collector?"

"A general, no less."

"So there'll only be one copy of the print. I won't find myself on a… oh, I don't know…" I skirted my hand along his desktop. "A seaside postcard, perhaps?"

Freddie's expression of obvious displeasure suggested I couldn't have chosen a more vulgar expression. "What on earth would make you say such a frightful thing?"

"I have family who might be…" I tailed off.

Freddie threw his hands up. "Mortified at the thought of their daughter earning a decent living for herself? If that's your only objection, don't give it a second thought. No one else need ever know."

That out of the way, I allowed myself to consider the practicalities. "And what does the general require, exactly?"

"Do I detect a weakening?"

I simply looked at him.

Freddie's attitude to my concerns was dismissive. "So stern! Just some perfectly straightforward shots. Disappointingly tame."

"If I agree, it will have to be on my terms. You know that I need somewhere to develop my own work."

"Listen, my dear, it's simply out of the question! I can't bear sharing my working space with anyone."

Using a phrase I had heard in the Miller's household, I ventured, "That's a great pity. I was about to propose an arrangement in lieu of fees."

His interest revealed itself with a sharp, involuntary intake of breath.

Stepping out of my gown I followed every instruction given to me. My mouth fell open on command. I elongated my body with an outstretched arm, pushed my shoulders back and exaggerated the line of my hip by crossing my legs. I felt no embarrassment, no shame. It was simply another modelling job. No worse than the occasions when there had been no private changing facilities, and I was forced to undress in front of other models. There was only ever the one occasion, but, though we may not realise it at the time, life pivots on the basis of impulsive decisions.

Holding my breath, I watched the developing fluid perform its magic. The first of the images Freddie had taken of me appeared, ghost-like. Flat paper darkened, misty patches turning to skin-tone, until its surface was populated with pores, raised veins, fine hairs, tiny lines, fleshy creases and their dark shadows. Hope evaporated. This was not art: it was the work I had hoped to avoid. Strictly science.

"If there wasn't a paper shortage we could have produced a collection." Freddie sighed at the injustice. "Perhaps next year."

There was little point brooding. It was a means to an end, I told myself; something never to be repeated. But, at the same time, it struck me that, given the opportunity to photograph women, I would produce something quite different. Something the subject could truly be proud of.

27 - LOTTIE'S STORY

LONDON, 1918

However successfully I imagined I had compartmentalised my two lives, refusing to re-tune itself, my body clock kept pace with the ebb and flow of tides. I was wide-eyed at dawn when, at home, I would have made forays to the beach to scavenge for kindling, fetched water, swept out the hearth and lit the fire, all before my day's work at Mr Parker's studio began. Chores that I had often performed begrudgingly now felt like freedoms. Freedom to leave the house, alone and in all elements. Not having to pretend.

Longing for purpose that my daily routines lacked, I sought refuge in back issues of newspapers and magazines. Between their covers, it was impossible to avoid wartime news. Never far from my mind, this was the 'reality' the Ministry of Information allowed: a strict balance, carefully censored.

I studied Ernest Brooks's photograph of a Red Cross volunteer helping a straining German Prisoner of War to sip from a tin mug. He might easily have been my tutor, Mr Parker, who so hated conflict and would have avoided it if he could.

As I looked at a picture of a Tommy, ankle-deep in mud, reaching for a shell from the top of a pile of ammunition, breath shuddered through my chest. My mind turned to another whose hands had previously reached for pebbles. In the photograph, the boy's face was devoid of emotion. And yet it was his indifference that demanded the greatest response from me. I quickly turned the page, unwilling to think of Alfie so hardened. It helped to focus on the use of symbols, what the photographer wanted me to feel.

Men setting up a makeshift camp in a still-smoking crater. Awful, and yet a human side of the conflict.

The silhouettes of men climbing ladders to repair electricity wires, a soldier below looking on, resembling the stained glass window at St Nick's depicting John at the foot of the cross.

For me, the most evocative photographs were taken by Frank Hurley, dubbed the 'mad photographer'. After declaring it was impossible to get war pictures of striking interest and sensation, he created photomontages, layering one negative on top of another. It wasn't that his manipulated images weren't true. He was simply trying to capture what was beyond the comprehension of those who hadn't experienced war first-hand: the scale of devastation; noise exploding all about. His photographs needed to speak for themselves and sometimes that required new truths.

In one picture, I saw jagged charcoal telegraph poles rising into the smoke-fuelled sky, forcing me to acknowledge an appalling contradiction. The tightening in my throat - the violent hatred I felt - at the sight of amputated trees was absent at the vision of a young soldier lying in a flooded shell hole. One arm over his head, the other limp across his chest: dead. In the background, a shell rips the earth apart, sending debris flying; a crater-in-the-making waiting to be furnished with the body of another young boy. The void in my chest filled with pity. Pity, yes, but not horror.

A neat stack of bodies surrounded by flies provoked a queasy fascination.

I turned another page: a line of boy soldiers marched up a hillock, their upside-down images reflected in the foreground. It is a beautiful evening and they are heading to the front.

Hurley's photographs taught me a new way of seeing. The image in my mind became more important than what I saw through the viewfinder. The challenge: how to get it onto the page. It was as if Lord Beaverbrook was talking to me personally when he spoke against those who dismissed the instant nature of photography, saying that it may well provide the most permanent record of all.

Far from something I did to kill time, I had to tear myself away from the photographs, often surprised to find I was not actually part of a scene I was focused on. But these were depictions of war. I craved normality. What inspired me to experiment were Julia Cameron's photographs of her maid, Mary Hiller. Photographed in profile with soft focus and atmospheric lighting, hair flowing over her bare shoulders, Mary became statuesque. Almost biblical. An ordinary girl made to look extraordinary.

Martha and I had become well-acquainted, if not friends in the truest sense. Close in age, we also bound by our distance from home. After Mrs Miller's mourning attire, she enjoyed the contrasting colours and varying textures of my cache of modelling clothes. On one of the rare occasions we found ourselves alone, an opportunity presented itself to act on an idea that had gradually been taking form.

As I recall, it was Martha who shyly introduced the subject: "Is it true you sometimes pose without any clothes on?"

Her question came as a shock. Given that there had only been the one occasion, I wondered who would have told her this, but Martha's presence often took me by surprise. She had the ability to move softly from room to room.

"I prefer to wear something, even if it's only the robe you had your eye on the other day."

I had caught Martha holding the sheer fabric - so fine it hid nothing - to her cheek. On seeing me, she had looked embarrassed and said primly, "That's not going to keep you very warm," closing the door of the wardrobe.

"I don't think it was designed for warmth."

"I can't imagine when you'd wear it. Why did you ask to keep it?" Her disapproving tone was borrowed from Mrs Bellamy, but then she nodded with realisation. "Your wedding night!"

"Why don't you try it?" Slipping it off its hanger, I now offered it to her. She took the delicate fabric between finger and thumb, making small circular movements. "Properly." I draped the robe around Martha's shoulders. As she swayed in front of the mirror, the light caught the tiny filaments, sparkling. I saw that the effect on bare skin would be to make it glow.

"You look quite beautiful."

"I do?" Martha asked turning sideways, a protective hand on her stomach, to admire her reflection.

"In fact, I've been trying to pluck up the courage to ask if I might take your photograph."

Horrified, flattered, calculating: a flare of her eyes was all it took for Martha to change from maid to model. "When you pose, you ask to keep the clothes, don't you?"

I raised my eyebrows, pretending to be slow to understand, but I wasn't so far removed from that Brighton girl on the promenade that I couldn't remember the attraction of the beautiful garments. She clutched the robe possessively at her throat.

"You'll have to do exactly as I ask."

"Now?" I watched her swallow.

"I suppose we could do it now," I replied, as if the suggestion had been Martha's entirely. "I'll set my equipment up while you change into the robe. Use the bathroom if you like."

Although I had no qualms about my own body, I had only seen paintings and photographs of naked women before - because, when Martha emerged, her chin shyly touching the top of her chest, more was revealed than was hidden. I hadn't asked her to remove her undergarments: she had done this of her own accord, led by her misunderstanding of what my job involved. There was a moment when I might have dispelled the myth, encouraged her to cover herself, but when she walked in front of the window, the fabric came to life and she was transformed, glowing. The immediate challenge was how to capture what I could see with my eyes: one of Botticelli's *Three Graces of the Primavera*.

"Take a seat." I pulled the stool at the dressing table back for her, took the pins from her hair and brushed it out. "First, we have to make sure you're looking your best." Normally hidden under a cap, her hair was surprisingly lustrous. I let a few locks fall forwards from her shoulders and trained the others down her back. "Have you ever worn rouge?"

Her reflection lifted its eyes to mine. "No, Miss!"

I picked up the brush. "With skin like yours, you hardly need any."

With little coaxing, Martha began to react in front of the mirror, angling her face and allowing herself to smile. At last, I asked her to pose for the photograph I wanted to take.

A square of sunlight had fallen into the room and, within it, liquid shadows cast by a magnolia tree were at play. I had Martha lie on her side, her head resting on one hand, eyes closed. Loose hair drifted over her face, a strand catching in her lips. I moved one of her arms so that it shielded her breasts and bent her legs at the knees, pulling them upwards to protect her pubic area; lifted the fabric where it had caught and let it settle. Her slight shaking betrayed the fact that she was giggling.

"What's so funny?" I asked as I took my place behind the camera.

"I'm supposed to be changing the beds, and here I am lying practically naked on the floor! What would Mrs Miller say?"

"Hold still, now. The light is almost perfect." Waiting until the sun danced on her and the overall effect was one of girlish innocence, I slowly exhaled and took the shot.

For some reason that wasn't quite clear to me - guilt, perhaps - I claimed that the photograph was a disaster. I think I frightened myself. I had the feeling this was something I might be good at - no, *more* than good - but I had no Mr Parker to ask for a professional opinion. I only had Freddie's photographs as a measure. He displayed no interest in the work I produced. It was true that I suffered from a lack of equipment, but I could detect a growing subtlety in my photographs that was lacking from his. To paraphrase Mr Parker, he had all of the technical understanding and none of the emotional. Freddie's portraits could have been of statues.

"It was a mistake to have you in the pool of sunlight." I answered Martha's whispered enquiry on the staircase.

"I thought you said it was perfect!"

"I must have made a mistake. The shot was overexposed."

"But your beautiful wedding robe..." She seemed distraught that I might think she had acquired it under false pretences.

"*Your* wedding robe." I squeezed her arm.

Inspired by images of home, I had two ideas for my first composite creation as I set to work alone late one evening in Freddie's studio, planning to work through the night. One was to superimpose Martha's image onto a negative of the beach, a sea-nymph washed up on the shore - a *Titian*, as Mrs Miller would have called her. My concern was whether my mermaid would look as if she was born of the depths, with her hair dry as bone. The other was to superimpose her onto a timeless pastoral scene of the Downs: lambs sheltering under a broad oak. I had in mind a picture of a sleeping beauty, the sheep she was dreaming of very much in evidence.

With no textbook to work from, I kept detailed notes of each experiment, timings and measurements of how I had superimposed the images, looking forward to discussing the results with my old tutor. My fears about Martha as a sea-nymph appeared to be founded. Although not quite earthly, she was better suited to a position beneath the trunk of a gnarled tree. The final image was as I had imagined: the golden glow of the early-evening sun; a girl innocently dreaming; translucent, blades of grass visible through her. Whether the grass had grown over her as she slumbered or if she, like the moss-covered trunk, was a product of nature was unimportant. Ethereal but organic, she had merged with the landscape to become one with it.

Having used Martha's image after lying to her, there seemed to be no way of showing my work to associates of Mrs Miller. Hidden in my portfolio, it was seen by no one until an advertisement about a photographic competition sponsored by the *Daily Mail* appeared, the theme, *What our Brave Boys are Fighting For*. If not the green grass of home and a girl, then what? The prize money was tempting, but it was the promise that the top 100 photographs would be displayed in a special exhibition at the National Portrait Gallery that proved too hard to resist.

On an impulse, I entered under the name Lottie Pye using my Brighton address. Call it the gesture of a homesick girl caught up in an internal game of tug-of-war. Call it stupidity if you will. Scant hope Ma would understand how nudity - or what passed for nudity in her opinion - could be justified; not even if she could look into the picture and find art. But I never allowed myself to imagine, not for one moment...

28 - LOTTIE'S STORY

LONDON, 1918

Life didn't grind to a halt because of the war, but inconveniences niggled. More readily expressed than the greater sorrows we stowed away, it was simpler to voice disbelief that the theatres were forced to close by ten thirty, in the same way that men returning from the front limited their complaints to grievances about bully beef rations rather than the daily brutality they had witnessed.

And then, after we learned about the slaughter of the Russian royal family, after Bulgaria withdrew from the war, after the fall of Damascus, there were whispers of a turning of the tides. Some dared talk of the beginning of the end. All that was needed was for boundaries to be redrawn and the terms of peace settled by men in suits. To my uneducated mind this begged the question: if it all came down to meetings and treaties, to signatures on pieces of paper, why had war been necessary in the first place? Why not the results of the 1914 Olympics? The answer: we needed to rid the world of evil.

It was just as well I kept my views to myself. To Mrs Miller's mind, the sinking of a passenger ferry called *HMS Leinster* just after President Woodrow Wilson had offered the Peace Without Victory deal showed the Germans in their true colours.

"They're animals!" she declared.

But, as we joined the tightly packed crowd to wave our flags outside Buckingham Palace at eleven o'clock on the morning of 11th November, hoping for a glimpse of the tops of royal heads, the Americans ordered an offensive that accounted for what would be the war's final 11,000 casualties.

At Wellington Square, released from her pledge, Mrs Miller proposed a toast. "To our brave boys!" Her clothing still sombre, the mood was tainted by memories. Four years ago we had all said it would be over by Christmas. Now that it was, all I felt was a deep sorrow. After a respectable period of time, Charlotte Lavashay excused herself, but it was Lottie Pye who threw herself face-down on her bed, her sobs drowned out by swollen waves of cheers that wafted through the open window. Heaving shoulders told of relief, sorrow for those who had passed, regret that I was not at home. But if I returned, what would be there for me? No Daddy waiting to comfort me; no Mr Parker to finish the job of turning me into a photographer. And no Alfie, whom I had failed in my promise to keep vigil.

Felicity (now a volunteer policewoman, respectable at last in a wide-brimmed hat more suited to a Boy Scout than a model) persisted in trying to encourage me. "*I won't say the money isn't handy, but what we wouldn't give to have you safely home with us. We are so afraid for you in London, firstly with the bombs and now with the influenza. The newspaper says there's two thousand dead.*" Ma was ailing, it seemed; her eyesight not what it was. Even ever-faithful Josie struggled to raise a smile from her, let alone rouse the old lioness. But all I could remember was the woman who had insisted Daddy chase rabbits, and I wasn't ready to forgive her yet. It was better, this new beginning, I reasoned: better that I kept my distance.

Splashing cold water on my face, I adopted a mask of

cheerfulness, but my choice of evening dress was pale grey silk. Sombre, the memory of a restless sea.

Entering the drawing room, I caught the tail of a conversation about the cavalry. John was shaking his head. "Word is, they'll shoot the horses rather than ship them home."

"I do hope you're wrong! Your father donated his willingly, but the man who puts a gun to one of them had better watch his back. Ah, Charlotte, my dear! A little sherry?"

I accepted the sweet medicinal liquid offered in a tiny glass from a silver tray. As it numbed my lips and warmed my throat I wondered if, perhaps, it was what I had been sickening for.

"I expect you young people will want to head into town for the celebrations."

"Not me. I'm in no mood for crowds after this morning's crush," John said and I breathed a sigh of relief. "Unless you want to, Charlotte?"

"I hardly know what to do with myself," I admitted.

The doorbell rang, sharp tinkling. Mrs Miller announced, "Ah! That will be Mr Irving and his son."

We waited a short while only to hear the sound again, this time longer and more impatient.

"Is there no Martha?" I asked, thinking it strange I hadn't seen her since she brought me my morning tray.

"Oh, my goodness!" Mrs Miller raised a hand to her mouth. "In all the commotion I had quite forgotten. She left after lunch. Her mother sent for her. It seems her brother has been reported missing."

"Today of all days!" John exclaimed.

"It may be the last we see of her. I called the agency, but, like everything else, I was informed we shall have to make do."

Still, no one moved.

"Shall I answer the door?" I volunteered. "Mrs Bellamy will be rushed off her feet downstairs and it wouldn't be right for you..."

Initially appalled by my suggestion, Mrs Miller mellowed when, looking around, she dismissed the limited alternatives. "Then, perhaps, if you don't mind awfully. I hadn't thought this through. Hopefully one of the other girls will want her old job back." She turned to John for comfort. "One assumes the munitions factories will close."

I opened the door, sounds of revelry spilling over the threshold: a volley of fireworks, exploding; a nearby peel of church bells; shouts and cheers. "Sorry to have left you out in the cold. I'm afraid we're short-staffed this evening."

"Ah! Good evening Charlotte… er…" Harmless and jovial, Mr Irving looked about as he stepped into the hall, uncertain what to do with his hat and coat.

"Allow me," I offered, and hung them on the brass stand.

"Oh, very kind, very kind. You won't have met my son, Robert."

"Delighted." I smiled at the uniformed young man, whose face was inclined as he made a performance of wiping his feet.

"Sent home from the Somme with a piece of shrapnel in his backside. Ha! It could only happen to him. Couldn't sit down for weeks."

Conscious of the potential for embarrassment, I looked at the son only briefly enough to notice his fair colouring and a stiffness in the way that he carried himself, no doubt due to his injury.

"Thank you, Father! I'll do my own introductions from now on, if you don't mind." Bemused, he appeared to be studying me, his frown adopting a lopsided shape. "I say, don't I know you?"

"I don't think so."

"Charlotte, come now! You're far too modest." Mr Irving touched my arm. "You can see her face anywhere these days. She's a model - one of London's finest."

"My ambition is to be a photographer." I stepped forward to relieve the son of his greatcoat.

"You're very talented, I'm sure." Lowering his tone to a level he thought was confiding, Mr Irving nudged my elbow. "But I'd rather look at a photograph of you than one you've taken of Mrs Miller's pals. Ugly sisters, the lot of them!" Then he disappeared into the drawing room, flinging open his arms: "Mrs Miller! What news!"

Several steps behind him, Robert turned to me. "I know plenty of people who would agree. You're shyer in person than I expected."

After John's frequent administrations with the sherry decanter had dispelled some of that shyness, and the air thickened with discourse and sweet-smelling cigar smoke, I tired of brushing similar comments aside. "Forgive me. Perhaps we have met and I simply don't remember."

"Your photographs fetched quite a price at the front. You were responsible for putting a smile on the faces of a good many pals of mine before they went over the top."

"I'm sorry, but I don't know what you're talking about." Denial didn't prevent the sinking feeling in my stomach: realisation that the photographs, supposedly destined for the general's private collection, must have been reproduced. After all of Freddie's assurances, he had gone back on his word!

Separated by the grand piano, with one elbow resting on a shoulder-height shelf against a backdrop of leather-bound volumes, John had been answering Mr Irving's enquiries about the family business (something I had discovered little about, the subject dismissed as 'dull' the minute I voiced any interest). His eyes strayed towards me, questioningly: I averted mine.

"There's no need to be embarrassed," Robert said. "None at all."

Mrs Miller's laugher rang gratingly across the room. I should have felt anger; instead I felt as if I were standing on a cliff-edge, waves pummelling the rocks below me. Lowering my voice, I asked, "Were there many of them?"

"Let's just say they were used as currency."

He seemed to think I might find this amusing. Instead I rocked forwards onto the balls of my feet. My view was of the sheer drop. If what Robert said was true about his pals, a good many copies would remain buried in French mud, but it was the thought of one stray print making its way to Brighton that horrified me; perhaps being sold to some seedy backstreet shop, the type that displayed hundreds of similar pictures in little chests, corners dog-eared where sailors had flicked through them, or - worse still - to the vendor on the pier. While I struggled to breathe, my thoughts went out to Martha, heading home to Wiltshire to comfort her mother. If I had been taken advantage of, hadn't I done the same to her? Although someone would have to know her very well to recognise her from my photograph, I had lied - to say nothing of failing to ask for her permission.

It took me a moment to absorb what Robert was saying.

"There was a Private who was keen to have us understand that you were his girl." I found that I had tightened my grip on the stem of my glass. "We didn't know whether to believe him but he produced a portrait of you. It was him who told us to call you Lottie."

"Alfie!" I gasped, reaching for the back of a nearby chair to steady myself. Even the sound of his name had the power to raise my spirits. "We grew up together." The description seemed important and yet inadequate.

"So he *was* telling the truth! What was it he said? 'The French can keep their *Angel of the Trenches*. It's Lottie who's going to get us Tommies through.'"

"When was this?" I asked. Again, I was aware from the way that John's cigar changed hands that I had distracted him from his conversation.

"Must have been the end of 1917. Just before I was shipped home."

If Alfie was alive a year ago, I had stopped my vigil too early!

"No news?"

I shook my head.

"Pity." With that solitary word, he quashed the hope he had ignited. For that alone, I would have found it in myself to despise him. "Decent chap. Mind you, we've lost a great many decent men." His eyes travelled to John and I saw the disdain in them.

I felt an unbearable sadness, aware, at the same time, of being under scrutiny from more than one quarter. Robert saw it too. "John's keeping a close watch. Don't tell me, you've swapped one brother-figure for another."

Refusing to take the bait, I explained. "I'm here as Mrs Miller's guest."

"I wonder what she would say if she knew you were the force's favourite pin-up."

"The photographer is a friend of hers."

He regarded his hostess quizzically but not without admiration. *"She's* upped her game."

"I'm not sure I understand your meaning."

Robert smiled across the room at Mrs Miller as he continued, minimising the movement of his mouth. "It can't have escaped your notice that Mrs Miller never approves of John's taste in women. I imagine it was her insurance policy. She's quite the master schemer."

I protested, "Mrs Miller has been nothing but supportive." But, at the same moment, I began to doubt. "Mr Irving," I asked, pointedly. "Do you still have the photograph?"

He tapped his breast pocket.

"You have it *here?*" I had assumed that the rectangular bulge was a cigarette case.

"I only brought three things back with me: your photograph and my New Testament fitted nicely into the little tin Princess Mary sent us for Christmas."

I told myself that my fear of blackmail was unfounded. Robert had had no idea we would meet. "I don't suppose you'd consider letting me have it?" I ventured, trying to sound calm.

"I wouldn't want to be parted from it, not when it's worked like a charm. Unless…"

Seeing Mrs Miller's silken approach, I raised my eyes in warning.

Mocking, he inclined his head, the slightest of bows. "…you'd consider coming dancing with me."

"Dancing!" Mrs Miller took him by the elbow, tucking one hand underneath and placing the other on top. "Now, that is a generous offer, isn't it, Charlotte?"

"I -"

"No arguments: you must accept. There hasn't been nearly enough dancing recently."

We walked into dinner, John and Mr Irving in front, the three of us following. As Mrs Miller congratulated Robert personally for the victory, I felt an uninvited hand settle on my backside. Hissing in Robert's ear, "Keep it. Plenty more where that came from," I quickened my pace and took his father's arm.

29 - SIR JAMES'S STORY

SHERE, 2009

Since Jenny had interpreted the photographs of my mother for me, something significant had shifted in our relationship. A fragile trust developed as the days shortened, another year coming to its close. Only that morning I had noticed a powdery frost clinging to the steps of the war memorial as I brought the milk in. No longer threatened by Jenny's curiosity, I remembered what it was to give a little and receive something greater in return.

"If I were you, I'd be asking if your father knew what your mother did for a living before he met her," she mused, examining one of the sets of photographs before assigning it a home in the filing cabinet. In recent weeks my dining room had been transformed into the hub of a business, my parents undergoing something of a reunion through the belongings they had left behind. Racing trophies, medals and models of cars; photographs, postcards and scrapbooks.

"Oh, I would imagine he did."

"What makes you so sure?"

"He liked to think he was unconventional." I laughed, looking at a photograph of him in his leathers. "He wasn't, in fact. On some things he was very traditional. That is, he kept one set of rules for himself and another for everyone else. But having a pin-up for a fiancée would have slotted very neatly into his self-image. He did so enjoy antagonising my grandfather. His father was a great one for his views on women. He never made a secret of the fact that he didn't think my mother was suitable marriage material - too late by then, of course."

"They eloped?"

"Not as such. No one dreamed of the lavish ceremonies we see these days. You did the deed quietly with whatever witnesses you could find, then made a formal announcement."

"Your father sounds like a rebel."

I chuckled. "A rogue, certainly. He always said he chose my mother because she was exciting." As I scratched my chin, I failed to add that he also told me he had married for love, something that, becoming increasingly sentimental with age, I found a rather wonderful admission on his part. Despite his win-at-all-costs attitude, my mother - or perhaps love itself - had been his one weakness. Not a bad character-flaw to possess.

Jenny was speaking. "So, your mother's was a real-life rags to riches story."

"No, no." I turned to rub my arthritic hands in front of the imitation coals of the gas fire. "She was a business woman with her own studio by then. Even before that, the Pyes had been respectable by anyone's standards."

"I was only using a saying. I mean, that sort of thing doesn't happen in the real world."

"Oh, I don't know! Many of the biggest stars of the era started out in poverty. And by that I mean real poverty, not how the word is bandied about today. You've only got to look at Clara Bow."

She looked at me blankly. "Who?"

"The original 'It Girl'? No, perhaps not. Then what about

Chaplin? He spent his childhood in and out of the work-house." My thoughts went off at a tangent. "Have you ever heard of Sylvia Ashley?"

Jenny shrugged, "Should I?"

"No - only that she was a prime example. She started life as Edith Hawkes of Paddington - a proper little cockney - and ended up a princess. All by knowing how to play the game. Of course, it helped that she was a great beauty."

"And what game was that?" Jenny asked cynically.

"Well, after a spell in modelling under the name of Sylvia, she thought she'd try her hand on the stage. Her audition for George Grossmith Junior was legendary. Asked to sing - a requirement she questioned for a chorus girl - she settled on the full version of the National Anthem. Naturally, convention demanded everyone jumped to their feet: her first standing ovation.

"Even without a leading role to her name, she made headlines. She hooked herself a blue-blooded aristocrat, Lord Cooper, and, despite opposition from his family, she married him. It barely lasted a few months but she decided the name Lady Sylvia Ashley rather suited her, so she hung onto it.

"Then she set her sights on Hollywood. And not just Hollywood but the king of Hollywood! She became Douglas Fairbanks's mistress. Although Mary Pickford had once been called a marriage-wrecker, they'd become the... who's that charming young lady who keeps adopting all those children?" I circled one hand to encourage the words.

"Madonna."

"I said *young!*"

"Look who's talking." Jenny grinned, while I clicked my fingers in frustration. "Angelina Jolie?"

"That's the one. They'd become the Brad and Angelina of their day. By the time the divorce was finally settled, Fairbanks only had three years to live. He left Lady Sylvia one million dollars richer."

"How convenient."

"With a title and money, she could have had her pick. She chose another British aristocrat. Not a good option, as it so happens."

"Didn't it last?" Jenny's face was ripe with mock sympathy.

I shook my head. "Then came wedding number four to our old friend Clark Gable. This was after the war. Sylvia was said to have resembled his wife, Carole Lombard."

She looked shocked. "The one who was killed in the plane crash?"

I nodded. "The very same. Despite Gable telling the press he'd never been happier, it didn't work out. After seventeen months Lady Sylvia filed for divorce.

"She married her Russian prince at the age of fifty. He was in the hotel business, which funded his expensive hobbies of car-racing and horse-breeding. This one was *'til death do us part*. Hers, sadly. She was buried under the name Princess Sylvia Djordjadze, a far cry from pretty little Edith Hawkes of Paddington." Remembering Jenny's mother, I refrained from mentioning that she had died of cancer.

"I think it's sad," Jenny said.

"How so?" I had only meant to amuse. "I thought she did rather well for herself."

"I don't call four failed marriages doing well!"

"Not quite up to Elizabeth Taylor's standards. Not that you could accuse *her* of marrying for money."

"Every time she changed her name, she lost something of herself."

"I suppose you'll be one of those women who insists on keeping her name."

"I hope so. I'd feel as if I had lost another link with my

mother if I changed mine. And, before you say anything, I know that might not make sense, because Jones wasn't the name she was born with. But that's how I feel."

I envied Jenny, the way she allowed her emotions such clear expression. "I can understand that. My mother abandoned her married name when she left my father. I suspect it was to minimise scandal, but it felt as if she deliberately distanced herself from us."

Taking one last look at my view of the square - decorated Christmas trees already displayed in the window of the gift shop - I drew the curtains, pondering my choice of story. Sylvia's was one of many I could have chosen, but something had made me opt for hers. It wasn't simply a tale of rags to riches: it was about separation. Sylvia only looked in one direction - forwards. My mother performed a neat U-turn. What had she found in her new life that frightened her?

Jenny had already changed the subject. "How did your father fund his racing habit?"

"Oh." I turned back to her. "Family money, a few winnings, business deals. He didn't win the big titles himself, but he built cars that won races. He was pretty shrewd for all his appearance of being a playboy." When I looked at Jenny, she had raised her eyebrows. "And, no, I didn't do too badly out of it. There's always been enough to live comfortably, even after... well, you've already read all you need to know about that."

"All the same," Jenny said with her old head on. "It must have been hard on you."

"I needed a friend to give me a good boot up the backside. 'James, you've made a colossal balls-up of the whole thing. Get over it.' Life goes on."

"Some friend!"

"Just what I needed. Things are only the end of the world

if you let them be. Remember that next time you're feeling sorry for yourself."

I felt foolish then, imagining the eight-year-old Jenny who had lost her mother. Some things not only feel as if they're the end of the world: they should be acknowledged as such. I was about to apologise when Jenny asked brightly, "When are we going to drop in on your mother?"

I liked her choice of words, the sense that it was a casual thing - but I hadn't anticipated company. "Who's this *we* you're talking about?"

She shrugged. "I've got to know her. I'd like to see where her story ends."

I was surprised to realise I didn't object. "Soon," I said.

"Next week?"

"Look here!" My tone was joking. "I don't know if you've noticed, but I'm an old man who doesn't like to be pushed into things."

"You're putting it off." She faced me, an equal. "And you just said that you need an occasional boot up the backside!"

That was when I realised Jenny considered herself to be a friend. Not one I would have chosen, but perhaps that fact alone highlights my foolishness.

"Next week." Though I wouldn't admit it, I was happy to defer to her. I snuck a look at her - a friend! - smiling secretly and then, taking my seat, I picked up the last two photographs I had been looking at. They had been set apart from the rest in an unmarked folder.

Satisfied, Jenny leaned over the table. "What have you got there?"

"I don't know. Two photographs that don't seem to belong together. One was clearly taken the day war was declared. And then we have this experimental shot that's really quite extraordinary. You have to look twice to see what's going on."

"I'll trade with you." She turned the photographs over and nodded. Each had an identical stamp on the back, not at all like the stamp of Parker's studio. "Here. I've got a scrapbook of newspaper articles. They're all about a photography competition. And I think you've just found the missing entries."

30 - LOTTIE'S STORY

LONDON, 1918

"Your tea and a letter for you, Miss." Crab-like, Mrs Bellamy elbowed her way through the bedroom door, the contents of my morning tray chattering. Seated at the side table wearing a dressing gown, I was poring over yesterday's discarded newspapers. "Not that I've got time to go running around after you, mind."

"Is there anything I can do to help?"

"Help!" She hooted. "You'd only get under my feet. Besides." Mrs Bellamy slid the tray onto the table. "Mrs Miller wouldn't hear of it."

I recognised Felicity's exaggerated loops on the envelope. Even though it made me homesick, news from Brighton was always something to be cherished.

Mrs Bellamy cast her all-seeing eyes over the room in search of something that was less than perfect and began to fuss with the curtains I had tied back. Gasping, she declared, "Have you seen the state of the square! All them paper streamers and beer bottles left lying around for someone else to pick up."

"You've got to excuse a little high spirits."

"High spirits! It's out and out vandalism, that's what it is. I don't want to tell you what I heard was going on in Trafalgar Square last night. It's just as well you were safely tucked up in bed."

"Did you do anything to celebrate?"

"Too much silliness if you ask me - and it looks set to carry on for a couple of days yet. 'Sides, I wasn't fit for anything after I'd finished downstairs - although not even that racket could keep me awake. I had my first decent night's sleep in four years! Now, I've things to be getting on with. No doubt you'll tell me if there's anything Martha normally does for you that needs seeing to."

Waiting for the door to close behind her, I tore at the envelope greedily and unfolded the delicate sheets of transparent writing paper, another casualty of wartime shortages. Scanning the pages, I barely believed what I read there. '*But now down to business. We have news! You have won first prize in a photography competition. You are to present yourself at the offices of the* Daily Mail *at Carmelite House, Fleet Street on 12th December at 9 o'clock with proof of identification.*' Someone thought I was good enough, not as a photographer's model, but as a photographer! Excitement welling: my shaking hands tightening their hold on the edges of the paper, I re-read the paragraph to make sure there was no mistake. I had thought it selfish to wish for something so badly when men were still dying on the march to Cologne. Pacing the room I acknowledged how much I had wanted this. Looking out over the square, I felt joy in the abandoned streamers and flags. But I also felt humbled, shaky in a way I would never have anticipated. There was a sobering postscript. '*We are so proud of you, Lottie - and I know that Mr Parker would have been too.*' I had at least lived up to one promise I had made. The credit mostly his, this was Mr Parker's award.

The sand in the egg-timer lasted only a few moments. Practicalities would have to be faced: Martha needed to be told; then Mrs Miller and John, who might feel that I had abused their hospitality; and Ma too.

But before those things, there was the appointment at the offices of the *Daily Mail*. For a girl with no birth certificate, providing proof of identification might have been a tall order, were it not for the photographic record in the *Brighton Gazette*. My life as Lottie Pye had been well documented.

And then, in the precise moment it seemed possible I might achieve what I had been working towards, I caught sight of my face reflected in the mirror. Robert Irving's comments from the previous evening echoed: *Don't I know you?* Other men might recognise me; men who knew the name Lottie. Sitting down at the dressing table, I doubled my hair over at the back, creating the illusion of the shorter hairstyle adopted by many girls, unflatteringly called *the curtain*. I couldn't disguise my face, but I could alter the way I looked sufficiently to introduce an element of doubt.

31 - LOTTIE'S STORY

LONDON, 1918

"Lottie Pye?"

Despite having waited to be called, the sound of my name - my Brighton name - spoken aloud in a sterile, echoing corridor startled me. "Yes!" I jumped to standing, clutching my portfolio under one arm.

"You seem uncertain." A walrus-faced man frowned at me with a bemused expression. "I must admit, given the maturity of your entry I was expecting someone older."

I gave an apologetic smile. "I'm sorry to disappoint you."

"Not in the least. This will make a far better story. May I offer you Lord Northcliffe's congratulations? My name is Worth." He extended his hand, and I took it briefly, inclining my head. "Shall we?"

Shown the way to a comfortable office where my photograph was displayed between two others, I was directed to a seat in front of a large mahogany desk. Following the direction of my gaze, Mr Worth nodded.

"As you can see, the standard of entries was extremely high. I'm sure some people will consider our choice controversial but, in the unanimous opinion of our adjudicators, yours was the strongest entry by far. Tea?"

"Thank you."

A strong brew was served, sugar lumps offered, before a second man joined us. Slightly younger, with a slick of dark hair and small round spectacles, it was apparent that he was on edge. Touching the blunt ends of my newly-cut hair nervously, I wondered if perhaps he recognised me. He extended a considerably colder hand. "Mr Arthur. I'll be taking minutes."

"So, tell us about yourself," Mr Worth invited. "Have you been taking photographs for very long?"

Dry-mouthed, I took a sip of tea, conscious of the rattle of the saucer caused by my unsteady hand. I began as bravely as I could. "I took my first photograph six years ago."

"And who, might I ask, are your influences?"

"Well, there's my tutor, Mr Parker, of course. He was always very keen to distinguish between the technical and the emotional sides of photography. But this particular piece of work was influenced by Frank Hurley."

"The mad photographer? This image struck us as being almost Pre-Raphaelite. Wouldn't you say so, Mr Arthur?"

The younger man seemed surprised to have been interrupted from his conscientious note-keeping. "I - I believe that's the description we used when we first saw it."

"Well, I'm flattered you thought so. It was Hurley's processes that inspired me rather than his subjects: the idea of creating a new image from more than one negative."

"So this is a montage? We wondered how you'd achieved the result. Is it difficult to do?"

"I have to admit that this was my first experiment."

"Really?" Mr Worth continued. "It's terribly clever. Tell me, what does your *experiment* say to you?"

I was uncomfortable at being asked to explain my work. It was like asking a magician to explain how he had managed to extract a rabbit from an empty hat. The difficulty was that, although I had been taught to perform the trick (what Mr Parker referred to as 'the technical'), the magic remained a mystery. Instinct told me that photography was the capture of a precise moment in time, not to be dragged out into a sentence or a speech. "Firstly, it's about the image of England we all carry in our heads, something that doesn't change no matter what else happens in the world."

They sat, expecting more. How to explain that my work had an energy of its own, something I didn't feel responsible for?

"And, of course, it's about the girl, who is so much a part of the scene that she seems to be growing from it. But it's also her dream." Tongue-tied by the effort of putting thoughts into words and arranging them in order, I was embarrassed to find I had spilled tea into the saucer.

Dismissing my concern as I edged it onto the desk, Mr Worth encouraged: "You were talking about a dream?"

I stumbled upon an explanation that fitted both my emotions and the theme of the competition. "It's about being homesick. Wanting to be home so badly that by closing your eyes you can transport yourself there."

"Charming - and most appropriate. Don't you agree, Mr Arthur?" He turned to his colleague, clearing his throat; what I would realise, in retrospect, was a cue.

Mr Arthur snapped another photograph on the surface in front of me. "And what about this one?" It was the photograph I had taken on the day of the outbreak of the war: the image of Brighton beach: the lovers in the foreground, the paperboy announcing the terrible news at the back.

"Where did you find this?" I was delighted and surprised that they had gone out of their way to obtain another example of my work. But they were newspaper men. They would have their methods.

"One entry per person, Miss Pye." Two pairs of eyes had

turned hard and cold. "That was the rule."

"You don't think I...?" I stammered, looking from one of them to the other.

Mr Arthur turned both photographs over and showed me the entry-stamps on the reverse: "Lottie Pye." He jabbed a judicious finger at my name.

"No matter how impressed we are by your technical ability," Mr Worth said, his tone almost apologetic. "I'm afraid you give us no option but to disqualify you."

"But that's not my handwriting," I protested, pointing to the back of the second photograph.

If not mine, then *whose?* I stood up, realisation dawning. My chest expanded; the corners of my mouth lifted. The men looked on in confusion at my reaction. They had expected embarrassment. An apology. Certainly not barely-contained joy.

"In accordance with the rules of the competition, we are entitled to the rights to the photographs..." Mr Arthur continued uncertainly.

"Do what you like with them!" I laughed, realising that winning wasn't the prize I had been hoping for.

"I beg your pardon?"

I almost danced as I picked up the photograph taken on Brighton beach. "Mr Parker is the only one who would have entered this on my behalf. Don't you see?"

The two men leaned towards each other, their foreheads almost touching as they exchanged whispers.

"This must mean he's back from France!"

I used the opportunity to look at the other photographs displayed on either side of mine. A shot of a mother and child, the child with a single tear on its cheek, sentimental and overdone. I wished I'd had the confidence to enter my photograph of Felicity and Harry, something honest and real without any need of manipulation. The other entry was of a picture-perfect English village, the angle of the approach road inviting the viewer into the scene. "Clever." I loitered in front of it.

Mr Worth cleared his throat, and I turned. "Miss Pye, you say you only entered one photograph in the competition - the winning entry."

"That's correct." I nodded, my gloved hands clasped in front of me.

"And you had no knowledge that the other photograph had been entered on your behalf?"

I shook my head. "Thinking about it, I wouldn't be able to assign the rights of the second photograph to you. *The Brighton Gazette* bought them. But, quite aside from that, it doesn't belong in the competition, does it?"

Mr Arthur could barely refrain from tutting. "Perhaps you'd be so good as to explain yourself."

"The competition was about what our boys were fighting for. That photograph was taken on the day war was declared. The fighting hadn't started."

"Miss Pye, this photograph was shortlisted in the final ten. Our judges thought the newspaper reference very clever."

At this announcement - two pieces of my work in the final ten! - my eyes were drawn to the placard: the boy had been selling copies of the *Daily Mail*. I could have laughed out loud. "Do you know? I hadn't even noticed."

"This is most irregular. I think we need to refer to Lord Northcliffe for a ruling."

"Can I go?" I asked, light-headed.

"Certainly. We'll have to get back to you about this."

"Gentlemen." Beaming, I could almost smell the combination of iodine, salt, brine, seaweed and vinegar. *I was going home!*

But as my footsteps echoed towards the exit, I heard the sound of a second pair sprinting behind me. "One minute, Miss Pye! One minute!"

I stopped; turned.

Mr Arthur rested one arm against the wall while he caught his breath. In view of his youthfulness, I had taken him to be the more junior of the pair, but now I wondered if I'd been mistaken; his display of nerves an act. His chest was heaving. "I think we can settle this without bothering Lord Northcliffe. If you are able to prove that someone else entered the second photograph without your knowledge, then the prize money, the press coverage and all the glory that comes with it will be yours. But if you can't prove what you say… well." He smiled, self-satisfied, as, fully recovered from his exertions, he righted himself. "You'll only have the press coverage."

"I - I don't understand."

"Allow me to elaborate. It's quite simple, Miss Pye. We've invested heavily in the competition. If you can't prove what you say, well..." He shrugged, as if the matter would be taken out of his hands.

"But you wouldn't!"

"The story of how you attempted to defraud a national newspaper? Now, that would be newsworthy."

32 - LOTTIE'S STORY

LONDON TO BRIGHTON, 1919

Mrs Miller let go of her spoon, and it clattered around the rim of her soup bowl. "You're leaving? When?"

"Tomorrow."

"So soon?" Ignoring the damage to her blouse, she dabbed at the corner of her mouth with a napkin.

"I'll drive." John glanced sideways at his mother, masking his concern by enthusing, "In fact, let's all go. You'd enjoy a trip to Brighton, wouldn't you, Mother?"

Hands poised mid-air, I clasped the handle of my own cutlery tightly. The thought of my neatly-compartmentalised life being exposed was inconceivable. "I couldn't let you use your petrol ration. Besides, it won't be a holiday. There are things I need to attend to." To say nothing of making amends for leaving without a goodbye.

"John, she's trying to tell us we'd be - what is it you young people say? - cramping her style. May I ask when we can expect your return?"

This appeared to be taken for granted, but I hadn't thought that far ahead. If Mr Parker was to reopen his studio, my loyalties would lie with him. Hesitant, I admitted, "I'm not sure."

"I have to say, it's most inconvenient. What with Christmas

just around the corner, I had been counting on your assistance."

Tight-lipped and subdued throughout the remainder of the meal, Mrs Miller had no opinion to offer on the headlines about the death of the actress Billie Carlton from an overdose on Armistice night. John had no more luck coaxing her into a discussion about the general election that was to take place the day after the next - for the first time, Mrs Miller would qualify to vote. This was what she, and countless other women, had fought for - only to prove themselves by rolling up their sleeves and keeping the country afloat.

As a compromise, I allowed John to drive me to the station. The car edged slowly forwards, its progress hampered by crowds who were reluctant to be parted, anticipating a glimpse of the King and Queen who had embarked on a seven-day tour of the capital. Entering the forecourt under the grand clock with little time to spare, John insisted on a rushed tea at the café, still decorated with celebratory red, white and blue bunting: "Humour me. For old time's sake."

Breaking off from an enthusiastic outpouring about a piece of the new hot dance-music he was learning on the piano, John grasped my hand. "You are coming back, aren't you, Charlotte?"

"I would imagine so," I replied, panicked into inventing a lie.

"You didn't seem very sure last night." He chewed his upper lip and nodded repeatedly as if convincing himself of some little-known fact. "This might be my last opportunity. It's never been the right time to tell you while we've been living under the same roof - Mother's seen to that! - but you must know how fond I am of you, Lottie."

The waves already beckoning, I needed no further complications. I remembered Mrs Miller's warnings that it was my job to let John down. The truth seemed as good a place to start as any. I took his hands in what I hoped would be interpreted as a sisterly manner. "Did I ever tell you how I was rescued after my mother was struck by lightning?"

But he was focused on pressing my hands to his lips.

"John," I protested, withdrawing them. "You don't really know me."

"I know everything I need to."

I attempted a light-hearted approach, smiling. "Your mother has made it quite plain that she has other plans for you."

There was a rush of steam as the train prepared to depart. *"Last call for Brighton."* I heard the shrill stutter of the whistle as the cry of the gulls echoed inside my head. From all directions, people scurried towards the platform, a hard press of bodies as they neared the gates. My place was with them.

"I really must go," I said, standing.

"Charlotte, I -"

"All aboard! Last call!"

Placing a restraining hand on his chest, I patted the place it came to rest. "I'll be back before you know it. We'll talk then, I promise." Balancing the luggage I had arrived with in one hand and a new case in the other, I moved towards the crush at the barrier.

My stomach was a knot of apprehension as I located a vacant seat and stowed my belongings on the overhead rack. What if Ma had already heard about my role as the force's pin-up? What if I was unable to convince the *Daily Mail* of my innocence? But those weren't the only things that troubled me. I looked out at the Thames through the grime of the carriage window, remembering the sixteen-year-old who had arrived, imagining London as a glamorous city: home to the Crystal Palace and the dome of St Paul's; the Savoy Hotel, Covent Garden Opera House and the Electric Cinema; of afternoon teas at Fortnum's followed by dinner at Simpsons in the Strand. But it had also been a place where ordinary people – and, like Martha, I was still one of them - were forced to load their possessions onto carts and move to who knows where. I departed with a sense of having betrayed them. Still a fraud, I had done nothing to contribute to their war effort. The only difference was that I was now a fraud with a London accent and a fashionable wardrobe.

The green of Epsom racecourse passed me by, stone quarries, then sprawling hospital buildings before we were submerged in dense woodland. Spat out into daylight, the brick arches of the Balcombe Viaduct spanned the Ouse Valley. I held my breath as we rode its narrow expanse. Once we had passed through another town, the Downs were spread out before us like a patchwork quilt: Wolstonbury Hillfort to the right of the carriage, Ditchling Beacon to my left, and, straight ahead, my first glimpse of the Clayton windmills. Then, propelled into a tunnel, deep within the hills them-selves, darkness. I imagined the trees and sheep above me, the English Channel in front of me, until, at last, home - and everything that meant.

My first obligation was to pay my respects to the sea, a bleak churning grey-green. I stood on the promenade at the place where my story began, Ma straining her voice above the storm to cry, *Madam!* And although I could see the expression of surprise on my mother's face as she turned, her features still eluded me. My mind wanted to superimpose Rebecca Lavashay's face on the memory, another composite creation. Perhaps that was the reason Hurley's work intrigued me. Who was I if not the composite of a series of images?

Breathing lungfuls of air laced with vinegar and shellfish, my view was tainted by thoughts of those who had crossed the Channel with Paris on their minds, only to be buried beneath French mud. At every corner, a young Alfie leaning against the wall, hands in pockets. *'Oi, oi, I see Lottie Pye's back from London, all hoity-toity.'* At the front, Daddy bent over the railing, his pipe clenched between his teeth. *'Not too grown up to kiss your Daddy, I hope.'* But they were shadows and ghosts. In search of something real and unchanged I walked by the fishermen's arches, nodding at men in heavy sweaters and oilskins, sitting on barrels, pipes hanging from downturned mouths, repairing torn nets, painting upturned boats with coats of tar and varnish. The smell of decay was stronger here than I remembered, and the damp in the air clung to everything it touched.

"Morning, skipper." I smiled at a wind-weathered face, bemused to find his sacred masculine space invaded by a young lady in a wool serge suit.

Even our shopfront was altered, the plate glass not as polished and the paving not as cleanly swept as it was when this little corner was the centre of Daddy's universe. The shop door stuck on its hinges, caught on the rush matting. The fact that I had attended Daddy's funeral didn't prepare me for the shock of finding Josie in his place behind the counter.

"Well, now." She took stock, hand on hips. "Look who the cat's dragged in."

What had I expected? "Hello, Josie." I was awkward, unsure how to behave.

"You'd best go up and tell your mother you're here."

Climbing the worn wooden treads, each replayed its own secret memory. From the kitchen doorway, I watched Ma bent over the blackened pot, a little more hunched, a little shorter than the image in my head. My eyes pooled. Ma was the one who had rescued me from a storm. She had given me a home. Lost her sons, one by one, and then her husband.

"Water needs fetching, young whippersnapper," she said without turning, pointing to the bucket. A hint of her old self.

"Yes, Ma," I said obediently.

Having expected Harry's voice, Ma's back stiffened. Her

own voice was altered, thick in her throat, when she said, "And then you can help me with the pastry. Not that you were ever much help. I hope you haven't forgotten how."

"Breadcrumbs. Fine as I can get them."

She sniffed. "I must have taught you better than I thought."

Putting down my bag, I took off my jacket and rolled up the sleeves of my blouse. When I reached for the handle of the bucket, Ma grabbed hold of my forearm, her grip surprisingly strong. "So you're back."

"For a few days, yes."

It took a few minutes for this to sink in. "Well, let's take a look at you." And she raised her eyes. "What in heaven's name have you done to your hair?"

One hand covered my bare neck self-consciously and felt for the ends, damply curling from contact with the sea air. "Everyone's wearing it shorter in London. It's easier to keep."

"I don't like it," she said bluntly. "Doesn't suit you."

I smiled, giving in to a few tears. "I've missed you, Ma."

"No one asked you to leave." And she returned to the work that stopped for no one, the work that had sustained her.

I felt obliged to offer the explanation that wasn't requested. "I couldn't just stay and watch." Attempting to regain control, I bit down on my lip. "Waiting for the postman to arrive."

Although she rolled her eyes, Ma's resolve was weakening. "But that's what our women have always done. You know that better than most. I lost count of the number of times I had to drag you away from the beach where you were standing with the fishermen's wives."

There was no avoiding the question at the front of my mind: "Is there any news of Alfie?"

She shook her head. "No news is good news. Remember that." Much-repeated words meant to offer comfort: empty.

Downstairs in the yard, I heard him before I saw him. Running feet and zooming noises punctuated by his impression of a Lewis gun. A joy to behold; young, golden-haired, Harry was playing aeroplanes, flying in circles, arms alternately wings and at the controls of the gun.

"Let me guess. You're a Handley Page."

"Lottie!" he shouted, completing a lap before he flew towards me and leaped into my arms, bony legs circling my waist. "I'm Jimmy McCudden and this," he stretched both arms wide, trustingly throwing back his head, "is my DH2 fighter. I've just shot the Red Baron down!"

I laughed, pulling his torso back up and crushing his small ribcage, glad of his warm body to hold fast to. "You're getting so heavy!" I staggered about, pretending he was too much.

"Don't drop me!"

"Where's your mummy?"

"Out catching criminals and dirty foreign spies." Already, he was wriggling free. "Nana Kitty made me move your stones."

"I expect they were in her way."

Taking me by the hand, Harry solemnly led me to the bottom of the yard, where he had constructed a wall of pebbles against the brickwork. He picked one up and let it fall from a height, making the sound of an explosion. *"Boom! Krhhhh!"* Games composed of fighter-planes and bombs. Barely old enough to remember peace.

I left Harry happily bombarding his stone fortress and filled the bucket. A cold torrent drenched the hem of my skirt and trickled between the cobbles in the spaces where moss grew and weeds forced their heads to the surface. This was reality: making yourself useful; little in the way of thanks. If I had wanted, I could have stepped back inside my old self as if a day hadn't passed.

With no fattened calf to be had, my homecoming celebration consisted of a meat pie and potatoes, served with a compulsory pot of tea. A chattering Harry, bouncing up and down in his seat, mouth full of food, demanded to hear all about Buckingham Palace and the guards in their actual bearskin hats, if it was true that the King was an actual German, and whether I had seen any actual Zeppelins. And for every response I gave him, he had a friend called Tommy Adams who had told him different and could prove it.

"Why ask if you *actually* already know, you little terror?" Josie demanded before turning to me. "There isn't much in this world that Tommy Adams doesn't know. Born brilliant, apparently."

But to be caught up in Harry's childish excitement was a gift.

The bell above the shop door rattled. Josie was the first to her feet. "Just a minute!"

A shout of, "Only me," followed. I smiled fondly at the familiar tone of Felicity's voice.

"Hush now!" Ma chided Harry. "You don't want us to have to tell your mother you haven't been behaving. Keep quiet and we'll surprise her."

We waited in silence, Harry, a finger on his lips, until her footfalls reached the top of the staircase.

"What a day!" Felicity blew out her cheeks as she removed her felt hat and smoothed her hair. "I'm parched. Is there any tea in the pot?"

"Someone's in your seat, I'm afraid," Josie said, rising from the table to fetch a cup from the dresser.

"Lottie?" Felicity stopped in her tracks. "Let me look at you. What a wonderful surprise!"

"What about you?" I held her at arm's length to admire her belted uniform with its shirt and tie and its side-buttoned skirt. "A policewoman!" I noticed that her eyes had filled and was touched.

"Have you come to show us your award?" She paused to tip her son out of his chair. "Up you get, Harry."

"Why?" he protested, his attempt to grip both sides of the seat failing.

"Don't answer your mother back!" Ma wagged a finger at him.

"Because I've been on my feet all day, that's why!"

When I explained that there would be no award until Mr Parker had cleared up the confusion over the double entry, Felicity turned her darkening eyes to Ma. "You haven't told her?"

Thin-lipped, Ma shook her head. "I thought it best it came from you."

A chill coursed down my spine, infecting my blood. "Told me what?" But there was little room for doubt as Felicity's lips moved while she crossed herself.

"Come along now!" Josie placed one hand on Harry's shoulder and steered him towards the door. "Let's give the adults some breathing space."

"Oh, wh-y?"

"Because I said so! You can help me in the shop. Time you started pulling your weight."

"Lottie," Felicity began, her mouth trembling.

"No," I whispered, unwilling to believe. *These* were the words she had concealed behind news of Harry's antics.

"It can't have been Mr Parker who entered the photograph in the competition." She shook her head. "It wasn't the sort of news I wanted to send by letter."

He hadn't been part of the fighting! So certain had I been of his safety that I hadn't spared a single prayer for him.

"Three months ago I arrived at the studio to find the building up for lease, so I paid his solicitor a visit. I'm afraid Mr Parker didn't return from stretcher-duty one night. I have a letter somewhere…"

Felicity faltered, covering her eyes with her hands, so Ma took up the thread. "Turns out his pal took a hit, so Mr Parker threw the injured man they'd been carrying over his shoulder and went on alone. He didn't make it back to the field dressing station. For a man who didn't believe in war, he was brave enough, I'll give him that."

Like Harry, I was tempted to demand, Why? But there was no one who could provide me with an answer. In the shuddering silence I counted up all of the things I owed him. My camera was a gift from him, my teaching his. Without Mr Parker, there would have been no photographs. Without his influence, I would have been living Martha's life.

"Have you heard anything from Mrs West?" Clinging to Felicity, I insisted, "Swear to me there's nothing else you've tried to protect me from."

She shook her head. "Nothing. Mind you, she doesn't read and she's too proud to ask her neighbours for help."

"I'll go tomorrow," I said.

"She won't thank you." Ma tutted.

"All the same." I would present myself to Alfie's mother, who didn't even have his body to bury, and give her the opportunity to tell me to get out of her sight. This was how things were done in Brighton.

"I need some fresh air, if you don't mind." I tore myself away from Felicity's embrace.

Collecting a pebble from Harry's battlements, I turned downhill to the seafront. The dusky sky was cloud-bound with only the thinnest slither of moon for comfort, but I was glad of the anonymity darkness offered. The smells of yeast, hops and tobacco, the heavy-handed chords of a piano and raucous singing, wafted out of an open doorway. Not ragtime rhythms, but *Tipperary, My heart lies there.* These were the boys who had been lucky enough to return, expected to slot neatly into their old lives, only to find they were no longer the same shapes as the holes they had left. The answer was to be found at the bottom of a glass.

Enveloped in growing darkness, I was guided by the lights of the Palace Pier. For the second time in twenty-four hours, after a gap of over a year, I stood on the beach, facing Le Havre. Mine the vigil of fishermen's wives, I stood tall, the December wind biting at my cheeks. The waves seemed louder than their daytime counterparts: travelling through the stillness; lapping at the pier supports; putting feelers out over the beach; carrying smaller stones in their wake; crashing against unseen rocks. How angry I was at the waste of it! It was there in my shoulders and fists. I screamed into the darkness, "*Why, Alfie? You were supposed to be my future.*" The pebble lay heavily in my pocket. I hurled it into the sea where it sank unseen with a hollow splash, taking its place on the seabed until a strong current washed it ashore or constant battering reduced it to sand.

Trudging. Crunching behind me. Closer now, I tensed at the smell of strong liquor and tobacco, and heard the sound of wet lips feasting on the neck of a bottle before it was flung aside, shattering.

"Out by yourself?" I felt hands clawing the front of my dress, reaching down towards my pockets; my neck muzzled with a face of bristle. "This is no place for a young lady."

My stomach tightened and fear coated the inside of my mouth. "I haven't got any money for you."

"It's not your money I'm after. Just a little of your company." He wrestled me down onto the pebbles, and I used the anger in my fists to fight him until, *slap!* Already raw with cold, my face stung; the breath knocked out of me.

"There now, be a good girl."

Forced down, the back of my head hit stone. I tried to cry out, but no sound came. His stale breath thawed the side of my face as a hand smelling of salt and sweat was pressed over my mouth and nostrils. I fought for air, lashing this way and that, the heels of my boots scraping, useless. He sat astride me, thighs clamped against my sides. The hand was removed, required elsewhere. The thud of blood in my ears and my ragged breathing masking all other noise, I told myself, *Keep quiet, be a good girl and he'll leave you alone.* But then his weight landed hard on my pounding chest. Hands tore at my skirt but it would not give. My spine was ground into the beach, my skin branded by brass buttons as he shifted his weight, and grasped my waistband, trying to force my skirt down. And if I tell you that I had no idea that his intention was rape I am sure you won't believe me, but it was so far removed from the closed-mouthed kisses of films, so unnatural and contrived, so primitive in all its panting foul breath. So mean. So pitiful.

In time I would tell myself that the man - whichever regiment he hailed from - was a disappointment to himself: that when he breathed the word, "Sorry," before rolling aside and staggering away in the blackness, it wasn't because of what he had done, but because of what he'd been unable to finish.

Thinking he had intended to suffocate me, I was surprised to discover that I was sitting up and rocking with both hands at my throat as I gasped for oxygen. My heels were still kicking, finding only pebbles to scrape against. Moments later, straightening my clothes, I stumbled up the beach. And like many a returning soldier, I held my silence, lying very still on the cot-bed in the kitchen; not wanting to add to Ma's worries or to put Felicity to any trouble on my account. Because bruises didn't warrant the attentions of a doctor who cost good money.

33 - SIR JAMES'S STORY

SHERE TO BRIGHTON, 2009

"I thought we'd take the route of the London to Brighton Vintage Car Rally." I glanced at Jenny in the rear-view mirror as we headed out of Surrey and south onto the A23. The road names were firmly imprinted on my mind from repeated journeys with my father, whose driving skills far exceeded his navigational techniques.

"Shouldn't we take a map?" I'd ask.

"This is my map." He tapped the side of his head: time to panic. To avoid outings that ended with dwindling farm tracks and lengthy recriminations, I consigned regular routes to memory: B2114, through Handcross Hill and Hammer Hill, B2115 to Whitemans Green, B2036 for Cuckfield, A273 for Burgess Hill, then back on the A23 at Pyecombe. They were filed between the nine times table and the words to *Jerusalem*. As well as being rewarded with the title of navigator-in-chief, it distracted me from the hand quivering ever-upwards on the speed dial.

"Bit of a trip down memory lane. My father owned a Wolseley made in 1899. Beautiful thing, she was. He kept her roadworthy for her annual outing. I inherited her, but I never had the patience. Or the mechanical skill."

"You got rid of it?" I saw the reflection of Jenny's eyes flashing at me.

"I gave her to Brooklands. It's a museum now, of course. I can go and see her any time I like."

We located the church of St Nicholas easily, pulling up alongside the flint wall. "Here we are." The handbrake carefully cranked into place in consideration of the steep incline, I glanced out of the window and paused. "I know we're not here to admire the architecture, but it's a disappointingly squat little structure for two people who like their steeples pointed."

Jenny smiled. "You always know you're home when you see St James's." Having smoothed her hair into position, she led the way through the wooden gate. "The graveyard's very overgrown."

Together, we surveyed the random collection of sunken headstones. "I wouldn't know where to start looking. I'm afraid I haven't thought this through at all."

"Let's try inside," Jenny suggested. "Someone must be able to help."

Entering the porch, she read the dedication aloud: "St Nicholas, Bishop of Myra, patron saint of fishermen and sailors, children, pawnbrokers and Russia."

"Huh! He's got his work cut out!"

Contrasting with the gloomy flint facade, the interior was light and spacious with just enough in the way of décor to avoid austerity. The heels of my shoes producing a satisfactory echo, Jenny maintained a respectful distance, clutching a delicate bouquet she had brought with her, a timid bridesmaid.

"Is this your first visit?"

"I beg your pardon." Turning, I was greeted by a lady churchwarden: short-haired, thick-spectacled, standing too close for comfort in an effort to keep her voice at a respectful volume.

"I couldn't help noticing you look a little lost. I always suggest starting your tour with our rather wonderful font.

It's twelfth century, one of our oldest treasures. Sadly, it was damaged in the seventeenth century, but you can still see three of the carvings. The one of the Last Supper is really quite unusual."

"Actually, we've come for your churchyard."

"Then, let me find you one of our leaflets." Opening a yellow two-fold she pointed to a paragraph halfway down.

"I'd better stop you. It's my mother's grave I'm here to see. I believe she's buried next to Phoebe Hessel."

She grabbed my arm, enthusing, "You must be Mr Pye!"

I decided not to correct her.

"I'm Monica. We're extremely proud of our two old ladies. Come this way."

I turned and raised my eyebrows at Jenny as Monica used both hands to lift the reluctant iron latch of a heavy side door carved with ancient graffiti, and started down a short dandelion-lined path. She came to a halt in front of a grassed area. "There can't be too many churches who can boast this sort of thing. Phoebe's gravestone isn't the original, of course. It was restored by the Northumberland Fusiliers in the Seventies." Phoebe Hessel's gravestone stood tall within a railed enclosure, wordy in the extreme. By contrast, my mother's was more discreet. "We stopped allowing burials here some time ago but, after your mother turned one hundred, she got it inside her head that she would like to be buried alongside Phoebe. She used to come here as a child and always loved her story. Our Vicar is a difficult man to convince but, seeing as they both lived to the grand old age of one hundred and eight, she was granted her wish." Monica patted me on the shoulder. "I'll leave you to it, shall I? I expect you have a lot to catch up on."

"Well. This is it," Jenny said.

The moment had arrived. Just as with the unveiling of the photograph album, her nervousness was apparent, mirroring my own.

"I must say, I'm intrigued. Let's see what Phoebe has to say for herself." We both shuffled to the left, and started to read.

"Born at Stepney in the year 1713," Jenny interrupted herself to say, "It's funny to think we're reading the same words your mother read as a girl."

I could almost see her, maybe at seven or eight, hiding behind the headstones. "But this is extraordinary! *She served for many Years as a private soldier in the 5th Reg. of foot in different parts of Europe and in the year 1745 fought under the command of the Duke of Cumberland at the Battle of Fountenoy where she received a bayonet wound in her arm.* If the Fusiliers paid for the grave to be restored, I assume there must be some truth in it."

Jenny resumed: *"Her long life which commenced in the time of Queen Anne extended to the reign of George IV by whose munificence she received comfort and support in her later Years. Died December 12th 1821, aged 108."*

"How about that?" I heard myself sniff involuntarily as I turned towards my mother's gravestone, and my mouth moved silently as I read.

Lottie Pye
1901 – 2009
"Time Measured with Stones"
I'll tell you no stories.
A story is almost certainly a lie.
Only this -
I was born of the sea
A child of the tides.
I was a mother, too briefly.
Living long enough to regret what I could not undo,
I stopped time
But never learned how to turn back the clock.

Jenny crouched to lay her small bouquet at the bottom of the stone. I thought she might say something but it seemed we both saw the words for what they were.

"I should have come earlier," I said at last.

Rubbing her hands, she cupped them together and blew into the small hole between her thumbs. "You came. That's what's important."

"There was such a long time when I might have got to know her." The dates stared back at me. "Years, after my father died."

Jenny slipped an icy hand into mine. Apart from the odd shake of a hand, it was the first human contact I could remember for a considerable period of time. I squeezed it gratefully. "You're freezing."

She hopped from one foot to the other. "Stupid really. I should have brought some gloves."

"We're not used to the sea air. Let's go inside."

"Don't you want some time on your own?"

"I've seen what I came for."

With a crunch of gravel, Jenny stepped backwards. I saw that she was holding her mobile phone out in front of her at an angle.

"What are you doing?" I asked.

"A trick your mother taught me: I'm stopping time." She thumbed more buttons and, satisfied, held the image of my mother's gravestone up for inspection. "There. You might want to read it again later."

Relieved to feel the slight increase in temperature inside the church, I felt a painful burning as my cheeks and ears thawed. Jenny appeared to have taken charge, locating the churchwarden who was speaking to an out-doorsy American couple, dressed optimistically in matching checked shorts and hiking boots.

"And here we have a very fine example of an oak roodscreen

dating back to 1480. I think you'll agree the carvings are exquisite." She raised a finger on seeing Jenny. "Excuse me, one moment…"

"I didn't mean to interrupt," Jenny apologised.

"I hope you and your grandfather found what you were looking for."

"Yes, thanks. Amazing, the other headstone, isn't it?"

"And all true, so they say."

"I was wondering, do you know anyone who might have known Lottie Pye?"

"Why yes, I do, actually," she replied. "I often visited her at St Leonard's."

"St Leonard's?"

"The nursing home where she lived for the last ten years of her life. They looked after her beautifully."

I hadn't expected to feel a pang of guilt. I stepped forward. "Perhaps there's somewhere we could have a cup of tea and a chat?"

"If you can give me quarter of an hour, I finish at noon. I'm very partial to a Starbucks. There's one just down the road if you turn right. I'll meet you there if you like." She left us to resume her tour.

"My idea of hell," I muttered dismally.

"I'll wait for the drinks." Jenny offered as we rested our elbows on the rounded counter beyond the tills. She glanced over her shoulder at Monica who was seated at the table we had reserved, wedged between two pushchairs laden with plastic bags and whose occupants were kicking their legs competitively. "Go and be nice."

"I'm not sure I remember how."

Sliding into a faux-leather seat too shallow for my bulk, I had the feeling of being trapped, but said to my beaming companion, "It's very kind of you to spare us some of your time."

"My pleasure. I was terribly fond of your mother." She clasped the straps of her handbag which was resting awkwardly in her lap, and sat with her knees pressed tightly together.

"Had you known her long?"

"Let me see." The pointed tip of her finger applied to her lips suggested careful calculation. "I was there for her one hundredth birthday, so I'd say - well, it must be about nine years."

"Nine years!"

"Sadly, I never met your father."

"Here we are." Bending her knees, straight-backed, Jenny lowered a laden tray onto the table.

"What's this?" I indicated to the corrugated red cardboard cups. "No cups and saucers?"

Jenny crouched down to pick up a stray squeaky toy. Both squirming children reached, grabbing. One of the mothers broke off from her conversation to say, "I'll take that. It's Henry's." The other child began to grizzle, a sound that threatened to turn into a fully-fledged tantrum.

"These are the Christmas cups," our friend, the churchwarden was enthusing, as if they were as traditional as candles at Midnight Mass. "I think they're rather jolly."

Jenny sighed at the sight of my face. "I'll see if they'll let you have a mug."

"I'd prefer a cup and saucer..."

"You asked for Tall," she said, over her shoulder. "Tall comes in a mug."

Monica and I were left alone to wince at each other, our backs uncomfortably straight. Moments later, after side-stepping through an obstacle course of Christmas packages, Jenny took her place at the table. "I had to tell them who you are to get this."

"I'm the customer," I said sulkily. "Not that it seems to count for much these days."

With a swift upending movement, she decanted my drink without spilling a drop, and prompted, "You're welcome," drawing attention to my bad manners. Jenny turned to Monica. "So, where were we?"

"I was telling your grandfather that I met his mother just before she turned one hundred." I glanced at Jenny whose mouth was itching to break into a smile. "That was when she moved to the home."

"She lived on her own up until then?" The prospect of relinquishing my own independence was already weighing on my mind, like an ever-present threat of blackmail.

The response came in a tone that was one of surprise. "Ever since your father died!" She leaned forwards conspiratorially. "She said she didn't miss her little bungalow, but I think you always do, don't you? You have to leave so many memories behind. She once told me her life was in boxes."

Jenny nodded knowingly. "Well, she wasn't wrong there!"

"Did she talk about her family?" I asked.

"Oh yes. She had your photos in a lovely double frame on her bedside table. Where she could keep an eye on you, she said." Monica sipped, leaving the trace of a foam moustache on her upper lip. "She spoke about your father often. He sounded like a fine man. Never feeling sorry for himself or taking no for an answer. And she spoke about you, of course."

I raised my eyebrows, interested to learn what she'd had to say, almost too keen to reinforce my original opinion of her. "Really?"

"Very proud of her James, she was. It was politics, wasn't it? I have to say, I'm surprised we've never met before. Such a shame there was no family at the funeral."

I bristled at the implication of criticism. "Then she can't have told you very much." From Jenny's fiery glance, I knew that I must have spoken gruffly. I deliberately softened my tone. "I'm afraid I never knew my mother. My parents

259

separated when I was very young, and I was brought up by my father. Not the man you were referring to."

The conversation at the next table stopped. Monica blinked. "Oh, I see…"

"In fact, I've only started to get to know her recently. Through her work."

I could tell the poor lady was clamming up, as if considering the possibility that the woman she had visited for the past nine years had been an imposter. "Her work?"

"She was a photographer."

"Is that what she did? She never spoke about herself."

"But she gave the impression she knew me well?" I examined the toes of my freshly-polished shoes.

"She was never short of news…"

With sadness, I said, "I can assure you, she knew very little about me."

"Apart from your letters," Jenny piped up. "The ones you wrote to your father. She had those."

"They stopped in the late Fifties."

Monica was clearly in denial. "But she told me all about your great friend. Sebastian, wasn't it?"

"Sebastian?" I asked. That was not the name of my *great friend*, as she put it.

"The two of you were at university together!" She leant over and took my hand, as if it were possible I had forgotten. "So sad when they insist on drinking. In a way, I think it was for the best that you couldn't persuade him to come home from Morocco with you."

"Dear lady." I withdrew my hand, searching for a title for the story that had familiar undertones. "My mother must have been confused."

The mothers at the next table began to loop woollen scarves around their necks and zip their children into layers of Arctic clothing. Glancing at her watch, Monica clearly saw an opportunity for escape. "Goodness, look at the time! I don't know where it goes once Advent begins." Turning to the mothers, she scraped back her chair. "You're overloaded. Can I help you with anything?"

After the commotion of replacement customers shoe -horning themselves - and the results of their compulsive shopping expedition - into place had died down, I allowed myself an indulgent sigh. "I don't imagine you tell your life story to someone sent by the church to visit. My father used to say that you deserve the lies you're told."

"That rings a bell." Jenny flicked open her mobile phone and called up the photograph she had taken of my mother's gravestone. "Here it is. *A story is almost certainly a lie.*" She looked at me intently. "You don't think your mother was confused, do you?"

"At her age, perhaps. On the other hand, she might have just borrowed a few characters from Evelyn Waugh. Ha!" I laughed without humour, the noise taking me by surprise. "I don't know if I prefer the idea that I was a fictional character in my mother's life, or that she deliberately span a yarn to satisfy someone else's curiosity."

Jenny looked at me blankly. "I don't get it."

"Evelyn Waugh mixed in the same circles as your young photographer friend, Beaton. And he wrote a very fine book called *Brideshead Revisited* about a young man named Sebastian Flyte."

"I saw the film!" Jenny said excitedly, holding up one hand. "He was played by Ben Whishaw."

"And who was I played by, I wonder?" I asked.

"I forget. But Michael Gambon was very good as your father."

"Typical! Always outshone by him."

The snort of high-pitched laughter from the table closest

to us grated and we found ourselves blinking at each other, wide-eyed.

"Come along, Granddad." Grinning, Jenny offered me a hand to extract me from the chair. "Let's get out of here. We can't come to Brighton and not take a look at the sea."

Bracing ourselves against the icicled wind, we walked along West Street which seemed to offer the most direct route to the front. Chin to chest, Jenny spoke through the crimson wool of her scarf, the red of her cheeks visible above it. There was a fine fall of white splinters that couldn't quite call itself snow. "I'm glad it's a black and white day. It feels like one of your mother's photographs."

"There's not much of Regency Brighton left."

"There's enough. You just have to look through the alley-ways between the houses to get a sense of it."

"I barely recognise the place," I said as we were deposited rudely onto a busy junction, confronted by diesel fumes and the smells of burnt sugar and stale frying oil. Despite this assault on the senses, I felt a small but perceptible change as I caught a glimpse of the waves; a calming, a settling of old scores. Something not unlike peace. After braving the expanse of bellowing traffic on King's Road, Jenny and I found ourselves above the beach between the bustle and neon glare of Brighton Pier and the shipwreck of the old West Pier, silhouetted against what little remained of the pallid winter sun.

"I've never been here before," Jenny admitted, crunching forwards towards the lonely remains of the pillars, while I opted for the solid footpath.

"Never been to Brighton!"

"My Dad likes his beaches to have sand. And to be hot." Jenny turned to me, her hair lashing her face but her eyes shining.

"On a day like today, I have to say: he has a point."

"How long is it since you skimmed a stone?"

"Oh, I don't think my legs are up to that. You go ahead."

But as she was crouching down on her haunches, she was distracted by a flurry in the sky: "Look!"

The heavens appeared to change their hue as a swirling shoal cartwheeled over the wreckage, fluid and ghost-like in motion, turning the sunset from rose pink to black to shades of grey. The swarm dispersed and regrouped, spinning synchronised shapes out of air like a Spirograph.

"Starlings," I said, a memory awakening in the recesses of my mind. "Now that's something I remember. It must have been here."

The memory said, "No, son, we can't see your mother today."

"But, Sir! Why not? She lives here, doesn't she?"

It bared its sharpened teeth. "Because we haven't been invited, that's why!"

My father had been stubborn, just as Jenny had suggested. That stubbornness had cost me a mother, and I was beginning to feel cheated. Cheated out of knowing someone extraordinary.

34 - LOTTIE'S STORY

BRIGHTON, 1918

"Whatever you're selling, I don't want it," Alfie's mother barked as she pulled the door inwards, looking more wearied than annoyed to be called away from the laundry she took in to supplement her widow's pension.

"How are you, Mrs West?" I asked, holding myself stiffly. "It's me: Lottie."

She blinked into the daylight to confirm my unlikely announcement. "Well, you've got a cheek! Abandoning your poor mother after everything she's done for you. Do you know the worry you've put that woman through?"

I hung my head and waited for the tirade to end.

"So what do you want?" she snapped, suspicious.

"I wondered if you've had any news about Alfie."

"News is what you dread, my girl. You come knocking, I expect the worst. Do you understand?"

I understood. I understood it didn't mean that you'd be let off the hook for not going knocking.

"Three of them: gone. Mrs Barnes had her son back last week, though he's not the same son she sent away. I'm told most of them are needed to stay on in this *army of occupation* of theirs. We're the last ones to be told what's going on."

Thinking what a fierce mother-in-law Mrs West would have made, I dared venture, "Hasn't Alfie written to you?"

"Now, why would he go writing to his mother when she can't read?"

"So you've not heard from him since he left? Surely…?"

"Surely my Jack could read them to me? Or my Billy? Oh, but hang on a minute. They've taken the lot of them. May they rot." She stepped over the threshold to spit on the pavement.

Alfie's home had been a noisy place, potent atmosphere charged with the honest sweat of a husband and five boys who had achieved varying degrees of manhood. Now Mrs West was alone, the house damp with the cold, and still. Beyond her, I saw the row of empty pegs in the hall.

I offered the only news I had: Robert Irving's sighting of Alfie in France.

"Do you know how long soldiers survive at the front?" Her tone was cynical, unimpressed. "Do me a favour: hold your tongue if you can't offer me more hope than that."

"I'm sorry to have troubled you," I muttered, stepping backwards. Coming had been a mistake.

"Oi! Where do you think you're off to?" Hands on hips, Mrs West moved aside. "I'll not have you telling that mother of yours I wasn't hospitable. Go through to the kitchen." It wasn't so much an invitation as an order.

The room was in half-darkness, the embers a dim glow, the contents of the coal bucket reduced to a thin layer of dust.

"I almost forgot," I said, reaching for the twist of paper I had brought. The habit of picking up fragments of coal on my travels hadn't deserted me. That morning I'd had a lucky find: a couple of pristine lumps lying in the gutter.

"Stick 'em on," she instructed. "All this advice to use less coal, less bread…" She shook her head, sniffed briskly. "Don't stand on ceremony. Sit yourself down."

I perched, my bruises still too fresh to have a colour; my grazes tender.

"Properly!"

Obeying, I could feel the mark of every button, each bruised vertebra, against the slatted back of the wooden chair.

"That's better! So tell me, how's your mother?"

I winced. "She's well, thank you."

Picking up the kettle using a once-white cloth scorched caramel in patches, Mrs West added water to the pot. "We'll let that take. And old Josie? She's a character, that one."

"I don't know what Ma would do without her. And as for Felicity -"

"Now there's a turn round. Common whore to police-woman!" Mrs West shook her head. "If it were anyone else, folks wouldn't have stood for it."

On another day, or with another opponent, I might have voiced my loyalties. Now, biting my tongue, I accepted the weak tea that was offered. Mrs West took none for herself. I couldn't see another cup.

"So, you've come home dragging your tail between your legs."

She thought I was a failure, and that was fine. Perhaps I was. Instead, betrayed by the sea, my decision had been made for me. "Actually, I'm just down for Christmas."

Mrs West raised her eyebrows. "Still think you're too good for us, do you?"

I wanted to ask how she could bear it: the empty sterile house, the waiting, the ghosts.

"There's no work for me here," I said.

"Plenty of work." She shook her head knowingly. "But you, you always thought you were different."

Not thought: told. I had been brought up believing it. I wanted to escape that mean little kitchen and the woman who had suffered so much that she was entitled to say exactly what she thought. I sat there for Alfie's sake, holding back tears that were prickling in the corners of my eyes, but she would go on: "Why people can't accept what they are is beyond me. Tom Sayers was the best man to come out of Brighton. Barely went to school, but he made the most of what he had. World Heavyweight Champion. One hundred thousand people turned out for his send off, trailing all the way from Highgate to Tottenham Court Road..."

"One hundred thousand," I repeated, stupidly. Daddy had loved to quote statistics from Tom's life. I could have reminded Mrs West that Tom Sayers moved to London at the age of thirteen, where he worked, fought and died. Brighton spat him out but they still took credit for him in the way men who never play football tell you they 'won' a match on a Saturday afternoon. Was it wrong to want to better yourself, whether it was with your face or your fists? But my chance was slipping away, the future I had carved for myself now as uncertain as my past. If I visited the gypsy fortune-teller on the pier, I could only see her predicting a shameful return and the likes of Mrs West telling anyone willing to listen that I had got what was coming to me all along.

35 - LOTTIE'S STORY

BRIGHTON TO LONDON, 1918-19

Delaying the inevitable, two weeks rolled into three before my return to London - and the threats of the *Daily Mail* which loomed large.

Meanwhile, in our house of women, we balanced on kitchen chairs to string paper chains made out of coloured scraps from the corners of the ceiling. In other households the much-anticipated first Christmas of peacetime was on hold. In truth, only a few lucky men - mainly the injured - had returned from the war. Stranded, many were still awaiting transport. Reunions with wives and sweethearts and meetings with children not yet seen, were delayed. Letters told how sick the men were of French soil, how they longed for old Blighty. Some wrote of mutinies after news that a return to England might not mean a return home, their skills required elsewhere. This was not what they had signed up for, or what wives had been given to understand.

Knowing we weren't waiting for the bell above the shop door to rattle and a man in khaki to appear, kitbag in hand, ours was the table many brought their woes to. (It was widely considered that, by leaving, I had forfeited any claim I might have had on Alfie.) I lost count of cups of tea poured, words of sympathy muttered, while my hidden bruises faded like a sunset from plum to yellow.

When I left, I allowed Ma to send me on my way with one of her pies: "In case you should go hungry." Harry had a shopping list for me: I was to send him a postcard of the guards at Buckingham Palace, ask Charlie Chaplin for his autograph and take a photograph of Tower Bridge opening for a big ship. For Josie, it was simpler: an awkward embrace and, "Don't be a stranger." Only Felicity seemed to instinctively understand that I was carrying a weight I hadn't wanted to burden them with. The words that I had intended remained unspoken. "Never be afraid to come home," she whispered as she kissed my cheek and then, laughing, dabbed at the stain of lipstick.

I didn't admit that, without the hope Mr Parker had provided, there was one less reason to return. And thinking of how John and I had parted, I had begun to persuade myself that my future lay in London.

Pulling into the station, the carriage window framed a view of him eagerly elbowing his way through the jostling crowd, one hand raised above collective head-height. I allowed myself to smile, glad that I hadn't rejected him out of loyalty to his mother.

"Charlotte!" After taking my bags, he lent me his hand as I stepped gingerly down the steps and onto the platform. "You look well, I must say. The sea air has done you good."

His talk of the sea reminded me that I felt older than when I last saw him those few short weeks ago. "It's good to be home." *Home!* I had said it. I hooked my hand under his elbow, letting him steer me through the commotion, towards the exit.

"There's someone I'd like you to meet."

"Alright." I hugged his arm to me, imagining some old school friend or family acquaintance. Perhaps cousin Edward who had failed to show.

But, his face reddening with pleasure, I followed John's gaze to a girl standing by the barrier. Dressed simply in a cloche hat and an elegant three-quarter-length coat with a fur collar, she raised her hand in excited greeting, not quite a wave, and placed two fingers on her parted lips, not quite a kiss. I tried to still my breath, aware that the conversation I had been scripting wouldn't be taking place. Instead, what should have been a private scene was about to be played out in front of strangers.

"Charlotte, I'd like you to meet my fiancée, Elizabeth." Putting down my bag, John let my hand fall from the crook of his elbow, turned to face me and replaced it with hers. The hand on his arm was displayed in such a way that it was impossible not to notice the diamond on her ring finger. And there she was, her sincere and smiling eyes appealing to me for approval.

"Do call me Bets," she gushed. "I know we're going to be the best of friends. J-J's told me all about you - don't worry, I know absolutely everything! He even told about the silly little crush he had on you. Of course, now I've met you in person I can forgive him for that."

My mouth was as dry as dust. "Engaged!" I said with all the humour I could muster. "But I've only been gone for three weeks."

We never know what we want until it's taken away. Sometimes I think we only decide we want something when we understand that it can't be ours.

"Isn't it just the maddest thing?" She laughed, hugging his arm to her, as I had done moments earlier. "I've literally been swept off my feet."

I wanted to say that John had a habit of doing that; that his mother couldn't have lost a minute after I left, issuing invitations to eligible debutantes.

"How did the two of you meet?" I asked as we moved

towards the exit and Elizabeth took me by the other arm, a barrier separating me from John.

"It was Christmas Eve, wasn't it, J-J?" She deferred to him, as if there was a chance she might be mistaken. "A party at my Aunt's. She was determined to make up for all those miserable Christmases we've had to suffer."

John opened the front passenger-door of the car and Elizabeth slid in, tucking her feet delicately after her. While she was rearranging the skirt of her coat, John's eyes met mine briefly, his clouding with confusion. "That leaves you in the back, I'm afraid. Would you mind awfully?"

"Not at all." I managed to smile, determined not to let him see the pain of my humiliation. Taking my place behind Elizabeth I looked down at my lap where my hands lay, lifeless.

I was glad to have the sound of the traffic - the bustle of horses and trams - hoping the need for conversation would be redundant. John's eyes were fixed firmly on the road ahead.

Oblivious to any atmosphere, Elizabeth swivelled and rested her elbow on the back of her seat, shouting over her shoulder, "I nearly forgot: well done, you! We went to see your photographs at the National Portrait Gallery."

Her words filled me with foreboding. "I had no idea they were already on display."

"They're monster good. Johnny and Mrs Miller are terribly proud, you clever old thing!"

"Yes, you dark horse." John's voice was a poor mimic of Elizabeth's enthusiasm. "If you hadn't told Mother about the name you used to go by, we shouldn't have known they were yours."

"To have won, out of all of those people! How does it feel to be virtually famous?" Elizabeth's laughter a silvery arpeggio, I forced a smile.

"Charlotte's been famous in some circles for quite some time," John replied, his tone noticeably frosty.

"Well, of course, I know that, Silly!" Elizabeth gushed. "But it's different to be recognised for your own photographs. At least, I think so."

I realised it would be impossible not to like her, which was probably the worst thing about the situation. And there she was, in front of me, her fingers alighting on John's arm.

"I know! We should go and see them now. Oh, let's!"

"I'd prefer to wash the journey off my face first," I protested.

"Nonsense," John said, swerving to change lanes. "You must be dying to see how they look."

Entering the gallery's marbled entrance hall, the interior was full of the hiss of joined-up whispers and the click of heels. Elizabeth led our party triumphantly, turning to make sure we were following close behind, hers the only uninhibited voice. "This way!"

Each echo had an echo of its own.

I should have felt excited; instead I felt sick to my stomach. My winning entry was at the centre of the exhibition. John stood stiffly by my side, hands behind his back, while Elizabeth was distracted by someone from her circle. To an observer we would have appeared companionable. Only I knew that he wouldn't look at me. He read the gilded inscription, "Lottie Pye," shaking his head.

"Who told you?" I asked.

"Robert Irving. He thought I should know."

Of course. I had refused him; this was his revenge.

"Hardly in the name of art, was it?" John spat. "*This* is art."

"Actually." My eyes stinging with tears, I held my head level. "It was only by having those photographs taken that I was able to negotiate time in a darkroom." An admission that I hadn't known where the photographs would end up would have meant appearing naïve. That, on top of everything else, would have been too much to bear.

"You only needed to ask, surely you understood that?" His

voice was a low staccato. "I blame my mother. She encouraged you."

I heard his sharp intake of breath.

"The girl," John said disbelievingly, peering closer still. "It can't be!"

There was little point in denial: "Martha modelled for me."

"Does she know she's here on display?"

I let down my guard, utterly miserable. "She had to leave before I could tell her. I had no idea I'd win. I only wanted to know if I was good enough."

John's powerful silence made me long for his criticism. Finally he said, "I wouldn't have found it so difficult to stomach if you had modelled for this sort of work. You've made her look quite beautiful. She's almost… ethereal."

"Divine, isn't she?" Pushing between us, Elizabeth shrugged with pleasure. "Everything else is so obvious: wives and fetes and sandcastles." She leaned closer to kiss John on the cheek. "I'm sorry to drag you away, but it's one o'clock, darling, and I need to be at the theatre by half-past."

"What are you going to see?" I asked, relieved by the change of subject.

She laughed. "A packed house, I hope!"

"Elizabeth is an actress," John explained. "She's starring in *Peter Pan* at the New Theatre."

"Oh, you do exaggerate! I've got the tiniest role."

"Nonsense. You're marvellous." He puckered his lips to kiss her and then turned to me, confirming my suspicion that this display was for my benefit. "She outshines everyone else."

"You see." She pushed him aside playfully and leaned towards me conspiratorially, cupping one hand over my ear. "He says things like that and I'm utterly helpless." Then, as if forgetting me entirely, Elizabeth turned back to John, fawning. "Actually, darling, I almost forgot to tell you. I'm going to audition for a fantastic new play by a young chap called Noel

Coward next week. He's a dead cert for the next big thing."

Once again, I was being punished. Mrs Miller hadn't arranged for John to meet Elizabeth. He had done it all on his own.

36 - LOTTIE'S STORY

LONDON, 1919

"Why don't you go in," John suggested, passing my bags to Mrs Bellamy, his hand already gripping the polished scroll of the banister as her shoulders dropped under the weight. "I have some correspondence I must finish," he said over his shoulder, taking two steps at a time. "Business."

The change in atmosphere immediately apparent, John had broken his habit of greeting his mother before attending to anything else. Mrs Bellamy returned my questioning gaze with a bland smile of denial, but little escaped her. She bent her knees and put both bags down. "Excuse me, Miss. I'll just rest my arms a minute."

"Has Martha sent news?" I asked, exploring a different thread.

"There's no news about the brother. Terrible business, if you ask me. She's to stay with her mother for the foreseeable."

"You must be exhausted, running the house single-handed!"

"I can't complain. I had a half-day off for Christmas shopping and another at New Year."

"I'd like to write to Martha if you have an address for her.

Oh, that reminds me. I have something for you," I said, delving inside one of the bags and retrieving the pie, wrapped in layers of greaseproof paper. "It's one of my mother's pies. She's famous for them in our part of the world."

Mrs Bellamy raised her eyebrows as though asking what need she would have for a pie when she spent all day in the kitchen. "You must thank her for me," she said in a forced voice with no pretence of gratitude. "I'll put your luggage in your room and turn down the bed, Miss."

"Oh, I don't know if I'll be staying -"

We had been here before. "While you make your mind up." Mrs Bellamy turned towards the staircase.

Looking at my reverse image in the hall mirror I smoothed my hair and then tapped lightly on the drawing room door.

"Come!"

Mrs Miller was reclining on the sofa, a fringed tartan blanket covering her legs.

"Is that you, Charlotte?" she said weakly, a handkerchief in one hand.

"John didn't tell me you were unwell!" I said, hurrying over to perch beside her.

"I'm fine," Mrs Miller insisted, sitting upright. "I've had a slight cold that went to my chest. It was two days before I could persuade Mrs Bellamy I wasn't dying of this terrible flu. Needless to say it was a perfectly miserable Christmas. John met you from the train, I take it?"

"Yes." I forced a smile. "He's gone upstairs to finish some work."

Sitting upright, she grasped my forearm with a cold hand. "So he introduced you to this fiancée of his."

"Yes." I determined not to allow my hurt and confusion to show. "She seems lovely."

Mrs Miller released me, laughing dismissively. "I've never heard such utter tripe! You're no fool, Charlotte. I want you to get rid of her."

I was taken aback by her bluntness. "I beg your pardon?"

"It would be more... palatable coming from you. I know what this is all about." She brushed my protests aside. "You've refused John and he's taken up with the next pretty little thing that came along."

"It isn't as simple as that."

"You need only use your charms..."

"No!" I said firmly, then lowered my voice again. "You told me I wasn't good enough for your son, in not so many words -"

"If I recall, what I actually said -"

"Hear me out, if you will, Mrs Miller. You needn't worry: John believes you. And that's without knowing the half of it. So, you see, nothing I can say would do any good."

Mrs Miller regarded me from an angle, blinking. "I think you'd better start from the beginning, my dear."

Keen to learn if there was any truth in what Robert Irving had suggested about her motives, I spared Mrs Miller little. "The evening Mr Irving came to dinner - Armistice Day - his son recognised me. At first I thought it was from my advertising work, but then he told me my photographs had made it all the way to the front line. In rather large numbers."

"If I'm to understand correctly, you are talking about some," she winced delicately, "of Freddie's less artistic shots."

"There *were* no artistic shots. But I think you knew that, didn't you?"

Swan-necked, she said, "I think we both did, my dear."

"I refused Robert because he made it clear what sort of girl he thought I was. So, obviously, he's made it his business..." It struck me that to include Robert in the dinner invitation might have been part of Mrs Miller's plan.

She tightened her mouth and made fists of her hands against a backdrop of tartan wool. "The spoiled brat! Never could bear to be told 'no'. Why are men such children?"

"But that's not all. The photographic competition -"

Mrs Miller was suddenly animated. "Yes, I *can't* understand *why* you didn't tell me. And you chose to use that perfectly dreadful name after we specifically -"

"*That* name," I interrupted, "Is how I'm known in Brighton. I wanted to make the people who care about me proud."

"Well!" Mrs Miller protested. "After everything I've done to help you!"

"And I *am* grateful." My voice caught in my throat. "Extremely grateful. Which is why I'm sorry that I will prove to be an embarrassment to you." I hung my head.

"Don't be absurd. Things like this blow over quicker than you think they will - although I'd like to give young Freddie a piece of my mind. You're talented, my dear. I've seen the way you unlock people's emotions. That's rarer than you might think."

Shaking off her compliments, I forced myself to continue. "Tomorrow, I must go to the offices of the *Daily Mail* and tell them that I have no idea how two photographs came to be entered in the competition under my name. And they will print a story saying that I attempted to defraud them."

Mrs Miller's brows knitted together in confusion. "Two entries?"

"There were two of my photographs in the final ten, both submitted under the name of Lottie Pye. I entered one - the winning entry. I thought my tutor must have entered the other on my behalf. That it meant he was back from France..."

"So that explains your hasty departure! Well?"

I let my head drop. "It can't have been Mr Parker."

"Oh, my dear. That handsome man. You were terribly fond of him, weren't you?" She patted my knee distractedly. "Well, the most straight-forward solution seems to be for me to say that, as your patron, I entered the second photograph on your behalf. I will say it was a simple misunderstanding. That I did it to surprise you."

"I can't let you do that. Your name will appear on the front of the newspaper."

"My dear, I know people who *pay* to get their names in the paper."

"I don't know."

She placed both of her hands on top of mine. "Well, I do. In fact, I insist. I won't allow you to undo our hard work! Who knows? The paper might be entitled to press charges."

I looked at her in disbelief. "You don't -?"

"But I'm afraid I do. There may be more than embarrassment at stake, Charlotte. Think about it."

I could do little else.

Later, I found John sitting at the grand piano in a haze of smoke, eyes half closed, cigarette dangling. A tumbler of deep amber liquid within reach at one end of the keyboard and an overflowing ashtray at the other, he was torturing himself over the complicated rhythms of a piece of American dance-music.

"Damn!" He hit a minor chord in frustration and, taking the cigarette between two fingers, threw back his head to drain his glass. "Charlotte! I didn't hear you." With a clumsy sideways shuffle, he patted the stool in the expectation that, as I had done many times before, I would sit next to him. Although I would rather have avoided such close proximity, I complied, our elbows touching. "They call it *Syncopation Runs Riot*. Something's run riot, that's for sure. Drink?"

I brushed his offer aside before reflecting that, after a day of shocks, a nightcap might be a called for. "Actually, I think I'll change my mind."

"Whiskey?" Without waiting for a response, he lifted the decanter and poured a generous measure into another crystal tumbler.

"Why not?" I held out my hand to receive the glass.

"Why indeed?" John clinked and then drained his. I had

never seen him drinking so hard and with so little pleasure. He didn't look like a man newly in love. I began to fear for Elizabeth. She didn't deserve to be used as a weapon.

Taking a nervous sip, I felt the whiskey do its work, warmth flowing from cell to cell. John flexed his hands and returned his attention to the sheet music. With a determined overlapping of fingers, he played the same sequence time and time again, experimenting with emphasis on different notes.

"See! I can't quite get it right."

"I liked Bets," I ventured into uncomfortable territory.

"Did you, now?" He slurred his words furiously. "So do I."

I attempted to keep things light. "I should hope so too, since marriage is on the cards."

"Completely on the cards," he said to an accompaniment of the opening notes of *Three Blind Mice*.

The warmth from the whiskey had reached my stomach. "I must say." I allowed myself what I judged to be a careless laugh. "I was so surprised by your announcement, I completely forgot to congratulate you."

"Not to worry, old thing. I rather surprised myself. Still, never too late." Seeing John lean towards me playfully, lips pursed, I turned my head away. He straightened up, returning his hands to the keyboard. The moment passed without further mention, except that his voice harboured an immature sulk. "Of course, Mother hates her."

"Naturally. She didn't choose her." But I was in no mood for consoling John. Having said what was expected, what I really wanted to know was how he could he cast his feelings for me aside so readily.

"She thinks we can all just go right back to the way things were."

I nodded. "It's high time I found a place of my own. If I were in Elizabeth's shoes, I would think it very strange that I'm still living under the same roof as you. Especially given what you've told her about us."

John looked startled. "I was talking about the war!"

"I see."

He stormed ahead. "Mother thinks we can pick up where we left off, as if these last four years have meant nothing." He shook his head. "Do you think we did enough?"

"You did your bit."

"But I didn't fight! Here I am, contemplating marriage, and all I can see is that confounded poster of a child asking, 'Daddy, what did you do in the war?'"

"What about me? I knitted a few socks! At least you'll be able to tell your children how you kept guard over St Paul's night after night."

"While half the men I was at school with are dead!" A bitter gleam surfaced in John's eyes and the edges of his mouth twitched.

"You can't think that way. You only need to feel guilty if you don't go on and do something with your life."

"Oh yes? And what would you suggest, Miss Lottie Pye? You and your..." His face contorted with a drunken sneer. "... dirty photographs."

Hurt, I stood and faced him over the top of the piano. "John, I know it's the drink talking, but that's unfair. There was only ever the once, and I was misled."

"The once?" John looked confused. "I presumed. That is, I thought..."

"You could have waited to ask. But three weeks was too long, wasn't it?" My stomach now a tight ball of glowing embers, it was the alcohol that gave me the confidence to berate him like this.

Rearranging his mouth, he refuelled his own glass. "Have another."

I blocked the neck of the decanter with one flat hand. "No, thank you. I won't."

An impasse reached, we remained in silence, my head

turned towards the door, John looking in the opposite direction. It struck me what a photographer might have made of that tableau, perhaps taken out of context, and how they might explain it afterwards. *I walked in on two lovers arguing, the man drunk, the woman aloof.* And then I felt foolish. John had always behaved as a gentleman. I had nothing to be angry with him about, no claim on him.

"I should say goodnight." I turned towards the door. "It's late."

A sharp note was struck. "Mother tells me you've got yourself into another muddle." It appeared that certain confidences were still being shared. "Says she'll sort it out tomorrow."

I paused with one hand on the door handle. "She's offered."

"I'd let her, if I were you. It was probably her doing in the first place."

The possibility had crossed my mind. Mrs Miller had unfulfilled ambitions that weren't satisfied by matchmaking for her son and entertaining polite company. She was keen to be acknowledged as the patron of a successful artist. "If I do that, your name might end up in print."

"Who could possibly want to read about me?" He laughed mirthlessly and returned to his punishing practice.

37 - LOTTIE'S STORY

LONDON, 1919

There is much to be said for notoriety - provided you don't give a damn what people think. In Brighton it had always been understood that God would forgive you long before the neighbours.

When the *Daily Mail* couldn't print their shock headlines, they took advantage of material that came their way from an anonymous source. Material that, whilst it didn't suggest I was a liar, brought greater shame on the family as far as Ma was concerned. She would never have believed I was a cheat but she had no option but to believe what was there in black and white.

The journalist had no doubt thought himself clever, comparing me to my winning photograph: a composite Jekyll-and-Hyde personality. He revealed that Lottie Pye was none other than London-based model, Charlotte Lavashay. But he went further, writing that Lottie Pye's navel was as famous as her face in certain quarters. There was no criticism. Although he refrained from suggesting that stripping off was every girl's patriotic duty, a discreet Union Jack had been printed across one corner of my photograph.

Distance didn't protect me from Ma's brittle recriminations, dictated to Felicity at length. It was best I stayed in London because she couldn't bear to set eyes on me. I felt pity for Felicity, having to put pen to paper when it was she who had told me never to be afraid to come home. And if that was Ma's verdict, I could only imagine Mrs West's reaction.

I had rarely felt so alone.

In the back of his Regent Street studio, Freddie creased the newspaper neatly, as was his obsession, and handed it back to me. "It's not so bad." There was no hint of embarrassment. "I must say, they've used one of my best shots of you."

I threw the paper down. "This is no joke, Freddie. What I do affects people besides myself." My expression was accusing. "After those other photographs were reproduced, how do I know this isn't your doing?"

He held his hands out in front of him. "You flatter me. I wish I *had* thought of it! It's not every day a business receives free advertising. Mind you, if you ask me, they've missed the real scandal."

I drew myself in, folding my arms. "And what would that be?"

"Isn't it obvious?" The shake of his head and forced exhalation of breath implied I was being extremely naive. "You're a professional, and yet you entered a competition for amateurs."

"I've had a few photographs printed, that's all!"

"You've been published, my dear."

"But it was you who said the locals didn't count!"

"Yes, about that. Remind me." He took me by the arm conspiratorially. "How was it you were introduced to me? *Model and photographer* if I recall."

He was right, I realised. Worse might follow. Having lost the moral high-ground, I snatched my arm away. "The word 'professional' implies profit. I was hardly making any money from it."

"And your portraits for Mrs Miller's circle. All *gratis*,

I presume?" As I opened my mouth to make further futile protest, he cut in, "Don't worry. Your secret's safe with me. On the bright side, you're in more demand than ever. Take advantage, darling. Put your glad rags on and get out there."

Sighing, I relented. "You're right."

"What do you say we go to the gallery together? I need to know if I should start worrying about the competition."

I entered the exhibition hall for the second time with growing anxiety. What if there was a series of articles? If the gossip columns took an interest? But when I saw how my work had been adorned, my feet refused to move. Tucked into its gilt frame were photographs and postcards. Those Mr Parker had taken in his Brighton studio and those Freddie had taken in his Regent Street studio. The montage had become a collage.

"Oh, my." As I bowed my head in shame, Freddie raised his eyebrows and did what I could never have done. Very deliberately, he marched up to the photograph and removed the postcards one by one. Tapping the edges to square them against each other he handed them to a uniformed attendant. "Yours, I presume." Then he craned his slender neck towards me and called across the echoing expanse, "Darling, when are you going to get that famous navel of yours over here?"

Heads twisting sharply, fabric rustling, whispers of, "I say, isn't that…?" "I do believe…" "Well I never! It is, you know."

The old feeling came back to me.

'I'll thank you not to stare.'

'It's whether you want to get used to it, that's the question.'

I missed my daddy.

The idea of flight was almost overwhelming. A hat! If only I'd worn something with a wide brim.

I could see mouths moving, but couldn't process the words coming out of them. The stretch of polished floor separating me from Freddie seemed impossibly wide. He held both hands out to receive me, a parent encouraging his offspring to walk. My head held self-consciously high, somehow I found myself holding both of his hands.

"Ready?" he whispered, under the pretext of an embrace, then louder: "Now! Tell me all about this glorious creature of yours."

Behind us, the few people who had loitered at a safe distance were edging closer, a second row forming behind them. Freddie flared his eyes impatiently, demanding a performance. I couldn't afford to disappoint.

Knowing that, I began tentatively. "She's my sleeping princess. I wanted to give her a timeless quality, a relief from the pace of change." My voice wasn't nearly as polished as it should have been after a year in Chelsea; undone by my recent return to Brighton - or the longing for home that my image conveyed to me.

He nodded with a downwards twitch of his eyebrows. "Go on."

Perhaps I needed to refer to the issue of nudity, rather than ignore it. "And I particularly wanted to celebrate the female form."

"Because, of course, you've been photographed yourself, haven't you?"

"Many times."

"Do you think that being a woman photographer is an advantage?"

"Clients need to be confident in the photographer's ability to show them as they would like to be seen, especially if they are to reveal something that would normally be hidden - and I don't just mean the physical. So, yes: when photographing women, I think that being a woman gives me a huge advantage."

"And the idea of combining the two images? How did that come about?"

"I wanted to merge my subject with the landscape so it

appeared that she was growing from it. I couldn't simply look through a lens to capture the picture in my head. There was no option but to experiment."

"I must say, I'm particularly interested in your sheep? Can you tell me what they represent?"

I shrugged. "I'm sorry to disappoint you, but they're just ordinary sheep. Southdowns, if I'm not mistaken."

There was a trickle of restrained laughter behind us and Freddie turned to the audience - for that is what it had become. "Tell me, ladies! Who among you would be happy to let Miss Pye create an image of you like this? Hmmm? Is it something you would hang in the privacy of your own homes?"

Amid sceptical looks from the men present, there was a general murmur of consensus.

"You see, I'd like to know if there would be a market for this sort of work, were it to be available on a commercial basis."

"Yes." One lady stepped forward. Not a particularly young lady, not attractive in any conventional sense. But good bone structure, well-dressed, and with a certain self-awareness. I saw immediately how I would light her. "I'd be very keen."

"And, in your opinion, would you expect to pay more than the cost of an ordinary portrait?"

The woman shook her head as if there was no dispute. "More, most definitely. This is art."

Freddie inclined his head. "Madam, I apologise on behalf of humble portrait photographers everywhere."

"I meant no offence..."

"And, as you see, I have taken none."

He turned to me, his back to the audience. My ordeal was over. "Charlotte, I didn't lie when I said that you're more in demand than ever. However..." He glanced slyly behind him to ensure that no one was eavesdropping. "Several of our, shall we say, *preferred* clients have cancelled their instructions. I'll leave you to guess who they are. But this..." He faced my photograph and jabbed a finger at one of my sheep. "This is your future, my dear. Come and work with me. Not as a model, but as a photographer!"

For the first time that day, my smile was genuine. Unlike Mr Parker, who harboured artistic aspirations, Freddie only ever professed to be a businessman. If he saw profit, it meant there was a living in it for me.

"After her! Don't let your first client escape."

38 - SIR JAMES'S STORY

SHERE, 2009

"What do you think of this?" Jenny asked, handing me a cutting from *The Tatler*. It was a discreet advertisement, a flimsy piece of paper, only a couple of inches of column height. 'Lottie Pye Limited, Intimate Portraiture for Women.'"

It fluttered through my fingers and I gave chase. "Charmingly put. Strange she reverted to her maiden name, don't you think?"

"I expect she was making the most of the publicity from the competition. It's not often you're slapped all over the front page."

"Thankfully, no. There was a time I was afraid to step outside my own front door for fear another reporter would be waiting to pounce." I sighed, remembering my own headlines: *'Sir James Hastings Resigns Amid Rent Boy Scandal'. 'Calls for Sir James Hastings to be stripped of his title'. 'Disabled Groups Say Sir James Hastings Should Keep His Seat'.* I wasn't brave enough to demand to know how my personal life was relevant to the job. Instead I denied everything, not knowing that one of those photographers had enough evidence on a single reel of 35mm film to send my career down the swanny.

"I had my picture on the front page of the *Dorking Guardian* once," Jenny offered.

"What terrible crime did you commit?"

"When I was in the Brownies we were invited to Buckingham Palace. I thought we were going to meet the Queen, but it was just a long coach journey followed by a quick tour with a footman. The highlight was McDonalds."

"Still. Quite an honour."

"I stole an ashtray." She bit her lip and shrugged. "Still got it, actually."

"Were you caught?"

"No. It was just the right size to fit in my uniform pocket."

"Good girl. Stick to the golden rule."

Still looking over my shoulder at the cutting, Jenny said, "I'm beginning to see the likenesses between your life and your mother's."

"You mean that neither of us was a stranger to scandal!"

She shrugged dismissively. "Something like that."

"I'll say it so you don't have to: my mother took advantage of her headlines whilst I hid myself away." I sighed. "Now we've got that out the way, pass me another folder, will you?"

Jenny thrust out her arm impatiently. "There you go again. Why do you always think I'm criticising you?"

I accepted the incoming folder meekly. "You're right."

She hadn't run out of steam yet. "It makes it very difficult to have a conversation with you."

"I can see that." Duly chastised, I suddenly felt like laughing. "That was a criticism, though, wasn't it?"

Jenny glared, then, with an exasperated shake of her head, relented.

Forgiven, I opened the flap and immediately recognised the face staring back at me. "Here we are: my father." I passed the photograph to Jenny. "Looking very dapper."

"The size of that moustache!"

"He looked like a devil, didn't he?" Somehow, I was strangely proud of that fact. If there was one thing I was discovering, it was that I had had two very interesting parents. There is no crime worse than being dull.

When you're young, the circumstances you live in are normal as far as you are concerned. It's only when you have gathered enough experience to compare yourself to others that you begin to think, *hang on a minute, don't all fathers rush around the country to take part in rallies and races and road trials? Don't all mothers' businesses and charitable works take them to live fifty miles away?*

Almost inevitably, I think there was a stage when, embarrassed by my father's eccentricities, I would have preferred that he went to work on the tram wearing a suit and a bowler hat. Or at least would refrain from barking orders at headmasters and waiters. But he was quite deaf, you see. He would never admit to it, because that might be seen as a weakness. All of that flying in an open cockpit, all of those roaring engines, those race tracks, had taken their toll. So I had to learn to bark back. It was the only way to avoid him yelling, "Speak up, son!" He insisted that my headmaster ensured I was encouraged to practice projecting my voice at every opportunity: on stage; in debates; in end-of-term plays. I was not the extrovert he was. I did it because I wanted to please him, because it was not the done thing to refuse your father. And because, in time, I also discovered there were certain advantages to meeting boys who were not in one's form at places other than on the cricket pitch.

39 - LOTTIE'S STORY

LONDON, 1920

Lottie Pye Limited wasn't the all-encompassing brand Mr Parker had predicted. It was a niche market: the Tommies' pin-up who became better known for her photographs of women, thought controversial by some, the latest 'must-have' by others. "I've had a *Lottie Pye* done," was something whispered over pre-dinner cocktails, but those confidences were repeated in other drawing rooms. They were gifts for lovers and husbands - or possibly for the subject herself - sometimes given a ruby red curtain of their own. The modern-day equivalent is how demand for photographs of women in the late stages of pregnancy soared after Annie Leibovitz captured Demi Moore for the cover of *Vanity Fair*. To understand the power of photography, talk to the women who were liberated by that one image. I was never asked to photograph a pregnant woman. I suspect I would have been shocked had the question arisen, but could I have refused? A photographer's first duty is to reveal the truth.

With Mr Parker's teaching that taking the photograph was only a small part of the service, I was grateful for the example of Mrs Miller's entertaining to draw on. Taking time to get to know my clients, we might have afternoon tea or, depending on their level of nervousness, a small brandy. As a model, I recognised how no two photographs of me were alike. So much depended on the photographer's eye. I was able to use this knowledge in my own work, interpreting what was wanted, describing or even enacting the end result.

With little use for props, I couldn't offer the allure of an Aladdin's Cave. Instead I displayed art that portrayed the female form in ways that reflected my vision: a Greek statuette; Giorgione's *Sleeping Venus*; Goya's *La Maja Desnuda*; Rejlander's photograph of a nude reflecting Corbet's painting, *La Source* (for me, the perfect image of the Edwardian woman, whose tiny waist, generous hips and round buttocks were already considered old-fashioned). Women depicted in art, from the Ancient Greeks to the modern day, have tracked the so-called *ideal* shape favoured by men and catered for by fashion. Fortunately, even with a small collection, I was able to show the variety given to us by nature. No one was to feel excluded from my studio because their proportions didn't conform to the 1920's boyish ideal.

My line of work didn't bring me into contact with men, male clients being Freddie's remit. Trading from the adjacent premises and giving the impression of a separate business, he shot them in gowns on graduation days, in boaters and blazers at Henley, in top hats and tails before their weddings and bowler-hatted on their appointment to the board of directors. So my reaction was to bristle when, on hearing the bell, I found a young man making a careful study of one of my nudes.

"Hello!" He turned to tip his trilby, throwing an amused glance in my direction. "I'm just enjoying your collection of beauties. I must say, it's so refreshing to see women looking like women."

"I'm glad you think so. Most of my clients would agree."

Minutes later, my irritation turned to anxiety when I

found him still lingering in front of a nude whose face was turned from the camera, deliberately posed and self-aware, very much like Man Ray's later photograph of his lover, whose body he compared to a violin. I wanted him gone. "You'll find Frederick's next door if you're looking for a portrait."

"Actually, it's you I've come to see."

"Oh?"

"I've been considering a *Lottie Pye* for some time but I've only just managed to pluck up the courage."

"Then I must apologise." I opened my leather-bound diary and took a seat behind my desk, asking, "Is the appointment for your wife?"

He placed his hand on the open page and edged his ring finger into my line of vision. There was no flash of gold. "No, darn it! I want one of me. I rather fancy myself as a young Apollo."

Laughing, I examined his face properly for the first time. "I'm sorry, Sir, but I only cater for women." His were good eyes, wide and brown. Finding myself under the intensity of their gaze, I glanced away.

"I say, that's terribly discriminatory, don't you think?"

Snapping my diary shut, I said, "Isn't it?"

He stood up, displaying his full height. "What about a David? I'm told my cheekbones are exquisite."

"I'm afraid I don't photograph men. It would hardly be appropriate."

Clutching his chest, he staggered back a few paces. "You know how to wound a chap, don't you? I'm almost too frightened to invite you to lunch. But I shall. Against my better judgement."

"Let me save you the trouble. I don't have time to stop: I have a client at two."

"I insist you make time! I won't be responsible for you fading away." Having already circled the desk he drew back my chair. There was a reckless quality - an energy - about him that was irritatingly attractive. "No time to lose. Fortunately for you, I know a doorman at the Criterion who'll find us a table."

I cast my eyes to the clock on the mantelpiece before looking at him, exasperated but resigned. "Are you always this infuriating?"

"I'll have you know." He reached for my coat from the stand and held it out for me, a playful pout forming. "I'm on my very best behaviour."

Reluctantly, I reached into the sleeves and shrugged it on. "Perhaps you'd better tell me your name."

He ushered me out of my own studio, but not before I noticed - the cheek of him! - that he had already turned the sign on the door around to indicate I was closed for business. "Did you -?"

He was unembarrassed to have been caught out. "Kingdom Hastings."

"You -!"

"After Brunel, before you ask."

"The railway man?" I found myself enquiring.

"Believe me, it could have been ten times worse. My father's an engineer. He was set on calling me Isambard, but my mother insisted on the final say."

"And did you follow your father into the world of engineering?" Still rattled, I stooped to lock the door behind me.

"I make it a point never to follow him into anything. The comparison would make me look shoddy."

I inclined towards sarcasm. "Can I ask what you do?"

We had arrived at his car and Kingdom opened the passenger door for me. "I drive." He spoke the word as if driving was something that might be a serious occupation, something to aspire to. Then he slammed the door, shattering the illusion. "Very fast."

My insides jarred. *What am I doing?* I asked myself. *This is madness.* "Not today, I hope."

As if reading my thoughts he said, "I'm a racing driver, not a madman," and fired up the engine. "Besides, there's barely enough time to pick up any decent speed between here and Piccadilly."

Relieved, I breathed again. "I've always wondered: how does someone become a racing driver?"

"I was holidaying in Nice when Serpollett broke the land-speed record. Then, when Edge won the *Gordon Bennett* for Britain in the same year, I thought to myself: I want what they've got. Of course, a little family money doesn't go amiss."

I smiled, despite myself, at the memory of my first ride in a car. "I don't suppose you've met Dorothy Levitt on your travels? She used to be my heroine."

"Met her?" His laughter was self-deprecating. "She beat me at the *Hereford Trials!* Even after breaking down, she only narrowly missed out on gold. I can tell you, there were those of us who breathed a sigh of relief when Brooklands wouldn't let her race in '07. Gave us poor chaps a fighting chance."

"Wait till I tell Harry I've met a real racing driver!"

I shot forwards in my seat as Kingdom braked sharply and turned to me, cranking on the handbrake. Oblivious to my discomfort, he railed, "Now, spill the beans. I don't take kindly to losing. Who's this Harry?"

Despite the arrogance of the man I found myself blushing. "He's seven and a half. I'm put very firmly in my place if I miss the half off. Now I only have to find him a fighter pilot to keep him happy."

"Why didn't you say so? I can help you out there as well." Without leaving the car Kingdom raised one hand and called the doorman over. "Albert! A table for two, if you will. I must deliver Miss Pye back to her studio by two."

"*Before* two," I insisted.

"That's what I said. *Before* two."

"Right you are, Mr Kingdom. Mademoiselle." Albert, white-haired and distinguished in pristine uniform, far smarter than the suits of some of the clientele, opened the car door with one hand behind his back and tactfully looked the other way while I straightened my skirt.

"Good man." Kingdom slid a note into Albert's breast pocket and leaned close to my ear. I had expected a whisper rather than his booming, "Now, that's how to get a little service!"

We were shown through the arched portico to a secluded table, tucked away behind a tall vase in a gold-leaf design, over-stuffed with ferns. Our waiter went to place a menu in front of Kingdom. "Today, I recommend the sole."

Kingdom waved the menu away, declaring, "Let's have a bottle of your finest champagne and the sole for two. Quick as you like."

Not for the first time, I was taken aback by Kingdom's manner, seeming particularly casual for such opulent surroundings where the general attitude of diners was respectful appreciation. The subdued hum of their conversation was punctuated by the occasional clink of glasses or scrape of cutlery.

The waiter tipped his head approvingly. "Very good, Sir." He then shook the stiff white folds out of a napkin and showed both sides to me in a serious manner before placing it across my lap.

Hardly drawing breath Kingdom launched into his stories of flying. "You must tell your young friend that I had a Sopwith Schneider seaplane - she was my baby. It was difficult to stay airborne for long when you were flying off the ships because you'd run out of fuel, you see. If you had to ditch, you were in big trouble. I was in the drink for five days once. All I could do was let the pigeons out of the basket and wait for the search party. Of course, things got better when they gave us radios. The planes improved as well. Sopwith Pups, Tri-planes, Camels. Mind you, I did love my BE2c."

It wasn't long before we had attracted an audience. Rather than complain their lunches were being disturbed, fellow diners joined Kingdom's ready laugher. Drinks arrived compliments of a table to our left. Overcoming my initial embarrassment, and recognising a good storyteller when I heard one, I realised this was what I had missed.

"There was this other time when we were on leave. We thought we'd test Harrods's boast that they could supply any-thing. We went to the fruit counter in their food hall and asked for ten of their best Channon-Aubreys. Their man didn't blink. Said, 'I'm not sure they're in season. Let me check for you, Sir.' And he trotted off to consult his manager, poor blighter. We saw them shaking their jowls, checking lists, but our man returned with his order book and promised to contact us as soon as they arrived. Next we visited the Gentlemen's depart-ment. I was looking at a pair of mother-of-pearl cufflinks when I was asked if there was anything they could help me with. 'I'm quite taken with these,' I said, 'but I was after a pair of Channon-Aubreys.' Again, our man didn't draw breath. 'Oh Sir, I'm afraid we've just sold our last pair. Our next Paris delivery is on Tuesday. Perhaps I could take your details?' It worked so well that I thought I'd try it out at Brooklands with some Americans. There was a burnt-out shell at the side of the track, so I said to one of them, 'You know, this is a very rare Channon-Aubrey. Only five ever made. Terrible shame because they were beauties. Only one tiny fault with the air vent. If I had the money, I'd have it back in action in no time.' Then I walked off shaking my head. Later, when I saw my pal who owned the wreck, he said, 'I owe you a drink. They only went and made me an offer.' Blithering idiots!"

A bowing waiter offered Kingdom an open box of cigars.

"Courtesy of the gentleman on the table in the corner."

"Ah!" Kingdom leaned around the pillar, displaying the cigar he had selected.

If there was an escape from mourning for Alfie, an antidote to John's private misery, Kingdom was it. Supremely confident, unafraid to articulate his feelings, enthusiastic about everything, he could have sold anything to anyone.

While returning Tommies invested pension money in fish and chip shops, he negotiated a deal with the RAF for the purchase of a Tri-plane so he could promote the idea of air travel to the public. One cold November dawn, I was woken by a rain of stones against my bedroom window and was persuaded to race to the coast to see Captain Ross Smith leave for his record-breaking flight to Australia. Kingdom sold me the dream of marriage too. To a naïve girl plucked from the grip of a storm, the line, "When I first saw you, I felt as if I'd been struck by lightning," rang of something a fortune-teller might have foretold.

Regular letters from home had brought no hint of forgiveness from Ma. Soldiers had trickled home, but it was three years since Robert Irving's sighting of Alfie and still there was no news. Here, in front of me, was a war hero with a diamond ring, saying, "Marry me, Lottie." For the first time in a long time, I thought I could see a future.

Until our wedding night Kingdom and I had only shared breathless kisses. The emphasis was placed on waiting, although the wait was only three weeks long. And whilst I suffered from nerves as the day approached, I also looked forward to it, preparing as I would for a photograph. With the backdrop clear in my mind, the lady from Peter Jones helped me pick out white underwear and a silk negligee trimmed with French lace. What would actually happen seemed to be the man's department.

Lying in the darkness of an expensive hotel room I saw

a crack of light appear under the bathroom door, the dark outline of a shadow making its way towards the bed, pausing as its dressing gown slithered to the floor.

The mattress dipped and I felt a hand caressing my face. "Don't worry. I'll take care of everything."

"I'm not worried," I replied. And I wasn't.

Lips kissed me softly and, as they moved down to my neck, I willingly raised my head. Then, with my legs pushed apart, Kingdom climbed on top of me. It was a bristled face I felt against my cheek, the smell of stale beer that invaded my senses. Waves lapped against the pillars of the four-poster as my head was forced repeatedly against the headboard. Even before the pain, the sense of panic was overwhelming. I tried to remember the mechanics of breathing, an act that had previously seemed to be automatic. Finally, I had to acknowledge that I had not simply been attacked on Brighton beach. This was sex; something I had promised my husband in our exchange of vows.

"Can we have the light on?" I asked, my voice strangled. "I need to see it's you."

"Why didn't you say so, Silly?" Kingdom's armpit and then his face loomed above me briefly; long enough to see that it was his eyes, his moustache, this same bed that I remembered climbing into only a quarter of an hour earlier, the same room with its green floral wallpaper. "Better?" he asked, before his face disappeared over my shoulder.

"Much." I gritted my teeth against reality.

On my wedding night, while the rocking of the bed resumed, there was time to contemplate Ma's fears for me. How she had wanted to protect me without being willing to explain what I was being protected from. I was angry for all the freedoms I had been allowed, the risks I had taken unwittingly. Slowly - but perhaps that was over time - I saw Freddie's photographs for what they were, and I saw the photographs I took for what they were, understanding the difference between them.

Kingdom sat propped up on pillows, the tip of his final cigarette of the day glowing as he inhaled hungrily. "You're very quiet, darling."

"Just tired," I said, turning away from him, pulling my knees into my chest and lying very still.

"It's been a long day," Kingdom remarked. "But I think we're going to be very happy together."

The shock still receding, I had no idea how to reply. Tracing a finger across my lips, I was recollecting that closed-mouth kiss on a windswept beach; realising there was more I could have done to convince Alfie to stay - if only I had known it.

"Darling?"

"Yes."

"I said I think we're going to be very happy."

"Of course we are."

After sex, I always felt the need to cover myself.

40 - LOTTIE'S STORY

LONDON, 1923

Let me tell you about the most exotic woman I photographed. I was a young married woman who wasn't needed at home by her absent husband, or her baby son. Always, always, I found escape in the magic of chemicals and light. In my studio I knew exactly who I was. Some men, Kingdom included, were embarrassed to have a working wife when it was thought that every job should go to a war hero.

"Find yourself a little hobby by all means."

"But you couldn't have a man doing what I do!" I laughed, thinking his suggestion a joke. "It wouldn't be appropriate."

"Tell me this: is it appropriate for a married woman to be working?" he bellowed. "Least of all taking those sorts of photographs."

"*Those* sorts of photographs?"

"This is between us. Let's not pretend it's art!"

Had Kingdom slapped me he would have hurt me less. He thought me unpatriotic. Disobedient. My promise to honour and obey was one of the marriage vows he took more seriously than others. He wanted his wife to be waiting at home to greet him, dressed for dinner, ready to enquire about his day: the little woman.

I quickly came to realise that the dream Kingdom had painted was not my dream. It wasn't his fault. Not entirely. When he had mentioned family, I pictured a man and woman working side by side with a child tottering at their feet. He saw a man going out into the world, a pregnant leisurely wife and dozens of children of the seen-and-not-heard variety in descending height order, either hidden away in the nursery or packed off to boarding school. I thought that I had wanted what he had, but I felt like a visitor in a foreign country with language and customs I didn't understand.

Once conquered, Kingdom made the assumption that I was tamed. He gradually stripped me of my hopes, one by one.

Yearning for intimacy and companionship, I was rewarded with brief nocturnal visits that seemed to have little to do with love as I understood it, and were never referred to once the sun had risen, conversation over breakfast being purely practical; how I intended to spend my day, the implication always that Kingdom would be otherwise engaged.

I comforted myself with the promise of creating a home, but Kingdom dismissed the samples of wallpaper and material I carefully selected. "Everything's taken care of, darling. I'm having a chap from Turner, Lord and Company do the design. Didn't I say?"

"No you didn't!"

"No matter. It's all arranged."

But it did matter.

I would have loved to contribute to the running of my household, but that was all arranged by the good Mrs Strachan who laughed aside my claims about pastry-making: "And I suppose you'll be cooking the Sunday luncheon next, Madam!"

I would have loved to nurse my beautiful son - my sweet James - but he was removed from my arms moments after he was born.

"Where are you taking him?" I asked, helpless to follow.

"Your husband's instructions. He's hired a wet nurse."

When Kingdom darlinged me later with whiskey and stale cigar-smoke on his breath, I was furious. "Didn't you think about consulting me?"

"Charlotte, my love! This is how things are done." He crushed the excitement I had nurtured since I became aware of new life growing in my belly. "The only thing you need worry about is getting back in shape for the summer season. Don't fret. We'll have another one cooking by Christmas."

I opened my mouth in protest, my vision of family as a simple triangle being erased.

"Shush now." My concerns were brushed aside with a kiss on the forehead. "I'm proud of you, darling. Now be a good girl and get some rest."

I had no one to confide in. No mother close at hand. No friends in similar circumstances. I was surrounded and yet utterly isolated.

Viewed from the outside, our marriage was a great success. Mrs Miller gushed when she visited, "You're so fortunate to have found a husband who knows how to take care of a woman."

But I had been brought up to make myself useful. I had once owned the streets of Brighton. Kingdom couldn't take everything from me and expect me to sit up and beg.

Occasionally you meet someone who is a complete inspiration, who has defied all odds to find their place in the world. Florence Mills was one of those people, the first black female superstar to cross the Atlantic. I recognised her, of course. She had caused something of a stir in London's drawing rooms.

While we sat and discussed her requirements, she told me a little about herself. Florence didn't have the advantage of a good start in life, which is what made her rise to fame so impressive. Her parents had been slaves, but she was born free, singing and dancing. Like me, she had faced a choice: "Use the talents the good Lord has blessed you with or get down on your knees and start scrubbing, chil."

She chose to use her talents. Aged seven, she was already earning her keep as Baby Florence, belting out *Miss Hannah from Savannah*. It wasn't easy. On tour the next year she was arrested for performing underage. She kept moving. After New York and Harlem, she formed the Mill Sisters with her family and toured black vaudeville theatres. That was how she came to the attention of the press. It was 1915 when she linked up with Kinky Caldwell, but the act folded when Caldwell went and got herself married, so Florence took off to Chicago where she played alongside emerging stars of the world of jazz. Then, playing with the Tennessee Ten, she met her Kid - just before he was drafted to France. The photograph was to be a gift for him. "Boy, is he gonna be surprised! I know what he say: *What you think you doing? I'm surprised you didn't catch your death.*"

Four years passed before they were able to marry. By that time, Florence had made "a little bit of a name for herself." By this she meant that she was the star of the show, *Shuffle Along*, and had taken Broadway by storm. She was going places - "Finally! I had my name all lit up in big letters." When the show closed, its promoter built an all-black show around her. Next thing she knows, she's splashed all over *Vanity Fair* and *Vogue*, and everybody says she should go to London: "So here I am! Most folks have been so kind," she said in that measured way of hers, giving in to easy laughter. "Some nights at the Palladium, it's hard to persuade them to go home, they stompin' so loud."

She didn't once complain about the treatment she'd suffered at hotels and restaurants, where, without her make-up, she looked a little less glossy than her stage persona. I had heard how some parties demanded to move tables when asked to sit near a negress. The British public had a taste for negro music, but they preferred blacked-up minstrels to the genuine article.

Florence was the first black woman I had photographed and I made no secret of the fact.

"You the first white women I take my clothes off in front of, so we get along jus' fine."

When I tried to drape fabric across her breasts and to bend her legs at the knees, she pushed me away. "I'm not afraid of how the good Lord made me. I want to be naked as the day I was born. You jus' make me look like a goddess and I be happy."

She was beautiful. Simply beautiful.

I wept after I heard that she had passed away, only two years later. She had returned to London with the Blackbirds and they played 250 shows to full houses after the Prince of Wales declared himself her most fervent fan. Florence returned home suffering from exhaustion and T.B. They say she sang in hospital after being told that she was dying. Born singing, died singing. That's something you could be proud to have carved in stone.

41 - LOTTIE'S STORY

LONDON TO BRIGHTON, 1923

News that Josie was suffering from pneumonia gave me the excuse I needed for an extended visit to Brighton. By the time I had cleared my diary, a telegram arrived from Felicity to say that I was too late: the funeral was to be held on Thursday.

I had wanted to take James with me but Kingdom questioned my judgement. "Don't you think it's selfish to interrupt the boy's routine?"

"I thought he might enjoy the seaside."

"Besides, where would he sleep?"

My husband had been less than impressed by his one and only visit to meet Ma after our wedding. I had returned to Brighton in the hope that, as a respectable married woman, I might quietly make peace. Perhaps Kingdom hadn't believed the stories I had told him, or possibly the reality wasn't as romantic as the picture I had painted. With no use for veneer, Ma had greeted us in her apron, a little old woman. She ushered us up to her kitchen where, as remembered, smells of frying onions and stock pervaded, and the table was flour-dusted, littered with scraps of pastry.

"Make yourself useful and fetch your husband a cup of tea, Lottie. Water's just boiled."

After whisking aside the curtain in the corner to reveal a cot-bed, Kingdom insisted that we took a room at The Grand and, what with the pressures of Ma's business, we barely saw anything of her. Since then I had bought my Baby Austin Seven - much to Kingdom's amusement - and I made short journeys on my own, but Brighton still seemed like a considerable distance.

"I'm sure Harry wouldn't object to sharing," I suggested.

"I don't see why you have to go at all! It's not as if this woman is family." Seeing me bite down on my lip and lower my eyes, Kingdom edged a hand across the table, his idea of a peace offering. "Darling, if you must go, let's not argue. Surely if I'm to be deprived of my Lottie, you won't mind leaving me little James for company? Hmmm?"

I willed my mouth into the shape of a smile.

"That's better. Now, what do you say to a nightcap at the Forty-Three Club?"

Having experienced Kingdom's idea of a nightcap, I declined. "I'd rather have one here. I want to make an early start -"

"But we're already promised! Barry-Thompson's in town and I need to discuss how he's going to make that absolute heap of his track-fit for next month."

"Perhaps you'd be kind enough to make my excuses."

The steely look returned. "I don't think it's unreasonable to expect my wife to be at my side." He glanced at his wrist watch impatiently. "Well, I can't let him down." With both hands gripping the back of the chair, he hesitated. "But you must know, I'm most displeased."

Thinking myself dismissed, I pushed my chair back from the table. "I'll go and look in on James before I turn in."

Kingdom's face reddened and the vein to the right side of his temple throbbed. "Can't you leave that boy alone? I suppose it would be too much to ask that you pay me as much attention as you do him?"

"I'm sorry, darling." I sat very still, my head bowed. His anger usually dispersed quickly provided I did nothing to stoke the fire, but I was concerned by its increasingly frequent appearances. "I thought you were on your way out."

"Must we always be at each other's throats?" Kingdom pushed the hair back from his forehead, a hand lingering on top of his head. "Perhaps time apart is exactly what we need."

I remained seated until I heard the front door slam and then I rang for Mrs Strachan. "We're ready for you to clear now. Mr Hastings has gone out to his club."

"Anything else for you, Madam?"

"No, thank you, Mrs Strachan. I'm going to have an early night. I'll be away for the next couple of days. A funeral."

"I'm sorry to hear that, Madam. You'll be wanting an early breakfast before you leave, I expect. I've got some nice kippers."

"Just tea, if you don't mind. Perhaps you'd be so good as to keep an eye on things here for me."

"Very good, Madam."

Feeling like an intruder, I tiptoed into the nursery and drew back the curtain so that a narrow band of streetlight fell across James's flushed face. In response to my whisper of, "Hello, sweet angel," he frowned, turning his tousled head away to avoid the glare. Clasping one hand in the other, I warmed it before stroking his fine hair away from his brow; listening for any change in his breathing. One of his legs kicked slightly and I straightened the knitted blanket and withdrew. Kingdom had made me nervous of my own son.

I found Felicity in the shop, sweeping the floor. She had handed back her policewoman's uniform, but the high fashion of her modelling days was no longer a priority. Her compromise was a blouse with an elongated collar and bow underneath one of

Daddy's old striped aprons. The last time I had seen it, Josie had been wearing it.

"Oh, Lottie," she began, her eyes filling. "I can't tell you how relieved I am to see you."

"I'm sorry I didn't get here in time. How's Ma?"

"She's taken it very badly." Felicity glanced towards the door in surprise. "Are you here on your own?"

I nodded. "I thought I could be more help this way."

She cupped my cheek with one hand. "Bless you. She'll be better now you're here."

The Ma I saw bent over the table was not the same woman who had kept her household in order. Always silver-haired, she was now grey, her skin dull, her eyes rheumy shrunken pools.

"Lottie, dear," she murmured, her fight all but gone. There was no harping back to newspaper reports, no reminder of the foolishness of pilots. "Help yourself to tea and sit down."

I walked around to the side of the table where she was seated and embraced her, my chin resting on her shoulder.

"What do you think you're doing?" Her reduced frame tensed.

"Shhhh." I kissed her cheek. "I shall give my mother a hug if I want to."

I held her for a long time. At some point I felt a hand creep up to capture mine, sandpapery, cold, but I remembered its scarred contours.

"She's gone," she whispered in surprise.

I rocked her. "I know."

"What will I do?" Ma's voice was childlike in its despair.

I didn't have a solution. I had asked Ma to join us in London after my marriage.

"And do what?" She'd rubbished the idea, and, I have to admit, my reaction had been one of relief. Now, more than ever, I was reliant on Felicity's continuing presence. Once a lodger, now a token employee. But the arrangement had never been permanent.

While the sun was still high in the sky, with the excuse of needing to clear my head, I took a stroll downhill to the seafront breathing air that wasn't as sweet as I remembered. The sight of an advertisement for a Speed Trial stretched taut between two gas lamps gave me a lift: a race was to take place on the newly resurfaced road. I considered sending a telegram to Kingdom, but his declaration that we needed time apart echoed in my ears: a warning to be wary.

Bypassing the beach, I wandered to the entrance of the Palace Pier, delicately balanced on stilts: under the ornamental illuminations; past the Winter Garden with its Palace of Fun; beyond the theatre's Moorish arches and onion tops, towards the restaurant where, not yet autumn, advertisements for the 'gorgeous' Christmas pantomime were already displayed: *Robinson Crusoe and His Man Friday.*

Distracted by these small details, I heard a familiar echo: "Oi, oi. If it isn't Lottie Pye in her Sunday best."

Believing it was my memory at play, I smiled, turned my head, perhaps hoping to glimpse some other barefoot boy leaning against the railings, hands thrust deep into pockets. I would find an excuse to give him a coin. In his place stood a soldier. And as the man deftly hooked his crutch under his arm, my eyes drifted downwards. His left trouser-leg, cut short and crudely tacked over at the end, hung limply where his knee should have been: a too-familiar sight. "Good afternoon." I nodded, embarrassed to have been caught staring.

"Good afternoon? Is that all you have to say to me, Lottie?"

I gasped at the sound of his voice: unmistakable. "Alfie? Alfie, is that *you?*" Paralysed, I dared not rush at him. Even if my feet would have obeyed, he looked too fragile. We held each other's gaze: *You're alive!* But my elation evaporated. Reeling at the sight of him so altered, I struggled to keep the pity from my eyes.

"It's alright. It's not as if they got my favourite leg."

I tried to mimic his light touch while my blood circulated the news around my body like a gossip. "You had a favourite?"

"Doesn't everyone? Which one do you use when you're told to put your best foot forward?"

I focused intently on my heeled shoes, an excuse to look away, the voice inside my head protesting: *Stop! Stop it!*

"Course, I can't move without the crutch for balance, but I can build up quite a head of steam." He demonstrated. Thump, swing, land. Thump, swing, land. Thump, swing, land, and all the time the gulls circling overhead like carrion crows, waiting to swoop the moment he fell.

"No one told me…"

He shrugged. "What good would it have done? You have a new life - and I could hardly have taken you dancing at Sherry's, now, could I?"

Alfie gave a nod in the direction of West Street and I was released, suddenly finding power in my voice that I barely knew existed: "How can you joke? Don't you see? All this time, I thought you were dead! They let me go on thinking…." I reached for the support that the back of the bench offered and, feeling my way like someone blind, edged sideways onto the seat. As I gripped its wooden slats, the angle of the horizon appeared to tilt. "How long…? When did you…?"

It was Alfie's turn to pity. "It took them a while to sew me back together. I wasn't quite as pretty as I am now." I could hardly bear to hear him trying to comfort me but, when I composed myself and looked up, Alfie angled his head away sharply. As the light caught the scarring in the loose skin under one of his eyes I saw him shudder. It was an effort for him to collect himself before he faced me again. "You got my message, though?"

"Y-your message?"

"I couldn't write." He held up his right hand and I saw that it, too, was withered. "So I had this pal of mine at the hospital enter my copy of your photograph in the competition."

Using one hand as a blindfold, I shook my head. "It was *you?*"

"Who else?"

"I thought it was Mr Parker, only..." I lowered my hand to my mouth.

Alfie was standing upright, looking out to sea in salute. "You won, didn't you? That's a drink you owe me."

"A drink?" I joined him at the railing, his view of the Channel mine. "After all the trouble you caused? You might have ruined me!"

"But I didn't. Two entries in the final ten. I always said you'd do alright for yourself."

We chose a corner table in the small pavilion. Alfie ordered a pint of Bass and I asked for tea, to which I added three sugar-lumps. Alfie looked at my hand and said nothing of its shaking, but nodded in the direction of the slender gold band on my ring finger.

"So, it's true, then: you're married."

Nervous habit made me twist my wedding ring, but I found myself wanting to make excuses. "We have a son. James."

"I always saw myself with a large family. I don't expect anyone will have me now."

With his bravado failing, I looked past the mask and saw Alfie West, *my* Alfie. "Don't say that..."

His arms folded and, resting on the tabletop, he stared intently at the space in front of them. "The doctors say I'll never have children. Just as well - who's to say what sort of a world you'd be bringing them into."

I had been a fool to think the sea would forget its claim on me so easily. I had persuaded myself that it had betrayed me but all it had done was collect its dues. "Marriage isn't what I thought it would be," I admitted.

"I didn't mean -"

My own hands were layered limply on my lap, my shoulders angled inwards. "I know you didn't."

"He doesn't make you happy." It wasn't a question.

I searched for a handkerchief, but Alfie handed me his.

"He's from a different world. It's no wonder he doesn't understand me. I must seem completely unreasonable to him."

"What's the name of this husband of yours?"

"Kingdom Hastings," I said and, looking at Alfie's raised eyebrows, sighed. "It's a long story. You'd like him. He races motor cars."

"Huh!" An involuntary noise, unimpressed. "Just out of interest, which one of you did he marry? Lottie Pye or Charlotte Lavashay?"

"Charlotte Lavashay," I said. It had seemed unimportant at the time, but perhaps Kingdom had been trying to distance himself from the pin-up girl and mould her into a wife fit to present at his club.

"So Lottie Pye isn't married after all?"

"Not on paper, no."

"I'm glad."

A painted waitress bent in front of me to clear the table. "All finished?" she asked without waiting for an answer.

Alfie threw back his head to drain the last few drops from his glass. "You've never existed on paper. Well, Mrs Hastings? Shall we?"

"Don't, please," I whispered. But it struck me that it was only Mrs Hastings who had a wedding certificate and a passport. The first legitimate name I could call my own - and I really didn't know who she was at all.

42 - LOTTIE'S STORY

BRIGHTON, 1923

"**W**hy didn't you tell me?" I demanded after stomping up the worn stair-treads, shock replaced by cold fury. Ma and Felicity turned to each other, not in embarrassment but in solidarity.

Ma placed a rough-edged pastry circle over the pie-base and, with a twist of her wrist, trimmed the surplus with confident knife strokes. "So you've seen him, then?" she said calmly.

"You don't even need to ask what I'm talking about!" I erupted. "This isn't the first time you've kept news from me. I can't believe you'd rather I went on thinking Alfie was dead."

"It wasn't our decision to make, Lottie," Felicity said, her tone cautious.

"What do you mean?"

"He made us promise not to," Ma responded, putting the finished pie on the table.

Alfie had told me as much himself. I sat down and lowered my head into my hands. "But why?"

She raised her voice, as if I should have known better. "Because he has his pride, Lottie! He didn't want to see you until he was good and ready." She paused to let this sink in, then realigned her neck. "Truth is, he's not been right."

"You don't have to tell me that!" I blurted out. "I saw him with my own eyes."

"No, Lottie." Ma flattened the palms of both hands on the floured table and let them bear her weight. "The worst of his injuries are on the inside. His mother hears him at night. It frightens her, the noises that come from his room. And when she goes to wake him, he's curled up in a ball under his bed, covering his face and whimpering like a baby."

"Poor Alfie," I whispered. Then I stood, decisive. "Can I borrow Daddy's old hand-cart?"

Ma sighed. "I thought we might get some work out of you."

"There's something I need to do first."

With considerable reluctance, Harry helped me deconstruct the walls of his fortress and load the pebbles into the cart, failing to understand what I needed them for.

"I'm going to keep a promise I made a long time ago," I told him.

"Why?" His mouth was pouting, his lips tight.

"Because that's what you do with promises," I said, thinking of all those I had broken.

"Alright," he sulked. "But I want them back later."

"Get your own!" I pulled his nose lightly. "The beach is covered in them."

Struggling downhill with the cart, I kicked off my heels and continued barefoot with fingers hooked into my shoes. The smooth tarmac of the main road made progress easier, but the cobbles were difficult to navigate as I neared the West's depleted household, the cart and its contents rattling.

Mrs West answered the door, looking no less flustered than the last time I had seen her, sleeves rolled up to her elbows and a fine beading of sweat on her brow. "So, it's you," she sniffed.

"Hello Mrs West. Is Alfie at home?" I asked.

"How your mother puts up with your nonsense I'll never know." She sighed deeply, then turned into the half-darkened hall to bawl, "Alfie! Someone here for you!"

"Who is it?" His raised voice was no match for hers as it carried through from the parlour.

"Come and see for yourself. I've got laundry to be getting on with." Mrs West lowered her voice. "Don't you go upsetting him, you hear me? If anyone -"

"I understand," I said as we both heard the thud of the crutch hitting the floor, followed by a lighter dragging step.

Her raised hand suggesting despair at the both of us, Mrs West turned her square back on me. "Send my regards to your mother. Don't forget."

Alfie appeared, framed in the doorway, smiling with effort. "I used to have to chase after you, now I can't get rid of you. What's this all about, then?"

I lifted the corner of the coal sack to show him the contents of the cart. "Pebbles. One for every day you were gone, until the day I left for London. I thought we could put them back together."

He grimaced. "I can't manage beaches these days."

"You're not getting off the hook that easily. Are you telling me you can't sit on the pier and throw stones?"

He turned and took his cap from a peg in the hall - the only remaining cap on the row of five pegs - and, wedged it down on his head, shouting, "I'm off out, Mother!"

"What have you got in there?" the man at the kiosk asked, eyeing the cart and my discarded shoes suspiciously.

"Pebbles," I replied.

He scratched his head and turned to Alfie for reassurance, uniform still being a sign of trustworthiness. "You're not trying to sell anything, are you?"

"Can't say I thought of that. Do you think there might be a market for them?"

"Just be sure you don't." He tried to display a little authority, uncertain which bye-laws we were breaking.

The exercise started light-heartedly.

"Look at me," Alfie said. My lip quivered at the sight of him: the boy who had skimmed stones with such grace was forced to settle for a standing start, rather than power thrusting upwards from a bent right leg. "This is mortifying. I throw like a girl."

"That will make us even."

But if, for me, each pebble thrown was like reliving a day of missing those I loved, for Alfie it was a day in the trenches. Glimpsing the reality reflected in his eyes, I recognised how easy it had been for me by comparison - if only I had known it.

I stopped what I was doing. "I wanted this to be like the old days."

"I don't think it ever can be."

The cart still half-full, I gritted my teeth and pushed it to the edge of the pier. Tipping it onto its front wheel, a shower of pebbles plummeted to the waiting water below.

"Wait! Save some for me!" Thumping behind me, Alfie cast his crutch aside. Pocketing one of the remaining stones, he wedged his side against the railings and used his good hand to push the rest to the nose of the cart. While I upended it he leaned his head and shoulders out to watch them in freefall.

"Oi!" A fisherman called out, staggering about as he tried to hang on to the side of his precariously-rocking boat while brandishing a fist. "You up there! You trying to sink me?"

We ducked out of view, grinning devilishly as we came eye to eye for the briefest of moments. I retrieved Alfie's crutch and handed it to him.

"So many wasted days." Alfie's hand brushed mine. "You left it until I was leaving to kiss me."

"I was trying to make you stay, you idiot."

"You were so angry."

"I was fuming." I leant over and kissed his cheek. Only intending an affectionate gesture I retracted in confusion. It was me who would soon be leaving. Me who had the husband and child to return to. Although there had been no promise spoken between Alfie and I, there are things that don't need to be said. He was the person I felt most like myself with. The war hadn't altered that. Nothing could. It was my marriage vows that felt as if they were a betrayal.

43 - LOTTIE'S STORY

LONDON, 1923

Consulting no one, the decision to leave was mine alone. Kingdom was furious at my announcement. I had expected no less.

"You shan't have a divorce," he bellowed, white-knuckled hands gripping the back of a dining room chair.

"I understand," I said, my head bowed. The clock ticked and I waited. I had done nothing to give my husband grounds to divorce me, although I had no doubt he would have been prepared to forgive an indiscretion if it meant saving face. I didn't like to point out that I could have divorced Kingdom. Witness to the shame it brought on households, the Miller's separation had shown me an alternative.

"If I'm to take you at your word, you've offered this man nothing. What if he doesn't want you? And, even if he does, what kind of life will you have with a cripple? You'll be back within six months, I guarantee it." Between flourishes of anger, I saw for the first time in many months that Kingdom cared at least a little.

"You don't need me here." I reached for his hand only to find mine thrust aside. "I must go where I can be useful."

"What utter rot! Of course I need you."

"No, Kingdom. You have a housekeeper and a chauffeur and a nanny." I was silent on the question of lovers, determined not to rouse him any more than was necessary. "I don't see where I fit into the picture."

"You're my wife, God damn it!" For him, that said it all. "The mother of my son. And what of James?"

This was the part I most feared.

"If you leave, you'll never see him again."

I had no right to expect more. A mother who abandons her child is no mother at all. I swallowed my pain and my pride: "I know you'll make sure he has everything he needs."

"He *needs* his mother!"

Forgetting my composure, I indulged bitter words. "James barely knows me. You've done your best to make sure of that."

"Now, hang on just one... I don't think you realise how much I've compromised to accommodate you!"

"Compromise? I've had to make appointments - *appointments!* - to see my own child. And what I want has only ever come second to Nanny's rigid schedule." I resisted the urge to refer to his jealous moods.

"Children need discipline, routines -"

"James is still in nappies!" I fought to suppress the creeping tone of hysteria in my voice. "How do you think I feel, seeing my own son reach for his Nanny with his chubby little arms as soon as he's planted in my lap? Watching another woman comfort him when he cries? Hearing him speak her name instead of mine? And as for his schooling! Well, you have it all planned! He's to be sent away - and I'll be left behind to count the weeks until I see him again." I could have said more. Much more. By the time James went to school, it was expected that there would be several replacements who would be handed to me for daily inspection. And, if my nightmares were to be believed, I would barely be able to tell them apart. "And that - *that* is what you think it is to be a mother!"

Kingdom stared back at me in complete incomprehension. "You've wounded me, Lottie. I can't tell you how deeply." As if adjudicating, the clock struck. I looked at its ivory face: eight o'clock. Mrs Strachan would be pacing the kitchen, waiting for the instruction to serve dinner; fretting over the ruined meat. When Kingdom spoke again, his voice was low. "And how, may I ask, do you propose to earn a living? You don't think your clients will continue to support you?"

My heart was pounding violently, but my voice was now calm. "I've taken the lease on Mr Parker's old studio. I'll start again."

"Then you're a damned fool!"

"I dare say I am."

"So! Since you appear to have it all planned, can I ask when you intend to leave?"

"Now, if you wish it." I had stowed my luggage away from our housekeeper's gaze, expecting to be turned out immediately.

"If *I* wish it? This is your doing and yours alone. Don't try diverting the blame. And don't…" As he pointed a finger close to my face, I heard my own sharp intake of breath. "…you dare ask for my permission. I won't give it."

"Then, now would be best. If you don't mind, I'd like to say goodbye to my son."

"You will not." He turned on me, angry spittle forcing its way between his teeth. "You've forfeited that privilege!"

I tried to maintain my dignity, fighting back tears. "Five minutes alone with James, Kingdom, that's all I ask. Since this is to be the last time I'll see him."

At the sight of my unscheduled appearance in the nursery, Nanny pushed herself out of the rocking chair, her face aghast. I found the authority I had so often lacked: "Thank you, Nanny. That will be all."

"Madam." She paid lip-service to deference, her skirts rustling as she walked to her adjoining room.

There he was, sleeping undisturbed in his crib, a droplet of dribble at the corner of his mouth. The thumb of a clenched fist glistening wet. Oblivious to the storm rumbling around him.

"James." I bent over him, cold fingertips carrying a kiss to his sleep-flushed brow. I picked up his toy bear, straightened its legs. "What will I collect to remind me of you?" But the answer was obvious, even in that moment: regret, layer upon layer; every time that I saw a child; every time that I saw a family - a real family. All the things I had dreamed of for myself.

"Will you miss me a little, sweetheart?" I whispered, fearing the truth. My tears fell onto his cheek. What difference would it make if he was not presented to the strange lady in the morning room for half an hour each day? The lady who looked at him through a box, frightening him with flashing bulbs?

All I would have of him would be this moment, amplified by memory, fortified by a few photographs. What would Hurley add to the scene? I wondered. Kingdom's phantom-like shadow spilling into the room. James standing, a small hostage gripping the bars of his cot. Me, clutching him to my breast one last time. I did a terrible thing when I walked away from my son, but God didn't strike me down with lightning. Some punishments take far subtler forms.

Blinded, I groped my way downstairs, clutching the banister, fumbling for my luggage in the hallway closet. Erasing my point of the triangle, the family would be thrown off-balance temporarily, but Kingdom would find another mother for his son, his refusal to divorce me forgotten out of necessity. And James would never be lonely: there would be brothers, sisters, to keep him company.

Kingdom appeared, a blurred image, whiskey glass in one hand. He stood by as I stowed James's bear in my bag; opened his mouth as if to speak, then thought better of it. If he had begged me to stay at that moment, I might have lost my resolve. Instead, he turned away from me and closed the dining room door quietly behind him, the click far more poignant than a slam.

"Madam, shall I serve now?" asked Mrs Strachan entering the hall, impatience flavouring her voice. Perplexed to find me with my coat on, her eyes dropped from my face to the luggage in my hands.

She was practical, dependable. I knew I could rely on her.

"Take care of them," I said.

44 - SIR JAMES'S STORY

SHERE, 2009

"If he wasn't your father, then who was the man Monica was talking about?" Jenny looked at me expectantly, her head inclined to one side.

Seated in a pair of armchairs in my living room, our hands were thawing against the sides of teacups while Isambard curled in his basket in the corner, observing. The gas fire's imitation coals were making a real crackling noise.

"My mother left us for a man called Alfred West. I met him once. It was the same occasion that I met my mother, although I didn't see the two of them together. He wasn't at all what I'd expected."

"How come?" Using both hands to raise the cup to her lips, Jenny sipped.

I sighed and closed my eyes, willing my thoughts to find their bearings. "I'd assumed she had left for someone richer, more attractive. You know how these things are supposed to work. Certainly someone who could have given her more than my father."

Jenny nodded, frowning.

"Not so." Already, I could feel guilt at the fact that the eleven-year-old in me had been repulsed by Alfred. By his puckered eye and the trouser-leg that turned over where his knee should have been. "Do you remember the photograph of the three children outside the photographic studio?"

"Not our man on Westminster Bridge?" Jenny asked.

"No, not him. I still can't work out where he comes into the picture."

"Shame. I thought we were onto something."

"I'm thinking of the bellboy. Something tells me that's him. I've found a number of pictures of the same lad. Although there seems to be a gap, the trail starts again several years after the war ended. Fetch the photo album from the other room and I'll show you."

Jenny deposited the green tome in my lap and knelt on the floor, one elbow resting on the arm of the chair. Isambard responded by repositioning himself by the other arm. I had been brave enough to fix the photographs of the early part of my mother's life in place, feeling confident that there were no more surprises lurking in boxes. Plucking a photograph of a man in uniform from its photo corners, I turned to the early pictures of the bellboy, and placed it beside them on the open page, then I set the album on the coffee table in front of Jenny.

"This was the man my mother left us for," I said, watching her face adjust.

I heard her breathe deeply and then swallow as she took in the face, the crutch, the folded trouser-leg. She searched the features firstly in the beaming boyish faces and then the old soldier's. After she turned the photograph over to find the date her face registered shock. "If he was the same age as your mother - and he can't have been much older - he was only twenty-five when this was taken. He looks like an…" She stopped mid-flow, turning the photograph back over to study it.

"An old man?" I nodded. "The war did that. It turned young men old overnight."

Looking up, she met my eyes. "Then it wasn't like you thought it was at all."

"No?"

"No! Your mother didn't reject you. She left because someone else needed her more."

"I can understand that as an adult, but I was only a boy. That didn't matter to me. *I* was supposed to be the most important person in her life. Do you remember how you told me that you just wanted your mother to be there when you got home from school?"

Jenny bit her lip and her hair fell forwards hiding her face.

"I would have liked that. Just once. My father told me there would be a next time. She only had to ask. I spent years waiting for an invitation that never came. And then I decided that I wouldn't go on like that, so I made a deliberate decision to forget all about her."

And then, with both Jenny and Isambard looking on, my shoulders shuddering, I started to cry tears containing the salt of many years.

45 - LOTTIE'S STORY

BRIGHTON, 1923

Stepping into the dim light of Mr Parker's office, I was greeted by an accumulation of dead bluebottles too numerous for the healthy population of spiders to dispose of. Deliberately ignoring them, I swept aside the limp velvet curtain covering the entrance to the studio, unable to recreate the feeling of unveiling Aladdin's Cave. My childish hope hadn't survived the loss of several brass hoops and the sophistication of London. The once-magical props reduced to a clutter of musty and mothballed relics, the task facing me seemed overwhelming.

You'll be back in six months.

"No, you won't." With eyes prickling, I scolded myself. "You wanted hard work, Lottie. Now you've got it."

I listed all of the things that needed to be done before I could consider opening the door: advertisements to be placed; cards to be printed; equipment to be installed; redecoration to be supervised. I cleaned and polished, hammered nails into walls, hung pictures. With rolled sleeves and physical activity I banished any self-pity I was harbouring and, if I occasionally caught a glimpse of a man in a black suit out of the corner of my eye, his presence was not unwelcome.

"Miss Pye." The decorator approached me, paintbrush in hand, not for the first time that morning. "The clock's ticking. Have you decided what we're to do with the exterior sign?"

I stepped outside onto the bleached flagstones and, biting my lip, stood surveying the shopfront: N M Parker; Parker's Photographic Studio.

"I'm sorry to press you, but we must have your decision. We've another job at Hove to start on tomorrow."

Like a photograph, the sign was a piece of the past existing in the present. Besides, Mr Parker had no other memorial on his home soil. "I can't bear to paint over his name. He was my tutor, you see."

"Can you afford to be sentimental? You'll want to use your professional name. It's free advertising."

He was right, just as Kingdom had been. I was under no illusion about my prospects. I couldn't rely on the support of rich clients for special commissions. My staple was to be bread-and-butter studio work and my rates needed to be keen. But I was decided.

"I appreciate your advice, but I've had enough change. *People* have had enough change. Parker's will stay as Parker's."

"Forgive me for saying so, Miss, but I think you're making a mistake."

"There must be another way." Looking at the half-hexagonal window-shelf behind the plate glass, I remembered the wonderful displays at Fortnum's and Harrods that changed with every season, and it struck me: I would make my own window display.

Following me back into the shop, the poor man scratched his head. "So I'm to leave it as it is?"

"Just a fresh coat of paint. And the letters outlined in gold. Like a shadow."

He shook his head. "As you wish."

"I do." The picture coming into focus in my mind, all I

needed to do was create it. "That's exactly what I wish."

With renewed energy, I searched through my portfolio for work that was recognisable as mine. Not only my award-winning photographs - which I hoped would be familiar to visitors from London and enthusiasts - but those that would show people my love for Brighton. I selected photographs that I had taken of the Indian soldiers: at prayer, resting, wielding cricket bats. Those I had taken of recognisable personalities: not just the rich and famous but Daddy sweeping the pavement outside the shop; the fishermen and their wives at market; our postman wheeling his bicycle uphill; the vicar scowling at a small child. My home town. The project gave me new purpose; not just hope, but excitement. My vision was of a gallery that locals would return to searching for themselves among the faces, something I hoped would help people realise that photography was not just for the few.

With my back facing the door, I was preparing for a visit from a local journalist when the bell clattered. I turned, finding myself face to face with Alfie. My features froze.

"Catching flies?"

I closed my mouth.

"I heard a rumour you'd taken over the old place and I came to ask if you've got a job for a man with one good leg and one good arm."

"Alfie." I was unprepared for this conversation. Not knowing how to announce my return - either to Alfie or to Ma, whose response I feared - I had put it off.

"Don't panic. I'm just here to take a look around."

I smiled guiltily. Had my reaction been so obvious? "Still in uniform, I see."

"I don't expect my old bellboy get-out will fit me. Still here, is it?" He shuffled forwards, casting his eye around the office. "Like coming home, isn't it? Except you've made a few changes." Then he pointed to a photograph on the wall opposite the door and said, "That won't do. It's one of my favourites of yours."

"Mine too. I want people to see it as soon as they come in."

"They won't see it at all, with that reflection bouncing off the glass! And you're the one who's supposed to understand light."

I stood beside him. "You're right. I haven't looked at it from this angle."

"Just as well I'm here." Balancing his crutch against the wall, Alfie lifted the photograph from its hook using his good hand. I swallowed as I wondered how he would manoeuvre himself, but the frame was not so large that he couldn't elbow his crutch into place and walk, albeit clumsily, as far as the desk. Grinning, he said, "Nothing broken. That went better than I thought."

The bell sounded again and he turned to greet my visitor, holding the door open. The man from *The Gazette* removed his hat with one hand and smoothed his hair with the other, whilst wiping his feet conscientiously on the mat.

"Do you have an appointment with Mrs Hastings?" Alfie asked with customary friendliness.

I stepped forward and offered my hand. "Lottie Pye. I use my professional name when I'm working." Nobody moved. As much to break the silence as anything, I said, "And this is my assistant, Alfred West."

"Alfie!" The man clapped Alfie on the shoulder. "Good to see you looking so well."

"You know each other?" I smiled, feeling foolish. "Of course you do. After London, I've forgotten what it's like to live in a town."

"You remember Charlie!" Alfie laughed, taking charge. "Charlie Brazier?"

The penny dropped. "You're *that* Mr Brazier? I never would have recognised you!"

"Pulled your hair and made you cry, remember?"

"I was hoping you might have forgotten." Charlie pointed at Alfie affably. "You gave me a black eye for that."

"I should think so, picking on Lottie!" He took Charlie's hat and, with a flick of his good wrist, landed it on the coat stand. "Why don't you two make yourselves comfortable. I'll see if I can't find where the tea's hidden."

"Upstairs, straight ahead. Everything should be on the tray."

"Righto. I think I'll prop that door open. Get rid of those paint fumes before we all pass out."

Charlie waited until Alfie had stomped out of the room, then lowered his voice. "Will he manage?"

I tried to look confident. "He'll be fine."

"I have to say, it's awfully good of you to find him a job. Alfie always could talk his way into anything."

"He was apprenticed to Mr Parker. Alfie knows the equipment as well as I do." Even as I said it, I saw the sense in Alfie's proposition. I was going to need help and there was no one I trusted more.

"But… I mean to say."

Trying to ignore the all too obvious shout of "Bugger" and the loud clattering that followed - there would be a few minor issues to overcome - I smiled at Charlie stiffly. "I believe we have an interview to be getting on with."

Looking flustered, he plucked a notebook from his inside pocket and, licking a finger, located his place. "Miss Pye, you've had your share of success in London."

"Lottie," I corrected him. "Seeing as we know each other. I've also had my fair share of controversy," I pointed out, having learned that directness tends to throw journalists off their guard.

"But why give up a blossoming business?"

"I rather hope I haven't given it up. I've simply relocated.

Brighton's always been in my blood. It's a large part of who I am. Do you know London?"

"I've visited once or twice." He moved his head from side to side. "Seen the sights."

"Then you'll understand what I mean when I say that it's hard to wake up with brick walls at the end of your road when you're used to sea and sky. London air tastes of smoke when I craved salt. They have pigeons instead of gulls. But most of all, the people I met just weren't family."

"Now that's an interesting reference, because you didn't know your own family, did you?"

"I think of all the people I care about as family. The fact that we're not related isn't important to me. Ma, Felicity, Harry…"

We had heard Alfie's slow approach and withdrawal as he thumped his way up and down the stairs several times. The curtain shouldered aside, he appeared in the office doorway red-faced with effort, the tea tray balanced on his forearms. I stood to relieve him of it, looking him in the eye, "…not forgetting Alfie, of course. Alfie, I was just telling Charlie that you're family as far as I'm concerned." I turned to slide the tray onto the table.

"I hear that you are married. Will your husband be joining you?"

"That isn't very likely. He loves his London club too much."

At this point, Alfie put his good hand on my left shoulder. I looked up at him and raised my own to meet it. "I'll be out the back if you need me," he said, and to Charlie, with humour. "You'd better make this a good article or there'll be another black eye for you."

When I turned back to Charlie he was fly-catching. Perhaps it wouldn't be the article I had hoped for, but we are accustomed to putting on brave faces in Brighton. The mayor is most insistent.

"I'm sorry." I smiled. "Where were we?"

He closed his mouth, tracing one finger down his list of questions. "How were you introduced to photography?"

"It was right here, in this studio. I used to run errands for Mr Parker before I became his model."

"And, can I ask, how would you describe your own work?"

As always, when struggling to articulate my thoughts, I turned to a visual image for inspiration. "A photograph allows a piece of the past to exist in the present. Mr Parker called the camera his time machine. He said he was stopping time itself. I'm sorry…" The moments when the mention of my tutor's name brought tears to my eyes still caught me by surprise. "I look at the images I took a few years ago and I see faces of those who are no longer with us, buildings that have been destroyed. Even children who grow up too fast."

Charlie shook his head. "Oh, they do that, right enough!"

"You have children?"

"Two boys. My oldest is three. Honestly, I don't know where the time has gone."

"Then you'll understand why I'm so distressed if I see an image I'd like to capture and I don't have my camera with me, or if I fail to reproduce it faithfully."

"You're obviously passionate about your work."

"It's my life."

"Can I ask, if you were really able to stop time, when would you have stopped it?"

The question floored me. Said by someone else its meaning seemed to have altered, the focus on moments I would have changed or erased. The instant before the lightning strike, my mother's head turning in surprise; Daddy crouched in a ditch alone in the dark before the car came hurtling round the bend; a stubborn kiss on a lonely beach; my decision to pose for the general's photographs; my final view of James sleeping as I stood in the doorway.

And, sitting in the chair that had belonged to my old tutor,

I wondered for the first time what Mr Parker might have thought of when a small girl asked him why anyone would want to stop time. What of the wife and daughter he so rarely mentioned? His own private memories, the moments he had failed to capture. What, I now suspected, had informed his choice to become a photographer. Perhaps what had convinced him of the sacredness of life.

"Are you all right, Lottie?"

"Yes," I insisted. I chose a cherished moment: something simple. The surprise and delight on Daddy's face as I hurled myself into his arms. "I was just thinking. It's so hard to choose just one, but I think I'd go back to see my Daddy."

"I remember him." Charlie nodded approvingly, scribbling in his notebook. "He was a good man."

"I couldn't have been luckier."

"Now, you were a model before you became a photographer. Can I ask, how does that influence your approach?"

"I have the advantage of understanding what the model and what the photographer contributes. Over the last couple of years I've worked almost exclusively with women, taking the time to understand how they see themselves."

"You've taken photographs of -" He thumped his chest as he cleared his throat, then his hand traced the circumference of his shirt collar. "Excuse me - nudes, have you not?"

"Not exclusively. But, when there is demand, yes."

"Can I ask why?"

"The same reason that an artist draws from life, I imagine: to learn about form. Because everything is so pared back, I've gained a far better understanding of lighting and exposure."

"I hope you don't mind if I press you. Why that particular direction?"

"It chose me. Women wanted me to recreate my winning competition-entry with them as the model."

Charlie glanced at his list of questions as if they might

come to his rescue. Following his gaze, I saw words written in capitals: *FORCE THE ISSUE.* "But why spend money on something they couldn't display in their own homes?"

"You'd have to ask them that!" I laughed. "But seriously, I like to think all of the photographs we created were suitable for display. I only ever take photographs of my subjects as they want to be seen. Frankly, I found the photographs of the women's Olympic swimming team far more shocking than anything I've produced. And I dislike the use of nudity in religious art, which people have no scruples about hanging in their living rooms."

Charlie's expression suggested distinct discomfort. He appeared to skip to the end. "Can I ask what you hope to offer your home town at this stage in your career?"

"Mr Parker understood that not everybody wants stiff, formal photographs. His were full of warmth and personality. He was also keen to embrace new technology. I intend to follow in his footsteps. I can see a day when ordinary people will own cameras and will use them to record their everyday lives. So as well as a studio, I've created a gallery for the community. I want to show people what's within their reach."

"I think I have enough material for the article." He reached down and opened his bag. "You know what I have to ask you now?"

Seeing his camera, I laughed. "Only if I can take yours."

Charlie protested. "What do you want a picture of me for?"

"For the gallery. Come through to the studio." I whisked aside the new curtain, the thickest ruby velvet I had been able to track down. "I'll show you where the magic takes place."

46 - LOTTIE'S STORY

BRIGHTON, 1923

Somewhere close by, a neighbour's child was wailing, its cries waning as it seemed to reach the point of exhaustion and then, finding a new source of energy, escalating: desperate. I realised it was a sound I had never heard in my London household, Nanny rushing to my son's side before his cries could filter through the door of the nursery.

"Lottie, I'm not sure I can..." In the darkness, Alfie pulled away from me and, breathing heavily, lay stiffly on his back.

"Don't worry." I blinked with unseeing eyes. Some maternal instinct made me want to get up and tend to the child. "It's not important."

I was determined that this wouldn't be a disaster. Too much was at stake. I had felt the need to embrace the reality of what I would grow to think of as my amputated family. Amputated, because my companion in life was no longer complete in body. Amputated, because I had chosen to separate myself from my husband and son. Amputated, because Alfie and I would never complete our own triangle. I had insisted that we both undress. For Alfie, even the removal of his shirt had been difficult. I had dragged his trousers from him. He lay on his back, neither responsive nor in rejection. "You're only saying that to make me feel better."

"Would you believe me if I said I wasn't?"

"Aren't you?"

"No." I rolled onto my side and supported my head with a hand, cupping his face with the other. I traced the roughness of Alfie's skin gently: he was tense but didn't flinch. "After our wedding night, Kingdom and I never slept in the same bed. We could never have had a conversation like this."

"Above all that, was he?"

"That's why I came back. I was forgetting who I was."

"Not for me, then?"

"And for you. Mostly for you," I admitted. "Have you ever… you know?"

"You and your questions! I'm glad it's dark, that's all I can say! When you said you couldn't have had this conversation with your husband, I was almost flattered. *Before* I knew this was what you had in mind."

"Say it quickly and get it over with. Cross my heart, I promise not to tell your mother."

"Once. In France."

Propped up on an elbow, I could just see the light from the hall reflecting on Alfie's puckered eye and I felt an immense tenderness towards him. "Was she pretty?"

"Now, how am I supposed to answer without getting myself into trouble?" He fidgeted, the commotion resulting in some minute adjustment of his arms and shoulders.

"She *was* pretty. I'm glad." Resting my head on his chest, I pushed my body against his. The skin of his torso was warm and smooth and I breathed him in. "Did you know, when I kissed you that time on the beach, I thought that was all there was to it?"

I felt strangely protective of this other person whose breath buffeted my forehead, whose chest rose and fell under my arm, whose veins pulsed so violently beneath his body's surface. I had vanity enough to think I had the power to heal him. A smile spread over my face. That was how we fell asleep.

When I woke next in the early hours, it wasn't to the sound of the baby's crying, but to a twitching, whimpering, then a sound so violent it wasn't possible to imagine the visions that accompanied it. Alfie's open eyes unseeing, in a state of half-sleep he moved as quickly as he might have done on two good legs, seeking safe refuge under the bed. I swung my legs out, moved the chamber pot aside and crept underneath, dragging the blanket behind me. The bare floorboards were cold and rough, and I tucked it under his bad leg, worried about the damage that his irregular jerking movements were causing to its fragile skin. We shivered together, his body angular and rigid where it touched mine. I had heard tales of men crying out for their mothers when they were taken like this, but, though he gave no indication he knew I was there, it was my name Alfie used.

"I'm here." I spoke the words repeatedly into the back of his neck, not knowing if he heard me or not. "Shhhh. I'm not going anywhere."

I was determined to be strong when he was weak. If this was how it was, so be it. The next night, I would be better prepared. I would lay spare blankets on the boards under the bed.

47 - SIR JAMES'S STORY

SHERE, 2009

When my shoulders had stilled and my tears had stopped falling, with Jenny and Isambard still looking on, I made the admission I had remained silent on: the one that most troubled me. "Alfred West wrote to me once."

"He *wrote* to you?" Jenny failed to tame the surprise in her voice.

I nodded, allowing my chest a slow rise and fall. "It was after my father died. He wanted to explain that my mother thought it best she didn't come to his funeral. Hadn't wanted to cause any more upset. His solicitors had been in contact with her, of course, but I didn't invite her to the service. I didn't see why I should when she'd never shown the slightest interest in us. They had found an announcement in the local newspaper quite by chance. The organisers of the London to Brighton rallies had placed it - my father had always been a great supporter of theirs. Alfred said that they had agreed he would attend on behalf of both of them."

"He was there?"

"Yes - not that I saw him." I shook my head. "The church was packed. Once I had carried the coffin inside, I sat in the front pew and didn't look backwards."

Although my head was low, Jenny must have observed how I pulled my upper lip in and bit it. "There's more, isn't there?" she asked and reached for my right hand.

I took a deep breath. "My mother didn't know that Alfred wrote to me. They'd had a blazing row, you see, and he took it on himself to go behind her back. I think the decision must have pained him. My mother had always claimed that the reason she wouldn't make contact with me was out of respect for my father's wishes. Alfred tried to change her mind after my father died, but she insisted that his death didn't alter anything: an agreement was an agreement. Alfred thought she was being stubborn. But more than that - he was worried she would live to regret it."

"He asked you to make the first move," Jenny said. It wasn't a question.

I hung my head. "I was too angry. I wrote to the poor man and said it was too late for all that."

"Did you ever hear from him again?"

"Oh, yes. He replied. A very kind letter. Said he was sorry, but that he respected my feelings." I met Jenny's eyes. "He assured me he would stop trying to encourage my mother. He told me he recognised it was too painful for both of us."

Jenny said nothing, nodding.

I felt the damp of Isambard's warm muzzle on my knee and looked down to see his saucer-like eyes peering up at me. "I think that Alfred West was a good man."

"Do you wonder why your mother didn't want to be buried next to him? Or with the Pyes for that matter?"

"I thought of nothing else all the way back from St Nicholas's. I never would have said this before, but -" I smiled weakly. "Let's just say you've put me straight on a few things. I don't think she thought she deserved to be happy. Not even in her choice of final resting place."

48 - LOTTIE'S STORY

BRIGHTON, 1924

I pushed Ma's shop door open tentatively, breathing in the frying onions and crisp pastry, smells that threatened to drag me back to the child I once was. George V's disapproving eyes glared down at me from his frame.

Felicity clattered to the bottom of the steps at the sound of the bell, wiping her hands on her starched apron. "Lottie!" Then she lowered her voice. "So, the rumours *are* true."

I took both of her hands in mine. "It's so good to see you. How's Harry?"

"Exhausting, that's how he is! And your little James?" she asked, moving her head so that she could look me in the eye.

"Please. Not now. I need to -" This was not the time to give way to tears. I needed to face Ma as her equal.

"Oh, Lottie, no!" My meaning clear, Felicity's eyes widened with concern. "What about Kingdom? Has he let you go so easily?"

"No." The corners of my mouth twitched. "There was nothing easy about it."

She glanced over her shoulder in the direction of the kitchen, whispering, "I wouldn't be surprised if Kitty has heard the same fishwives' tales that I did. Do you know what you're doing?"

"I've been away too long, Felicity."

"It's Alfie, isn't it? She whispered, squeezing my hands.

I met her gaze, desperate to know if I had her support, and she smiled that same frayed smile of hers.

"I always knew there was something special between you." Felicity followed the route my eyes took towards the staircase. "Best get it over with. You'll have a rough ride ahead - and not just from Kitty." I felt the warmth of her hand on my arm. "Believe me, I know what people here are like."

But I had already left it too late. Ma greeted me with fury born from holding her head high in the face of gossip-mongers. "Come to show your face, have you?" Standing in the doorway of the kitchen, her face was already red and clammy from standing over a pot. She adopted the stance I recognised so well: hands on hips, feet hip-width apart. Yet to reach boiling point, she had been saving herself. "So!" Her nod was all-knowing. "You went and married your playboy and now you've left him!"

"I've come home, Ma."

"Your home is with your husband and son." She shook her head, punctuating her words with jabs of her finger. "Your decision! Your choice!"

She turned her back on me and walked into the room. I followed, protesting. "That was before I knew Alfie was alive!"

"'*Til death do us part*, you promised. Not while it suited. Always leaving as soon as things get difficult!" Her words rained down, one after another and, just as her stories did, they took on the rhythm of dough being pummelled. Work couldn't pause, even for an argument. "And why here, where you bring shame on both families? Don't you think Mrs West has been through enough, is that it?"

"It was you who taught me that being useful is important!"

"Hah!" She expelled the sound as if accused of an atrocity. Her second attack was more pronounced. "I taught you about the importance of family. Loyalty. What about your little boy who needs you? I don't know why I'm wasting my breath. I should have known you wouldn't have a maternal bone in your body, just like your own mother. No sense of sacrifice."

There was more if I had cared to listen, but it was there: an echo. *Just like your own mother.*

"Like my own mother?" I interrupted, uncertain if I had heard correctly.

Ma startled as if slapped; sat down at the table. Put her head in her hands. "Out of my sight!" she ordered, her voice flat and bitter, but, more than anything, aged. "I can't look at you."

No longer contrite, I grabbed one of her arms and pulled her hand away from her face. "Tell me what you meant!"

She inhaled deeply before snapping back, "Your Daddy was right. You begged me for fairy tales, so that's what I gave you!"

"What do you mean, Ma?" I was quieter now, my stomach turning in apprehension.

She extracted herself from my grip with the nervousness of a child expecting punishment. "Your Daddy didn't know the truth." She nursed her arm. "I never told him."

I sank onto the hard wooden seat of the chair next to hers. "Are you saying that the story about the storm wasn't true?"

"The storm was true enough."

"But the lady on the promenade? My mother -?"

"Dead." She crossed herself. "Though she wasn't your mother."

"But your hands…" I grabbed at them, peeling back her fingers to reveal what I had always taken as proof of Ma's love for me.

"I was stupid. Picked up the pot without using a cloth." My eyes followed hers to the blackened handle of the saucepan on the fire. "I was on my way to have them looked at when the rain began." Pausing, Ma beseeched me. "I didn't want to tell you like this."

I felt no pity. "Were you *ever* going to tell me?"

"Perhaps. If you hadn't left like you did."

So this was how it was going to be, blame batted from her side of the court to mine. "The truth, Ma, you owe me the truth!" My elbows made careless circles in the dusting of flour.

It is far harder to begin a story than you might think. You might say, "Start at the beginning," but sometimes there is no obvious beginning. You just have to begin. Ma began with a policeman called George.

"You remember him. The one who came to tell us about your daddy's accident?"

Impatient, I failed to see the relevance of his appearance. "Yes?"

"George had a sister - Constance May - younger than him by some years. People thought her simple, but show her how to do a job and she could do it well enough. She went into service at the age of thirteen. A good household, so they thought. Anyway, Constance May got herself into trouble - the eldest son - and was thrown out. She couldn't show her face at home, so she went to the workhouse where she gave birth." Ma met my eyes directly and nodded, eliminating any lingering doubt. "The day of the storm, I was walking along the promenade on my way to the doctor's - that much was true. Lightning caught my eye and drew it to the beach. There was a young girl crouched down low, half hidden between the upturned boats. By this time the centre of the storm was heading our way.

"I called out, but couldn't make my voice carry over the sound of the rain. As I made my way down the steps, I could see the girl loading pebbles into an old flour sack, and there was movement inside. My immediate thought was that it was kittens and I couldn't bear to think of them being drowned."

She hesitated. "Do you want me to go on?"

I nodded with a helplessness I hadn't felt since I was a child who wanted nothing more than everything to stay exactly the way things were.

"It was only then that I recognised Constance May. She was shivering wet, her eyes wild, and I asked her how she'd got like that." Ma pawed at my arm. "Are you sure, Lottie?"

"I have to know."

"Yes, I think you probably do. I only wish -" She swallowed the end of her sentence and nodded: *so be it*. "She said to me, 'I waded out up to my waist but I couldn't make her sink. The tide brought her back.' People often referred to objects as 'she', so I didn't think twice about her choice of words."

One hand at my collarbone, I could barely whisper, "My God."

Ma was blinking hard at the table top as though she couldn't believe her own words, but they had gathered a momentum of their own. "I said to her, 'Go home and get dried off, Constance May. I'll do that for you,' thinking that she would leave and I could take the kittens. 'I can't ever go home,' she said. It was then I realised that the mewing I could hear wasn't kittens: it was a child. Trying not to let my panic show, I said, 'Let me take a look.' Constance May didn't resist, so I said, 'What a beautiful baby. Do you think I might hold her?' Her face lit up and she said, 'I don't suppose you'd like to keep her? Only you mustn't tell no one she's mine.' Then, before I realised what she intended, Constance May got up and walked straight back into the water. I had to fight her to pull her out of there, hanging onto the clothes on her back. She only stopped struggling when we heard a crash of thunder. It was as if the whole world was coming to an end. There was a blinding flash and I thought I saw something hurtling off the pier. I had no idea what it was - to be honest, all I was interested in was finding us some shelter. Then came the sound of shouting and shrieking, lots of it. I knew people would be distracted, so I said, 'We'll find somewhere safe for you, I promise.' By then Constance May was so frightened it was easy to convince her to let me take her by the arm.

"Who should we meet at the top of the stairs but her brother, George. 'Can't stop,' he said. 'I'm on my way to an emergency,' but I told him, 'There's an emergency for you right here,' and that was when he saw his sister. George had five daughters of his own and couldn't take another child, but he knew I had lost my boys. When I offered to give you a home, he thought it would be for the best. We persuaded the nuns at St Mary's to take Constance May -"

"The home for penitents?" I interrupted.

"That's right. She wouldn't hear of going to her mother's or back to the workhouse. The only other option was the asylum, but that was a dreadful place. It was George who dreamt up your story after someone grabbed me in the street and said, 'You saved the baby. Thank the Lord. We all saw the carriage go over the edge and thought it was drowned, poor thing.'

"George persuaded a coastguard to take him out by boat, but they didn't hook a carriage or a baby. Only a three-wheeled bicycle with a basket on the front. There was so much commotion that no one ever questioned the story, least of all your Daddy. When he commented on my hands, I had all but forgotten about them. It was him who bandaged them, suggesting it must have been the residual current that burnt me. You know how he was with science. I didn't like keeping anything from him. I just said that I had done what anyone in their right mind would have done - which was the truth."

I was numb. If I wasn't the daughter of a prostitute, a fine lady from London, or an aspiring actress, *who was I?*

And then it dawned on me. "My mother: is she still alive?"

Ma nodded. "She still lives at St Mary's. I see her every week."

And, of course, I realised. My mother was Ma's charitable cause, her Sunday outing.

"You can't go telling people. If you do, it will have all been for nothing." It was Ma's turn to grab me by the arm. "It wouldn't do any good, going to see her," she said. "She doesn't remember."

"What's my name? My real name?"

"You had no first name when I found you, but your mother's family name was Ellis."

"And my father? Does he have a name?"

"I never asked." Her voice was curt.

But she had been in service. A good family. "It wouldn't have been so hard for you to find out."

She turned on me, a little of her fight returning. "I didn't want to! Don't you see? I didn't want to lie to your daddy any more than I had to!"

"Surely there was gossip -"

The shake of her head was most insistent. "I've never mixed with women who gossip, Lottie. You know that."

"But you let Daddy spend good money on advertisements - money the business couldn't afford. You allowed Daddy to trawl through the columns week after week, knowing he wouldn't find anything!"

"I didn't know that for a fact. There was always the possibility your father would come looking for you."

He hadn't wanted to. That much was clear.

I don't know how I managed to get up and walk down the stairs. The need to get outside and breathe must have carried me.

"Lottie?" Felicity looked up from her cleaning of the counter, cloth in hand.

Grasping for the door handle, I hesitated. "Did you know a girl called Constance May Ellis at St Mary's?"

"Little Connie? The cleaner? You met her. That day on the

steps with me, poor sweet thing. She managed to take offence at something you said, do you remember? Is everything alright?"

"Everything's fine," I said, and then I made my way to the seafront to revisit the place where my story began, eyes open for the first time.

I sat on the shingle, gripping my knees and rocking. It was the place where Alfie and I had always taken refuge when the world around us had gone mad: next to the feet of the pier - the place I had so carefully avoided of late, but the only possible place to be. The hypnotic effect of the tide did its job. My breathing slowed to its rhythm. The foam of the waves crept ever closer, my feet already damp, but I was barely aware of its timid passage. There, time stopped of its own accord.

I sat up abruptly as something landed violently in the pebbles beside me - Alfie's crutch. It heralded shouting so intense it was as though I had suddenly taken my fingers out of my ears. "*What are you doing, sitting here in the wet? Didn't you hear me?*" I blinked up at Alfie helplessly. "I've been shouting for ages. Harry said his mother told him I must come and look for you, that it was urgent. No clues. Just 'Find her!' So, come on. What's so important that you couldn't come up the steps to meet me? You know this is the *one* thing - the one *thing!* - I need help with."

I saw the distance Alfie had travelled: down the steps and across the expanse of shingle. All on his own. And then I could see no more.

"What is it, Lottie? I shouldn't have blown up at you. Now, there's no need for that. Nothing can be this bad." He dropped down awkwardly, some feet behind me.

"Can't it?" I wailed.

He held out his arms. "Get yourself over here in the dry. Come on."

I shuffled backwards and he folded his arms around my shoulders.

"Now tell me."

"I can't -"

"Yes you can. Let the wind carry the words out to sea."

And, for the first time, I recounted the tale of how my own mother had tried to do away with me. After listening in silence, and without interruption, Alfie shook his head. "My mother always said she was from St Mary's. That must be how the gossip started."

The home for fallen women.

I was aghast. "Your mother knew?"

He shrugged. "More likely to have been a good guess. She always did have a sixth sense. I preferred your Ma's version."

I began to shiver violently. "All those years, she lied to me!"

"She was protecting you." He smoothed my salt-encrusted hair with his good hand. "But more than that: she was protecting your mother."

"She says I asked her for fairy tales and that was what I got."

"For goodness' sake, you were a child!"

"Every decision I've ever made was because I thought I was someone else."

"Listen to me, Lottie. A name doesn't mean anything. So far I've met Lottie Pye, Charlotte Lavashay, Mrs Hastings and now this Lottie Ellis, and do you know something? You're the same person you always were. Still my stubborn red-head."

My hands reached for the cold, smooth curves of stones. "It's not just a name. Don't you see? I have no idea who I am!"

Alfie's hold on me tightened. "I know this changes things. Not being wanted is different from being orphaned, I understand that. You'll be thinking of James - and perhaps even Kingdom now you know you have a link to his world."

I twisted round to protest. "I -"

"Shhhh! Let me say this: if you want to go back to London and take care of your little boy, I'll understand."

"I -"

"For barking out loud, let me finish, will you? Even if you don't want to hear this, I need to say it. I'll always know you came back for me. You kept your side of our bargain."

I shook my head. Ma was right: I didn't have a maternal bone in my body. It had taken the sound of my neighbour's child's ragged cries to make me think it peculiar that I had never heard my own son's. Thank goodness he was safe, where I could do him no harm. "I don't deserve James -"

"That's nonsense, Lottie, and I won't have you saying it. Not after you've taken care of me the way you have. But there will come a day when perhaps you need to think about the story that your husband is telling your little boy. Because he'll have to tell him something."

I should have listened, but with everything else drowning in doubt I clung to one certainty - that, somewhere in the muddy water of morals, I was putting the past right.

49 - LOTTIE'S STORY

BRIGHTON, 1925

I met my mother twice. Once as a child, once as an adult.

It had been many years since I stopped searching for her face in the crowd. There was another face I looked for. Fooling myself that I was collecting images for the gallery, the lens of my camera seemed to settle on every stone-skimming, bony-kneed boy under a certain age. Even when I didn't go out into the world, they peered through the studio window, leaving greasy fingerprints in the fog from their breath; they sneaked into the office for a glimpse of the 'funny man with the leg'; they begged me for errands to run, hoping to earn tips. On the days I didn't feel the need to keep my distance, I rewarded them with a glimpse through the lens beyond the ruby velvet curtain, and their delight reminded me of my first glimpse of the magic I had insisted was science.

To begin with, the boys were the only people who came: acts of disobedience and rebellion. Alfie and I were a curiosity. Living together openly, people felt more comfortable referring to us as 'the Parkers'. We never felt the need to correct them, because we had both come to realise that Mr Parker had thought of us as his children, giving us opportunities when the alternatives were too hard to contemplate. Among people of our own age or over, I was the town Jezebel, some-one who had always thought herself above rules. Tolerated only because of Alfie, who had always been well-liked and was thoroughly dependable, even to the point of limping back from the dead to comfort his mother.

Felicity was the only person I turned to for advice: she understood what it meant to be looked down on. "Hold your head up. Never apologise. But make yourself visible in the community. Volunteer for the jobs no one else wants to do and do them well. Never boast, just keep doing them. People come round, but it takes time."

"What sort of things should I volunteer for?"

"You remember my appointments?"

"Yes?"

"I used to visit the people in hospital no one else would go and see. Those who'd been turfed out of the workhouse. People without family, or whose family wouldn't see them because they had something contagious. I spoon-fed them when they couldn't feed themselves. Gave them bed baths. Held their hands."

I looked at Felicity and thought about how she had been happy to let people think what they would. She smiled at me. "Never feel you have to explain yourself when you know the truth."

It was some time after I began my rounds of visiting that I realised someone was missing from my list.

"George," I said, entering the police station one September evening as the light was draining from the violet sky.

"What can I do for you?" He looked up from the desk cheerfully and I watched his Adam's apple move. He knew me, and he knew what people said about me. "Lottie." His voice was strangled. "I didn't expect to see you."

"If I ever wanted to know, would you be able to tell me my father's name?"

I heard his sharp intake of breath, his hesitation.

"I don't - not now. But if I ever felt the need?"

George cleared his throat and licked his lips nervously. "I'd be able to tell you."

An understanding.

"I'd like to meet my mother," I announced.

He said nothing, locking eyes across the desk.

"Now - if you don't mind. I don't want to cause any trouble. She needn't know who I am."

George wiped his mouth with the back of one hand, sniffed, then pushed himself to standing. "Gregson! Watch the front office for me."

"Where are you going?"

"Out!"

We walked the short distance to Queens Square in silence but for the sound of our footsteps. It seemed there was little to be said between an uncle and his niece. The lie had been washed away but not the twenty-five years in between.

The door of St Mary's was answered by a blinkered nun who greeted George with some surprise. "It's not your usual day, Sergeant Ellis."

"I know it's irregular, but I'm working this Thursday."

"I see." She looked at me, hands clasped in front of her, waiting for an explanation to be offered.

"This is…" He hesitated.

"Mrs Hastings." I offered my gloved hand, respectable when I chose to be. The nun responded with a curt nod.

I had little time to reflect on how I was feeling as we were shown to a door with a small grille in it, one of many identical openings on a long stretch of echoing white-washed corridor. I remembered two young women appearing drunk, free from the oppression of having spent too long indoors. "We live very simply here, Mrs Hastings." The nun turned to me, before knocking. "Constance May! You have visitors."

The door opened inwards and I saw her: an expectant pair of eyes, which quickly retreated when she realised that her brother wasn't alone.

"Take a seat," George said to me in a warning voice, then spoke with a gentleness I hadn't detected in him before. "Connie, this is a lady photographer who's come to see you."

Her lank hair was long and grey, worn loose and tucked back behind her ears. She perched on the narrow metal-framed cot with its threadbare covering, knees angled towards George. Her eyes darted from one point to another, as if she were tracking the movement of a fly, never settling for more than a moment. She clasped and unclasped her hands, the nails bitten to the quick, fingertips raw.

"I don't want my photograph taken." She turned towards me, her expression almost spiteful.

I carried my camera with me out of habit, an extension of myself. Covering the lens with my hands I assured her, "I won't take your photograph."

I needed no photograph to remind me. The eyes were wide-spaced, ice blue, the skin alabaster, as skin can only be when it doesn't see the light of day, the mouth thin and drawn. This was a face that cared nothing for appearance, aged beyond its thirty-nine years as if time advanced at an accelerated rate within the closed walls of St Mary's. The spacing of her features wasn't at all like mine. Mr Parker's grid would have been of little use - but I recognised my hairline, the direction of growth, my nose, perhaps my chin. There was a baby-like quality about the face, an innocence despite its lines, but nothing remained of the pretty young woman I had seen stepping out of the front door all those years ago.

"I don't want you to take my photograph." Like a child, she sought the reassurance of repetition.

George sat on the bed next to her and patted her conjoined hands. "No one's going to do anything you don't want while

I'm here." An enviable display of solidarity.

I noticed that she had taken the once-white pillow from the bed and pulled off its cotton cover, which she twisted in her hands.

"Constance May," I ventured. "How long have you lived at St Mary's?"

"My whole life."

"All your life?" Surprise crept into my voice. But I remembered that Ma had told me Constance May - my mother - had little memory of her life before she came here. There would be no answers from her.

She glanced at George, who nodded, encouraging. "My whole life," she confirmed with confidence.

"What about your family?" I asked.

She rocked back and forth. "Three meals a day if I make myself useful."

"Well," I glanced about the room. "They certainly look after you." Apart from the single bed with a wooden cross on the wall above it, there was a bedside table with a copy of the bible and a hairbrush, and the wooden chair I was sitting on. Little comfort. No sign of personal possessions that might provide clues as to how a life was lived. When I looked back at my mother's face, her focus was the far corner of the small room. She had no interest in me, not even out of curiosity. I had invaded this intimate space without invitation. There was no place for me in it.

"I should go," I said, standing.

George turned to his sister: "I'll stay a while, shall I?"

She responded by resting her head on his shoulder, peaceful at last. Her hair fell forwards, covering half of her face.

"Goodbye, Constance May," I said, not expecting a response. After closing the door, I hesitated. Glancing back through the grille, the one eye I could see was wide open, staring directly at me. A shudder ran though me, the sort you might attribute to someone walking over your grave. From where I was standing, the pillowcase draped on her lap resembled a flour sack. One that might be used to drown kittens.

Standing there, I understood something very clearly, something not even Alfie had pointed out: the fact that my mother had been taken advantage of while in service was the reason Mr Parker's scaremongering had caused Ma to doubt herself. And without that doubt taking root I couldn't have avoided the life of a domestic servant. Or perhaps worse - this half-life of my mother's. So, although she had wanted to do away with me, had I been born to someone else, I might never have become a photographer.

Feeling the need to be near Ma, I found her in the half-darkness of the dying fire, darning what appeared to be one of Daddy's old brown socks.

"I've seen my mother," I announced.

Her eyes flared with anxiety.

I crouched down and took her hands. "It was something I needed to do and now it's over. You were right not to tell me the truth when I was younger. I wouldn't have been able to cope."

She nodded. It was all I would receive by way of an apology. "And what about your family in London?"

"My place is here with Alfie, Ma, and I need you to accept that. I'm good at what I do and I intend to make a success of my business. And when you can't manage the shop any more, I want to be here to take care of you. Just like you took care of me."

When she didn't reply, my eyes settled on Daddy's pipe, high on the mantelpiece. Following my gaze, Ma stood and stretched up to fetch it. She placed its curve firmly in the palm of my hand, folding my fingers around the bowl. I breathed in the scent of stale tobacco.

"You should have something to remember him by."

"But what else do you have of his?"

"I only need to close my eyes and he's beside me. You're the one who's always needed something to look at."

50 - LOTTIE'S STORY

DITCHLING, 1987

It was November 5th: Bonfire Night. Alfie and I were sitting at home with no option but to listen to the volley of fireworks that screeched across the night sky. His face and torso were hidden behind the newspaper. I disapproved of his choice of reading material. Degrading pictures of women and the publication of photographs intended to ruin lives, under the guise of public interest! Lester Piggott was their latest victim. Not enough that the jockey had been sent to jail for three years, they were intent on tearing him apart limb by limb. Given the work we had done together - the life that Alfie and I had led - I thought he should have known better.

The cats cowered under the coffee table, making themselves as small as possible by tucking in their legs tightly. Occasionally the tabby shifted her weight like a hen hatching eggs, while the other rolled his black tail disapprovingly. Alfie had never taken to the cats. I'd caught him throwing empty tins at them from his chair - and that was another bone of contention. You should have seen him when he came home from the doctors and was told he'd have to use a chair.

"Bloody witch doctor doesn't know what he's talking about! I walk in on my good leg to ask about one of those hip replacements they gave old Joe down the road - who's hardly used the damned thing, by the way - and he says to me, 'But Mr West, you've only got one leg.' 'Only one?' I says to him. 'I must have been robbed.'"

"Alfie, you didn't!"

"I've made better use of this one leg than most people make of two. Stands to reason it's going to wear out quicker. It's discrimination. I can't see why I'm not entitled to the same treatment as those old buggers, if not better. 'Know how I lost this?' I asked him. 'Fighting for King and Country.' He had the cheek to tell me my fighting days were long gone."

Alfie was proud. The doctor wouldn't have understood what it took for him to ask for help. Or what it took out of him to be told he'd have to address the world sitting down from there on in. Still, he enjoyed the motorised buggy the council provided. The 'boot' was just the right size to smuggle a four-pack of beer when he went for his daily jaunt to the war memorial to pay his respects to his father and brothers. Wreaking havoc on the pavements, he'd race the boys on their bikes. Thought I didn't know, the devil. That contraption was supposed to have a top speed of ten miles per hour. I think he got one of the local lads to turbo-charge it. And why not? There are only so many ways you can get your kicks after your body fails you.

Where was I? I get so forgetful these days. So we were listening to the neighbours (who enjoyed nothing better than to set fire to something in their back garden, cremating meat in the summer or keeping us up half the night come autumn) when Alfie rustled his paper and said, "Lottie Pye, you're looking particularly lovely this evening."

"What is it now?" I set my book down on the arm of the chair, its creased spine facing upwards. The interruption was an annoyance. I'd been meaning to re-read *Brideshead Revisited* ever since they turned it into a television series with that lovely young actor. For some reason, I felt the story connected me with my James. Since Kingdom's death, it had been rare for me to experience that connection. Say what you will, Kingdom always kept me up to date. There were those dreadful newspaper articles in the Sixties, which made me want to write to my son and comfort him. But my husband had named his terms. When I walked out of the door I accepted that I would never see James again. Kingdom's side of the bargain was unspoken. He didn't replace me. Sometimes I think it would have been better if he had, but I never had to worry about James calling another woman 'Mother'. Kingdom was gracious enough to allow me glimpses through letters and photographs - and that one time when my son was standing there right in front of me, so small and lost that I almost reached out to touch him. But James didn't know me. I framed the image of an anxious child looking back over his shoulder and carried it with me. A reminder that I had no right to cause further confusion in my son's life.

"Seeing as you're asking," Alfie continued. "I'll have one of your finest cups of tea. I'd get it myself, but -" and he looked down at his missing leg, shaking his head sorrowfully.

I narrowed my eyes. "That old excuse."

We had our routines, as two people who had lived together for fifty-five years do.

"Is a man not allowed to try?"

I sighed and pushed my bones out of the armchair. My elbow cracked as I leaned on it.

"You want to see a doctor about that," Alfie quipped.

"Don't push your luck." I thought I was old then!

I left him laughing to himself, resembling the Brighton boy I had known, and trailed my hand along the stacks of cardboard boxes that contained my life's work. The collection I had made for James. Each day a new image.

"I wish you wouldn't," Alfie used to say.

"I have to."

"I know that. I just don't like to see you torture yourself."

"It's my work."

"So you say."

They lined the hall and, stacked high, piled deep, they filled every crevice in the bungalow. Alfie threatened to set fire to the lot of them at least once a week, but he knew what they were.

Distracted by a spot of washing-up in the kitchen, I can't have been gone for more than five minutes when there was an ear-splitting explosion, loud enough to shake the walls.

"Jesus!" I heard Alfie shout as Blackie shot out of the living room and dashed across the kitchen tiles, seeking refuge in the corner under a chair.

"I'll have a word with them in the morning," I muttered to myself, and went to try and tempt him out with a scrap of left-over sausage. Then I set the tea things on the tray and walked back through, probably chattering. Something about a lack of respect for animals, or people who haven't experienced war not being able to understand.

I saw what remained of the rocket on the rug, set down the tea tray and bent stiffly to pick it up, one hand on the small of my back. A piece of tattered red paper attached to a stick. Harmless enough.

"Do you see? This thing actually came down..." And I turned to show Alfie the remnants. "...the chimney." There he was, one hand across his chest, his head slumped to the side. Eyes still open. And to think that I'd been worried about the cats. Since the war failed to finish him off, Alfie had always seemed invincible. "I won't write," I said and I kissed him hard on the lips.

When I dialled 999, I said, "They've killed him," and hung up.

From those three words, they tracked me down, sending

half of the local police force. But not an ambulance. Not a single doctor.

I must have gazed up at them, confused. "Madam, did you call us?" a blue uniform asked.

"I think I must have. Through there." I pointed.

They tell me I begged them not to take him. I don't remember now. It sounds like the sort of thing I might have done. What else would you do when the person who was your whole life is taken away from you? The only person who could remind me who I was. They left me his empty chair. In the flowerbed to the left of the front door I found a stone. Not smooth like the pebbles on the beach, but a rough-edged flint, broken to expose the inner scallop-shaped core. I placed it in the still-warm indent of his chair. That was more than twenty years ago.

I used to think the sea was calling me home. Now I wonder if it wasn't always the dead whose voices I heard.

Stories. I have three, but only one of them is true.

I took my pen and began to write in a spidery scrawl, '*Time measured in stones.*'

51 - SIR JAMES'S STORY

SHERE

Although the exhibition had been Jenny's idea, it had turned into something of a joint project. I may have missed my mother's funeral but it wasn't too late to pay tribute to her work. We had advertised in the local paper and in *Surrey Life*: 'I Stopped Time: A Retrospective. A photographic exhibition featuring the work of Lottie Pye, whose private collection dating from 1911 sheds new light on life in the early part of the 20th century. Her son, Sir James Hastings, has carefully selected 150 images from many thousands, including intimate family portraiture, Society and fashion shots and her award-winning entries in the *Daily Mail*'s photographic competition, first displayed in the National Portrait Gallery in 1918.'

Surprisingly, I had been telephoned by a man by the name of Martin Douglas who claimed to have inherited an original Lottie Pye.

"I'd be delighted if you'd show it," he said. "I've never known what the devil to do with it. I mean, where do you hang a naked photograph of your mother?"

I was sympathetic. "Where indeed?"

"I'm afraid it's been in the loft for years. She always swore she'd take her revenge on me when she died. I had no idea *this* was what she had in mind. She was always so damned upright, if you know what I mean."

"Oh, I do."

"She was a member of the church choir!"

Martin had arrived as scheduled with his mother tucked under his arm, sealed in bubble wrap.

"But she's beautiful!" Jenny had said on her unveiling, with customary enthusiasm. It was a straightforward photographic shot rather than a montage, but the lighting and pose had all of the hallmarks we'd come to recognise as my mother's work. Not nude, but draped in translucent fabric. I showed him the studio-stamp on the back of other photographs.

"It's the genuine article," I said.

"Are they valuable?" he asked with surprise.

"I have no idea," I admitted. "I suppose we might find out this evening. Would you want to sell?"

He laughed. "Do you think anyone would take her off my hands?"

Jenny's concerns were of a more practical nature. "I'll go and make her a plaque and then we'll find a good spot for her."

Out of Martin's eye line, I could see her frowning. In choosing mountings for the exhibits, Jenny's aim had been to let the photographs speak for themselves, rather than give them gilded cages, but this frame was an original. I wondered if she doubted her intuition. Then again, Jenny's frown might simply have been for anyone who would consider giving away what memories they had of a mother, particularly one that showed a previously unseen side of the young woman she once was.

"Do you think people will come?" I asked Jenny.

Standing by the door to the village hall, she clutched

a small pile of the leaflets she had designed. A thick black woollen coat covered her thin black dress, heels in the place of trainers, and she was dancing about in the draught of the porch.

When I had seen her half an hour earlier, I had been shocked by the transformation. "Good God," I gasped. "You look absolutely stunning."

"*She* took me to Guildford shopping." Brushing aside the compliment, Jenny confided, "I thought she was going to do the whole 'I'm not trying to replace your mother' thing, but she only wanted to buy me a new dress for this evening. Talk about making me feel guilty!"

"Well, you put me to shame. I'm going to change out of this ancient suit and tie and find something to do you justice."

And I had taken my tux out from its layers of protective plastic and brushed it down.

"Of course they'll come. We'll have to turn them away."

Outside, the sparkle of fairy lights and flashing blue icicles brightened the bleak mid-December evening, the occasional whoosh of tyres breaking through the silence. In the echoing hall, I sucked air slowly through the empty pipe. I had been a smoker once although I had given up years ago. It was only in the past few weeks that I had taken to using the pipe I had found among my mother's boxes as a comforter. My front teeth were a good fit for the indentations in the stem. I felt my pulse quieten and the nerves I always experience when waiting subside.

Slowly, a stream of people trickled into the hall, loitering at the drinks table to choose between mulled wine or bubbly from our local vineyard at Denbies, hands hesitating over identical mince pies. Quietly proud, I saw Jenny's father pointing out her handiwork to his girlfriend, their elbows grazing. I counted over sixty heads, many of them from the village, nodding to the Smythe-Jenkins and agreeing with

Mrs Adams's "Isn't this nice!" before the double doors were forced open as one. A large group of youngsters, fresh from the William Bray, arrived at the last moment filling the back half of the hall. I was rather worried they might prove disruptive but, as Jenny turned to greet them, I realised they were her class from college, there to offer support.

Jenny nodded encouragement from her halfway position and I tapped the microphone, stepping back as it growled at me.

"Ladies and Gentlemen, I'd like to thank you for tearing yourselves away from your Christmas preparations - and, I believe, *The X Factor* finals - to join us this evening for a celebration of the work of Lottie Pye: my mother. For reasons known only to her, she chose to leave me her photographs. Boxes of the blasted things! What you see on display is only a very small fraction of my inheritance. My mother was a stranger to me during her lifetime, but I have come to know her - as I hope you will too - through her photographs.

"What has surprised us is that some of the older photographs appear to show very modern attitudes. Many show brand new inventions that we take for granted: the pioneers of engineering, of aviation and fashion. Some of you may find her experimental composite shots or her photographs of women, which include the first black American superstar, Florence Mills, particularly interesting. But, for me, it is her depictions of everyday life that I find the most moving. When you look at her photographs, you see the world through her eyes.

"Before I leave you to enjoy yourselves, I have one very special thank you. Everything that you see here this evening - the layout, the frames, the exhibition notes, the labels - everything down to the drinks you are holding in your hands, have been arranged by a very dear friend of mine. Jenny Jenny Jones." As I bent down to pick up a large bouquet of yellow flowers, there were cheers from the back of the hall. "Where are you hiding, Jenny? Come and take your bow."

She made her way through the crowd, face flushed, and she fingered a strand of hair at the corner of her mouth at the sound of a shrill whistle. "You didn't need to," she said in a low voice as she took the flowers and kissed me on the cheek.

"Oh, yes I did."

When she tucked her free hand into the crook of my arm and turned to face her audience, I saw that she was searching for her father's face. He had joined her classmates, matching them with the volume of his clapping and the stomping of his feet. Beside him, the girlfriend took pleasure in his delight. I raised my glass in a toast. "Enjoy," I said stepping down from the podium.

Later, after the initial buzz had subsided, Jenny's father sought me out. "Terry," he introduced himself, extending one hand. "I want to thank you for giving Jenny this opportunity. It's brought her out of herself these last few months."

"No, believe me: it's she who deserves the thanks. She's been a breath of fresh air. I'm actually very glad she persuaded me to do this."

"It's quite a collection you have."

"Yes," I smiled, glancing round at what we had accomplished. "Yes it is. I think we whittled it down rather well."

"Listen." Terry appeared awkward. "You've probably made plans, but Jenny wanted me to ask you, if you're not doing anything for Christmas...?"

"Well, that's very kind of you." The realisation that I would have politely declined only a few months before didn't escape me. "You do know I come as one of a pair?"

Terry shifted from one foot to another. "Oh, your partner would be welcome, of course."

"My dog." I smiled. "Isambard."

"Ah, yes. Jenny's mentioned him."

"I can't abandon him for the whole day."

"Extraordinary," a voice said from behind my shoulder.

"Excuse me one moment," I apologised to Terry and turned to see a man in a turtleneck and sports jacket. "Let me introduce myself. I'm Giles Tremayne, a collector."

"And what do you collect?" I asked as we shook hands.

"Photographs. Love to see the entire collection. Why don't you give me a call?"

I declined the business card he offered. "Actually, I don't think so: it's not for sale."

"I'd like the opportunity to persuade you to change your mind."

"I'm afraid you'd be wasting your time."

Pressed up against people at all angles, I was relieved to find Jenny by my side. "You should hear the comments! I think we've earned our degree."

"I've just had an offer for the entire collection."

"You wouldn't sell, would you?"

"I don't think there would ever be a right price."

Jenny smiled, said, "Full marks. That is the correct answer."

She span away from me, a sleek starling becoming one with the swirling, churning mass. Something in the way she moved, her hands raised above her head to part the crowd, made me wish I had a camera to frame her. I blinked and, in that instant, it was as if I was experiencing a flashback, although I knew it wasn't a memory of anything I had experienced. That was the moment I became a photographer.

ACKNOWLEDGMENTS

I drew inspiration from a number of sources, including the amazing body of work of my favourite photographer, Lartique, and the extraordinary life of the model-turned-photographer and photojournalist, Lee Miller.

In researching historical facts I used *Consuming Passions* by Judith Flanders, *Lost Voices of the Edwardians* by Max Arthur, *Bright Young People: the Rise and Fall of a Generation 1918 - 1940* by D J Taylor and *We Danced All Night* by Martin Pugh, as well as Brighton folklore from a variety of sources.

I must admit to taking liberties by putting words into the mouths of real characters, but I hope I have done so respectfully and in historical context. The story of Channon-Aubrey was told to me by Alan Peck, and it was Evelyn Waugh who led me to Florence Mills.

Apologies to the *Daily Mail,* who have been so very generous to me, but whose name was used for the sake of historical accuracy.

Heartfelt thanks are due to all of my readers, but especially the Hilary Johnson Agency, Helen Enefer, Sarah Marshall, Harry Matthews, Delia Porter, Amanda Osborne, and my sisters Louise and Anne, all of whom helped enormously in the final edit. In closing, I must apologise to Matt for testing his patience by turning our dining room into an office. I promised to put it back in one piece every evening before you got home: I lied.

ABOUT THE AUTHOR

Jane Davis is the author of six novels. Her debut, Half-truths and White Lies, won the Daily Mail First Novel Award and was described by Joanne Harris as 'A story of secrets, lies, grief and, ultimately, redemption, charmingly handled by this very promising new writer.' She was hailed by The Bookseller as 'One to Watch'. Jane's favourite description of fiction is that it is 'made-up truth'.

She lives in Carshalton, Surrey, with her Formula 1 obsessed, star-gazing, beer-brewing partner, surrounded by growing piles of paperbacks, CDs and general chaos.

For further information, to sign up for pre-launch specials and notifications about future projects, or for suggested questions for book clubs visit www.jane-davis.co.uk.

A personal request from Jane: "Your opinion really matters to authors and to readers who are wondering which book to pick next. If you love a book, please tell your friends and post a review."

Made in the USA
Middletown, DE
17 March 2016